ONCE
TWICE BURNED

ONCE BITTEN, TWICE BURNED

CYNTHIA EDEN

KENSINGTON PUBLISHING CORP.
www.kensingtonbooks.com

KENSINGTON BOOKS are published by

Kensington Publishing Corp.
119 West 40th Street
New York, NY 10018

All Kensington titles, imprints and distributed lines are available at special quantity discounts for bulk purchases for sales promotion, premiums, fund-raising, educational or institutional use. Special book excerpts or customized printings can also be created to fit specific needs. For details, write or phone the office of the Kensington Special Sales Manager: Kensington Publishing Corp., 119 West 40th Street, New York, NY, 10018. Attn. Special Sales Department. Phone: 1-800-221-2647.

Kensington and the K logo Reg. U.S. Pat. & TM Off.

ISBN-13: 978-0-7582-8408-2
ISBN-10: 0-7582-8408-X
First Kensington Trade Edition: May 2014
First Kensington Mass Market Edition: December 2017

eISBN-13: 978-0-7582-8409-9
eISBN-10: 0-7582-8409-8
First Kensington Electronic Edition: May 2014

10 9 8 7 6 5 4 3 2 1

Printed in the United States of America

ACKNOWLEDGMENTS

Thank you so much to all of my wonderful readers. You are just incredible!

Thank you to Eden's Agents! (What would I do without you?)

For my editor, Esi—it is always a pleasure!

For the fabulous Justine—oh Justine, you inspire me every time our paths cross.

Thank you to all of the wonderful people I have met on my writing journey. I hope that you all enjoy the phoenixes and the dark places that they will take us.

ONCE BITTEN, TWICE BURNED

CHAPTER ONE

Betrayed.

The knowledge burned through Ryder Duncan's gut like acid, burned almost as much as the horrible, consuming hunger that had gnawed at him over the months he'd been held captive in this hell. The hunger that *still* ate at him.

He paced his cell. Ten feet wide. Twelve feet long. He'd paced this same path over and over again.

And he couldn't fucking get *out*.

His hands punched into the nearest wall. The walls of his prison were all made with heavy, thick stone, and even his enhanced strength couldn't break through them. Though he'd sure tried his hardest to punch his way out. For his trouble, he'd gotten broken and bloody knuckles.

Blood.

Without fresh blood to fuel his body, he was just growing weaker every day. At this point, Ryder knew he was operating on instinct. Primitive drive.

For someone like him, the most primitive drive was *bloodlust*.

Ryder stilled when he heard the sound of footsteps approaching his cell. Guards. Coming by to taunt him. If they would just make the mistake of stepping into his cell, getting close enough for him to touch . . .

I'd drain them dry.

His fangs were fully extended in his mouth. The hunger was too intense for anything else. Some vamps could go for days without feeding, no problem.

He could handle days.

He couldn't handle weeks. *Months.* The bastards were starving him, and starvation was one very painful and cruel way to kill a vampire.

He clenched his fists and turned away from the door. He didn't want the guards to see how close to breaking he was. If they saw, they would be afraid, and then they'd never step inside his cage.

The footsteps grew closer. He tried to calm his rushing heartbeat so that he could focus on the prey that approached, but the frantic thunder echoing in his ears wouldn't slow down.

When he got out of his prison, he'd make his betrayer pay. Not an easy death. One that took so very long.

A bright light flashed on above him, and Ryder held himself perfectly still. He knew what the light meant. The humans outside were watching him through their two-way mirror. He turned his head, the move taking a strange amount of effort, and Ryder glanced at that mirror.

He'd tried to shatter it. Hadn't worked.

The men who'd built this place had known just how to supernatural-proof their prison.

"How are you feeling, Ryder?" a voice asked, one tinged with the slightest hint of the South. He knew that voice. Dr. Richard Wyatt. The warden of this hell.

Hell was a so-called research facility—the Genesis Facility.

Humans thought the supernaturals inside this place had volunteered to be test subjects. Day and night, experiments were performed on them. The experiments that were supposed to help good old Uncle Sam develop a bigger, stronger fighting force—before Uncle Sam's enemies created that force and beat 'em to the punch.

Maybe some of the supernaturals *had* been stupid enough to volunteer as guinea pigs. Ryder hadn't volunteered. He'd been tricked. Betrayed. Drugged. He'd woken in this cell, been kept prisoner for too long, and he wanted *out*.

One way or another, he would get his freedom back, even if he had to kill every guard in the place in order to get it.

"Come in," Ryder growled back to Wyatt. "And I'll show you." He'd been longing to rip out Wyatt's throat.

The doctor laughed. "I'm afraid that's not possible, but I am growing concerned for you."

Bullshit. The doctor was fucking Frankenstein—one who was obsessed with experimenting on the monsters who were already in the world.

But soon enough, those monsters would be coming for him.

Ryder had the sadistic prick marked for death.

"I've never seen a vampire go so long without food. Most die of starvation long before this point."

And there was a tidbit most humans didn't know. Folks usually thought you had to stake a vamp to kill him. Or behead him. But those were the fast ways to die. If you wanted a vamp to suffer, you made him go without blood. Slow starvation. He'd wither before your eyes.

I'm not withering.

Because he wasn't your average vamp. Wyatt had realized that, so the real games were probably about to begin.

"How is it that you're still standing?" Wyatt wanted to know with that annoying, clinical curiosity of his.

"Come in," Ryder invited again as he snapped his teeth together. "Find out."

Silence. Then, "Open the door," Wyatt ordered, and Ryder blinked, stunned. They were opening his cell door? His muscles trembled in preparation. The first person to come through that door was already dead, the fool just didn't know it. He could move fast, so fast, now that the drugs were out of his system. He'd have his teeth in the guard's neck within seconds. And as soon as he got that blood in him . . .

I'll come for you, Wyatt.

Metal grated as the door opened.

"I don't want you to starve," Wyatt's voice explained from the speaker above Ryder's head. "Your death would teach me nothing new. So I'm giving you sustenance. Try not to damage her too much."

Her?

Ryder whirled around and lunged for the prey at his door. But it wasn't a guard who came inside. No, the guard *shoved* the woman over the threshold even while the man—a sweating, balding mass of fear—shot backward and slammed the heavy door shut again as quickly as he could.

Ryder's hands curled around her arms. The scent of fresh flowers surrounded him and the woman—tall, slim—tilted her head back as she stared up at him in absolute horror.

"Don't hurt me," she whispered. *"Please."*

He could already taste her blood. His hands tightened around her arms. Ryder hadn't expected . . .

He could hear the throb of her blood. *Drink it. Drain her.*

If he put his mouth on her, Ryder wasn't sure he'd be able to stop.

And, Wyatt, damn him, he knew that.

Ryder's gaze raked her face. Wide, scared eyes. Dark brown. Deep. Golden skin, skin that looked as if it had been kissed by the sun. She had delicate features, a curving chin, high cheekbones, and a small nose. Her lips were trembling, full, tinted the faintest pink.

His gaze dropped to her neck. A lovely neck, with the pulse pounding so frantically.

Her hands slammed into his chest. *"Don't."*

"Go right ahead, Ryder," Wyatt's voice droned, like a father giving a child permission to play with a favorite toy.

She's a human, not a toy.

Even though he knew plenty of vampires who thought humans were just playthings—good for food and fucking—that *wasn't* the way Ryder thought. Not anymore.

She shook her head, sending the heavy curtain of her hair—brown but shot with red highlights—over her shoulders. "Mister, you've got some real big teeth, and I'd appreciate it if you kept them *away* from me."

Her voice was husky, low, and sexy. It whispered with an accent he'd heard before, down in New Orleans. Smoky. Rolling.

"Please," she said again, as her hands pushed against his chest.

But he couldn't let her go. Ryder inhaled again. She smelled so good. He knew she'd taste even better. "Just a few sips," Ryder told her because he was past the point of pulling away. The hunger was too strong. It wasn't the man who wanted her blood. It was the beast who had no control.

She yelped and kicked out at him.

He barely felt the blows.

"Take as much as you need, Ryder," the doctor's satisfied voice told him. "She's all yours."

He grabbed the woman, twisted, and forced her back against the right wall. They were across from that damn two-way mirror, and his bigger body easily shielded hers, blocking her from Wyatt's view. "I'm . . . sorry." He barely managed to grit the words, but he had to say them. He hated her fear. Hated that he was the one who made her afraid.

She stopped struggling. "Don't be sorry, just let me go."

The thunder of her blood was the best music he'd ever heard. "Haven't . . . fed . . . too long."

"I'm not your midnight snack." Her words were brave, but he saw the fear in her eyes. "I'm a person, dammit! Now let me go."

He couldn't. His head lowered toward her throat. "I'll hold on to my . . . control." Ryder hoped the words weren't a lie. "I just need a little . . . blood."

There was nowhere for her to run. She was pinned to the thick stone behind her and trapped with him in front of her. But she shoved her head back against the stone as she tried to put a feeble distance between them, and, unfortunately for her, that move just had the effect of exposing more of her throat to him.

"You can't be real," she whispered. "Your teeth . . . your eyes . . . *none* of this is real. They drugged me. I'm hallucinating."

If only. Poor lady. She'd probably had no clue about the monsters that walked in this world, not until Wyatt had tossed her into hell. "Just . . . hold still. It'll be . . . over soon."

Just a few sips.

"No!" She screamed, then she rammed against him, a blow that was surprisingly powerful. Powerful enough to send him stumbling back five feet.

His ass hit the floor because he'd never expected that kind of attack from her. Humans weren't strong enough to toss vamps around like that.

The intercom crackled. "Ah, now, Sabine, that wasn't part of the deal. I told you that if you provided nourishment for my guest, then we'd discuss your freedom."

Her chest heaved. A nice chest, he noticed, even through the rage and hunger. Full breasts.

"I'm not nourishment!" she yelled as she glared into the two-way mirror. "You can't do this to me! I have rights!"

"Your rights don't exactly apply here." Wyatt didn't sound concerned. Why would he? The guy had the might of the U.S. military backing his little "experiments."

The worst fucking mistake the paranormals had ever made was coming out of the closet. But some idiots just couldn't keep quiet. They'd shown themselves to humans. Gotten tired of living by the old ways—or hell, maybe even technology had been to blame. Too much advancement. Cameras everywhere. Eyes always watching.

It was hard to hide the beast inside when Big Brother was *always* spying on you.

So they'd come out, and now there were freaks like Wyatt who thought they could harness their paranormal power. Use science to make magic into their weapon of choice.

"If you aren't cooperating, Ms. Acadia, we can always take you back to your cell." Wyatt's voice lowered and he said, "Guard, retrieve—"

"I don't want my cell! I want to go home! I want—"

Ryder pounced. In an instant, he had her in his arms. He twisted her hands and secured them behind her body. She was struggling, definitely using more than just human strength, but he was prepared for her this time. She wasn't getting away.

"I won't hurt you," he told her. And Ryder hoped the words weren't a lie. Sometimes, the bite could bring a woman pleasure. A better release than sex.

Sometimes, the bite could bring pain. Worse than torture.

He didn't want her to hurt.

His mouth was desert dry. His fangs fully extended and aching. He could already taste her.

I just want her.

His tongue swept over her neck. Sampled, then he sank his teeth into her throat.

The woman—Sabine—gasped against him. Her body arched into his as the first tender drops of her blood spilled onto his tongue.

"Make sure the recording is operational." Wyatt's voice seemed to come from far away. "I want to get every bit of this."

But Wyatt and what he wanted didn't matter. Sabine's blood was on Ryder's tongue, and her blood was like nothing he'd ever tasted in all of his years of existence. Not just warm—the blood was hot. Spicy. Rich with flavor. He wanted to lap it up, to savor it.

To gorge on it.

His hands hardened on her. He'd meant to take just a few drops.

He wanted to lift his head away. Wanted to so badly, but *her blood was too good*.

He drank more, greedy now. Desperate. Her blood flowed through him, heating his body from the inside out and sending tendrils of power pulsing through him. Some humans tasted of wine. Some of the euphoria that came from drugs.

No one had ever tasted like her. Life. Sex. Pleasure. Everything he wanted was right there, in her blood.

He drank deeper.

"S-stop." Her voice was weaker than before.

He didn't want to stop. He'd looked for this—he'd always wanted this taste. Craved it, when he hadn't even known what he was missing. His body seemed to be growing stronger, the muscles tensing, with every drop of her blood that he took.

She sagged against him, and Ryder scooped her into his arms, holding her even when her head fell to the side and her breath rattled in her chest.

More.

More.

At first, he thought the urging was just inside of himself, but then he realized that bastard Wyatt was the one urging him on.

And the woman . . . Sabine wasn't fighting him any longer. She barely seemed to be breathing.

He jerked his head away. Stared down at her in disbelief. He hadn't taken that much, had he?

But he couldn't remember how long he'd been drinking. He only knew—

I still want more.

He lifted her higher against his chest. Held her cradled in his arms. There was no more weakness for him. Only strength. But she . . .

Her lashes were closed.

A fear unlike any he'd known before had his whole body tensing. He'd just found her. Ryder knew he couldn't lose her this soon. *Not. Now.*

And sure as hell not by his own hand. Or teeth.

He brought his wrist to his mouth. Slashed open the flesh. He knew what she needed. "Drink for me." She'd be all right once she drank his blood.

"No!" Wyatt's voice thundered out. "Stop! Put Sabine down and back away."

"Fuck off." He lowered them both to the floor so he could better tend to her. But he kept her close as he put his wrist to her mouth. "Drink." She'd just need a little of his blood, and she'd heal.

If she'd just drink . . .

An alarm began to sound. Voices shouted over the intercom. Then footsteps rushed outside of his door. The guards were finally coming in to face him.

Now was the perfect time to kill them. But if he moved away from Sabine, she'd die. She needed more of his blood. She needed him to survive.

His eyes narrowed on her face. *What are you?* She'd been afraid, but she'd still fought him. She'd stared at a monster and asked to go home.

Now she was almost at death's broken door.

"Get away from her!" Wyatt was shrieking now.

She wasn't drinking. He pried open her mouth. Forced drops of blood onto her tongue and then massaged her neck, trying to make Sabine swallow. *Live.*

The guards grabbed him, trying to yank him away from her. *Hell, no.* He threw them back. Heard thuds when they hit the walls.

"You have to swallow the blood," he told her, voice dark and rumbling with command. "Come on!" *I didn't mean to do this*. She'd been so afraid. He'd told her that he'd hold on to his control.

But the beast that he was hadn't been able to hold on. The beast . . . Ryder . . . he destroyed. That was his life. All he knew. And he'd destroyed her, too.

His vision seemed to blacken. She was the only thing he could see in that growing darkness. Beautiful, so still.

His head sagged over her. *"Please."* Now he was the one to beg. He'd tasted heaven, and he'd tossed her to hell, all in one instant of time.

"Get away from her!" Wyatt's voice wasn't on the loudspeaker any longer. It was right there. In the room with him.

Kill him.

Ryder's head jerked up. He bared his fangs.

And . . . and felt her mouth move lightly against his wrist. She was trying to drink, to take his blood.

Sabine was fighting to live. *Yes.*

His gaze snapped back to her. "That's it! Come on, just drink some—"

Gunshots blasted. Bullets drove into his chest. One. Two. Three. The force of the hits had him falling back even as his blood sprayed the wall behind him.

"I *told* you," Wyatt raged as he lifted his weapon. *Wyatt had fired?* "Back away from the female subject!"

Ryder ignored the pain and reached for her again.

"Stop him," Wyatt ordered. Ryder realized the guards were back on their feet. "Shoot him until he stops moving. The bullets won't kill him, but they can put him down for a time."

Then the bullets exploded, popping like firecrackers

over and over again as they sank into Ryder's body. His chest. His arms.

He hit the floor. Blood seeped from his wounds. Pooled around him on the stone floor.

"Enough!" Wyatt lifted his hand. His eyes went from Ryder to Sabine.

Her head had turned and her eyes—wide open, still alive—were on Ryder. He could see the life in her gaze. She was trying to come back to him. *Trying.* She just needed more of his blood.

Her hand had lifted. Was she reaching for him? Ryder gathered every single ounce of strength that he had. "My . . . blood . . ." Only a little more, and she'd be fine. He could save her. Her death—unlike all the others—wouldn't be on him. He started crawling to her through the blood.

"She's gonna live," one of the guards muttered. "I thought he was supposed to kill her."

He could be more than a killer. She could be more than a victim. Blood soaked his clothes. The power he'd gotten from her rich blood was gone, stolen away by a hail of bullets.

"He did kill her." Wyatt's voice was flat. "We just have to wait for her to die."

No! "Can . . . help . . ." He was almost to her side.

"Chain him," Wyatt ordered. "He's too weak to fight you. Chain the vampire and let him watch."

Their arms grabbed him. Jerked him away from her. But he wasn't as weak as they thought, not even with the bullets lodged in his organs. Ryder fought them, clawing and snapping with his fangs. Half a dozen guards had to jump on him and yank him back to the far wall. Then they locked thick chains around his wrists, trapping him. The guards hurried back as soon as those locks snapped in place. They were bloody now, too—from the wounds he'd given them.

When they moved away, he saw her again. Her chest was struggling to rise. Her eyes were still open.

"Don't . . . do this," he growled as he strained to break free.

Wyatt walked around her, staring down at Sabine as she sprawled on the floor. "Why do you even care? Shouldn't she just be food to you?"

Ryder didn't speak. He wouldn't tell this bastard anything about himself.

"I think one of the bullets must have ripped into your heart"—Wyatt didn't sound particularly concerned—"you're bleeding far too much. Hmmm . . . I should have considered . . . will that wound to the heart kill you?"

No. It wouldn't. He was healing already.

"I didn't intend for them to shoot you in the heart." Wyatt frowned at the guards. "Errors like that cannot be tolerated here."

The guy was psychotic.

A bullet to the heart wasn't normally an error. It was murder.

"You're just . . . gonna watch . . . her die?" Ryder yanked at the chains and didn't care when they cut into his wrists. He'd heal. He always healed.

She won't.

"Yes." Wyatt nodded and offered an almost-absent smile. "Yes, yes, I am."

Her eyes were on Ryder—her eyes . . .

He saw the life leave them. Actually saw a veil of nothing sweep into her stare. *"No!"* He yanked at the chains, twisting his hands, breaking his wrists as he fought to get free. He smashed his fingers as he tried to jerk his hand through the ring that bound his wrist. He didn't feel the pain as he struggled.

Dead.

"Exit," Wyatt snapped, *"now."*

The guards started hauling ass. They were leaving her like that? Just sprawled on the floor like a broken doll?

Maybe there was still time. His right wrist shattered. *Maybe*.

"If I were you, I wouldn't move," Wyatt advised Ryder with a quick frown as he paused by the door. "This is her first change. I have no idea how powerful it will be."

Ryder didn't understand the bastard. He was moving, all right. *Won't give up. Won't—*

The door slammed shut behind Wyatt and his men. And . . . the scent of smoke teased Ryder's nose.

What the hell?

His gaze snapped back to Sabine. Her eyes were still open, only her eyes weren't dark brown any longer. The brown was changing, turning to a gold, then seeming to burn red.

Red like fire.

The scent of smoke deepened around him. Ryder pulled his broken right hand free. Now the other—

Her body began to burn.

He yelled then, roaring her name, but the fire didn't stop. It blazed hotter, higher, and swept over Sabine's slender form. The white-hot heat from the blaze rushed over his skin, almost singeing him. Sprinklers erupted with a powerful spray from overhead, and the water drenched him but did nothing to stop the blaze that consumed Sabine.

His breath rasped out. Ryder stopped fighting for his

freedom. There was nothing to be done now. No one could come back from those flames.

So there was nothing for him to do in the end but watch the fire burn, to hate himself for the monster that he was, and to wish that Sabine Acadia had never had the misfortune to walk into his prison.

But then something began to move within those flames. *She* moved, and Ryder realized that Wyatt's experiments were just getting started.

Because even though she'd just died right in front of him, even though Sabine was burning, it sure looked like she was trying to rise from the fire.

CHAPTER TWO

The flames were all she knew. Burning so hot, but not hurting her. She saw fire—red and gold, so bright. She tasted ash.

The flames grew higher.

Pain and rage and fear and hate began to churn within her. Something had happened to her. Something bad. She knew it, but she couldn't remember exactly what had happened.

She couldn't . . . remember much of anything.

Just the fire.

But then the flames began to die away. Slowly, the fury of the fire became just a flicker, then faded to mere wisps of smoke around her bare feet.

She stood in some kind of room. With heavy, perhaps stone walls. She instinctively knew the walls were made of stone—but she didn't know *where* she was.

Fear made her heart beat faster. Her gaze searched the small room, flying from the left to right and she saw . . . him.

Against the back wall, stood a bloody man, blisters

on his skin, his eyes—a wild green, bright and fierce—locked on her. There was disbelief in his eyes, shock carved into the hard, chiseled planes of his face.

And there was a chain around his wrist.

"How the hell," his voice rasped out, deep and rumbling, and sending a shiver over her skin, "did you do that?"

She just stared at him. He seemed familiar. Her head tilted as she gazed at him. They were alone in the room. He was hurt. She was . . .

Naked?

Frowning, she glanced down at her body. Maybe she should cover herself, but she didn't. The fury inside her left no room for modesty.

Destroy.

Burn.

Whispers that came from within.

She took a step closer to the man.

He lifted a hand toward her. A broken, twisted hand. "I thought you were dead."

I was. The same whisper in her mind.

"Sabine, what happened?"

The name echoed in her mind. *Sabine.* An image flashed in front of her. A man, with dark red hair and a wide grin, chasing a little girl near a river. *Sabine, you're too fast for me! I can never catch you.*

Her head began to throb. "Who are you?"

His eyes narrowed. "You don't remember me?"

She shook her head. "Why are you chained?"

"Because they wanted to stop me from getting to you."

She stilled. The ache in her head grew worse. Swelled higher. The rush of blood within her veins felt like the burn of fire.

The man stood just a few feet away from her. He was tall, muscled, and covered in so much blood. She glanced down at her own body. Not a drop of blood was on her skin. Her gaze rose back to meet his. "Where are my clothes?"

Surely she hadn't just been . . . naked . . . with him.

"They burned away." His shoulders straightened. He was a big one, tall, with thick shoulders and a muscled chest. A *bleeding* muscled chest. "You died, then you burned."

A shocked laugh came from her. "You're crazy." She wasn't dead. And he . . . his intense gaze caused the faintest flickers of fear to grow in her belly. As she stared at him, her body started shaking, a small tremble that seemed to come from her heart and reverberate through every muscle. Sucking in a deep breath, she spun away from him and rushed toward the door. The guy was chained up, and he had to be that way for a reason. Since he couldn't move, it seemed to make pretty good sense that she get away from him. Her hand lifted and she pounded her fist against the door.

Fire immediately swept out from her hand and blazed a path up the door and toward the ceiling.

Screaming, she leapt back, even as the sprinklers erupted overhead.

"There they come again." His dark mutter.

The icy water drenched her. She tried pounding on the door again. More fire, fire that didn't so much as singe her fingertips, but the door didn't open.

Trapped.

She shook her hands, trying to stop the fire. Flames *couldn't* be coming from her fingers. That wasn't possible. This was just a nightmare.

She looked at her hands and saw—more fire.
Nightmare.

She screamed and spun around to stare at the man.
Except he wasn't a man. His fangs were bared—*fangs!*—
and he was straining as he ripped his left wrist out of
that cuff-like chain. She heard the crunch of bones and
she flinched, but he just gave a growl and wrenched his
broken hand free.

Then his gaze met hers.

"Who are you?" she whispered.

"Ryder." He lifted his right hand. Pressed it to his
bloody chest. Bones snapped and popped. Then he used
that right hand—nausea rolled within her—to snap his
left hand and its fingers back into place.

She raised her own hands before her. The fire flickered above her fingers—freaking her the hell out—but
she shouted, "Stay away from me!"

He wasn't coming toward her. He was digging something out of his chest. Clawing at his chest and pulling
out something small and black. He clawed at his chest
again and again. The objects that he pulled from his
flesh—at least seven of them—looked like bullets.

Ryder dropped them. "Hope you're getting a good
show, Wyatt."

Who was Wyatt?

The throbbing in her head was driving her crazy.
Burn. The fire above her fingers flared higher. She
slammed her hands against the nearby wall and the
flames shot up the stone instantly, heading to lick at the
ceiling. "What is happening to me?" she whispered. A
scream seemed to echo inside her head.

"Sabine."

His voice cut through that scream. Her head turned

toward him. Their eyes met. He was stalking toward her. Closing in. "Stop the fire," he told her, his voice quiet.

"I-I don't know how!" Tears leaked down her cheeks. Her hands stayed on the wall. She was afraid that if she lifted them up, she'd shoot the flames right at him.

Part of her wanted to hurt him. Part of her wanted to just hurt and destroy *everything*.

But another part . . . another part was lost. *Help me*.

The flames continued to rise up the wall. The man—Ryder—kept coming toward her. He had to feel the heat from the fire, but he didn't look afraid.

Powerful. Dangerous. But not afraid.

Since flames were shooting from her hands, shouldn't *she* be the dangerous one?

Her nails dug into the wall.

"Stop the fire, Sabine," Ryder told her again, and her breath heaved out.

"Don't you think I would, if I could?" Her head shook frantically. The scream in her mind was back. Was that her scream? "I can't! I—"

His fingers curled around her chin and stopped the shaking of her head. She was afraid that the fire would spread to him, so her fingers shoved harder against the wall. His body surrounded her. She kept her hands on the wall. He was touching her, and she was too terrified to touch him. "Get away from me," she whispered.

She couldn't even begin to guess at the emotions in his eyes as he gruffly said, "I want to help you."

"Why?" She understood *nothing* that was happening. "Why are we here? Where are we?" The flames seemed to burn hotter, while his touch on her skin felt curiously cool. Almost soothing. "You know me, right? We were here together?"

His fingers stroked her skin.

"Tell me!"

"I know you," he said. His head lowered to her. "Don't let your control break. Fight this."

Fight the fire? The scream inside? *What?*

His lips took hers. The kiss was the last thing she expected, and her gasp of surprise slipped into his mouth. The kiss was soft, gentle, even as the fire raged on the wall near her. The sprinklers kept pouring water on them. Water that dripped over her face and held her frozen against him.

No, it wasn't the water that kept her immobile.

His mouth pressed lightly to her lips. His tongue stroked inside, caressing her, tasting.

Her heartbeat drummed in her ears, but the scream in her mind began to quiet down. Still afraid, her nails dug deeper into the wall.

His fingers slid down her neck.

A memory nagged at her. An image.

His head, bending toward her.

"Please . . . don't . . ." Her voice. She knew it was. Her memory.

"Let me help you." His whisper against her lips. "Trust me. I won't hurt you . . ." Ryder's words were rough, ragged.

Did she imagine it or had he said . . .

I won't hurt you . . . again.

But he wasn't even close to hurting her now. His lips were light on hers. So soft and gentle and she wanted to kiss him back. To taste him. To forget the fire and just feel him.

"I know what you are." His lips feathered near the edge of her mouth. "I know."

Slowly, his head lifted. The water had soaked his hair dark. Droplets clung to his thick lashes. Slid down his cheeks. High cheeks. Such a handsome, sexy face. A face made to tempt a woman to sin.

Her gaze followed those drops of water. Fell down to his lips. Sculpted, sensual. But then—then— "You have fangs."

Did his lips curl in a faint smile? The smile was so brief it was hard to tell for sure. Then he said, "And you're burning the room around us."

She blinked up at him.

"Pull it back, love," he told her. *"Pull it back."*

She didn't know how.

He kissed her again. "Focus on me."

She wanted to, but it was hard with the giant wall of flames just inches away. "You should move away."

Ryder shook his head. "I won't leave you. I won't *watch*."

She didn't even know what that meant.

"Breathe," he told her. "Slow. Deep." His hand moved to rest over her heart. "Too fast," Ryder told her. *"Breathe.* You're safe with me."

She wanted to believe him. The scream in her mind—it had quieted so much, but her nails still dug into the wall. She focused on getting her breaths to match his. *In. Out. In.* The fire appeared to be shrinking. The flames were flickering.

"Good." His voice seemed to rumble inside her. His touch—his hand—it was cool against her overheated flesh. The edge of his thumb slid over her breast, and she gasped at the contact.

The flames flickered again.

She wanted to grab his hand and yank it away from her flesh, but she was afraid to touch him. If he burned like the wall did, he would be dead instantly.

But he was tensing before her. His head tilted even as his gaze flew toward the door. "They're coming."

They?

He dropped his hand.

The water kept falling on them.

"Stay behind me," he ordered. "No matter what happens. Stay *behind me*."

She yanked her hands away from the wall. Fisted them and shoved them behind her body.

The door was opening with a screech of metal that hurt her ears. There were men there. Men who wore thick, heavy white suits and giant masks that covered their heads.

What in the hell?

The men had guns in their hands, and their weapons were aimed at Ryder.

"Do you really want to dig out more bullets, Ryder?" a low voice asked. A voice that came from above them. Her head jerked up, and she saw a small speaker in the middle of the ceiling.

"Not really," Ryder drawled, "so I think I'll just kill these bastards instead."

And he lunged forward, moving in a flash despite the blood that still covered him. He was injured, hurt so badly, and—

He killed a man while she watched. Yanked the gun from the guy's hands. Turned the weapon back on the man in white and shot him. Blasted him in the heart and then aimed the gun on the others. "You should move faster," he told them.

They were trying to fire. Shooting with their weapons, and she lifted her hands, wanting the nightmare before her to stop.

Flames flew from her fingers and headed right for Ryder and the others.

The flames licked over Ryder's back. He didn't even stop attacking.

I'm sorry!

The flames hit the other men. The men in those heavy white suits, but the fire didn't hurt them.

"You'll have to burn hotter than that," the voice on the speaker said. "Their suits are reinforced, and your temperature is far too low."

What?

"But if you keep the flames going, you may very well kill Ryder," that droning voice told her.

She dropped her hands.

Ryder had another guard on the floor. The man's neck had been broken.

Ryder glanced over at her.

She screamed a warning at him. More guards were coming. They fired at him.

But the new guards weren't using regular bullets because no blood appeared when he was hit.

"Those tranq darts can take out anyone," the voice she already hated told her, "even a monster as strong as Ryder."

Another guard lifted his weapon and fired at her. Ryder roared and grabbed him. The man was dead before he hit the floor.

And she was hit. A tranq dart was in her chest. Her knees gave way.

"No point fighting," that annoying voice blasted out from the speaker. "Like I told you, the tranqs can take out anyone."

Her shoulder slammed into the floor. She tried to

push back up to her feet, but she couldn't get her limbs to work right.

Ryder was falling, too. Falling, but still fighting. Another dart sank into his neck.

Then his head hit the floor. The *smack* of his skull had her flinching and reaching out to him.

I've reached for him before. The memory was there, just beneath the surface of her mind.

He groaned when his body collapsed on the floor. A guard went to step over him—

Ryder's hand flew out, tripping the man. "I'm not . . . out yet," Ryder growled. "Stay the . . ." His fist slammed into the man's mask, "hell away from . . . her."

Her heart was slowing down. It felt like she had mud in her veins, not blood.

Ryder had yanked that man closer to him, and as she could only lie there and watch, Ryder buried his fangs in the guy's throat.

Drinking from him.

Her neck began to ache.

Another memory was there, trying to push through.

"Get her out!" The shout blasted from the intercom. "Now!"

The men not unconscious or dead hurried to obey. Ryder was too weak to hold them all off, but he took two down.

Two others grabbed her. Fire sputtered from her hands, but it didn't burn their suits. They dragged her out, hauling her right past Ryder.

He snarled in fury and tried to reach for her, but she knew the tranq must be having the same effect on him.

Mud inside. Can't move.

Ryder grabbed one of the fallen men. Sank his teeth into the unconscious man's throat.

"I'll . . . find . . ." Ryder's voice was following her. Her gaze found his. Blood stained his mouth. His victim lay on the floor beside him. Two puncture wounds marked the man's throat.

"I'll find . . . *you* . . . *Coming* . . . *for you*!" Ryder growled after her. She wasn't sure if his words were a threat, or a promise.

Maybe they were both.

Then she was outside of that small room. The men in white lifted her onto some sort of gurney. They strapped her in and rolled her down a hallway. Fluorescent lights flickered over her head.

She tried to break free, but the drug was still slowing her down.

A door opened. The scent of bleach and antiseptic hit her.

Another room.

"Let . . . go," she whispered.

Then a man leaned over her. Tall, dark, with green eyes.

Not like Ryder's eyes.

This man's eyes were a cold, arctic green. Chilling.

"You're lucky we got you away from him in time."

She didn't feel lucky.

"Sabine, I'm sorry for what he did to you."

Sabine. There was the name again.

He smiled. "You don't remember, do you? That happens sometimes, after a rising."

It's the Twilight Zone. She remembered that show. The images of it flashed through her mind in quick succession. *I'm in it. Someone. Get. Me. Out.*

"Your memory will come back soon enough. Once

you've rested." He shined a light in her eyes. Touched a hand to her skin and then jerked his fingers back, waving them as if they'd been singed.

She'd like to do more than singe him.

"How did it feel?" he asked her as he inserted a needle into her arm.

"What?" She gritted out at him. That needle was freaking huge, and whoever this man was—*I hate him.* The knowledge was there. Lost memory or not.

"Dying," he said, as if it were obvious. "How did it feel when Ryder killed you?"

Her heart seemed to stop. "You're crazy." She wasn't dead. She was talking to him. Living. Breathing.

And Ryder hadn't killed her. He'd been there to help her. He'd tried to calm her down so the fire wouldn't rage out of control. He'd done his best to protect her from the guards.

The man's lips tightened. "You'll tell me soon enough. This was just the first of our experiments." He pulled the needle from her arm. Nodded to someone that she couldn't see. "You'll beg to tell me."

She wasn't begging him for anything.

"Just as you begged Ryder to let you live. But he didn't, did he? He just took your blood and left you to die."

The fury had drained from her. Only fear remained. "Why are you doing this?"

He reached out to touch her face, but hesitated. *Don't want to get burned, do you?*

But Ryder hadn't gotten burned when he touched her. He'd held her, kissed her. He hadn't been afraid of her fire.

"You can help to change the world."

"Let me go."

"You can save lives. Make miracles. And really, is death too much to ask from you?"

He turned away before she could tell the crazy bastard that, yeah, death was too much to ask.

"It's not like you won't just come back when you die."

His words were tossed back at her. She couldn't see him anymore. The straps pressed her against the table and the drugs held her still.

"You're weaker than the other one," he said. "That isn't a bad thing, don't worry. I know how to make you stronger. All you need are a few more deaths."

In. Sane.

"We'll start soon, don't worry. But I need to check on the vampire. See what your blood has done to him."

Ryder had drunk from her? The bastard in the lab coat had said . . . *Did he kill me?*

No, that was crazy. She wasn't dead.

Or was she?

Because this place, with its stark white ceiling, with the men who shot at her, and with the *vampire* who killed in front of her . . . this place sure seemed like hell.

They dragged out the bodies while he was still weak. They moved fast because they were smart. Even as the last body was hauled out of his cell, Ryder was already pushing to his feet as his body fought the poison in his veins.

The SP tranq. How he hated that bitch. Damn Wyatt for every creating the drug that could knock even the most powerful of supernaturals on their asses. The SP tranq was tailored for Ryder and his brethren, guaranteed to temporarily immobilize even the strongest monsters out there.

And it *was* only the supernaturals that Wyatt cared about. This lab, the cells, they were all designed to hold supernatural beings so that Wyatt could experiment on them.

Ryder now knew exactly why Sabine had been brought to his cell. Wyatt had wanted to gauge Ryder's reaction to her, and Sabine—well, she was just another one of Wyatt's experiments. A victim, one who didn't even seem to realize just what she'd *been*.

Not until she'd died.

Sabine Acadia.

After drinking Sabine's blood, the guards' blood had tasted like stale bread in his mouth. She'd been life. Warmth. Spice and wine.

He stalked toward the two-way mirror. Drove his fist into the surface. "Where is she?"

He'd promised Sabine that he'd find her. He would. He'd leave Genesis, but he'd be sure to take her with him.

Then they'd both burn this hellhole to the ground. Sabine would be so good at that burning.

"I know you're there," he snarled at his reflection, and he did know that Wyatt was watching him. Ryder had tried to play it cool and not let the scientist realize just how enhanced his senses truly were, but screw that ruse.

He could *smell* the bastard in that other room.

"Where'd you take her?" His fist pounded into the mirror once more.

The intercom crackled. "Why do you care, vampire?"

He knew the question came because he wasn't supposed to care about anyone or anything. As a rule, he didn't care—that was the reason Wyatt hadn't been able to break him.

Don't. Care.

"You know what Sabine is, don't you?" Wyatt asked him.

Yes, he knew. She shouldn't have existed. She should have only been a myth.

But vampires were supposed to just be myths, too. *And here the fuck I am.* "I know you're playing with fire. So when your ass gets burned, you'll only have yourself to blame."

Silence. The kind that said he'd pissed off Wyatt. That was the kind of silence he liked, but then Wyatt said, "That was her first death. Her first rising. I don't believe Sabine had any idea just what she was."

Hell, after that fire, she hadn't even realized *who* she was standing there, her body naked, sexy and perfect, but her eyes looking so lost and confused.

He'd wanted to protect her. Protecting wasn't his bit. Killing was.

I'm the reason she died. Wyatt had tossed her to him like a fresh piece of meat before a starving dog. "You knew what would happen when I tasted her blood."

"Ummm . . ." He heard the scribble of a pen as it scratched over paper. Wyatt, taking his notes. Always recording and analyzing every word and deed.

The human doctor who was supposed to take genetics to the next level. Supposed to create the perfect soldier—hell, those had been Wyatt's exact words to him. *With the power of the beasts here, we can create a military force that will be unstoppable.*

Wyatt sure liked to play with fire. *Watch that, asshole, or you'll get burned to ash.*

Even before he'd been captured by Wyatt and his goons, Ryder had made it his mission to learn as much as possible about Genesis, and the man at the helm of the organization. The newspapers had been full of glowing stories about genius scientist Dr. Richard Wyatt and his plans to use Genesis as a research facility that would aid the U.S. government.

Ryder had looked past those flashy stories—stories designed to fool humans and lull them into thinking that everything was okay, that they still lived in a safe world.

A world in which the supernaturals could be used and controlled.

Yes, he'd looked deeper, and he'd discovered that paranormals were being abducted and forced into Genesis. Once inside Genesis, they didn't get out.

I will, though. I'll break free. Did the government realize how far Wyatt was going, in the name of his so-called research? Ryder bet they did, and the human suits just didn't care.

In his experience, supernaturals were highly expendable to humans.

Silence filled the room, then Wyatt finally said, "Vampires don't just drink blood, they drink power."

Ryder cursed. Like he needed a lesson on what his kind did. If Wyatt ever realized just who Ryder was . . .

I'll never get out of here.

Not an option for him.

"I knew Sabine would have plenty of power for you."

Enough power to drive him crazy from the rush. He'd never tasted anything quite like her. Probably never would again.

"Her fire didn't burn you."

Wyatt's words sank into Ryder, and he tried to show no change of expression. He'd hoped the doctor had missed that part of the experiment. He should have known better.

"The fire went right over your back, but you have no wounds."

Ryder smiled into the mirror. *Where is she?* "You know vamps . . ." He slapped his chest. The bullet wounds were gone. "Fast healers." Especially him.

"You didn't heal. You just didn't get burned." Wyatt sounded annoyed then. Big deal. Ryder was way past the point of being *annoyed*.

"Why don't you come in here?" Ryder invited him. "Check me out. See for yourself." *So I can rip open your throat.*

"You drank her blood . . . hmmm . . . was the blood what gave you immunity to her flames?" Now he figured Wyatt was just talking for the hell of it. "It must have been."

Ryder's back teeth ground together.

"Vampires burn as fast as witches, but *you didn't burn*."

Ryder saw the promise of death in the reflection that stared back at him. Wyatt would see that promise, too.

"We'll have to experiment more." Now Wyatt was talking to the others who were with him. More sadistic jerks in lab coats. The ones who cut open the paranormals and pieced them back together. Well, mostly, anyway. Ryder knew the paranormals being held weren't always allowed to fully heal or even survive.

And they said *he* was the monster. At least he didn't play with his food.

"Once she wakes up and she remembers . . ." Yes,

Wyatt was definitely talking to his flunkies. "Take her to the other vampire."

Sabine.

Ryder didn't move, but his fangs were suddenly burning in his mouth. "Don't fucking *dare*." Another vampire? Of course, he'd known more of his kind were being held. But another vampire and Sabine?

Look what I did, and I'm the oldest of our kind. A younger vampire would never be able to hold back. A younger vampire would hurt her, rip her skin. Tear her throat wide open.

Then she'd burn again.

The speaker crackled. "Is there a problem?" Wyatt's calm voice. Bastard, he knew he was baiting Ryder. "Not forming an attachment, are you, vampire? Because I thought you were incapable of attachments."

Yeah, well, he'd thought the same thing, but Sabine was changing the game for him. She needed him, and, for once, he was going to protect someone—not just someone, *her.* "Bring her back to me." Gritted out.

"And if I do, what will you give me?" Wyatt wanted to immediately know.

It was a devil's deal. One that Ryder had known would come, but he had no choice. His hands dropped to his sides. He stared straight ahead. When he concentrated hard enough, he could see Wyatt through the glass. The fool didn't know it. The doctor was smirking. His stance too cocky. His flunkies weren't nearly as close to the glass. Because they were afraid.

Despite the guy's IQ, Wyatt didn't seem to have the sense to fear.

When death comes, you won't be so cocky. You'll be so afraid then that you piss yourself.

Death would be coming soon for Wyatt.

"What will you give me?" the doctor asked again.

No choice. "Whatever the hell you want. Just *give Sabine back to me*."

Silence. Wyatt's gaze drifted down to his notes, and the men behind him shifted nervously. Then, finally, once he'd proven that he thought the power was his, Wyatt's stare rose to meet Ryder's. "Deal."

CHAPTER THREE

Seven days. Seven long, fucking days, and then they finally brought her back to him.

"Stand against the back wall," Wyatt's voice ordered, seeming to echo in the small room. "If you make a move to attack any of the guards, we'll kill her."

Again.

The word hung in the air. Ryder wasn't in the mood to watch her die so he marched toward that back wall. He lifted his hands, showing that he wasn't attacking anyone, *yet*. And he waited.

The footsteps came. He caught the faint scent of flowers. Still? Light, sweet. Even after everything, she still smelled of flowers? Then the metal grated. The door opened.

Sabine stepped inside.

She was dressed in loose, gray sweats and a T-shirt. Her long hair tumbled around her shoulders. Her eyes were wide, nervous, and her dark stare instantly locked on him.

The guard behind her pressed his gun into her back.

Ryder's gaze jerked to the man's face. He knew that guard—Mitchell. Barnes Mitchell. A prick who liked to dole out pain.

I'll give you pain. It was a promise Ryder planned to keep.

Sabine took a few steps forward. The door swung shut behind her, the hollow clatter of the metal making her jump.

Ryder lowered his hands.

She shook her head. "Don't even *think* of coming at me with those fangs again, *vampire*."

Ah, so her memory was back. His gaze swept over her. He was glad there weren't any flames around her this time, but he had to confess that he'd sure enjoyed the sight of her naked body.

His cock was hard just thinking about her lush curves.

Control.

Too many eyes were watching them, and he'd already revealed too much weakness to Wyatt.

"If you can keep your fire in check, *phoenix*, then I'll try to keep my fangs to myself."

She frowned at him. "What did you call me?"

His heart slammed into his chest. "You don't know, do you?"

A small shake of her head.

Fuck. Wyatt had let her die, and the woman hadn't even known that she'd be rising again. She must have been so afraid.

His gaze fell to the floor. Her blood still stained the heavy, stone tiles. "I'm . . . sorry." The words sounded harsh to his own ears. He couldn't remember the last time he'd apologized to anyone.

"Sorry for what? Biting me? Drinking my blood?"

Like a damn moth, he headed for her flame. *So beautiful*. Her shoulders stiffened as he approached and one foot edged back. Poor phoenix, there was nowhere to run. Wyatt had made sure of that.

"I'm sorry I couldn't save you." Too many had died over the long centuries of his existence. He hadn't stopped death but with Sabine, things were different. *She can come back*. She'd given him a second chance.

Her breath whispered out. "You . . . you made me drink your blood." He noticed that her small hands fisted.

If she wanted to take a swing at him, he'd let her. She sure deserved some payback. "It was the only way I could think of to help you. Vampire blood is very powerful. It can heal, just about anything." And the blood *had* been working, until the guards had dragged him away from her.

Mitchell had been one of those guards.

After the guards had chained him, Ryder hadn't been able to break out of the chains fast enough. She'd died.

Burned.

Her fist lifted. He didn't even brace for the blow. Sure, a phoenix was powerful, but he'd take—

Her palm flattened on his chest. Her fingers were still warm, far warmer than an average human's, and the heat seemed to sink into him.

Made him want her even more.

"Your heart's beating." Her gaze held his. "I can see you breathing. I-I thought vampires were supposed to be dead."

Hollywood hype. "I think *un*dead is the popular term in use."

"And are you, um, undead, I mean?" Her hand still pressed against him. So close to his heart. "Were you a human who died and came back as a vampire?"

"It didn't work quite that way," Ryder murmured. Things hadn't worked that way, not for him. That was all he'd say then. All he could say, with Wyatt and his doctor brigade watching. His hand lifted and curled around her fingers. "Do you know where we are?"

Her laugh was bitter, but the sound of it still had his body tightening. "Hell?" Sabine asked.

"Close enough." His gaze cut to the mirror. "You know we're being watched."

Her head inclined. "Wyatt." She said the name with fury and fear. "Why is he doing this to me? I didn't volunteer to be here like you—"

Now it was Ryder's turn to laugh. "Love, do you really think I volunteered to be kept in this hole? To be starved? Tortured?" Oh, Wyatt did enjoy his little experiments.

Her hand trembled in his grip.

"I was taken," he told her flatly. "Set up. Betrayed. Drugged." That damn SP tranq.

Her long lashes flickered. "I was taken, too. Kidnapped. They grabbed me when I was going home and threw me in the back of a van. The next thing I knew, I was here, and they were—they told me if I came in the cell with you, then I'd get to go home." Her voice dropped. "I just want to go home."

The longing in her voice twisted his heart. The heart she'd thought he didn't have. *Wrong, love. Vampires breathe, their hearts beat. We can love. We can hate.*

We can kill without hesitation.

She'd seen him do that already.

"Why won't they let me go?" She whispered, probably hoping that the microphones wouldn't pick up her words.

He pulled her into his arms. She gasped and tried to fight, but he just tightened his hold. Ryder put his mouth against her ear and barely breathed the words as he spoke, "Because they know what you are. They suspected before, but now they have proof."

She shook her head.

"You're a phoenix. You can die, burn, and rise from the ashes." There wasn't any time to build up to this reveal. Knowledge was power in this world, and she'd need as much of it as she could get in order to face the battles coming her way.

She stiffened in his arms.

His lips brushed over her ear as he said, "You're powerful, and that makes you very dangerous. Wyatt isn't going to let you go." No matter what promises the man made. "The only way we're getting free is if we free ourselves." His tongue licked lightly over the shell of her ear. He couldn't help it. The woman was too tempting.

He also needed to give Wyatt a show, to distract the guy from wondering about the words Ryder was whispering to Sabine.

Her hands were on his arms, and at the touch of his tongue, her nails bit into his skin. "S-stop."

"You can do it," he told her, knowing the words were true. "You just have to burn hot enough." She could be the ticket out, for both of them.

He moved his head, letting his nose nuzzle along her cheek. Then his lips were just an inch away from her mouth. Not touching her, not yet. "Burn hot, love, *burn*."

"I don't—I don't understand what's happening. A phoenix? That's—that's a mythical bird."

Most myths were based on truth. There was no denying what he'd seen with his own eyes. "When you die, you'll burn and you'll come back. Again and again." He wanted to taste her. That was why Wyatt had agreed to let her come back. Wyatt wanted to watch his two test subjects interact.

No, Wyatt wanted more than to just see them interact. The guy was all about his experiments. About creating a being who would be unstoppable.

You want us to fuck. You want to see if it's possible for a vampire and a phoenix to reproduce. 'Cause if we could, wouldn't that make the perfect little supersoldier for your army?

"I didn't even know my own name." Her stark confession. She was lost. Scared. "When the fire cleared, I couldn't even remember who I was. I was lost. There was . . . you."

He had to kiss her. Ryder's lips feathered over Sabine's. She gasped lightly at the contact, but didn't pull away. Her nails were still pressing into his arms, and when his tongue slid into her mouth, the sting of her nails was a sweet pain.

Then she kissed him back. Her tongue was hesitant at first, but she quickly grew a little bolder. Stroking him. Tasting him.

His cock swelled even more and pushed against her. This was what Wyatt wanted. For Ryder to seduce her. To take her.

All part of the deal.

The guy had even sent in a small bed, when Ryder had been sleeping on his floor during all the other long days and nights of his captivity. The bed was supposed to make the fucking easier.

And though Ryder wanted her—*hell, yes*—he wasn't about to fuck on command.

Not for Wyatt. Not for anyone.

His mouth pulled away from hers. "What did Wyatt tell you?"

"That—that there were more experiments to come."

Yes, there were. The experiments wouldn't stop, unless *they* stopped them. "You have to call up the fire."

"Ryder!" Wyatt's snarl blasted through the speaker.

Screw him. "Call up the fire, and none of the guards will be able to hurt you."

She shook her head. "They'll drug me. They keep injecting me."

"Burn hot enough, and the drug won't be able to get to you." If she had a wall of flames in front of her, if she burned with all of her power, then she'd be safe.

Her gaze was so confused and scared. She didn't understand. Dammit. The guards would be coming soon. So he grabbed her. She yelped and punched at him, but, in an instant, Ryder had trapped her against the far wall and, just like before, he used his body to block Wyatt's view of her.

"One of your parents had to be a phoenix, too." Because what she was—it was in the blood. "They must have told you—"

Her eyes were stark, whispering with pain. "My real parents abandoned me when I was two years old."

That sure explained how she hadn't known that she was a supernatural. She'd been totally clueless, completely unprepared for Wyatt's torture. *Unprepared for me*.

"I don't want to be a monster." Her words were hushed.

He stiffened, knowing that his next words would be brutal, but she had to face facts. "Too bad, because you are." They didn't have time for a pity party. He had to get her to embrace the beast within her. They needed that beast for their survival. She couldn't pretend to be human—being human wouldn't save their asses. Being an unstoppable machine of fire and fury? Oh yes, that would buy them a ticket to freedom. "You need to learn how to call up that beast that lives inside of you. Because Wyatt has big plans for you. Plans that involve you dying and screaming and him using you to create a whole new army."

She shook her head. "You want to hurt me, too." Her lips were red from his kiss. "You want—"

"He's going to give you to another vampire."

The color bled from her face.

"Your blood . . . there's something about it." *When I taste it, I just want more.* Because it tasted like pure, hot power flowing on his tongue. The best wine, the wildest drug, all rolled into one.

He held her shoulders against the wall. Ryder had to make her understand what was happening—and why she needed to pull up the phoenix inside. "He's going to make sure you die again."

She blanched. "No, I don't want to! *Help me.*"

He wanted to. Ryder was tearing apart inside. "I will. You trust me, and I'll help you." He hadn't helped anyone else in a century, but he'd just given his word to her. *A second chance.* "We have to get out of the facility."

The only way out was through Wyatt.

The guards were just steps away from the cell. He could hear their shuffling footsteps.

"You're breaking our deal," Wyatt told him through the speaker, sounding not too shocked.

Ryder tossed a vicious grin over his shoulder, a grin aimed at the two-way mirror. "What are you gonna do? Kill me?"

The door opened. Ryder's gaze jerked to the left. The armed guards stood in the entranceway. They weren't wearing their fireproof suits, but they were all heavily armed.

"Maybe we'll let you watch as we kill her," Wyatt said. Of course, he wasn't with the guards. The guy was far too much of a coward to come and face him when Ryder was strong.

The guards lifted their weapons. Aimed them at Ryder's body. He was shielding Sabine, blocking her so that the guards couldn't even see her body.

"New deal," Wyatt thundered out.

He wanted that man's head.

"Drink her blood, Ryder, or I'll find a vamp that will." The weapons stayed pointed at him.

"This hardly sets the mood," Ryder drawled lightly even as his fingers tightened on Sabine. *No other vampire could drink from her.* "An audience isn't really my thing."

The weapons weren't lowering.

"No! You can't do this!" Sabine pushed against Ryder. "We have rights! You can't just lock us up like this!"

Ah, she was still singing *that* song, was she? Still clinging to her humanity, when they needed her beast out. "Wyatt doesn't think monsters have rights."

You're a monster, love. Face it. He got that she didn't want to give up the illusion of safety that humanity entailed, but Sabine needed to look around. They were prisoners, she'd *died,* and the only way out was through her flames.

She didn't want to believe that she was just as much of a beast as he was, but there was no point denying the truth. The woman could freaking burn. Die and burn and live again. Not a talent that the average human possessed.

"Take her blood, Ryder," Wyatt ordered him. "Take her blood, *now*."

There was a feverish intensity in the words. An intensity that made Ryder worry . . . just what had Wyatt done? Why was the scientist so determined for Ryder to drink her then?

He didn't take his eyes off the guards as he asked Sabine, "Did he give you something before you came in?"

"They've been injecting me with drugs all week."

When he drank her blood, he'd get dosed with whatever brew was in her veins. His fingers fell away from her shoulders.

"I don't want you drinking from me," she told him. Her shoulder brushed against his as her body pressed closer to him. "I've been having nightmares about you every night."

Great. So he was the big, bad boogeyman to her. What else was new? But, really, there was no other way for her to picture him. *I drained her.* The guilt still ate at him. The woman was right to hate and fear him. Hell, she should probably get in line on that score. Plenty of humans—and vampires—felt the exact same way.

He just wished that he didn't have this need for her. The need had to be coming from her blood. Some kind of side effect that was messing with his head. Temporary, surely?

"I can hold on to my control." The words were flat, and he hoped they were the truth.

Her gaze slanted up at him. "Didn't you say that last time?"

Last time he hadn't known that a phoenix was being offered to him. He focused on the guards as he made his demand. "I want a wooden stake." Like they wouldn't have plenty of those handy. In this place, the smart guards should have them all tucked in their boots.

If they were smart. He actually wasn't certain that any of the guards qualified as smart. If they had any brains, they wouldn't be keeping him captive. They'd know to run, fast and hard, away from him.

Because he wouldn't be in a cage forever, and Ryder made a point of always getting payback.

"Why?" Wyatt demanded. "Why do you need a stake?"

Ryder cast his gaze to the two-way mirror. "Because if I can't stop drinking her blood, then I want her to stake me."

Sabine gasped.

Ryder smiled. "Like you said, it's a new deal."

"You're insane," Sabine told him, words tumbling out quickly. "I might be new to this whole supernatural bit, but even I know that vampires aren't supposed to *ask* for stakes."

He shrugged. "You'd rather I just drink from you without—"

"*I want that stake!*" Sabine shouted.

"Fine," Wyatt bit out. Static crackled for an instant on the intercom, then Ryder heard the guy say, "Mitchell, give the man his stake."

A few tense moments later, Mitchell, body sweating and twitchy, edged into the room. He pulled a stake from his back pocket.

The guards should have used these when they tried to take her from me before. Instead of shooting him, they should have staked him. But Ryder knew why they hadn't. Wyatt had wanted him alive then.

Now? Now it looked like the guy was still playing with him.

Let's play, bastard.

The stake was the first weapon that he needed.

Mitchell tossed the stake to him. Ryder grabbed it with his right hand. "Now get the hell out," he ordered the humans with bared fangs. "Before I decide to drop some bodies to the floor."

They got the hell out. Weapons or not, they were still scared spitless.

Who has the power, Wyatt? He knew the doctor would see the challenge in his eyes. Wyatt kept him locked up tight because he knew that if Ryder ever got free, the humans in Genesis would all be dead.

That's why you want me to take her blood, isn't it? Because it's all about control.

Ryder was ready to rip that control away.

He caught Sabine's wrist with his left hand and pulled her toward the bed.

Her heels dug into the hard floor. "Oh no, you're not—"

He was. They were.

He pushed her onto the bed. She immediately bounced right back to a sitting position on the mattress. He almost smiled at her. The woman was fast.

He was faster.

He pushed the stake into her hand. Her fingers closed around it, and she stared up at him with dark eyes that looked as if they could steal his soul.

Not that he had a soul to steal.

Not anymore. He'd lost that long ago.

He knelt in front of her, pushing between her legs. She swallowed but didn't speak. His fingers wrapped around hers, tightening her grip on the stake.

Then he lifted the weapon to his heart. If this act didn't earn her trust, he figured nothing would.

The experiment between the vampire and the phoenix was progressing far better than Richard Wyatt could have hoped.

He watched the two of them through the observation glass, anticipation filling him.

Sabine had the stake against the vampire's heart.

The door opened behind Richard. "You think she's gonna kill him?" the guard demanded. There was no missing the eagerness in Mitchell's tone.

"Doubtful."

"But he drained her!" Mitchell snapped. "The woman's got to want some revenge! She should want to hurt him!"

Like you do? Richard knew that Mitchell hated the vampire. Mostly because the man knew just how powerful Ryder was.

We hate what we fear.

A lesson he'd learned long ago. His father had taught him that lesson when Richard had been a child.

"She won't kill him." Richard knew the truth was actually that Sabine couldn't kill the vampire. Ryder was the fastest vamp that Richard had ever seen, and plenty of the undead had been brought through the doors of Genesis.

Ryder wasn't like those others. At first, Richard had thought that Ryder was just another test subject. Another vampire that could be used as a genetic donor for his experiments but Ryder's reflexes were too fast. His body healed *too quickly*. He didn't need the weekly blood supply that the others required in order to keep living.

And the man's strength was incredible to behold. He'd ripped the heart right out of one guard's chest. An unfortunate incident, but one that had taught them all—

Never get too close to the vampire.

During his observations, Wyatt had quickly realized that Ryder had not appeared to have any weaknesses. Certainly not any attachments. He killed guards who made the foolish mistake of coming to him. He drained them with a brutal efficiency. He never showed remorse or guilt.

Wyatt had begun to think the fellow might be a sociopath, in addition to having the curse of being a bloodsucker.

Then Sabine had entered Ryder's cell, and he'd seen the dangerous intensity ignite in Ryder's gaze.

Ryder had fed from her, but, when she'd been near death, the vampire had seemed to . . .

Break.

Wyatt tapped the glass in front of him. The two figures appeared frozen. The tip of the stake pushed hard into Ryder's chest. The vampire had one hand on Sabine's thigh while his other hand locked around Sabine's fist—the fist that gripped the stake.

"Drink up," Wyatt murmured. Ryder had to drink. The more blood that he took from her, the greater his weakness—and possibly his strength—would become.

It was a catch-22, but it was for the good of science.

As for Sabine, she'd begin her own transformation soon enough.

Ryder probably thought the big plan was for Sabine and the vamp to fuck. To breed.

Wyatt wasn't interested in creating a new life. He wanted transformation, not birth.

When Sabine took in Ryder's blood, how soon would she transform? Was it even possible to make a phoenix into a vampire?

I'll find out. His fingers pressed the button for the intercom. "Time to drink, Ryder."

The vamp's shoulders stiffened, but the hand on Sabine's thigh rose, and a few seconds later, Ryder brushed back Sabine's hair and bared her throat.

CHAPTER FOUR

"**W**ait." Fear churned in Sabine's stomach as she stared into Ryder's eyes. When a vamp was about to sink his teeth into a girl's throat, he shouldn't look so . . .

Reassuring. And, um, sexy.

Especially when said girl had a stake pressed to his heart. Why the heck had he given her the stake? Her fingers trembled around it. After what he'd done, maybe she should drive it into his chest but . . .

I need him. The truth was there. Desperate. He was her only hope in this nightmare. The vampire scared her, but the man named Richard Wyatt? He terrified her. He *liked* to hurt her.

Ryder had said that he'd help her. The vampire was the only one that she could trust.

Provided he didn't drain her dry. Her fingers tightened around the stake. "Aren't vampires supposed to have some power to control the minds of their victims? Can't you just make me forget what you did before? Make me—" Sabine broke off, unable to say the last.

He finished for her. "Make you want my bite." The words were deep and dark.

She almost shuddered. The last thing she wanted right then was to feel his teeth sinking into her throat. She hadn't been lying about those nightmares. He'd been starring in her dreams all week. Not those lab coat–wearing jailers and their constant needles. Ryder.

Fangs. Fury.

Only after he bit her in her nightmares, sometimes, he did . . . more. Things that didn't scare her, but turned her on. She swallowed.

"Would you want me to take your will away?"

She realized he hadn't actually answered her question. *Could* he do it? Could he take the memory away?

But with all the crazy crap that was going on already, did she want to add mind control to her list?

No, thank you.

"It took me three days to remember who I was." She licked her lips. His gaze dropped to her mouth. Lingered. His gaze seemed to heat. "So no, don't take the memory away." It had just been desperation talking. "I don't want anyone to ever mess with my mind again." Because she was convinced that Wyatt had done something to her. He'd made her forget.

Hadn't he?

Ryder's hand seemed heavy against her throat, and his thumb was stroking her skin. A small, circular caress.

"You don't seem as—as wild as before," she blurted. It was true and reassuring.

His gaze rose back to meet hers. "I drank from four guards when they took you away. Before you, it had been months since I fed."

The twisting in her stomach got worse. "If you try to

take too much from me, I *will* kill you." Fair warning. She remembered his unbreakable hold. The terror that had clawed through her.

"To stop me, just drive the stake into my heart."

The rough edge of the wood rubbed against her fingers.

His head began to lower toward her neck.

"No!"

He froze.

"Um, not the neck, okay? Bad memories. Really bad." Like there were any good memories of this place.

But Ryder nodded, and the overhead light glinted off the dark gold of his hair.

He took her left hand then and lifted her wrist toward his mouth. "Better?"

In the grand scheme of things? Probably not. But her wrist was a better option than her neck. Her breath rasped out. She was so in over her head. *A vampire. He's a real vampire and I'm—I don't know what I am.*

Monster.

His lips feathered over her skin. Sabine jerked and her fist shoved the stake against him. Not *into* him, but—

Ryder was watching her with that green stare. A stare that seemed so intense that it actually made her feel like he was looking *into* her. Then he quietly ordered, "You must trust me. I won't let you down again." A grim pause then, "Stop thinking about what happened before."

Her laugh was weak. "That's a little impossible."

"*Sabine.*" He said her name like it was a caress. The way a man would say it in bed.

They *were* in bed. She was, anyway.

"Close your eyes," he told her. "Think of something good."

There was nothing good there. They were prisoners. No one knew where she was, and Sabine wasn't even sure of *what* she was any longer.

The right corner of his mouth hitched up. "Your eyes aren't closed."

The vampire couldn't be teasing her right then. The blood of the men he'd killed—*her* blood—stained the floor. But he was lightly holding her hand. Gazing into her eyes. Looking at her like a lover.

"You need to let the fear go."

"Easy for you to say," she muttered. "I didn't sink my teeth into you and not let go."

His smile vanished. "No, you didn't." He pressed a kiss to the inside of her wrist.

She closed her eyes.

Now you do that?"

Sabine didn't answer him. Something good. She had good memories rattling around in her mind, now that her memories were actually back, anyway. She could pull some of them out.

"Where were you the last time you were happy?" Ryder asked her.

The image slipped through her mind. The dark bar. The laughter. The blues music that hung in the air. Rhett's music. "New Orleans." Her home. The only one she'd ever known. "At my brother's bar."

His breath rushed out. "You have a *brother*?"

The memory wanted to drift away. She held it tight. "N-not blood. The people who adopted me—my parents—they already had Rhett." Rhett had been the reassuring constant in her life. Always there. Always watching out for her. With her eyes closed, she could see him so easily in her mind. "He was playing the blues, and I was dancing behind the bar." The whole family had been there. Laughter. Voices mellow. She'd been swaying to the music, thinking how lucky she was. "I sang with him." Her lips curled. "I sound like a dying frog when I sing. Half the crowd left instantly."

His laughter came, surprising her, and her lashes flew up.

He looked different when he laughed. Still dangerous, but *different*.

He drained your blood. Don't go weakening around him.

"Hold that memory," Ryder told her as his laughter faded away.

She closed her eyes again.

His mouth was on her wrist. Pressing lightly. His lips parted. His teeth sank into her wrist, and there was only the faintest flash of pain, not nearly as bad as the prick of Wyatt's needles, then Ryder's mouth tightened on her skin. He was sucking her flesh. Taking her blood.

The fear rose within her once more.

Hold the good memory.

She tried to hold it. *Singing in the bar. Rhett shaking his head as he told her that the blues just wouldn't ever be for her. Her mother had waved her on. Sabine had laughed until her sides ached.*

His mouth seemed to harden on her wrist as Ryder took *more*.

The memory flew away from her as her eyes shot open once again. The stake was slippery in her sweaty hand, but she wasn't about to let that thing go. *"Ryder."*

His eyes were open, too. Open and locked right on her. His pupils were swelling as he stared at her, swallowing up the green of his eyes. So much hunger was in that stare. Hunger, desire.

A dark lust.

Her heart raced in her chest. "I don't want to hurt you." Was that the truth? Or a lie? She wasn't sure. *He hurt you.* The stake pressed down harder. "But I will." Sabine let the stake draw blood, just to show that she wasn't making an empty threat.

Say it and mean it. Her father's advice. *Don't take shit from anybody in this world.* A favorite mantra of his.

Ryder's fangs slowly lifted from her skin. His tongue swiped over the small wounds he'd left behind, lightly lapping at the skin.

The rasp of his tongue shouldn't have turned her on. It probably should have given her more nightmares. *A vampire. Drinking from me!*

But Sabine could admit to herself that the bite *had* turned her on. Her nipples were aching and heavy, and arousal had her shifting and arching her hips slightly.

One more lick, and his head rose. "Your taste is incredible."

Right, what was that, like a vampire pickup line?

He glanced down at the stake. Maybe he was just now realizing that he was bleeding, courtesy of her. It seemed only fair that they'd both drawn blood. He reached for the stake, but then his body began to sag.

She tried to grab him. The stake fell to the floor, and so did Ryder.

His eyes were closing. "What . . . did . . . you . . ."

She hadn't done anything. Had she? Sabine crouched at his side. "What's happening?" She'd been the one on the floor after the last bite.

Ryder started to shake—hard, heavy convulsions.

Then the cell door flew open. Guards stormed in, with their weapons raised.

"Get back!" one of them yelled at her.

She held Ryder's hand tighter. Sabine didn't even remember reaching for his hand, but now she was holding on to him for dear life. "Something's wrong with him!"

"No, my dear," Wyatt said as he pushed through the guards. "He's having the exact response to the drug that we'd hoped."

Drug? Understanding dawned. *The drugs they gave me.*

"Get his blood," Wyatt ordered the man on his right. A smaller guy with nervous hands and bright, red hair. The man's lab coat swirled around him as he hurried forward.

Sabine grabbed the stake. "Don't you touch him!" She held the stake up like a knife.

Wyatt laughed. "Shoot her."

What?

The guard at Wyatt's shoulder shot her. Sabine screamed as the tranq dart embedded in her chest.

She tried to hold on to the stake, but it rolled right out of her suddenly numb fingers.

The redhead was crouching over Ryder now, taking the vampire's blood and filling up test tubes. A *lot* of test tubes.

"Take the female subject back to her room," Wyatt ordered.

Sabine's body was about to crash onto the floor when two of the guards hoisted her back to her feet. Well, okay, her legs weren't exactly steady, so when they started walking, her feet dragged behind them.

"Good job," Wyatt told her with a small smile. "I knew you'd be able to get to him."

Wait, *what?* Her body might not be working right, but her mind was still functioning pretty dang well. Wyatt was making it sound as if she'd been working with him.

Her gaze darted back to Ryder. Of course, his lashes would have flickered and started to open right then. His green stare was far too aware as it locked on her.

He's awake. Which meant . . . *They're dead.*

And, wow, the guy sure hadn't been out for long.

Her expression must have given her away because Wyatt suddenly swore and grabbed for the blood-filled test tubes. *"Get her out of here!"*

They hauled ass getting her out the door. Wyatt was on her heels, more guards rushing behind him.

And the redhead who'd taken Ryder's blood—

She managed to turn her head and lock her gaze on him.

The redhead didn't make it out.

The metal door closed on his scream.

Lethargy pulled at Sabine's body, but she forced her eyes to stay open. They'd just hit her with one tranq this time, surely she could fight this.

Her head sagged forward. *Or not. Dammit.*

She hated to be so weak.

The guards began to haul her away.

"No!" Wyatt suddenly snapped. "She needs to see this."

She tried to slap at them, but her hands just fluttered in the air like useless birds. Then she was in another room, one with dim lights and lots of computers and machines.

"*Look* at him," Wyatt ordered as he took hold of her chin and forced her head back up.

Sabine blinked and stared straight ahead. At Ryder. She was looking through the two-way mirror.

Ryder was in his cell, and the redheaded man was in front of him. Ryder had one hand on the man's throat. It looked like the redhead was begging.

"See what he is?" Wyatt demanded, his fingers pressing hard into her chin. "Do you see why he can't be free?"

Ryder's eyes narrowed. Uh-oh. Could he hear them? It sure looked like he had. Wyatt hadn't even been speaking into the microphone, but Sabine was certain Ryder had heard the scientist's words. *Enhanced vamp hearing. Very enhanced.*

"Open the cell door!" Ryder roared. "Or you can watch as I rip his throat open."

The guards holding her shifted nervously.

Wyatt stepped away from her and bent over the small microphone. "You can't be set free," Wyatt said, voice snapping. "You're far too dangerous. By keeping you here, we keep the humans in the world *safe*."

Ryder sank his teeth into the redhead's throat. The guy screamed and tried to fight, but he was no match for Ryder.

"We-we can't just let him die," the guard to her right muttered. He was sweating. She could almost smell his fear.

"That's Jim Thomas—he's got a wife," another guard muttered. "A baby coming."

Wyatt stared straight through the glass. With a supreme effort, Sabine managed to keep her gaze open and on Ryder.

Ryder's head lifted. Blood dripped from his mouth. "Next time, it won't be just a bite. I'll rip his whole throat open."

She knew his threat was real. So did the guards.

"That vampire's too dangerous," one said, the sweaty one on her right. "He needs to be put down."

Wyatt's head jerked toward them. "That would be a waste, Donaldson."

"He's killed our men!" Donaldson fired back as his fingers dug into Sabine's arm. "He's about to kill Jim! He can't be controlled."

"Of course he can." Wyatt sounded annoyed, as if he were talking to a small child. His mouth was still close to the microphone as he said, "Just take out your gun and put it to her head."

Nausea rolled through Sabine. The guard hesitated.

"Do you want to watch Jim Thomas die?" Wyatt pushed.

The guard lifted his gun. The barrel pressed into Sabine's temple.

"Good," Wyatt murmured. His gaze darted back to the observation window.

Ryder had frozen. He knew exactly what was happening in that observation room.

"If you don't let the doctor go, then Donaldson will put a bullet into Sabine's brain."

Ryder's claws—*he had claws bursting from his fingertips*—dug into the doctor's throat. "So what? You shoot her, she burns, then she comes back."

Wyatt actually smiled at that response. "Yes, but we both know that death hurts, don't we? Do you want her to suffer, vampire?"

Ryder didn't speak.

If Sabine had been able to do so, she would have shouted, *I don't want to suffer!*

"Perhaps you do." From Wyatt. Considering. "Perhaps you enjoy her pain." Wyatt waved his hand toward Donaldson. "Go ahead, shoot her."

Donaldson hesitated. Sabine tried to fight the nausea and the lethargy and the heart-numbing fear. "D-don't," she managed to gasp. "I have . . . family . . . too."

Donaldson's blue gaze cut to the glass. To Ryder.

"Do it!" Wyatt barked.

Donaldson looked back at her. "You aren't human." He said the words as if he were trying to convince himself. His finger began to squeeze the trigger.

Jim Thomas flew into the two-way glass. Ryder had tossed the doctor straight at them.

"Take the gun fucking away from her head," Ryder snarled.

Donaldson lifted the gun.

"Get the asshole out of here," Ryder said, shoulders heaving, as he jerked his thumb toward the door.

The vampire just saved me. Tears stung her eyes.

Wyatt inclined his head toward Donaldson. The guy nodded and rushed to claim his friend. But as soon as Donaldson stepped one foot inside Ryder's cell, the vampire attacked.

He grabbed Donaldson, tossed him around like a rag doll a few times, and then shoved the guard's own weapon right against his temple.

"That was a mistake," Ryder growled at him. "You never, *ever* put a gun to a woman's head." He drove his teeth into Donaldson's throat. The guard screamed and tried to fight.

Wyatt just watched. Then, after a moment, he sighed. "Briggs, shoot the woman."

Briggs—the guard still holding her—stared at Sabine with wide eyes.

And he didn't reach for his gun. Sabine knew why.

Don't want to wind up like Donaldson, do you?

Wyatt must have realized the guard wasn't obeying because he whirled around, grabbed the man's gun, and pressed it against Sabine's chest.

Then they heard the laughter. Ryder's laughter. Sounding crazed.

Wyatt paused, then looked over his shoulder.

Ryder had hauled both men—still alive, barely, from the looks of them—toward the cell door. The men lay in a crumpled heap. Ryder was on the bed. His hands behind his head. "Come and get them," he called, voice almost mocking.

Then he just closed his eyes.

The drug was pumping fast and furiously through Sabine's veins, and, even though her arms and legs felt leaden, her heart raced so hard that her chest hurt. "He let . . . them go." *Now let me go.*

"Yes," Wyatt murmured. "He did."

So why hadn't the guy dropped his gun?

"But today's experiment isn't over yet." Wyatt stared right in Sabine's eyes. "Let's see how long it takes for your memory to recover this time."

Even though Ryder had freed the men, Wyatt was going to *shoot* her. Sabine tried to struggle but her body wouldn't listen to her mental commands.

"Briggs, take her back to her room. Strap her down."

Her breath rushed out in desperate relief. He wasn't going to shoot her. He—

"Then shoot her in the heart."

Briggs hauled her out of the observation room, and Ryder's roar of fury followed her.

* * *

The blood was bitter on his tongue. Too harsh. Too metallic. Not like hers. *Not like Sabine's.*

Ryder stood in the middle of his cell. Head bowed, shoulders sagging, a deliberate pose of defeat.

His fangs were burning in his mouth, and he wanted to spit out the blood that he could still taste.

What the hell? A vampire never turned away blood, but this time the blood had just been a means to an end. Not the sweet, powerful nourishment that he usually craved.

The observation room was empty. The dead silence from the other room told him that no one was watching him then.

Because you're off torturing Sabine?

He wanted to bellow again with his fury. Instead, he closed his eyes. He sucked in a deep breath, and he tried to reach her with his mind.

He'd taken her blood twice. The psychic link should exist between them now. Their blood link. Not all vampires could forge those bonds with their victims.

He wasn't all vampires. *Wyatt, you fool, you should have left me the hell alone.*

Now Wyatt would die. Everyone who'd helped him would die.

Because Ryder wasn't some fresh vamp who'd been newly turned.

I am ancient. I am power.

I am death.

And he used all of his power right then, trying to reach out to Sabine, to make sure that she was still alive and—

A wall of flames.

He couldn't reach her mind. He could feel her. The fear. The fury. But there were flames stopping his mind from connecting to hers. The blood link between them wasn't strong enough to get past the flames that shielded her mind.

His hands clenched into fists as his eyelids flew open. No one had ever been able to escape his blood link. Not demons. Not witches. Not djinn or shifters.

But the flames just burned brighter in his mind's eye. There was no getting to Sabine. He *couldn't* reach her.

He wondered if anyone could.

Ryder forced his hands to unclench. If he couldn't get a psychic link to Sabine, then he'd just have to get a physical link with her. She could resist the blood bond but others wouldn't be so strong. Humans were particularly susceptible to the link.

Oh Thomas . . . And Ryder pictured the redheaded doctor in his mind. Jim Thomas.

The doctor's blood beat in Ryder's veins. Blood that didn't satisfy. That just made him hunger all the more for Sabine.

He couldn't question that growing hunger, not then. He had to focus on his escape.

Jim Thomas. He felt the doctor's presence instantly as he locked on the terrified human. He'd bitten other humans while he'd been at Genesis, but the rage had been in control then. Ryder had bitten, drunk, and killed.

This time, his control had been stronger. He'd left the humans alive. *The better to use them.*

Wyatt didn't understand the monster that he had in front of him. Didn't understand the power of the beast.

Despite all of the security and guards, Genesis wouldn't hold Ryder.

Not now, now when he had his own prey to help him escape.

Ryder closed his eyes once more as he focused his energy. Darkness, just for an instant, then . . . then he was *seeing* through Thomas's eyes. The blood link was very strong. *Humans*. Sometimes they had their uses.

Thomas was in a white room. A redheaded woman with a stethoscope draped around her neck stood before him. Patching up the wound on his throat? The bastard was lucky he'd gotten such a light bite.

If I hadn't wanted to keep you alive, I would have ripped out your throat.

Thomas stiffened and whimpered, and Ryder knew the man had heard his thoughts.

That's right, human. I'm in your head. I can read your mind. See every fear that you've ever had.

Thomas opened his mouth. "The vampire—he's—"

Shut up. Ryder's instant command.

Jim Thomas's lips clamped together.

The doctor in front of him frowned. "Are you all right, Jim?" Her voice was clipped, a tight NY accent. Old money. Her fingers smoothed over his bandage. "Did the vampire hurt you anywhere else?"

I have no other wounds. Ryder pushed the thought into Thomas's head.

"I-I have no other wounds," the guy said instantly.

Ryder felt the pulse of the human's surprise. And his fear. The fear was like a thick fog in the man's head.

That's right, Jim Thomas. I'm in your mind, and you won't be able to get me out. I am in control. You should never have walked into my cage.

Because now the doctor was his bitch.

Thomas whimpered.

The woman's eyes narrowed. "I think you need a sedative."

No, Thomas getting knocked out for the night wouldn't suit his purposes at all.

Get up.

Thomas jumped off the exam table.

Tell her to fuck off. Ryder smiled, and kept his head down. It wouldn't do for any of the cameras to catch his expression. No one was watching now, but Wyatt would no doubt review the footage from his cell.

"Fuck off, Vivian," Thomas said as he shoved by the other doctor.

Her gasp followed him.

Thomas was appalled at himself. Flushing. Shaking his head.

Oh right, because saying that makes you feel bad, but torturing vampires and shifters—you don't ever feel a bit guilty for those crimes?

Thomas's heart raced faster, and, surprise, surprise—Ryder did sense guilt in the man's mind. Guilt and the dark knowledge that if Thomas didn't do his job, Wyatt would go after his wife. His unborn child.

So you let us all suffer in order to keep them safe?

Thomas had no answer, but maybe that was because he couldn't speak. Ryder had frozen his tongue and mouth. All Thomas could do was walk down the long hallway, glancing to the left and the right so that Ryder could learn the schematics of the facility.

Come to me. Ryder shoved the thought into Thomas's head and knew it would be a compulsion. *Cut the surveillance feed from my room. Open the door. Get me the hell out of here.*

And Thomas rushed to obey. A puppet on a string. A puppet with no will. No control.

Oh, that wasn't technically true. Thomas's mind was still functioning. Ryder could feel his psychic screams but . . .

You can't stop me.

Not with the blood link in place. No one could stop him.

The human went into the surveillance room. A guard turned toward him with a smile. "Hey, doc, heard that bastard vamp took a bite out of you—"

Go for his throat.

Thomas attacked him. Punching and clawing. The guard wasn't expecting the attack, and because of that, Thomas's rather feeble hits were able to take the man down.

Thomas, you should try working out sometime. It wouldn't kill you. Ryder smiled. *But I might.*

Thomas left the guard sprawled on the ground. A few taps of his fingers across the keyboard disabled the surveillance on Ryder's cell.

Ryder lifted his head. Now, he didn't care if anyone saw his grin.

Come to my cell. Get the damn door open.

Because he needed out of there. Ryder had to get to Sabine before Wyatt and his sadistic band of scientists tried more of their experiments on her.

Thomas all but ran back to him. The guy's fingers trembled as he swiped the key card over the control panel. The lights flashed green. The door opened.

Ryder lunged forward. He grabbed Thomas by the throat. "That wasn't so hard, was it?" Ryder asked as he slid from the human's mind.

Thomas whimpered. The guy did a lot of that.

"I could kill you right now," Ryder whispered to him. It would be so easy. A jerk of his hand would snap the human's neck. Or he could use his fangs to rip open the man's throat.

Jim Thomas's eyes were wide and desperate. "P-please."

Ryder threw him across the room. Thomas's back slammed into the wall. "Hope you like the cell." He stepped out of that containment hell. Shut the door. Heard the whir of the lock click into place.

I'm letting you live. Be fucking grateful. Thomas would be able to go back to his wife.

Ryder was being merciful. A fairly new concept for him. And he didn't even know why the hell he was bothering.

The child. The whisper came from inside of him as he hurried down the hallways. *You know what it's like when a child grows up alone.*

Yes, he knew all too well.

He inhaled as he ran, pulling in all the scents around him. The cold scent of antiseptic. Bleach. The rotting stench of death. So many dead bodies. Wyatt had been a busy man.

He inhaled again. Caught the wilder, woodsy scent that Ryder knew came from shifters—that scent drifted from upstairs.

But the scent of fire . . . the scent of woman . . . the sweet but rich scent that he'd come to associate with Sabine—that scent came from dead ahead.

Ryder rushed forward. He expected to walk right into the room that housed Sabine. Instead Ryder entered an observation room. Two white-lab-coat-wearing bastards whirled toward him when he entered. Three seconds later, they hit the floor, unconscious.

Ryder looked out of that tinted glass. Another two-way mirror. He stared at Sabine. She was strapped to a table, while a guard headed toward her. The man had a gun in his hand.

Donaldson. Ryder recognized the guard instantly, and not just because he had a blood-soaked bandage at his throat. The guard's bitter blood flowed within Ryder. The man—with his too short hair and tight, furious features—stared at Sabine with hate.

Are you pissed because I took a bite out of you? Ryder shoved the thought right at the guard. As with Thomas, forming the link with this human was effortless. All he'd needed was the blood, and, of course, to actually let the humans keep living long enough to use the link.

Donaldson stiffened.

That's right. I'm inside of you now. There's no getting away.

The guard's trembling hand lifted the gun. This guy was stronger than Thomas had been. *There's no use fighting. You're not powerful enough to stop me.*

"Please, don't!" Sabine yelled as she yanked against the straps that held her down.

Ryder could easily read Donaldson's thoughts. *She's not human. The bitch deserves this pain. She'll hurt, she'll die, then she'll come back again.*

It's not like she can ever really die.

The guard's thoughts enraged Ryder. *No,* Ryder pushed into Donaldson's mind as he grabbed the cell key card off one of the fallen doctors at his feet. *She won't die, and you won't hurt her. So stop pointing that gun at her. Point it at your own damn self.*

Ryder swiped the key card at the control box on Sabine's cell. The lights flashed, and he ran into the room.

He found Donaldson standing near Sabine's restrained figure. The guard had the barrel of the gun pressed against his own chest. Donaldson's eyes were wild, and he screamed, "Stop! Stop me!"

Sabine wasn't screaming. She just stared at the guard in wild horror.

Then she looked at Ryder. Her lips shook. "What's—what's happening?"

He rushed to her. Yanked away the restraints and pulled her into his arms. "You're safe."

She shook against him even as she wrapped her arms around him and held Ryder as tight as she could. As if she'd never let him go.

No one had ever held him like that. Most were too eager to escape him.

She knows what I am. What I can do. What I did to her.

And still she wants me? His chest ached. *My second chance.*

His arms curled around her. "I'm going to take you out of here." Take her out, then come back to destroy the place. Wyatt wouldn't get away with his sick experiments any longer.

She nodded against him, and her silken hair brushed over the side of his neck. He inhaled her scent, bringing it even deeper into his lungs. The scent soothed the fury that had been boiling to such a dangerous degree within him.

"I want to go home," she told him, the words a whisper. She'd longed for her home before.

He eased back just enough to stare down at her. She didn't seem to realize it yet, but her "home" wasn't going to be a real option for her, not anymore. She'd changed.

The humans at her "home" hadn't.

But he found he couldn't crush the faint hope in her eyes.

Then her gaze darted to the guard and her dark eyes widened in alarm. "What is he doing?"

"Can't stop!" Donaldson yelled before Ryder could speak. *"He's in my head."*

Ryder pulled Sabine up to her feet. "Forget about him." He wouldn't give the order for the guard to shoot. Not until Sabine was out of the room. No sense in her seeing that blood and gore.

But I'm not letting you go, Donaldson. You put a gun to her head. You were about to shoot her, both in my cell and now, with her tied down like an animal. Do you think I'll let you live after this?

Tears leaked from Donaldson's eyes. No, the man didn't think he'd be living past these last few moments.

Ryder pushed Sabine toward the door. "Come on." He didn't know how long they'd have before his escape was discovered. An alarm could ring out at any second.

But Sabine stopped walking. The woman froze against him. She looked over at Donaldson, then back at Ryder. "He doesn't . . . why is he pushing the gun against his own heart?"

Because I'm telling him to do it, love. And as soon as you leave the room, I'll tell him to pull that trigger.

Ryder shrugged. "Maybe he just can't live with the crimes on his soul. Bet he's played attack dog for Wyatt plenty of times."

And he had. Ryder could see the memories. So many dark, terrible deeds. Donaldson had killed before. Shifters. Witches.

As long as they weren't human, did you think their deaths didn't matter?

Donaldson gave a faint nod.

Wrong answer, bastard. They mattered.

Sabine's fingers caught his hand. Squeezed. "Whatever you're doing, *stop*."

He blinked at her in surprise.

"Don't be like them. Don't kill just because they do."

So misguided. He wasn't killing because the humans had started a battle. He was killing because that was his nature. You didn't tell the snake not to strike, and you didn't tell the vamp not to kill.

"Promise me," she said, shaking her head and still refusing to move when he gave her a harder shove. "Promise that you won't kill him. Just leave him here, lock him up in this cell, and let's go."

Ryder didn't like to make promises that he couldn't keep. In fact, he never made a promise unless he was sure that he could follow through on his words.

Others had broken their vows to him. They'd paid. In blood.

"If you don't give me your word," she hesitated, then said, "I won't leave with you. I-I'll find my own way out. I'll stay until I'm sure you're gone, sure that you won't kill him, then I'll escape."

He lifted his hand. Stroked the silk of her cheek. Watched with interest as her pupils dilated. Sabine had such a fast, primal response to him. Did she realize that?

I have the same response to her. "My love," he breathed the words, "that man was about to put his gun to your heart and pull the trigger. You don't need to feel sorry for him."

Her gaze searched his. "It's not him I care about. It's you. Be *better* than the ones who hold us here."

He wasn't better. Would never be. She just didn't understand who he was yet. What he was. Despite what he'd done to her, she didn't understand.

Sabine stared up at him, hope struggling desperately to shine in her eyes.

He found he couldn't destroy that hope. "He won't die by my hand. Not right now."

But when he came back to Genesis, once Sabine was safe . . . Ryder lifted his head and met Donaldson's wild eyes. *I will come back then. I will make you suffer. The bullet would have been too fast anyway.*

Donaldson grew even paler.

Stay here, Ryder ordered him. *Don't take a step until I come back and tell you to move.*

The guard's whole body tensed as his muscles locked down.

Sabine's breath heaved out. "Thank you."

He liked her gratitude, but he'd be taking more than just a "thank you" from her.

His fingers twined with hers as they hurried from the room. Donaldson didn't call out after them. He couldn't. He couldn't do anything unless Ryder ordered him to do so.

Now you know what it's like to be helpless. As Ryder had been helpless when he'd been forced to watch Sabine die right in front of his eyes.

Their footsteps raced down the hallway. To the left. To the right. A guard stumbled out, directly in front of them.

Ryder caught the guy. Grabbed him, then punched him out with one hard knock of his fist. Too easy. The humans were his prey now. Nothing could stop him.

No one.

He'd be free, and Sabine would be at his side.

Then those at Genesis would be the ones to scream and beg.

CHAPTER FIVE

Sabine didn't know where they were going. And as long as Ryder was getting her out of the pit that reeked of death, she didn't care. Her heart slammed into her chest and her lungs heaved as she rushed to keep pace with Ryder.

The guy was *fast*. But then, he was a vampire. She figured superhuman speed must be part of his package. Not a bad package to have, once you looked past the whole blood-drinking and fangs bit. He pulled her hand, yanking her toward a metal door on the right, and then they were rushing into a narrow stairwell. She stumbled inside with him, and the door clanged shut behind them.

"How much longer are we—" she began but Ryder pushed her against the nearest wall and put his hand over her mouth, effectively cutting off her words. She stared up at him, too conscious of the loud drumming of her heart, the sound seeming to fill her ears.

"More guards." He whispered the words against

her left ear. Barely a breath of sound. She could have sworn she felt the light rasp of his tongue on the shell of her ear, and Sabine stiffened. Not with anger or disgust but with a sudden stab of desire that she hadn't expected.

It was strange. Her body felt primed, too tense, aching, and it had felt that way ever since Ryder had taken her hand and pulled her off that exam table.

She hadn't thought anyone would be coming to her rescue. Sabine certainly hadn't expected a vampire with fierce eyes and bloodstained clothing to rush to her side.

But he had.

Maybe there was someone she could trust in this nightmare world, after all.

Ryder killed you. Wyatt's words rang through her mind.

Um, and maybe not.

But she did remember Ryder trying to give her blood during that terrible encounter. He'd forced his blood into her mouth. Urged her to drink.

The vampire just confused her.

Footsteps thundered by outside.

"Since you want me to let those fools live"—another whisper against her, and, yes, this time she was *sure* that was a light lick of his tongue—"then we'll play the game nice and softly."

It wasn't a game. It was life or death. Her life. His life.

She turned her head, pulling away a bit from that mouth and the tongue that was making her body tighten. Ryder—he was so big. Tall, dark, and dangerous—a description that definitely fit him.

He wasn't like any man she'd ever met before. Mostly because she'd never met a guy with fangs and claws.

He's a vampire. Not just some average guy. *Admit that to yourself.*

He was a vampire, and his mouth had just moved down to the curve of her throat.

Sabine couldn't help it. Every single muscle in her body locked when she felt his lips on her throat. The muscles locked in fear and desire. She shook her head and he freed her mouth. "Don't," her own soft order.

His lips pressed against her throat. "I'm not taking a bite."

Good. He'd better not be.

His head rose. His eyes met hers. "Unless you want me to . . ."

Heat pooled in her belly.

His nostrils widened a little bit, and he smiled. The fluorescent light above them revealed the brightness of his green eyes and the sharp points of his fangs. "Sometimes, the bite can feel good."

She swallowed, then shoved against his shoulders. She wasn't sure which one of them was more surprised when he staggered back. "And sometimes it can kill." Wow, where had she gotten that kind of strength? She'd just shoved him a good four feet. His back had bumped into the metal banister. If the guards hadn't drugged her, would she have been able to use that kind of strength on them before?

His gaze raked over her. "Remembered that part, did you?"

No. "Yes," she lied at once, wondering how much she could get him to reveal. Her actual death part was still rather foggy for her.

He glanced toward the locked door, then his gaze rose up, scanning the stairs that led to the second floor. "I was starving. They hadn't fed me in months."

This was supposed to make her feel better? He'd actually attacked her. Hardly the start of some epic relationship.

"I tried to give you my blood," he growled out. "If you'd just been able to take a few sips, you would've been okay."

The image of his face—dark, desperate, *Let her drink!*—flashed suddenly through her mind, and Sabine sucked in a sharp gasp of air.

Maybe there was a reason she couldn't remember those last moments before the fire. Maybe she didn't want to remember.

"But it was all part of Wyatt's experiment," Ryder muttered. "He wanted you to die, so he could see you rise again."

Goose bumps were on her arms. "I don't understand any of this."

He inclined his head toward the stairs. "The guards are gone. Come on, we need to go."

She wanted to keep talking. He knew more about her, she realized that. The knowledge was in his eyes, in the way he glanced over her body. *Phoenix*. He'd called her that before. The only phoenix she knew was a mythical bird. She had to get Ryder to tell her more. To explain to her just what she was.

He was the key to so much, provided, of course, he didn't kill her again.

Ryder had already headed up the stairs. She glanced at his wide back. Trusting him would be stupid. She wasn't stupid. Most of her memories had come back, and, so, okay, she didn't fully remember his attack on her. *I don't want to.*

Sabine just wanted to get out of this crazy hell, and to do that, she had to follow the vampire.

Follow him, work with him. Trust him?

Her fingers curled around the metal stair railing. The stairs squeaked beneath her feet as she hurried and climbed up behind Ryder. For better or scary-as-hell worse, they were together now. Maybe they'd both manage to get out of that place alive.

Are vampires even alive?

She had so much to learn.

Wyatt took his time scanning the notes he'd made on Sabine. She'd recovered nearly all of her memories after just three days. Fairly fast, considering that she'd just been through her first rising. She had amazing potential.

Test Subject Twenty-Nine is showing remarkable recovery skills. He quickly jotted down that notation. He couldn't wait to monitor her after the second rising.

Wyatt glanced down at his watch. Donaldson should be shooting her at any moment. He put the papers aside, not wanting to miss the experiment. His pace kicked up as he hurried toward the observation room adjacent to Twenty-Nine's cell.

Think of her as Twenty-Nine. When he'd first brought her in, he'd been thinking of her as Sabine. An amateur mistake. He knew better. But when she'd first come in, she'd looked human.

They're numbers. Subjects. Not people. Because he'd referred to both Sabine and Ryder by name, he'd noticed that his staff had started to refer to them that way, too.

You can't see them as individuals. As men. As women.

That was a huge mistake. His father had taught him that. His father never saw the humanity in his subjects. They were numbers, not names.

The beings in his lab were test subjects. Nothing more. Nothing less.

Donaldson had hesitated when Richard gave him the order to shoot Subject Twenty-Nine. He'd hesitated because he'd started to see her as a woman, not the monster she was.

I'll have to brief all the staff. Only numbers from now on. No names. The new recruits he had coming in would learn this lesson from the very start.

You were less likely to feel sorry for a number.

The door to the observation room slid open. "How is the test proceeding?" Richard began, then jerked to a stop when he realized two of his staff members were unconscious on the floor.

His gaze flew to the two-way mirror. The exam table was empty, but the room wasn't. Donaldson stood, statue-still, in the middle of the room, with a gun pressed to his heart.

Son of a bitch.

Richard rushed forward and pressed the button for the alarm.

They'd just reached the top of the stairs when a shrill alarm pierced the air. Sabine clamped her lips closed to hold back her instinctive cry and pushed behind Ryder. But instead of opening the door that was just a few precious feet away, instead of getting them the hell out, he spun back around and caught her arms.

"Guards are coming," he rasped.

Her eyes narrowed. She could almost hear the fast thud of footsteps. Wait, she *did* hear them.

His head jerked up. He looked to the left. The right.

Then his stare came back to her. "I can kill them all." Said with absolute certainty.

Her heart clenched. She didn't know these men and women. Maybe they were as screwed up as Dr. Richard Wyatt—every time she saw him, her skin crawled. But what if they weren't? What if some of the guards truly didn't understand all that was happening at Genesis? Was that even possible?

"Don't," she whispered.

Ryder shook his head. "That's a mistake." His gaze locked with hers. "But we'll play it your way, for now."

Then, instead of shoving open the door and getting out of the stairwell, he turned toward a grate behind them. He kicked out and the grate fell inward. "Get in," he told her. "Crawl forward fifteen feet, take a left, then punch out the screen you'll find in front of you."

How did he know this stuff?

But she didn't question him. She just hauled ass. Bending low, Sabine pushed into the entranceway. Some kind of air duct. She crawled forward even as she mentally kept up a hopeful refrain of *No rats, no rats, no rats*.

Like the rats were all she needed to worry about at Genesis.

Something grabbed her ankle and hauled her back. She didn't cry out, but she bit down hard on her bottom lip as her hands slapped against the metal walls around her. There was nothing to hold on to as she was pulled back.

"I said fifteen feet," Ryder growled at her. "Turn here."

Oh yes. She turned. The air duct became even narrower. Sabine knew that Ryder's broad shoulders must have been a tight fit, but she didn't glance back. Her hands slapped against the grate. Before she pushed it down, she peeked through the narrow openings and gazed below her. No sign of the guards.

She shoved the grate down. It fell and landed on a desk. Barely waiting a second's time, Sabine jumped right after it.

Her gaze swept the room. Heavy shelves. A big desk. No pictures. A lab coat hanging on a hook near the closed door.

Ryder landed behind her. "Don't worry," he said. "Jim Thomas isn't going to be heading in here for a while." His voice oozed confidence.

Glancing over her shoulder, Sabine demanded, "How do you know? What did you do to him?"

He offered her a wide grin. "I took a little bite out of him."

"Did you kill him?"

His sigh was long and low. "No. Why do you always seem to think—"

"Because you killed me." Her words froze him as he reached for the lab coat.

Ryder hesitated, then looked back at her. "Back to that, are we? I've told you they'd starved me."

As far as excuses went . . .

"And I didn't expect your *taste*."

Um, come again?

He spun toward her. Actually, he was stalking toward her. She was still crouched on the desk. Sabine scrambled down. "I don't know what you're talking about, vampire." She said the word deliberately, in order to remind herself of what he was.

Ryder rolled his eyes. Seriously. The guy rolled his eyes. "So what, now you're gonna think like *them?* I'm not a person, just a thing?"

Shame burned her cheeks. "I—"

"Whatever," he drawled, then lifted a brow as he said, "Phoenix."

She just looked back at him.

He stopped in front of her. The desk was behind her, pressing lightly against the back of her thighs. Ryder's intense gaze searched her face. "You don't know, do you?"

She shook her head. "Is that . . . what I am?"

He put the lab coat down on the desk. His head cocked to the side. His gaze seemed to grow even brighter as it raked over her.

"I feel like I've been frozen for the last thousand years."

Thousand? There was no way she'd heard that part right. Ryder *couldn't* be that old.

Duh, Sabine. Vampire. He could definitely be that old.

"And when I tasted your blood, for the first time in so long, I felt warm again. You did that. Your blood . . . hell, it seemed to make me live again."

She wasn't sure what in the heck to say in response to that.

"You taste like spice. Heat and honey. Pleasure." He leaned toward her. Her hands curved under the edge of the desk. "You taste like everything I had while I walked the earth as a man, everything I wanted, and I fucking *crave* you."

His hand caught her chin. Tipped her face back up. "The bloodlust—the *lust*—consumed me when I tasted you. I didn't have control. There wasn't time for control. I needed you too much."

She wet her lips. Her heartbeat was racing in her chest, the wild thunder echoing in her ears. The too-aware tension in her body seemed to be a normal occurrence when she was around him. "And now?"

The hunger in his eyes was her answer. Her fingers tightened around the edge of the desk. She was so far out of her element here. "Don't eat me." The words jumped from her because Ryder looked as if he wanted to devour her.

One blond brow rose even as his cheeks seemed to hollow, to sharpen with a predatory appearance she hadn't noticed before. "So very tempting."

The alarm was still ringing, muted since they were in the office, but she still heard it easily. "They're looking for us." *So you don't have time for a bite. Keep those teeth away from me.*

"Let them look. The longer we stay in here, the more the guards will disperse as they break up and search the facility."

His gaze had focused on her mouth.

Her own eyes kept dropping to his mouth, too, and it was only partially out of fear.

"I'm prepared now," he told her. "I swear, I won't ever lose control with you again. I give you my word."

She didn't exactly want to test that theory. And she didn't *exactly* believe him. "Get me out of this place."

His eyes rose. Met hers.

"Please," she whispered.

He could do it. She knew he could. With his enhanced senses and his speed and strength, Ryder could get her to safety. He could easily avoid the guards, find the exit, and get her away from Genesis.

Only the guy wasn't moving.

His mouth kicked up in the faintest of smiles. "What will you do for me, lovely Sabine, if I do?"

What? The guy was trying to barter over her freedom? Now?

"Perhaps a kiss," he said. That smile of his was still there—still a bit predatory. "Surely that's not so much to ask?"

No, not so much. Not in the big life-or-death grand scheme of things. Since she'd been expecting him to request a pint or two of blood, a kiss seemed fair enough. "Get me out, and I'll give you the best kiss you've ever had." An easy promise.

Ryder shook his head. "Give me the best kiss I've ever had . . ." Was there a taunt in his words? Yes, there was. "And *then* I'll get you out of here."

She didn't have time for this crap. Her hands flew up. She grabbed his shirt front and fisted her fingers around the material. "Fine." Then Sabine jerked the vamp toward her. His lips had parted in surprise. *Didn't think I'd do it, did you?*

He should have known better than to challenge a New Orleans girl.

She pressed her mouth against his. Thrust her tongue past his lips. Back in high school, she'd been the first-base queen. Her too-protective older brother had made sure she didn't get to round third base too much, but kissing . . . oh, she'd had plenty of practice on those hot Louisiana nights.

Ryder stiffened against her. She figured the guy

hadn't expected such a fast response from her. Good. She liked catching him off guard.

Her tongue licked across his lip, then slid back into his mouth. A growl built in his throat and his hands wrapped around her hips. Then his tongue was stroking hers. The kiss grew rougher, her heart beat even faster, and she stopped worrying so much about her perfect technique and just kissed him.

Hot. Wild. The kind of kiss that made her toes curl.

She sucked his tongue.

His hands jerked her hips toward him. Since she was on the desk, he was right between her legs, and there was no missing the thick bulge of his arousal. The vampire came with all the right equipment. So very right.

And big.

"We . . . have enough time . . ." He muttered the words as his mouth tore from hers.

Sabine blinked up at him. She wanted his mouth back on hers. He could kiss even better than her eleventh-grade boyfriend of choice, Leo Rouchoix. Leo the Lips . . . that had been his nickname back in high school.

Ryder's hands went to her waist. To the top of her sweats.

Wait, hold up, he'd said they had *enough* time?

She grabbed his hands. "No." Sabine shook her head, trying to shake away the lust. Trying to, and failing. "We're getting out of here." The alarm still beeped, and though Ryder seemed to think this room was a safe hiding spot, she didn't want to risk being discovered right in the middle of sex.

Not that she was having sex with the vamp. Not on the desk. Not in the middle of their escape.

Just *not*.

A muscle flexed in his jaw. "Do you know how much I want you?"

Um, she could feel how much. Impressive. But the vamp needed to prioritize. "I gave you the kiss."

His gaze dropped to her lips. No missing the heat in his green stare.

"Now you get us the hell out of here."

His head tilted. He didn't speak.

"Ryder . . ." They'd had a deal.

He lifted his hand. "The hallway outside is clear now. We can go." Ryder stepped back.

Just like that. Her heart was about to burst out of her chest, and Ryder was suddenly as calm as you please. Well, hell.

Had he just been trying to distract her? Keep her quiet until the guards outside had left? He could have just said "Quiet" instead of asking for her kiss.

His finger smoothed over the line between her brows. "The kiss was more fun."

Her heart froze. "You can read my mind." Her voice emerged as a horrified whisper.

Those sensual lips of his—lips she could still feel against her own—quirked briefly. "No, love, not yours."

Did that mean he could read the minds of others? She *had* to learn more about vampires. When she'd started to hear the whispers about them in New Orleans, about *all* of the supernatural creatures, she'd ignored most of the stories. Because most of them were BS. Huge exaggerations. Scary stories to frighten children.

But now, she sure needed to separate the fact from the fiction pronto.

"Your thoughts are easy enough to see on your face." He picked up the white lab coat again. "Put this on. You'll blend in better if we're spotted."

He turned away. Began digging in a nearby drawer. He pulled out another lab coat. Yanked it on.

Her fingers dug into the fabric. *Not yours*. That phrasing had been deliberate. She had to ask the question that had been burning through her. "What did you do to that guard downstairs?"

His back was to her, but she saw the sudden stiffness of his shoulders. "I stopped him from killing you." Said quietly. He glanced over at her. "You're welcome."

She licked her lips. Dammit, she *tasted* him. "You made the guard turn that gun on himself. You were in his head, weren't you?"

A slow nod.

"How did you—"

"I'd delay the escape for a fuck," Ryder said, the hard words cutting like a knife, "but not to play Twenty Questions. It's time for us to get the hell out of here."

Her eyes narrowed.

He lifted his hand and offered it to her. "Unless you want to stay?"

She wasn't taking that hand yet. "I want to make sure I'm not going to find myself suddenly aiming a gun at my own heart." Because she'd seen the desperate fear in Donaldson's gaze. Sabine didn't want to wind up on the receiving end of whatever scary mojo Ryder was working.

When she'd been snatched by Wyatt and his psycho team, Sabine hadn't exactly had time to pack her gris-gris. And her aunt Rya had worked so hard to create that satchel to protect Sabine. *I could sure use its protection right about now.*

Ryder stared at her. His eyes were so bright. His face tense.

"What?" Sabine muttered. "I think it's a fair concern." Especially considering the events she'd witnessed with her own eyes.

"If I could control you, your hand would be holding mine right now." He said the words with an annoyed air. "I *can't* get in your head. Not even with the blood I took."

That was good, right?

"I tried to get into your head."

She gulped.

"There was a wall of fire blocking your mind. It kept me out—is *keeping* me out. I'm betting it will keep every paranormal out."

Her hands had fisted, the better to hide the faint tremble of her fingers.

"So I won't be making you shove a gun at your own heart. I won't be making you do *anything* that you don't want to do." He exhaled on a long sigh. "Now, can you take my hand?"

She headed toward him. Her shoulder brushed his arm. She forced her right hand to unclench, and she lifted it from the pocket. Her fingers touched his. A hot charge seemed to pulse from his skin to hers.

"Lead the way," Sabine whispered.

Her fingers curled around his.

"Donaldson, drop the gun," Richard barked as he rushed into the cell.

Donaldson dropped the gun. The other guards swarmed in, searching the area.

"They're gone," Donaldson gasped out. "Been gone . . ."

"And you just let them walk away?" Fury spiked within Richard. "You were supposed to shoot the woman, not free her."

"I-I didn't . . . The vampire came in. He let her go."

Obviously. "While you just stood there." The man actually was still just standing there. Richard waved his hand. "Get moving, Donaldson. We're locking down the facility. We're going to find them." He turned away. "They won't get out of Genesis."

Richard had taken two steps before he realized Donaldson wasn't moving. Richard glanced back over his shoulder. The guard stood frozen in the middle of the room. His eyes were wild, his face taut. Sweat covered him, but the man wasn't stepping forward.

"Come along, Donaldson," Richard snapped. He didn't have time to waste coddling a guard. The man had been attacked. Yes, yes, traumatic, no doubt, but he was fine now. No injuries that Richard could see, except for the bandaged bite mark on Donaldson's neck. The wound still appeared to be bleeding, judging by the way the red stain was spreading on the white cloth.

"Can't," Donaldson rasped. "Not until . . . Ryder's back."

What? Richard spun around. His gaze swept over the guard. Donaldson's body was shaking, but the man was *not* so much as inching forward. "Come *here,* Donaldson."

All of the other guards were dead silent.

Donaldson shook his head. *"Can't!"* He shouted this time, his frustration breaking him. "I can't move a step, not 'til Ryder gets back!"

Richard knew his own eyes were widening. He tried to school his expression even as excitement filled him. "Why would you follow his orders?"

The other guards were avid. Watching too much. Hearing too much. Richard waved them away. "Go join the others! I want a search of every room at Genesis!"

The guards hurried to comply. Richard waited until they were gone, then he asked again, "Why obey him? Did he threaten you? Your family?"

"He's . . . *in my head.*" The horror of those words was reflected in Donaldson's eyes. Eyes that appeared to be filling with tears.

Richard remembered the way Donaldson had stood when he first burst into the room. "He made you put the gun to your own chest, didn't he?" Richard didn't want to let the excitement get the better of him. He'd hoped this would be the case. For so long, he'd searched for a vampire who'd mastered this particular talent. His search had yielded no success, until now.

Donaldson nodded. "I could . . . feel him." His hand lifted and his fingers rubbed against his temple. "It wasn't me up here. Just him."

Richard smiled. "It was the bite." Smart vampire. The attacks on Donaldson and Thomas had been part of an escape strategy.

Jim Thomas . . . you attacked him because you knew he'd have access to the key cards. He was your ticket to freedom.

Richard realized he'd underestimated Ryder. He wouldn't be making that mistake again.

Richard bent and picked up the discarded gun. "Do you still feel Ryder in your mind?"

Donaldson didn't answer. But then, wasn't that answer enough?

Richard glanced over his shoulder. They were alone. Donaldson deserved to hear this. "There are stories . . . some vampires are old enough, powerful enough, that they can actually control the minds of humans."

He'd just thought that was a legend. He'd hoped it was truth, but had discovered no evidence to back up that particular power, until this moment.

"He's controlling me," Donaldson whispered. A tear streaked down his cheek. "Stop him!"

Oh, now that was the tricky part. "It's the blood," Richard said. With vampires, wasn't it always? "He didn't take control until he had your blood." Otherwise, Ryder would have escaped sooner. He would have just taken control of the guards at any point and used them to do his bidding.

But though Ryder had killed a few guards when he'd first been contained at Genesis, the vampire hadn't been allowed to get within biting distance of any Genesis personnel, not since those early, desperate weeks. And since he hadn't been able to bite them . . . *You couldn't control them*.

Until a fatal mistake had been made. Until Thomas and Donaldson had gotten within the vampire's deadly reach.

During his time at Genesis, Richard knew that plenty of other vampires had tasted the guards. They'd had their blood—new guards often made foolish mistakes.

They got too close to their prey. One nip of the teeth was enough to guarantee that they'd be better prepared in the future.

Those vampires had never been able to take over the minds of their prey.

Those vampires hadn't been like Ryder.

What makes Ryder different? He had to find out. Ryder could very well be the vampire that he'd sought for so long.

The key.

The cure.

Richard's fingers tightened on the gun. "You're his puppet now. Whatever Ryder says, whatever he so much as thinks, you'll be compelled to do." Even turning against his own teammates. Hell, the guy would kill his own family if Ryder told him to do so. The proof was plain to see.

Donaldson had put a gun to his own chest.

Very, very interesting.

"Help me!" Donaldson begged. "If you find him, if you kill him, I'll be free, right?"

Yes, he would be free then, but Richard shook his head. "I have no intention of killing Ryder." What purpose would that serve?

The cure. He'd looked for a vampire like Ryder, searched since he was little more than a child.

Containment of Ryder would be priority one. They'd need more of his blood. Humans would have to be injected. More test subjects lined up and—

"Help me!" Ah, now Donaldson was shouting again.

It was hard to think when someone shouted like that.

Sighing, Richard lifted the gun. He fired. The bullet

blasted into Donaldson's chest, a direct hit to the heart. The man fell to the floor.

"Now you're free," Richard murmured. He stared dispassionately at the body. Donaldson had been dead from the minute Richard realized he was under Ryder's control. Donaldson would have been a weakness for Genesis. Ryder would have manipulated the human. Used him to attack.

"Sorry, Donaldson." Richard turned for the door. "But it's for the good of science."

CHAPTER SIX

Genesis was a maze. At least four levels, though Ryder was betting more levels waited downstairs, far below his own prison. So many cells. Far more than he'd realized.

Too many prisoners.

"There are others trapped here," Sabine said as she walked closely by his side. Ryder kept his head down. They'd been lucky enough to walk right past two guards without those guys even giving them a second glance.

You just saw the lab coats and you didn't bother to look at our faces.

Richard had hired those guys for their bulk. Not so much for their brains.

"We should get them out," Sabine told him, voice soft.

"I'll come back," he told her. Not on a rescue mission. But a mission to make Richard Wyatt scream in agony.

She glanced toward him.

"We'll turn the corner up here," he told her, inclining his head slightly, "then we'll go in the room on the left."

"I thought we were going for the exit."

Boots pounded behind them. More guards. Would these guys be as clueless as the others? Hopefully. If not, then he'd just kill them.

"We are heading for the exit," he explained, keeping his voice low. "I can smell fresh air coming from that place." His nose was even better than a wolf shifter's. Actually, since he'd taken Sabine's blood, *all* of his senses seemed to be working overtime.

"Walk faster," she told him as she started to double-time her steps. Had she heard the guards, too?

They rounded the corner.

Ryder kept following that fresh air scent. He didn't want to run. He wanted to turn and fight all those fools following him. To have a bloodbath just like in the old days.

But I can't risk her.

So he clenched his teeth and shoved into the room on the left.

A small window waited. One covered with bars. An office. Barely ten feet long. It smelled of humans. There were half-eaten snacks scattered on a table. A break-room?

A breaking-out room. He headed for the window. Yanked on the bars.

The footsteps were coming closer.

The bars snapped in his hands. "Come on!" He all but tossed her through the window.

But then another alarm began to blast. One that was coming from the exterior of Genesis. *Got it rigged so no one gets out, huh? Too bad, we're out.* Ryder shoved his own body through the narrow window. Chunks of plaster and brick rained down on him as he broke not just the window, but the weak wall surrounding it. Unlike the walls in his cell, this room wasn't reinforced. Probably because it wasn't a place for prisoners.

Before he'd even cleared the window, Sabine grabbed his arm. The woman was actually trying to help drag him out of the building. Cute. He didn't need any help. "Run!" he ordered.

She kept her hold on him. Didn't run until he did. Unexpected. It looked like Sabine wasn't the type to leave a partner behind. He'd remember that tidbit about her.

Then they were rushing toward the line of trees before them. Guards raced into their path, ready to cut off their escape. The guards had big, shiny guns.

Big fucking deal. He had big, sharp teeth—and he was about to let his claws out. Claws that would make a shifter envious. Had, actually, on plenty of occasions in the past.

He grabbed Sabine's arm and shoved her behind him.

"Stop!" one of the guards yelled. "Raise your arms and—"

Ryder didn't stop. Bullets tore into his shoulder and stomach.

He kept running. Grabbed the nearest guard. Broke his arm. Took his gun. Shot back at the others who were foolish enough to still be trying to stop him.

And, even though he'd tried to push her back, Sabine was there. Fighting at his side. Snatching up a gun when it fell from another guard's hands, and then whirling to fire—because they had more company coming at them from the south.

A quick glance showed Ryder that Wyatt had sent a heavy force outside. He easily counted ten guards—and there, in the middle was Richard Fucking Wyatt himself. "Shoot the prick," Wyatt snarled at Sabine.

And damn if she didn't.

Sabine raised her gun. Aimed. Fired.

Richard tried to dodge at the last minute, but the bullet still ripped deep into his chest.

The woman was one very fine shot.

But when she fired, all of the guards lifted their weapons.

Ryder snarled. He grabbed Sabine and turned, cradling her in his arms.

A hail of bullets hit him. Thudding hard into his back. Some even ripped out of his chest as they tunneled all the way through him. He held his body steady, refusing to buckle as the agony burned through him. So many bullets.

Keep her safe. Keep her—

Sabine gasped and her body jerked within his arms.

"Stop! Stop! Dammit, put down your weapons!"

That voice. No way. It couldn't be . . .

Footsteps pounded toward him. Ryder didn't turn, not yet. He'd wait, let them think he was weak, then he'd whirl and attack.

"Ry-Ryder . . ." Sabine shuddered against him. "H-help . . ."

His gaze dropped to her. Her face was so pale in the bright sunlight. Her eyes too dark. And . . .

He eased his body away from hers. Blood soaked her shirt.

His blood. It had to be his blood. He'd taken the bullets to protect her.

Her body sagged.

It . . . wasn't just his blood.

Her blood.

The guards were surrounding him then. He didn't give a fuck. Carefully, Ryder lowered Sabine to the ground. The grass was green and soft—and already getting soaked with her blood.

There were bullet holes in her chest. He'd tried so hard to shield her but *the bullets went through me and into her.*

"You're dead," he promised, savagery rising in him, a dark force that he didn't try to control.

Sabine's eyes widened. She tried to speak.

No, not you . . . Not. You.

His fingers were so gentle as he stroked her cheek.

The guards were dead. They were the ones he was sending to hell. He bit his wrist. Let the blood flow. Brought the wound to her mouth. He wasn't letting her die. Wasn't going to watch her burn.

"Are we really doing this again?" that familiar voice drawled. A voice that *should* belong to a dead man.

Sabine's lips feathered over his wrist. She was drinking. Good. *Yes.*

But his head turned and—sure enough—Richard Wyatt was striding toward him. Wyatt's shirt was red with blood, the guy's face appeared strained, but he was advancing just fine.

She hit him in the heart. I know she did. Even if she hadn't, no human could be up and walking after a hit like that.

Not human.

Wyatt's lips quirked a bit as he met Ryder's stare. "Move away from Twenty-Nine, and let's get back inside."

Twenty-nine? What the hell?

One of the guards sprang at Ryder.

Enough.

Ryder surged to his feet and broke the guard's neck. Shattered the collarbone of another and grabbed the bastard's gun. Fired—

Fire?

"I don't believe your blood can stop her death this time," Richard murmured as he cocked his head to the side.

Ryder whirled back around. Sabine had taken his blood. She should have been all right. She should have been—

No heartbeat. He didn't hear Sabine's heart.

And he could already smell smoke.

"No!" He fell to the ground beside her. More guards were coming. Screw them. He'd told Sabine that he'd get her out of that hell, but she was about to burn anyway.

"It's easier to contain her before the shift." Richard's voice. "Dose them both. Keep firing at her until she begins to rise. You'll have to time the attack just right."

Her skin was heating beneath his touch.

He felt sharp pricks on his back. Harder punches, too. The backup guards were dosing him with that SP tranq. Right then, he didn't give a damn. He wasn't moving from her side.

Not until she was back with him.

She rose once. She'll rise again. "Come on," he whispered to her. *"Come back!"* Because he didn't know exactly where Sabine went when she died and part of him was afraid to find out.

Afraid . . . when he hadn't feared anything in the last thousand years. Not since he'd put the last of his family in the ground.

Not until now. Until her.

"Sabine!" Her name was a roar. A desperate order. The SP tranq was already flooding through his body. How much of the drug had they pumped into him?

Didn't matter. Nothing mattered but her.

"Sabine." Softer now. More of a plea.

Her lashes began to flutter.

Yes. She was coming back to him. As soon as her eyes opened—

Her lashes opened. Her eyes were so dark and deep when they met his. Dark . . . at first.

Then a ring of red appeared in her eyes. A red that looked like fire. The ring spread. Flared hotter. The red expanded until flames consumed her eyes.

"Now you"—he had to lean forward to hear her whispered words—"run . . ."

Beneath his hands, her skin continued to warm as the fire flickered higher in her eyes.

Run.

He tried to stand, but the SP tranqs had numbed his body. He fell to the ground beside her. That was where he wanted to be. Close to her. *Close*.

Flames erupted, covering her flesh. The heat blasted across his skin. Several of the guards cried out, and he saw them, burning. *How does it feel?*

The guards hit the ground and tried to roll in an attempt to put out the fire.

But that fire wasn't dying.

Neither was Sabine.

As he watched, she rose. Covered in those flames, *she rose*. The fire was flying out from her body, hitting guards, seeming to deliberately attack them while none of those red-orange streaks were coming at him.

Because his phoenix was controlling her fire.

He'd never see anything more beautiful or more deadly, and he knew that he never would again.

"Shoot her!" Wyatt screamed. "Shoot her until she goes down!"

The remaining guards were trying to shoot, but the SP tranq couldn't penetrate the wall of fire around her.

Ryder's eyes wanted to sag closed, but he forced his gaze to stay open. Sabine had the strength right then. This was her moment. She could . . . "Get . . . away."

Through the flames, he saw her head turn toward him. Her hair seemed to be floating in the fire, and a rough brush of wind—*hot wind*—whispered over his skin.

"Now's . . . your . . . chance," he managed. He wouldn't be able to stay conscious much longer. But he didn't have to last long, just until she escaped. "Go!"

And she did. Sabine—his phoenix—turned and rushed into the woods. The flames around her dimmed as she reached the trees.

"Shoot!" Wyatt yelled.

More SP tranqs were fired at her.

But Sabine disappeared into the woods.

She'd gotten away. Hell, *yes*.

His head fell back against the ground. Ryder stared above him. The sun. Big and bright, and, right then, fucking gorgeous.

He could always think clearly when the SP tranq hit him. He just couldn't move his body an inch. It took all of his strength to keep his eyes cracked open just a few minutes more.

Vampires were supposed to hate the daytime. It made most of 'em weaker.

Not him.

The tranq was doing that all by itself.

Then he couldn't see the sun. Not because his heavy lids had finally closed, but because Wyatt stood above him, blocking the view. "Don't worry," Wyatt assured him. "We'll get her back. I'm sure that last shot hit its mark."

No!

Wyatt offered a smile. "Perhaps if you cooperate fully with my experiments, I'll even let her visit your cell once more."

Ryder tried to turn his head so that he could look over and see the woods. Sabine had gotten away. Wyatt was a lying sack of shit. He was—

A guard was carrying Sabine's limp body from the trees.

"Oh, didn't I mention?" Wyatt murmured. "I had guards waiting in the woods. Just as a precaution. They had orders to dose her with the SP tranq until she went down."

Son of a—

"When you wake up," Wyatt told him, "you're going to be very, very hungry."

His lashes were closing.

"Sorry, but I'm afraid I'll have to drain you nearly dry. For science, of course."

Science could fuck off.

His eyes closed.

I'm sorry, Sabine.

He'd promised her freedom. One way or another, he'd find a way to keep that promise.

Sabine was naked.

When Ryder opened his eyes, she was the first thing

he saw. What a damn fantastic sight. His body hard-ened and he lunged for her.

Only to be yanked back—before he could touch that smooth skin of hers—by the heavy chains that wrapped around his wrists.

Sabine flinched. She lifted her head, and her eyes—dark once more, no longer flaming red—met his.

His memory flooded back. The escape. The fire. Her. "You didn't get away."

She just stared back at him.

Hell, did she even know who he was?

She'd pulled up her knees. Wrapped her arms around her legs. Sabine was shielding her body from him.

A good idea, because the lust cutting through him was already reaching a fever pitch, after just a few seconds.

Physical lust . . . and bloodlust.

Because he didn't just remember their failed escape attempt. He remembered being strapped down. Remem-bered Wyatt shoving needles in his arm and draining his blood. Draining and draining until it had felt as if there was nothing left inside of him. Until Ryder was just a hollow shell. *No blood*.

After that kind of torture, he should have been no more than a beast. A wild creature that only wanted to feed. That was what Wyatt had wanted him to become.

Ryder backed away from her, retreating until his shoulders hit the wall. *Won't attack her. Can't*.

"I . . . fed you." Her voice was hushed.

Ryder blinked, not sure he understood.

Sabine lifted her wrist. He could see the narrow slice that cut across the faint line of blue veins. "I fed you while you were asleep. I thought I'd be able to, ah, con-trol you better that way."

Ryder could only shake his head. That had been too risky. When it came to a starving vampire and feeding, *control* didn't exactly apply. And when he was unconscious, anything could have happened. "You remember me this time."

Her hand dropped. Went back to curl around her knees. "It's been five days since we tried to get out. My memory—I didn't lose all of it this time, and what I did lose, yes, it's back." Her gaze was stark. "I died again."

He wanted to touch her, and, despite the blood she'd so generously given to him—*I can taste her. There's a sweetness in my mouth*—he wanted to sink his teeth into her delicate neck and drink.

Sabine wasn't safe with him. She needed to be in another cell. Needed to be *far* away.

"Wyatt said that sometimes I'll remember who I am. Sometimes I won't. If I—if I die enough, he thinks I'll totally lose myself . . ." He saw her throat move as she swallowed. "Wyatt said—"

"I don't give a shit what he said!" Okay, maybe he shouldn't have snarled the words. Her flinch had shame knifing in his gut.

And realizing that, dammit, he was naked, too.

Playing a new game, are you, Wyatt? What, now the guy wanted them to fuck?

Ryder sucked in a deep breath and tried to calm his fury. His gaze flew around the cell. Same room. Same inner pit of hell. But if he was back there, then that meant Wyatt and his cronies had retrieved Jim Thomas. If the guy was still at the facility, then maybe he could use him.

"I think Wyatt wants me to lose myself. To just become the—the phoenix." Her shoulders were hunched.

"That's not going to happen."

Her gaze met his. "Yes, it is."

She was so beautiful that she made him ache. Beautiful, strong, a creature of myth.

And Wyatt had stripped her and tossed her into a cage with a bloodthirsty monster. All for his twisted science.

Sabine's voice was husky as she said, "Wyatt told me that I will die, again and again, and rise in the fire . . . rise until the only thing left is a monster that just kills and destroys everyone in its path."

Wyatt was a talkative bastard, in addition to his million other sins. Heaving out a heavy breath, Ryder walked to her. The chains trailed behind him. He needed more blood in order to be strong enough to break those chains.

"I can't pretend this isn't happening. My life . . . everything's changed." She shivered and glanced at him. "And you know the worst part?"

Having a naked vampire standing over you, wanting a bite of you so badly his mouth is watering?

No, she didn't realize how desperate he was becoming. Maybe he could play the caring role a bit longer. If he was lucky. If she was.

Her eyes squeezed closed. "I've been to hell."

He didn't speak.

"When I died, I-I remembered this time. The fire is so hot. It surrounds me. Burns and burns and burns and it has to be hell. I go to *hell*."

He reached for her arms. Pulled Sabine up to her feet. "No, love, this cage we're in, *that's* hell. And, I swear to you, we will be free."

She shook her head. "We tried, we—"

He kissed her. His lips brushed over hers, silencing the tangle of her words. He wanted to thrust his tongue deep, to sink into her, but if he pushed, he knew he wouldn't be able to pull back.

With her, his control was too weak.

So he kept the kiss simple. A bare press of the lips. A soft caress against her mouth.

Just enough to give him a taste.

Just enough to have him hungering for so much more.

Then his head lifted. "Don't be afraid."

She stared back at him. Such big, dark, beautiful eyes. But then, he'd thought her eyes were beautiful even when they burned with red and gold flames. Sabine swiped her tongue over her full lower lip and confessed, "They wanted me to use my body to seduce you."

Seducing me wouldn't be hard. No way had she missed the big erection pointing toward her.

"They said that if you answered my questions, if I got you to tell me your secrets, that I'd be let go."

He wanted her mouth again. Because he wanted it, he stepped back. "I'll tell you anything you want to know."

But she shook her head. "They're lying. All Wyatt can do is lie." Her gaze met his. Her cheeks were flushed. "He's not human. I shot him in the chest—" Breaking off, she spun to face the mirror. Her hands slapped against the glass. "I saw him get shot in the heart! His men must have seen it, too! *He's not human!*" Now she was screaming.

He grabbed her shoulder. "Stop, he'll come—"

She whirled and wrapped her arms around him. "I want him to come." The rain of her hair covered her face as she turned her head toward him. "They only let me see you because I promised to seduce you. To learn your secrets." She gave a quick shake of her head.

"But I won't betray you. I just wanted to help you. You helped me, you were the only one who did."

"Sabine . . ."

"I knew that you'd need my blood."

She'd come to save him?

"Maybe now that you have it, you'll be strong enough to get out."

He heard the guards coming. Wyatt had realized his little plan had just gotten screwed.

But Sabine hadn't.

"Come back for me, okay?" She tried to smile. If he'd been human, Ryder was sure that smile would have broken his heart. "When you're free, promise to come back for me."

The guards wrenched open the door. They came in with their guns up. "Step away from her!" Wyatt shouted.

Ryder turned toward him. Bared his fangs. "Why don't you come and make me?"

Wyatt merely smiled back. "Fine. She's behind you. I'll just have the guards shoot until the bullets blast through you and penetrate her flesh again and—"

"How do you want to die?" Ryder asked him, genuinely curious as he made his plans. "It's going to be a slow death, but do you want me to start by cutting your flesh away? Or—"

"Death doesn't come so easily to me." Wyatt's mouth tightened. "If it did, do you think I'd be here?"

Interesting response. "So that's a yes for cutting your flesh away?"

The doctor's cheeks flushed dark red with what Ryder suspected was raw fury. *Not so clinical now, are we?* "Let Twenty-Nine go," Wyatt snapped.

Twenty-nine?

"That's me," Sabine muttered, sounding disgusted. "Because I'm not a person anymore. Just a number." Then she walked around Ryder.

The hell she was just leaving. He grabbed her arm. "Don't go with them."

She gave him a faint smile. "I was wrong about you. For a vampire, you aren't so bad."

Yes, I am.

"You've got a real killer bite, but there's more to you than just that." She searched his gaze. "Don't forget me," Sabine told him. Then she shrugged away his hand.

His gaze followed her. So hungry and wild and, he knew, desperate.

Wyatt shrugged off his lab coat and offered it to Sabine. He pointed to the guards behind him. "I want her transferred to the second facility."

A second facility? *Hell, no.* "Sabine!"

She looked back at him.

"You're not a number," he snapped.

She was so much more.

Her head inclined. "And you're not a monster."

Then she left him. The guards led her out of the room, and Ryder noticed they were careful not to touch her skin. Probably because they were afraid she'd fry them.

He hoped that she did.

Wyatt didn't exit the room. He stood in the doorway, lingering after the others were gone. "Were you the first?"

Ryder glared back at him.

Wyatt's lips tightened. "Don't you understand what I'm trying to do?"

"You're trying to get your kicks from torturing paranormals?" Yes, that bit was obvious. He more than *got* it.

"I'm trying to *cure* us!" Hushed, as if he were afraid someone, somewhere, might overhear.

Ryder slanted a glance at the observation mirror. "Us?" Sabine had been right, but then, he'd suspected that truth for a long time. When Sabine had fired her gun, Ryder had seen the truth with his own eyes. Her bullet had plunged into Richard Wyatt's chest.

But the guy was still alive. Humans didn't recover so quickly.

"No one's in the observation room," Wyatt said, voice rough. "Do you think I'd risk talking while others could hear?" Wyatt bent down and yanked out a pair of jogging pants from a duffel bag at his feet. "Fuck, put these on." He tossed the pants to Ryder.

Raising a brow, Ryder yanked on the pants. "Guess that little naked scene didn't work quite as you wanted, huh, asshole?"

Wyatt's eyes narrowed. "You think you've helped her? If you'd had sex with her, maybe gotten lucky enough to get her pregnant, you would have helped us all."

"Guess I'm not a helper that way." Ryder gazed back at him. "What happened to the whole, 'I'm not interested in birth, but transformation' bit?"

"That was before," Wyatt replied flatly.

"Before?"

"Before I knew just what you were!"

"The fangs and blood-drinking didn't give me away?" Ryder asked, baiting. "And here I thought we'd long ago established that I was a vamp. Your science really must not be that good."

The flush deepened on Wyatt's face. "I knew you were a vamp, but I didn't know you were the first."

"Back to that, are we?"

"A child with your DNA, Twenty-Nine's DNA—that *would* be a transformation."

Or an abomination, depending on the person you asked.

Wyatt yanked a rough hand through his hair. "Don't you get it? We need a cure!"

"I'm not sick. I don't need anything." He'd never been sick. Never would. A vampire didn't—

"I'm not the only one who did experiments." Hushed. And yes, Wyatt tossed a nervous glance over his shoulder. *Thought the big boss wasn't worried about someone overhearing him.* "Some of those experiments, they went damn wrong."

Ryder forced a shrug. "Then I bet you terminated them." Wasn't that the guy's MO? To terminate his failed experiments? When he'd broken free, Ryder had caught the scent of death. Bodies. So many.

A rough laugh escaped Wyatt. "Sometimes, it's harder to terminate experiments than you think." His eyes blazed at Ryder. "Imagine vampires who didn't retain their humanity. Vamps who were just killing machines, beasts with fangs and claws that have only the most basic of primal instincts—the instincts to kill and feed."

Ryder didn't let his expression alter. He did casually pull on the chains, testing them.

"Those aren't going to break." Wyatt waved his hand with a disgusted air. "It's a new metal, one we're having to use on another subject, too. Subject Thirteen has proven too strong."

"Subject Thirteen," Ryder repeated. So the mad

doc was giving them all numbers now. "What's he? A vamp? A shifter?"

Wyatt's eyes narrowed. "Cain's like Sabine, of course." *A phoenix*.

"Just stronger," Wyatt shook his head. "I'd hoped that Cain—Subject Thirteen—might be able to stop the—"

"The vampires? The ones who've gone all primal on you?" Ryder cut in, voice mocking. His gaze lasered in on Wyatt's. "All vamps have fangs and claws. That's not exactly a newsflash." He raised his own growing claws. "So forgive me if I don't give a shit."

"These vampires are different. Don't you get that? Every tooth is sharpened to a killing edge. Every tooth is a fang." Wyatt bit out these words. "Their claws are long, black, sharper than knives, and they never retract. The vamps stay in killing form, day and night, and the hunger they feel can *never* be quenched."

Ryder's brows climbed. "Sounds like someone made the wrong kind of monster." *Bastard, is this why you took my blood? To make more of them?* Because the world needed more monsters.

"You could be the cure for them. Maybe the cure for all vampires." Wyatt wiped a hand over his sweaty forehead. Huh. Looked like the doc was starting to fray at his edges. "You *are* the first, aren't you?"

"No, not even close," Ryder said, voice as mild as could be.

Wyatt frowned at him. "Liar. You think I don't know? I saw what you did to Donaldson—"

"And where is he?" Ryder had to ask. He was vaguely curious about the guard. He'd tried to reach out to him a moment before and felt nothing.

"Dead." Said without a hint of remorse.

Figured. "And the doc? Thomas?" Ryder hadn't tried

to link with him yet. He wanted to wait until he didn't have an audience.

"Jim Thomas is a test subject now."

Poor human. Yes, Ryder was almost feeling sympathy for him.

"Those vamps," Wyatt muttered. "We have to find a cure for them."

"Yes, well, good luck with all of that." Ryder crossed his arms over his chest, and the chains rattled. "Maybe if you'd let me the fuck out of here . . ." *And if you gave me Sabine* . . . "Maybe then I'd be in more of a helping mood."

Wyatt shook his head. "The blood they were given—the blood wasn't pure enough. That must have been why they had the breakdown with their cells."

Ryder forced his muscles to remain loose and relaxed.

"They were soldiers . . ." Was Wyatt just talking to himself now? Looked that way—crazy jerk. "Their minds should have been strong enough. Their bodies strong enough. Vamp and Lycan DNA—they were going to be stronger."

Hold the hell up. "You spliced vamp and shifter blood?"

Wolf shifter blood," Wyatt snapped. "Lycan—"

"And you created some crazy-ass monster that you can't control? How can you be surprised by that?" That was what happened when you played God. You created the devil.

Hell came to earth.

"*You* can be the cure."

Ryder shook his head. "You kill your test subjects left and right. Why the hell haven't you just taken these

"You can try to kill me." Wyatt's voice drifted through the speaker. "But I told you, I'm poison."

Then they'd both die.

"Now I have to go see about your lovely phoenix. If you won't cooperate"—Wyatt sighed—"maybe she will."

Then there was only silence. The frantic beat of Ryder's heart, and the knowledge that Sabine would be hurt. She'd be killed. And all he could do was sit in this cage and wait.

The rage built within him. Grew. With every second that passed, the man he was lost more and more control.

I can be fucking primal, too.

Wyatt was about to see just how primal the first vampire could be.

CHAPTER SEVEN

They left him alone in his cell for three weeks. Ryder counted the moments as the hunger grew within him. Sabine had tried to help him by giving him blood, but it hadn't been enough. Wyatt had taken too much from him during all of those long, desperate, draining hours.

Need more.

His fangs burned in his mouth. His gut clenched with a hunger that wouldn't stop, and he began to wonder . . .

When he'd been out, just what had Wyatt done? Taken blood, yes, but had the bastard injected him with something? The hunger was stronger, so much more intense than anything he'd felt before. And it certainly wasn't the first time that an enemy had tried to starve him.

But it was the first time that he'd hungered so completely for the blood of one person.

Need Sabine's blood. He was salivating, wanting it— *her*—so badly. He'd yelled for her. Roared. But the jerks in white lab coats hadn't come near his cell.

He'd tried to reach Thomas's mind, and he'd made contact, right before a guard had blasted a bullet into the guy's head.

So much for Wyatt's talk about Thomas becoming an experiment. They'd exterminated him quickly enough.

Ryder paced back and forth in his cell. Rage and hunger built. Sabine. He thought of her too much. She was consuming him, just like the hunger. She was—

He heard the faint rustle of footsteps. With his teeth clenched, he whirled toward the observation mirror. *Not watching.* No one was in there. Ryder stared back at his twisted reflection as a faint odor drifted to him.

His nostrils twitched. That scent . . . "Fire," he rasped. *Sabine?* His phoenix?

Then the footsteps were rushing away.

Ryder's wild gaze darted to his door. The chains were gone. He'd smashed through them. There was a faint *click* and hiss from outside of his cell. *The lock.*

He lunged forward.

And a gun lifted. A woman stood in the doorway. Her blue eyes were big and frightened, and her dark hair tumbled around her shoulders. He ignored the gun as his gaze zeroed in on her neck.

Hunger.

"Don't bite me!" she yelled.

His gaze jerked back up to her face. A pretty face. Pleasing. But . . .

I want Sabine. The woman before him was a means to an end. His ticket out. So he'd bite, he'd feed, and she wouldn't stop him. Gun or no gun.

"I'm here to help you."

His eyes narrowed. She sounded as if she meant the words, but he wasn't buying her line. It was just another one of Wyatt's games. Another lie. Like the twisted vampire story—primal vampires, his ass. "So says the woman with the gun aimed at my chest." He tried to keep his voice even so she wouldn't realize just how much fury surged in him.

She blinked and made the mistake of glancing away from him as she looked at her gun. "Look, that's just to—"

He ripped the gun out of her hand and shoved her back. His hand fisted in her hair as he yanked her head to the side. The perfect position for feeding. *"Hungry . . ."* And he was. Starving. But he wouldn't drain her. His control was there, hanging by a thread. He'd get power from her blood. Enough power to strengthen his body and get out of the pit.

"I'm . . . helping . . ." the woman said, sounding both angry and afraid. *"Trying . . . to . . . help . . ."*

She could help plenty by giving up her blood. Only he hesitated, not able to sink his fangs into her because in his mind, Ryder could see Sabine. Sabine had been so afraid the first time she'd come into his cell. "Need . . . you . . ." The words weren't for the woman in his arms. He *couldn't* bite her, a knowledge that pushed through his rage and hunger. He needed Sabine.

Only Sabine.

Before he could free the woman, hard hands grabbed him and yanked him away from her. His body flew through the air and thudded into the far wall.

"Too fucking bad," a big, angry bastard snarled at him. "'Cause I saw her first." The man's dark eyes glittered with fury. And . . . fire?

Ryder's attention was caught by those eyes. He'd only seen that circle of fire once before—in Sabine's eyes. As he watched, the man with the burning eyes turned and offered the woman his hand. Huh. The guy must be her protector.

Except the woman didn't take the offered hand. She glanced over at Ryder.

"You have to get out of here," the bruiser with the burning eyes said to her.

Ryder rose. Took a step forward.

The guy tensed. His gaze cut to Ryder. "Touch her again," the male snarled, "and I'll turn you to dust."

He'd like to see the guy try.

The woman still hadn't taken the fellow's offered hand. Ryder knew now that she wasn't working with Wyatt. Whatever was happening—these two were on their own.

The dark-haired guy grabbed the woman's wrist. He pulled her close. "Come on." They turned for the door.

But the lady was hesitating. "There are others." Her words reminded him of Sabine. She'd cared about the other prisoners, too. "They're trapped," the woman said, voice shaking, "and—"

An explosion shook the building, a blast that had cracks racing across the walls and ceilings.

Ryder tensed, then he heard screams. Screams that echoed and reverberated, seemingly calling out from all around him. Was Sabine screaming? He had to find her. Ryder rushed forward, shoving his way past the bruiser and his woman.

This time, no one would stop his escape. *I'm coming for you, Sabine.* A promise was a promise.

More explosions rocked the building and the screams rose.

* * *

Sabine stared up at the light above her. A small light, far too bright. At first, that light had hurt her eyes. In a room of darkness, it had been the only thing she'd seen. Her body was strapped down. No, chained down. Chained with a metal that could resist fire.

Because she'd burned before. More than once.

A whimper slipped from her lips. She knew her name because the voice that sometimes floated in the room—that voice called her Sabine. She didn't know where she was. Why someone kept hurting her.

She just knew the fire.

She pulled at the metal bonds. They wouldn't give. Her wrists were raw and bloody and she couldn't get free.

There had to be more than this for her. Why couldn't she remember? She'd had a life.

But it was gone. All she knew now were days and nights of fire and pain.

And the urge to destroy. To attack and kill . . . those urges grew stronger in her every moment.

Sabine jerked once more on the bonds. The coppery scent of her blood rose to fill her nose.

An image flashed in her mind. A man. Blond hair. Chiseled features. A faint smile tilting his lips. For some reason, when she saw that image, Sabine thought . . .

He likes blood.

She shivered. Her skin was cold. They wouldn't give her clothes. The clothes just burned away. Everything burned.

Sabine heard the crackle of static drift in the air and knew the voice was going to come again.

"This time," the voice announced—a female voice. One that was always flat and so cold, clipped with a hard accent—"this time we've been instructed to use gas on you. I've been assured that the process shouldn't take long at all."

The process. Sabine bit her lips. There was a hiss of sound and the air around her changed. Developed an acrid odor. The scent burned her nose.

Her throat.

A tear leaked down her cheek.

She held tight to the image of the blond man. It was the only image that had ever come to her.

He likes blood.

That knowledge should have scared her, but she was long past the point of terror. As she choked and shuddered, Sabine just thought . . .

Find me. Because somewhere deep inside, an instinctive knowledge told her that man was coming for her.

Chaos. Fire. Hell. But . . .

No Sabine.

Ryder's hands clenched as he watched Genesis burn. He'd taken blood—plenty of it—from the guards who were fleeing. But the blood tasted wrong to him. Sour.

Sabine.

The scream was in his head. She was the one he needed, but he couldn't find her. Genesis—there was nothing left there. Everything would soon be ash.

It was the *second* lab that he needed. Wyatt had transferred Sabine there. Ryder just had to find the place.

But the guards he'd fed on, they hadn't known about the second lab's location. He'd ripped into their minds—*they hadn't known*. The place was shrouded in secrecy and—

The big, dark bruiser from before was back. Ryder watched as the guy stalked right through the fire. The woman was in his arms.

The woman . . . *she'd tried to help me*.

In his rage before, he hadn't thought she was truly there to free him. But she had been. Not there to torture and destroy, but to help.

So he owed her. For the moment. Ryder braced his legs and called out, "Let her go."

The man's head snapped up even as his hold on the woman tightened. "I knew letting you live was a mistake." Disgust and rage were ripe in the man's voice.

Ryder swiped away the blood that dripped down his chin. He'd gorged too much. *So why am I still hungry?* He bared his fangs as he advanced. "She . . . saved me." Ryder managed to grit out the words. "I won't let you hurt her." Sabine wouldn't want the woman hurt. The woman—she kept reminding him of Sabine.

The guy frowned and gazed down at the woman. She appeared dead to the world, but Ryder saw the soft rise and fall of her chest. Still alive, just unconscious. Unconscious and in the arms of a phoenix who'd just torched Genesis. She wasn't exactly in a safe place.

Then the bruiser looked back up at Ryder, and fire burned in the man's eyes. *A fire just like Sabine's*. "I'm guessing you're lucky number thirteen," Ryder murmured.

The phoenix glared at Ryder and warned, "You don't want to tangle with me."

Actually, no, he didn't. He wanted that phoenix to get far away from him, but the woman . . . "She's human." He gave a hard shake of his head. Then he lied and said, "I don't know what the hell you are, and—"

"She's not." The words were shouted at him. The guy's grip on the woman just kept tightening. *Cain*. That was the name Wyatt had mentioned for Subject Thirteen. Cain needed to ease up or he might wind up hurting her.

And she wasn't human? Then what was she? She'd certainly smelled human to him. "Doesn't matter," Ryder said as the phoenix advanced on him. "I won't let you hurt her." Saving the woman had suddenly become too important. Why? *Because I can't save Sabine.*

No, no, he *would* save her. He wasn't giving up on Sabine, not yet.

Cain studied Ryder as if he were insane. *Yes, buddy, I am. Don't push me anymore.* Then the guy said, "I wasn't the one trying to eat her."

Ah, valid point. But that was okay. Ryder had a point of his own to make. "No, you're just the one who wants to fuck her."

Cain's eyes narrowed to fiery slits. This phoenix seemed to have more power than Sabine. Wyatt had already said that Number Thirteen was stronger. With vamps, age brought increased power. Was it the same situation for a phoenix? Sabine hadn't known *what* she was. The first death and rising had stunned her. This guy knew the score.

He also seemed to be able to control his fire. Wasn't that intriguing?

Before the male could escape with the woman, Ryder deliberately stepped into his path.

The phoenix sighed and told him, "If you don't move, you're dead."

Like he hadn't heard that a time or twenty before. Controlling the impulse to roll his eyes, Ryder advanced. "You can't—"

Fire seemed to surge right out of the guy's hand. The flames flew at Ryder, spinning in a deadly ball. Ryder yelled and jumped to the side. The blazing ball missed him, but as he lay on the ground, a whip of fire circled him, caging his body within the crackling flames.

Then the phoenix told him, "If you ever come at her again, you'll feel the full force of my fire." There was a deadly promise in the words. "And you won't have time to scream then. You'll just die."

Ryder stiffened. First up, he *hadn't* screamed. Yelled in fury, fuck yes, but screamed? *No.* The very suggestion was insulting.

And second, the bastard was just *leaving* him there. Leaving a vampire trapped in his worst nightmare. Flames that wouldn't die.

The flames were all she knew. Burning bright and hot in red and gold. Surrounding her. Seeming to come from within her.

The fire terrified her. So did the screams that she could hear. Or was she the one screaming? It was so hard to tell for sure.

She was supposed to remember someone. Something. A man?

The idea was there, whispering beneath the screams, but then she forgot him.

Forgot her own self.

The fire burned and burned and burned.

Fury cut through her. A killing rage. *Destroy everything. Everyone.* She wanted to hurt and punish.

But though the fire burned so hot, she couldn't move her body.

Burn, burn, burn.

The fire crackled. She started to laugh. Soon she couldn't tell the difference between that crackle of fire and her laughter. Maybe there was no difference.

Son of a bitch. He had to get out of the flames. More humans would be coming soon. It would be rather hard to ignore the giant blaze for much longer.

He couldn't wait for the flames to die.

Ryder sucked in a sharp breath and tasted the smoke. This would hurt, but he'd survive, provided he moved fast enough.

The flames were a thick wall around him, easily eight feet high. The phoenix had planned his trap carefully. It made Ryder suspect that the guy had faced off against vampires before. Faced off against them, and no doubt killed them with his flames.

Ryder wasn't in the mood to die.

Pain won't stop me. He'd grown too used to it over the years. It was a companion now.

Ryder's muscles tensed, then he ran forward, racing through the fire. The flames burned his pants, the shirt he'd jerked on before, then the fire raced over his skin.

Ryder dove for the ground. He rolled, spinning, as he tried to put out the fire that covered him. His clothes were charred, chunks missing, but so what?

He rose, then frowned. There weren't any burns on his body. Not even any blisters. The fire had touched his skin. He'd been sure of it but—

Ryder lifted his hand. *No burn.*

The flesh of a vampire burned quickly. Fire was one

of the best weapons against a vampire. Only he hadn't burned.

Maybe the fire just hadn't been able to touch him because he'd moved so fast.

No, I felt the heat on my skin.

Brows rising, Ryder walked back toward the circle of fire. His jaw tightened, and he shoved his hand right into the flames. The fire instantly surrounded his fist. He waited, counting . . .

One, two, three, four, five.

Ryder yanked his hand back.

No burns. No blisters. No marks at all. In disbelief, he stared at his unmarred fingers.

Sabine. Just what had his lovely phoenix done to him?

When the flames finally died away, she found herself strapped to a hard, metal table. No, not strapped. She twisted her head. The bindings holding her down were made of metal, too.

Her body was naked.

She felt both hot, a churning from inside of her, and ice-cold, a chill that came from outside of her body. Goose bumps covered her arms.

Static crackled. The sound made her head ache. Her gaze flew up—far, far up. At least twenty feet above her head, she saw a big, bright light.

Just that light.

"The fire lasted much longer that time, Sabine," a cool, calm voice told her. "You must be getting stronger."

Sabine? Who the hell was Sabine?

"Rest for a while. There have been some . . . developments." The voice seemed to echo in the room. "We may even have a job for you soon."

Why had they restrained her? "Where am I?"

A sigh slipped into the room. Not her sigh. A sigh that came from the voice. *She's female, just like me.*

"You always have the same questions, Sabine." Now there was a hint of annoyance in the voice. Impatience. "Rest." An order. "The next test will be different."

A test?

"We'll find out if you truly are getting stronger with each rising. The fittest will survive."

The fittest what?

But the static crackled again. Then . . . silence.

"H-hello?" she cried out.

No answer.

She twisted beneath her bonds. Pulled and yanked. Her left wrist cut open when the metal tore into it.

The scent of blood teased her nose.

He likes the blood.

She stilled.

And remembered.

I am Sabine. She thought of the cold woman's voice. Of hell and pain.

I am Sabine.

She stared up at the light. Remembered screams and death. A nightmare that wouldn't end. And that voice . . . that cold voice.

You will die. A promise.

Because her beast was out of the cage, and there would be no going back.

Time passed. The bonds holding her eventually were removed—the woman's voice told her that they were programmed to release once her body reached a certain core temperature.

Food was brought to her. Pushed through a narrow opening at the bottom of her door. She ate. Barely tasted the bland meal.

She paced her room. Walked the small confines again and again. They'd given her clothes, jeans and a T-shirt and even tennis shoes. Maybe they were trying to make her feel normal now.

Only she wasn't *normal*.

The man's image would whisper through her thoughts every now and then, but she never let her expression alter.

They thought her memories were gone.

You thought wrong.

Because when she'd come back after her last death, her memories had returned completely.

She heard footsteps approaching her cell. After her deaths, her senses had sharpened, too. She could catch the faintest of smells and hear the softest of whispers.

You don't know what I'll do to you.

She didn't let her smile break free. Sabine stilled and waited.

The door opened. Sabine didn't rush for the door. She didn't do anything. They thought they'd trained her. Broken her.

They were wrong.

A woman walked inside. A woman with sleek red hair that was twisted up on her head. She wore a lab coat, carried a clipboard, looked perfect and pretty.

But she was rotten inside. Sabine could smell that, too.

Guards flanked the woman, and, big surprise, they had guns trained on Sabine.

"I-it's time for a test." The woman's voice trembled. It had never trembled before.

Sabine lifted a brow. *Are you afraid to be in here with me? You should be.*

The woman—she smelled of antiseptic, blood, and fear—locked her gaze on Sabine. "I can give you freedom."

Her words were not what Sabine had expected.

"There's a monster out there. A dangerous, vicious beast. He has to be stopped."

Sabine was already looking at a dangerous, vicious beast. Just one that wore the skin of a human.

"He's like you," the lady told her. Then her jaw dropped as she seemed to realize what she'd said.

'Cause, yes, calling me a dangerous, vicious beast will make me want to help you.

"Why aren't you talking?" the woman demanded. She seemed unnerved by Sabine's stare. Good. The redhead's brows shot up. "*Can* you talk?"

"Yes." She just didn't want to waste words on the bitch.

The redhead sighed, as if in relief. "Our facility has been breached."

Was that why the lady was sweating?

He's coming for me. The thought had Sabine's heart squeezing. Ryder had given her a promise. Freedom was close. Close enough to taste.

"We know our director will be targeted for assassination." The woman's fingertips had whitened around her clipboard.

Their director? Ah yes, must be that dick, Wyatt. He'd come to see her a few times. Come to gauge the success of his precious "research."

The redhead's eyes narrowed on Sabine. "We want you to stop his attacker."

Seriously? The bitch was crazy. Sabine wasn't going to stop him. She'd applaud the guy. Give him a freaking standing ovation.

As the silence stretched, the redhead finally seemed to realize that fact.

Uh, hello? I'm the captive that you've been torturing and killing for days. Why, oh why, would I ever help you?

"You remembered this time, didn't you?" the woman asked as she eased back a step. "Wyatt said that could happen. That sometimes you'd rise with your memory there. It just hadn't happened before, so I thought . . ." Her voice trailed away.

Sabine just kept staring at her.

The woman cleared her throat. "Actually, that might make things easier," the redhead murmured, but she still made a point of getting closer to the guards. The woman slanted a quick glance at the guard on her right. "We still have the tail on her brother, right?"

My brother. Sabine fought to control her expression. They were looking for a weakness. She wouldn't give Genesis one.

But the crazy bitch was still talking. "Make sure our watcher knows that if Sabine doesn't complete this task, a bullet should be put in Rhett's head."

Fire burned in her gut. Heating and churning and *boiling* as fury and fear clawed at her.

"Now *that* got your attention, didn't it?" the woman said, sounding satisfied. "I saw the flash of fire in your eyes."

"I'll *give* you a flash of fire," Sabine promised, knotting her hands into fists.

The woman jumped back a good two feet. Her shoulders brushed the cell door. The guards lifted their weapons.

Sabine had been playing with fire lately. Conjuring it from nothing. Letting balls of flame roll in her hands. The practice helped to pass the time.

Now, deliberately, she let the fire rise from her palm. The ball hovered over her hand. "Look what little trick I learned."

Though they already knew this. They'd been watching her through their cameras and their two-way mirrors.

"Do you *want* your brother to die?"

Sabine forced a shrug. "Maybe he'll just come back." She even managed a smile. "Like me."

One perfectly arched red eyebrow rose. "Since you were adopted and he isn't your blood brother, I find that highly doubtful." She gave Sabine a wide smile. "But let's go see." She turned to face the door.

"No!" The word broke from Sabine, and the redhead looked back, all Cheshire-cat satisfied.

Damn her. "Why are you doing this?" Sabine demanded. "I'm a person. I have *rights*!"

"You're a weapon. And you're about to be used."

Very, very cold bitch.

"Your target is a man named Cain O'Connor. He'll most likely be with a woman—Eve Bradley." The redhead held up her clipboard. There was a manila file on that board. The lady pulled it free, then tossed the file near Sabine's feet. "You can find their pictures in here. Look at them. Memorize them, then go and *find* those two."

Sabine didn't look down at the file. "And if I do, you'll let my brother go?"

The redhead nodded.

Sabine heard the shrill cry of an alarm. The woman was right—it sounded like the second Genesis facility had been breached.

"Kill O'Connor. Leave the woman alive."

Sabine rolled her shoulders. "Then you leave me and my family alone?" Not that Sabine could trust her but . . .

"I give you my word."

What choice did she have?

Sabine let her fire die. Wisps of smoke floated above her hand. Slowly, she walked toward the woman. "Who are you?" she asked. The redhead with the upper-crust New York accent, one that spoke of old money, had never told Sabine her name.

"Doesn't matter." The redhead licked her lips. Her body had tensed at the alarm's cry.

To Sabine, the woman's identity mattered very much. A scientist, a doctor, a sadistic torturer. She was going to track this woman.

Sabine stared at her a moment longer, then she bent to pick up the file. She opened it, and her gaze fell to the photos inside. The male—Cain O'Connor—had gold skin, dark eyes, and hair that was almost black. He stared back up at her with an undeniable fury.

Yes, she could relate to that particular rage.

The woman's picture showed sparkling blue eyes. Smooth skin. Dark hair. She was wearing a lab coat, just like the one the redhead had on.

Was Genesis killing its own now? Hardly surprising.

The alarm seemed to shriek even louder.

"He'll be going for Wyatt's office. You'll find him on the third floor." The redhead was backing out of the room. The guards were starting to sweat now, too.

There was fear in all of their eyes.

Sabine could hear screams coming from a distance. Screams. Yells. Growls?

"If Wyatt dies, if you don't stop O'Connor . . ." The redhead stopped and glared at Sabine. "I'll know, and I'll make sure that a bullet finds its way into your brother's head."

Then she was gone, running away with her guards flanking her sides. Sabine's cell door was left wide open. The alarm continued to shriek.

She looked down at the pictures once more. Was this what she'd become? A killer for Genesis?

She'd had a normal life once.

She'd been a photographer. She'd taken so many pictures, mostly all in her beautiful New Orleans. She'd shown her work at galleries. Set up a website and even been able to make a fairly decent living doing what she loved. She hadn't gotten rich, but she'd gotten by.

She'd had a home. Friends. Family.

Rhett. No, Rhett wasn't her blood brother. But what did blood matter? When she'd broken her leg at six, he'd been there, holding her hand, talking to her, until the cast was set. When she hadn't made cheerleader at thirteen, he'd been there. Telling her that she was better off. That she was too good for the team and that the cheer captain had just been jealous of her skills.

He'd been wrong, of course. She hadn't made the team because she straight-up sucked and because, during the routine, she'd accidentally punched the captain, Kristi Martin, in the face.

At sixteen, he'd been there for her again. When her boyfriend had gotten drunk and a little too handsy—not respecting her first-base rule—Rhett had, well, he'd kicked Johnny's ass.

He'd *always* been there for her.

I'll make sure a bullet finds its way into your brother's head.

Sabine's breath whispered out. She knew that she would do whatever was necessary in order to protect Rhett.

Even if it meant letting her monster take control.

Even if it meant killing.

CHAPTER EIGHT

Fucking chaos. That was all he saw. Chaos. Screams and growls filled the air as Ryder fought his way through the second Genesis facility. Locating this place had been a real bitch, but he hadn't given up. Sure, he'd betrayed some people. Killed others during his hunt for information. *My hunt for Sabine.*

But he'd gotten there. He'd found Wyatt's hiding spot, and Sabine *had* to be there.

He'd make Wyatt reveal her location because Ryder was not leaving without her. From now on, Ryder planned to keep Sabine at his side.

Need her.

The hunger that he felt for her had only grown since he'd escaped from his prison at Genesis. Something was wrong with him. He was certain of it. Wyatt had done something to him. Ryder had taken the blood of others since first biting Sabine—drained plenty of 'em—but no matter how much blood he took, it didn't satisfy him. There was always a hunger inside of him. A craving for *her*.

He rushed down the hallway, stopping outside the door he knew would lead to Wyatt's office. He could smell the bastard inside. Ryder also knew that a trap waited for him behind that door—*I can smell your guards, too, Wyatt*—but he didn't care. They were all about to see just how strong he was.

But Ryder didn't kick his way inside the room. Why waste the energy on a fancy entrance? He opened the door quietly, slowly. He'd take his time and see just what Wyatt had planned.

The floor creaked beneath his feet as he entered the room. Wyatt had his back to him. The guy was leaning over his desk. Oh, but it would feel good to rip open the jerk's throat.

Wyatt leaned forward a bit more and his hand slid under the edge of the desk. In the next second, the door to the office slid closed, sealing them inside. Then Wyatt spun toward him. The guy had some kind of gas mask on, and Wyatt sneered, "Your mistake, phoenix—"

Ryder rushed toward him. *I'm not a phoenix, asshole. And you're dead.*

Shock widened Wyatt's eyes. "Wh-what—"

Gas drifted from the small vents in the ceiling. Ryder glanced up at that smoky gas. Right, that would explain the mask. Since Wyatt had obviously been expecting someone else to come busting through his office door, the guy had set the wrong trap. The gas didn't have any effect on Ryder. That horrifying knowledge was bright in Wyatt's gaze.

Before Ryder could grab Wyatt and sink his fangs into the jerk's flesh, a narrow door to the right slid open. Five guards rushed out, their weapons clutched tightly. They also wore the masks, as if that would keep them safe.

Ryder snarled and attacked. The fury that had built and built for days within him erupted. Fangs and claws slashed. The guards weren't going to stop him. The guards—some that he recognized from his time at Genesis—weren't ever putting him back in a cage again. They weren't going to hurt *anyone* else again.

Their bodies slammed into the floor. Their blood covered him.

The hissing of the gas continued. Wyatt was clutching his mask, looking as if fear had frozen him.

Ryder locked his gaze on the bastard, and taking one slow step at a time, he closed in on the guy. *No escape.* This reckoning was long overdue. "You have something of mine, Wyatt," he said, snapping his teeth together, "and I want her *back*."

Wyatt tried to punch at him. Like that was impressive. Ryder punched back, hard enough to send the mask flying off Wyatt's head. Then Ryder put his claws on Wyatt's face. "Where. Is. She."

Wyatt started to laugh then. "Addicted, aren't you?"

Ryder sliced the skin on Wyatt's left cheek. The laughter didn't stop. So he sliced open the doctor's right cheek. Matching wounds.

The blood flowed and Wyatt tried to fight him again.

Fool. "I can kill you quickly," Ryder said, "or I can do it slowly. Either way, you aren't getting out of this room." Actually, he'd already planned for the slow death, but why tell Wyatt that?

Wyatt's face was red, mottled. And when he lifted his hand to swing at Ryder, the move was slow, uncoordinated. Ah, the gas was kicking in. "Won't . . . kill . . ." Wyatt muttered.

"Hell, yes, I will," Ryder snapped right back. He'd take extreme pleasure in gutting the guy.

But Wyatt shook his head. "The gas . . . won't . . . kill . . . me . . . just . . . sleep . . ."

Wasn't that fucking fabulous to know. *"Where is Sabine."* Not a question. A snarled command.

"Dead," Wyatt whispered, his voice hoarse. "Dead . . . over and over . . . dead."

Ryder sank his teeth into Wyatt's throat. Why waste any more time? He'd take his blood and *make* the bastard lead him to Sabine.

The instant that Wyatt's blood slid onto his tongue, Ryder knew something was wrong. His body began to shudder, no, to spasm. He couldn't control the spasms. Couldn't stop them. Ryder tossed Wyatt across the room.

Wyatt slammed into a window, breaking the glass with his head, and the guy sucked in deep gasps of breath. Fresh air that came through the broken window.

Ryder spat out the man's blood. It didn't help. His body continued to spasm and he fell to the floor. *What the hell?*

"Told you . . . before . . ." Wyatt gasped, "I'm . . . poison." Wyatt rolled over to face him. "The others . . . the en-enhanced ones could . . . smell the poison. Knew to . . . stay away."

Fuck. The story the guy had spun about the primal vamps was true. But then, deep down, Ryder had suspected it was.

I'd just hoped like hell that it was BS.

Ryder's hands flattened on the floor. It felt like his insides were ripping open, but at least the spasms had stopped.

"And that's what . . . h-happens . . . with just a few . . . drops . . ."

Ryder lifted his head. Found Wyatt smiling. "Guess what would . . . happen," Wyatt said, "if you took . . . more?"

Using every bit of energy he could drag up, Ryder pushed to his feet. "I don't have to use my"—hell, he *hurt*—"fangs to kill you. I can do it with my bare hands."

And he would. Each step was brutal, but Ryder made his way across the room. He grabbed Wyatt and yanked the bastard up toward him. *"Sabine."*

"Want . . . her, do you?" Satisfaction rolled in the words. The mad scientist, pleased with the results of his experiments.

"What did you do to me?" The question burst from him. His claws slashed into Wyatt. "Why do I need her so much?" So much that when he closed his eyes, he saw her. He couldn't escape from his need. Not in dreams. Not in blood.

There was no place that she didn't reach. That she didn't haunt.

"I did . . . nothing . . ."

Bullshit.

"The beast . . . did it all. You don't know what you are . . ." Wyatt's voice rose in pain when Ryder drove his claws into the guy's side. "I . . . do. The *first*."

"I'm gonna be the first one to send you to hell, that's for sure!"

"She's your match. Without her . . . you'll . . . insane . . ."

What? He'd go insane? Now it was Ryder's turn to laugh. "I'm already there." The pain in his gut had lessened, but he wasn't about to make the mistake of letting Wyatt's blood anywhere near his fangs again. "So tell me where to find her or you're about to see just how it feels to have your skin peeled away."

Then Ryder heard a scream. Long and high. And he smelled smoke.

"You don't have to find her." Wyatt's head sagged. "She's coming. Vivian and I—we set her after the other . . . phoenix. Got to see . . . which stronger . . ."

"Always experimenting, aren't you, bastard?" Ryder put his hand over Wyatt's chest. Without his heart, he'd like to see how the guy kept living. "You won't experiment anymore."

Wyatt's lashes lifted. His body stiffened, and suddenly, he didn't look nearly so weak.

Wyatt shoved Ryder back. "If you kill me, you won't find out which of your own damn vampire group *sold you out* to me."

No, definitely not so weak. Had he *ever* been weak? Had the jerk just played him?

Ryder's body tensed.

"Do you think it was just chance that you were taken? *You?* When there are so many vampires out there?" Wyatt's voice mocked him. No more weakness. No more stutters. The guy was a damn good actor. He'd just been delaying . . . until what? *Until he smelled the smoke.* "Your own kind sold you out. Some didn't want to be monsters. Some wanted a cure."

"A cure you promised them?"

"A cure I was close to finding." Wyatt's hands fisted. "So close . . . until Cain O'Connor brought down Genesis. The phoenix burned my facility to the ground. He destroyed all of my research!"

"Yeah, cry me a fucking river. I'm betting you had plenty of backup research to keep you busy. Hell, all you did was retreat to this facility." Enough talk. Time for the kill. He lifted his claws.

"They're out!"

The fast words didn't give him any pause. Ryder shoved his claws into Wyatt's chest.

Wyatt groaned. "The vampires . . . the primals . . . most of them are dead, but some got out. They aren't contained any longer."

The hell they were. He wasn't about to believe another lie.

"I was trying to . . . fix them."

Ryder's claws jerked back. Wyatt's body swayed.

But the doc kept talking. "You were the first. Your blood was . . . pure. I thought the pure blood would . . . fix what was broken."

"Did it?" Not that he was buying this but . . .

Wyatt's gaze held his. Blood streamed from his wounds. Somehow, the guy was still on his feet. Were his wounds healing? Maybe. "I gave it . . . just to three of them," Wyatt muttered. "Needed a . . . test pool. They grew stronger and more . . . savage."

Not what he'd been hoping to hear.

"Primals have . . . a strong psychic sense. They pick up emotions . . . needs . . . your blood tied them to you."

Wasn't that grand?

"You want her blood . . . they feel what you feel . . . *they want her*."

This shit just got better and better. "Then they're dead." Simple. Because no one else would take Sabine. He was there to protect her. To claim her.

"Like me, they're . . . not so easy to kill." Wyatt looked down at his chest. Ryder knew his claws had sunk past flesh and bone. But Wyatt was still on his feet. Still talking. "My blood . . . it will keep them away. It can *hurt* them."

"Yeah, well, I'm betting I can *hurt* them, too."

Wyatt shook his head. "Not if they get to your . . . phoenix first."

They wouldn't.

Wyatt's hand flew up and locked around Ryder's wrist. *"I wish you could kill me."* The words were growled with a dark intensity. His eyes glittered. "I didn't want to be this way. I was a kid . . . I begged him not to change me, but he said I had to be stronger."

What the hell?

"Stopping my heart won't stop me . . . You'll have to try harder." Wyatt's hand tightened on him. No, he was lifting Ryder's hand, and trying to shove Ryder's claws back into his chest. "I've tried, too . . . I wanted a cure. I wanted to be *free*."

The doctor was breaking apart right before his eyes.

"The urges come to me. I can't control them. I . . . hurt people. Not just the subjects. Humans."

Ryder yanked his hand out of the guy's grip and stepped back. "Then I guess you're as much of a monster as me."

"No, I'm *more*." Desperate. Wild. "And I am what he made me."

"He?" Wyatt wasn't going down from his wounds. Whatever this guy was . . . he had a whole lot of strength and healing power.

"My father." Wyatt's smile was cold and evil and sad. "He liked to . . . experiment, too."

Son of a bitch.

Ryder heard the thunder of footsteps in the hallway.

More company, coming for them. Only the company heading their way . . . that company carried the scent of fire.

Not my phoenix. He'd never forget Sabine's scent. Flowers, sin, woman. But he also recognized this scent . . . it belonged to the male phoenix he'd met at the first Genesis facility. Subject Thirteen. Cain. Like Ryder, Cain wanted to get his pound of flesh from Wyatt. They all wanted vengeance. Every test subject Wyatt had tortured—*we all want our payback.*

"If you want death, then I think I can deliver it." Ryder stared into Wyatt's eyes, searching for truth. Did the bastard really want out of this world? Was that just another trick?

Wyatt's lashes flickered. Ryder caught the scent of fear.

He backed away from the doctor.

The scent of fear lessened. Ah, Wyatt thought he was safe. No, he was bait. "Cain is coming for you."

He'd follow the odor of Wyatt's blood. He'd find the bastard, and Cain would use those flames to send the guy to hell.

And if Cain came into the room, then . . .

Sabine will follow right behind him.

Wyatt had told him that Sabine was coming. The guy was working another experiment. Seeing which phoenix was stronger.

Cain was in the hallway. Sabine would be on her way after him. It was just a matter of waiting for her.

"I hope you enjoy the fire," Ryder muttered as he turned away. He didn't need to see the bastard die. He just needed the job to be done.

"It's not blood that . . . was the cure." Wyatt's voice

stopped him. "It's Sabine. Her tears. A phoenix's tears . . . found out . . . really heal . . ."

Ryder didn't look back. Why stare at a dead man? He slipped out of the room and got ready to wait.

Hurry, Sabine, I need you.

The cages were open. The beasts out. Sabine saw death all around her. Guards fighting. Dying. Beings with claws and fangs attacking.

She tried to jump away from them. She didn't want to fight. There was only one man that she had to find.

"Bitch, you're one of them!"

Hard hands grabbed her. She looked up into the wild eyes of a man—no, not a man. He had fangs and claws—claws that were cutting into her hips. The light glinted off the vampire's bald head.

"Let me go!" Sabine cried out. She'd put on a white lab coat. Thinking it would let her slip by the guards, just like last time. Only now, the lab coat marked her for death because it wasn't the guards that she had to worry about. She needed to fear her fellow prisoners.

"I'll make you *beg!*" His claws dug deeper, and she gasped. She'd had enough pain. Too much.

Her hands curled around his wrists. "No, you won't." Then she let her fire out. His hands heated beneath her touch. Burned. The man jumped back, screaming.

He didn't attack again. He was too busy trying to put out the fire that licked at his skin. Sabine yanked off the coat. Blood had already appeared in thick patches on the white material. She tossed the coat aside. Kept hunting.

The woman had told her to go to the third floor. Others were fleeing, rushing for freedom.

Instead of running out with them, she continued going up.

Another stairwell. More attackers. She kept her fire ready. When they saw it, everyone stayed the hell back.

Then she was reaching for the door that would lead her to the third floor. The scent of death and blood was so strong there and—

She screamed when she was grabbed from behind. Grabbed, and then shoved up against the nearest wall. The vampire she'd burned—he'd tracked her. There'd been so much blood in the air that she hadn't smelled him, so many other thudding footsteps that she hadn't heard him. Before she could scream again, he sank his teeth into her shoulder and tore into the flesh.

Her hands were between them. The fire burned from her fingertips, and Sabine shoved a ball of flames right into his chest.

He fell back, tumbling down the stairs, and the fire consumed him.

Don't think. Don't feel.

But it was the first time that she'd ever killed anyone. Bile rose in her throat.

This is what I've become.

Sabine swallowed. Pressed a quick hand to her bleeding wound. Her first kill, but not her last. She still had a job to do. Her target. Sabine turned around and with shaking, now bloody hands, she shoved open the metal door that led out of the stairwell. *Find the target. Kill him.*

As she headed down the hallway—one already reeking of blood and death—a tall, dark-haired male rushed from one of the offices. His face was locked in tense lines of fury, and she recognized him instantly from his photo, even before she saw the flames in his eyes.

Cain O'Connor.

He's the one like me. Another phoenix. Another who could die and rise and kill with fire.

He was the one she was supposed to destroy. She wasn't even sure how that was really supposed to work. Could the fire of one phoenix kill another? Because if it couldn't, Sabine was figuring that she would be pretty well screwed.

Body tensing, Sabine let her fire out. Not just a little ball this time. She wanted to be safe. A circle of flames wrapped around her as the power of the beast that lurked inside began to push past her control.

Through the flames, her gaze met O'Connor's. On a sigh, she said, "I'm supposed to kill you." What if her flames didn't work against another phoenix? How would she take him out then? How would she protect her brother?

But he shook his head. His hair, a little too long, brushed over his shoulders. "I'm not here to hurt you."

Laughter broke from her. "Of course you are. They're all here to do that. To kill me, again and again." Her chin lifted. She could do this. She *had* to do this. "Only I'm tired of dying. Maybe it's your turn now." His chance to face the fires of hell. Sabine lifted her hand and sent a line of flames racing toward him.

But the guy gave a little wave of his hand and her charging fire just . . . stopped.

Her lips parted. *He's stronger than I am.*

No strain showed on his face at all, and smoke just drifted lightly in the air.

Her stomach knotted. The fear that twisted in her gut wasn't for herself. *I'm sorry, Rhett.*

Cain held her gaze. "You're not the only one who's tired of dying," he said, his voice deep and rumbling.

Ryder's lips brushed over her neck. "Missed . . . you." He pushed against her.

She pulled away and stared down at him in surprise. His neck—how had it healed so quickly? Even with her blood, that level of healing was amazing.

Impossible.

His gaze narrowed as he stared up at her. "Did you . . . cry for me?"

She felt the wet tracks on her cheeks. Sabine nodded. In her twisted new world, he was her only constant. The idea of losing him had terrified her. It *still* terrified her. She needed to know that Ryder would be there for her.

His hand tightened around her wrist. "Don't ever cry for me again. Don't ever fucking cry for *anyone*."

His words hurt. She'd helped him. Why was he so angry with her?

Then the werewolf in the hallway growled again. Ryder's head jerked as he glanced at the battle in progress. The werewolf was leaping forward to attack.

Ryder tore away from Sabine. He rushed down that hallway and grabbed the guy's feet, sending the attacker falling face-first onto the floor.

The guy turned with a snarl, his features tight, animalistic, as he prepared, no doubt, to go for Ryder's throat again.

Sabine raised her hand and sent a blast of fire out from her fingertips. The fire came to her so much easier now. As if it were always waiting, just beneath her skin.

Ryder leapt back, avoiding the blast of those flames. The fire circled the now howling werewolf, closing in on him. The guy swiped out with his claws, then whimpered when the fire bit into him.

He would soon be doing more than just whimpering.

Sabine focused on her flames and prepared to tighten the net.

"No!" a woman shouted as she rushed from an open door. The same office that Cain had exited. The woman was slender, with long, dark hair, too pale skin, and desperate eyes. *The woman from the photo. Eve Bradley. I'm supposed to let her live.* The woman's eyes were on Cain O'Connor. "You can't do this to him!"

Cain grabbed her arm. "It's not my fire," he said.

No, it wasn't. *The flames are all mine.* Sabine slowly walked around the beast and stalked toward Ryder. He was close to the other phoenix, too close for her peace of mind. So she headed for them, and, within her circle of fire, the man's head jerked up. He snarled—a true animal cry—and just . . . charged at the fire.

Fine, if you want to die, then be my guest.

But the werewolf leapt right over the flames. Flames that had to be at least six feet high. He jumped right over them.

"Get out of the way!" Ryder yelled at her.

Sabine realized she'd made a mistake. She'd tried to move closer in order to protect Ryder, but she'd just put herself right in the path of the beast-man.

Maybe she could send her fire—

Claws sliced into her stomach. Deep. Brutal.

She fell, slamming into the floor and feeling the wet warmth of her blood soak the tile beneath her. For a moment, the entire world seemed to stop. Or maybe that was just her heart.

"*Sabine.*" Ryder rolled her over. This time, he was the one who gasped. She didn't need to see the damage to know that her wound was fatal. She could already feel death coming for her. After dying so many times, she recognized death's touch. Recognized it and hated it.

Her lips trembled. Sabine shook her head. "Don't . . . want to die again." It hurt too much. When she came back, what then? Would she be lost once more? Would she wake with no memory? Knowing only the taste of fire on her tongue? She didn't want to be lost again.

She didn't want to be dead.

I don't want to be a monster.

"Help . . . me," Sabine whispered.

Ryder pulled her into his arms. Her blood soaked him, too. "I will. I swear, I will."

Her gaze slid to the left. There was fire. Shattering glass. The werewolf had just jumped through a window. Good. She hoped he broke his neck when he fell. If he didn't . . . "Kill him," Sabine whispered.

Ryder pulled her tighter against him. "We can stop the blood. You'll be fine."

No, she wouldn't be fine. Neither would Rhett. *What if I forget him?*

She could hear that cold, female voice telling her . . . *I'll make sure that a bullet finds its way into your brother's head.*

"Kill the phoenix," Sabine whispered. Her hands grabbed Ryder's shirt. "Kill him for me."

Ryder frowned down at her.

"Wyatt—"

His nostrils flared. "That bastard is already dead."

Then so was Rhett. She'd failed.

Her lashes started to sag. She struggled to keep them open, for just a few moments more. The world spun around her. Ryder—he'd lifted her up, stood, had her cradled in his arms. "Hold on," he told her. "You'll be okay."

"Can you handle her?" a deep voice called out. She forced her eyes to focus. Cain. He was staring at them. Frowning at the gaping wounds on her stomach.

You know I'm dying, don't you?

Ryder turned away from Cain and headed back toward the stairs. "Always," he said.

A lump rose in her throat. "Don't want to . . . forget you . . ."

They were in the stairwell. "Don't worry, love, I won't let you."

She wanted to believe him.

But she couldn't.

CHAPTER NINE

Fuck, fuck, fuck!

Ryder kicked open the heavy, gleaming silver door, figuring that the room inside would be a lab. A narrow bed waited in the middle of the room under bright lights. Not so much a bed as an exam table. Trays of instruments were scattered around the room.

Handcuffs?

I hate this place.

But he had to take care of Sabine and he had to do it *now*.

Carefully, he put her on the bed. His teeth clenched as a pain-filled gasp slipped from her lips. The werewolf—yeah, that guy who'd attacked her had been a freaking werewolf, just one not quite like any shifter that Ryder had ever seen before—had done a number on her. She was bleeding out right before his eyes.

"I want you to drink my blood," he told her. Ryder caught her chin. Forced her gaze up to his. That gaze was so weak. No flames. Just darkness. *"Sabine,"* he snapped out her name, trying to force her focus back to him.

Only she didn't focus on him.

She didn't focus on anything. Her eyes began to roll back into her head. No! He used his teeth to tear open his wrist, then he shoved his hand toward her mouth.

"Vampire . . ." A woman's voice sighed out the title. "This didn't work before. Why would you think it would save her now?"

His head whipped to the left. A redhead stood in the doorway. A female with cold, perfect features wearing a white lab coat. Correction, a *bloodstained* white coat.

The woman sagged against the wall. Then she tried to push forward as she took a step toward him.

"Who are you?" Ryder demanded even as he kept his wrist at Sabine's mouth. He wasn't giving up. He'd never give up on her.

"I'm Vivian . . . Dr. Vivian Sutton . . . and I can save your phoenix. You . . . help me . . ." Vivian offered, breath heaving and her face tightening with a flash of pain, "I'll help you."

Ryder's gaze fell back at Sabine's still face.

"The tears . . . are they still on her cheeks?" The doctor tried to keep her voice flat, but Ryder heard the crack of emotion. Desperate hope. "I saw . . . the footage from the security camera. She cried for you." Her footsteps shuffled closer. "Are the tear tracks . . . still there?"

He didn't answer. He knew what the woman wanted. *The tears were the cure.* Wyatt's words.

And Sabine's tears—*they healed me.* When he'd been in that hallway, it hadn't been her blood that had brought him back. It had been her tears. So that part of the phoenix story was true, too. The tears of a phoenix could heal.

He glanced over at Vivian. "You're dying," he said to the doctor. There was so much blood pouring off her. She probably only had minutes left.

Her chin lifted. "So, is . . . she . . ."

Sabine's lips feathered over Ryder's palm. *Maybe she isn't.*

"The tears . . . they can't, *won't* heal a phoenix's own injuries, but they can heal *me*." The woman came closer, leaving drops of blood in her wake. "They can heal me . . . then I can heal her."

The fingers of his left hand slid over Sabine's cheek. So soft. Sweet silk. He'd missed her so much. A constant ache had filled his chest.

It wasn't about Sabine being some kind of second chance at redemption for him. It was about Sabine being—

Mine.

"The male . . . he would never cry—"

"No matter how many times you killed him, huh?" Ryder threw at her.

Sabine's lips moved against him again. Then her teeth—sharper than he remembered, bit into his wrist.

Yes!

But he didn't let the doctor see his relief.

"She was different . . ." Those footsteps kept shuffling closer. "Sabine cried each time she died."

The fucking bitch dared to tell him that?

"She begged for us to save her . . . Sometimes, she'd even beg for you."

His teeth snapped together. The woman was digging her own grave with her clinical, sadistic words.

"Then she'd cry when she rose." Her breath heaved out. The scent of blood deepened. "Maybe it's because she was so young. The first phoenix we captured, hell, we can't . . . even tell how old he is. The Immortal," Vivian whispered.

The Immortal? Was she talking about Cain?

"He didn't break. Subject Thirteen . . . didn't break, either . . ."

Fuck. Cain was Subject Thirteen. So that meant, hell, there was *another* phoenix lurking around some-place?

"They didn't break. Sh-she did. And I need her tears . . . need more of them . . ."

Ryder kept his hand at Sabine's mouth, but he sensed the attack coming from the doctor. He waited, waited, then he twisted his body. His left hand came up and caught the stake that the bitch had tried to shove into him. "I'm not drugged," he gritted out. "I'm not in a cage. So you can't control me, and you sure as hell can't kill me."

He snapped the stake in his hand. His gaze drifted over her as his nostrils flared. "You took a shot in the chest, huh? From one of the *monsters* or from your own guards?" Because they'd broken. He'd seen them. Shooting at anything or anyone who got between them and the red exit signs.

When the prisoners broke free and you'd been the one playing jailer and executioner, you had to know your ass was about to get tortured before death. *Run, run, humans. Run*.

But wherever they ran, the monsters would find them.

"You're already dead," Ryder told her, because the

wound to her chest was too deep. "And it's an easier death than you probably deserve."

He pushed her away.

But she shook her head. "Th-there's a syringe. A formula . . . it can stop the fire from consuming her!"

Desperation shook the words. A desperate woman would say anything, especially if she thought her lies would help her to keep living.

"Give me your . . . blood!" Vivian's voice was weakening. "Give it to me . . . and I will give you . . . the formula . . ."

Ryder stared at her, barely holding back his fury. If Sabine didn't need to keep feeding from him . . .

His jaw locked and he managed to growl, "The fire won't take her."

Vivian shook her head. "It will! Your blood . . . won't stop her change, it won't—"

"Three times," he said.

She shook her head again.

"For humans, it just takes one blood exchange for the transformation." For a human to take a last gasp of air as a mortal, and to awake as a vampire.

Her eyes widened. "You didn't—"

"For Sabine, since she was far from human, it took three exchanges." Maybe because her DNA was so strong. The vampire blood had needed time to sink into her cells. To bond. But the proof was unmistakable. When he glanced over her body, he saw that her wounds were closing. She was drinking his blood. She had *fangs*. Her teeth were sharper because they weren't normal canines any longer. His Sabine had transformed with this blood exchange.

He hadn't managed to stop her from dying that first

terrible night in his cell. But Sabine would never die again.

His blood guaranteed it.

He didn't expect Vivian to charge at him. But she did. With an infuriated scream, the redhead slammed into him and tried to pull Ryder away from Sabine. "Stop!" Vivian shrieked. "You're ruining her!"

With his left hand, he shoved her back, and never took his right wrist from Sabine's mouth. "I'm saving her. She doesn't want the fire." And how did Vivian have this strength? With that bullet wound to her chest, she should be barely managing to stay upright.

Not attacking.

"You'll make her . . . less . . ." The last word was a hiss.

He stiffened. "You have five seconds to get out of here, or I'll kill you." He never liked hurting women, but that Vivian—she'd hurt Sabine. The doctor was already dying.

"Bastard!" But Vivian's feet stumbled toward the door. "You'll regret this! She'll…hate you! She had the power of a god . . . and you're turning her into just another . . . bl-bloodsucker!"

His head turned. His gaze met hers. "You should be on the ground. Choking on your own blood." The wound had slowed her, yes, it was bleeding, almost gushing blood, but . . . Calculation had his eyes narrowing. "What are you, doctor? Are you an experiment, too, like Wyatt was?"

"W-was?" Her lips trembled. Grief flashed in her eyes.

He offered her a cold smile. "Guess you didn't watch that part on the security footage, huh? Go upstairs. See him for yourself."

She turned and fled. Still moving *too damn fast*.

But he didn't care about her. He only cared about Sabine. He looked back at her. Im-fucking-possible, because he'd never seen a vamp heal so quickly, but her wounds had already closed. Her cheeks were pink.

The third time had been the charm. She was locked with him now. Tied—body, blood, and soul.

He wasn't ever going to let her go. He didn't think that he could. Ryder's need for her had grown too strong.

As he stared at her, Sabine's eyelashes flickered.

"Look at me, love," he whispered as he leaned over her. "Let me make sure you're still with me."

Her mouth pulled away from his wrist. He didn't even glance at the wound. Her lashes lifted, and her dark eyes stared back at him.

No fire was in that gaze.

Just a darkness that seemed to see into his soul. The dark had never looked so warm or beautiful.

"Ryder?" She whispered his name. "What—where are we?" Then her eyes widened as she jerked upright. Her hand flew to her stomach. "He—he gutted me!"

Ryder wrapped his arms around her. Pulled her close to his chest. "You're safe."

But she shook against him. "I know this place . . . they used to experiment on me here."

Fuck that. He lifted her into his arms. "We're getting the hell out of here. No one is ever going to experiment on you again. I won't let anyone hurt you." A vow.

Her hands curled around his neck. "I feel . . . strange."

Because her body was transitioning. He'd heard of a few shifters being transformed over the years. Once they'd become vampires, they'd never been able to call up their beasts again.

Some said vampirism was a virus. An infection that spread with the exchange of blood. Humans were easily infected. Other paranormals just weren't as susceptible to the virus.

"You've lost a lot of blood," he told her, not wanting to explain what he'd done. Not then. "But you'll be okay."

Her head rested over his heart. "The fire was coming for me, but you stopped it."

His hold on her tightened.

"Thank you."

After all that had happened, the last thing she needed to do was thank him. When she realized that she was a vamp, Ryder knew she wouldn't exactly be thrilled.

Not when Sabine just wanted her human life back. How many times had she told him that she just wanted to go home?

He didn't speak as he carried her from the room. There was a thick blood trail in the hall. As if someone's bleeding body had been dragged away. There was also no sign of Vivian.

Growls and shouts could still be heard coming from the building. Smoke drifted in the air, and the crackle of flames grew louder.

Maybe the other phoenix had decided to burn this place to the ground. It seemed a fitting retribution.

Ryder held tight to Sabine and made his way from the wreckage and the hell. No one stopped him. No guards appeared with their guns. The guards who hadn't died had all run by now. And the paranormals left knew better than to fuck with him. Especially when he had his mate in his arms.

She is mine. To him, the truth was undeniable. *Always*.

Now, he just had to make Sabine realize that she needed him, too.

The vampire came at her, with his deadly claws and his too-sharp teeth. Vivian screamed, but there was no one to help her. No one to care.

When he opened his mouth and gave a guttural cry, she saw the vamp's teeth—every tooth was razor-sharp. Not just his canines. *Every. Single. One.*

She kicked and she punched, but he just held her with hands that bruised and knife-like claws that cut.

Vivian knew what he was. He was one of the freaks. One of the "bad experiments" that should never have seen the light of day. Wyatt had told her that most of the primal vampires had died in a recent fire, but this one—

"We wanted to help you!" she yelled. Not we, but Wyatt. He had wanted to help them . . .

The primal vampire's teeth sank into her throat.

The pain made her body jerk and shudder. She was going to die. She knew it. Her body could only survive for so long. She wasn't a vampire. Not a shifter. She just—

The vampire fell away from her, choking.

Vivian's hand went to her throat. Her blood trickled down her neck.

The vampire's face had twisted. He had his hands on his stomach, and he was the one screaming then. In agony.

Her breath rushed out. It had worked. Wyatt had told her . . . he'd said his blood was poison to the primal vampires. He'd said—

She lifted her hand. Stared at the bright red blood on her fingertips. *I'm poison, too.*

Wyatt had never appreciated the power that he possessed. She'd watched him. Seen so much.

He didn't die from gunshot wounds. Could move so quickly. Was so strong.

She'd found the records on his experiments. She hadn't been able to duplicate them perfectly, but she'd come pretty close with her own formula.

A tightness filled her chest. The gunshot wound was finally closing.

Vivian stared at the drops of blood on her fingers. It looked like she had gotten closer to that duplication than she'd realized.

She laughed then because she was going to survive. The vampires couldn't hurt her. With her new power, no one could hurt—

The primal vampire grabbed her and wrapped his hands around her throat. Vivian struggled to suck in air. She couldn't breathe, she—

The vampire burned in front of her. Firing up instantly, then turning to ash. The ash drifted over her as she screamed.

Then she realized that death was before her.

The Immortal. She'd never been allowed to get close to him, no one had, because the man had been deemed so dangerous, but she'd seen his picture before.

He stood before her, just a foot away. His eyes burned with flames. His skin was burnished a deep gold. His hair was pitch-black. He watched her. He smiled. He lifted his hand to her—

"No!" Vivian yelled.

"Why?" He seemed curious. "You enjoyed giving death to others."

She shook her head, frantic. She tried to back away, but the wall was behind her. "Y-you shouldn't be out!" They'd had him locked up so tight. *No escape.*

He shrugged. His gaze fell to her chest. No, to her healing gunshot wound. "And you should be dead. Been experimenting on yourself, hmm?" He lifted a brow. His hand was still between them. "I guess you'll only have yourself to blame for what's coming."

"Don't touch me!"

He glanced at his raised hand. "Are you sure? I don't think you're going to like what happens next. Death will be easier."

"I don't want to die!" Why was her stomach suddenly cramping? Her teeth burning?

His head cocked. "I think you got the formula . . . wrong."

Her breath seemed cold in her lungs.

"Your blood was poison, but you weren't immune to their bite. That part—you made the mistake there."

How did he even know this?

"You're becoming like them."

Hunger clawed at her. Ripped her in two. Her gaze fell to his throat as a red haze seemed to cloud her vision. She could hear his heartbeat. The rush of his blood.

Blood. Her mouth had become bone-dry.

"The change is faster than I thought it would be."

Feed.

She lunged for him.

And never even felt the fire that took her life away.

Ryder braked the pickup truck in front of a small wooden cabin. A stream trickled nearby, the faint sound of the water teasing Sabine's ears.

"Where are we?" she asked.

Ryder glanced at her. "Somewhere safe, for now."

She wanted to believe that, but "safe" wasn't exactly a concept she understood anymore. Compounding her fear, she felt so weak.

She climbed from the truck and put up her hand to block the bright rays of the sun. So bright. Too bright? Probably just seemed that way because she hadn't seen the sun in such a long time. The folks at Genesis hadn't exactly been keen on letting the test subjects out for morning strolls.

That's over now. I'm free.

Ryder took her arm. "Come on, let's get you inside so you can rest."

She nodded. But resting wasn't what she felt like doing then. She was tired, yes, achingly so, but at the same time, just the touch of his hand against her arm had sent a shaft of desire pulsing through Sabine's body.

What was up with that? After everything that had happened, the last thing she should be thinking about was sex. Yet it was the main thing that pushed into her mind.

Need.

Want.

Ryder opened the cabin door. It was darker inside, but the sun's rays spilled through the windows and let her see the small space easily. A small space that was filled with a very big bed. One that looked like heaven. Her gaze darted around. A couch. A TV.

A bathroom. Sweet heaven on earth—*a bathroom*.

"Are you hungry?" Ryder asked her, his voice quiet as he shut the door behind them.

Sabine shook her head but part of her *was* hungry. Just not for food. She glanced over at him. Licked her lips.

Her heartbeat kicked up. And her nipples tightened.

What. The. Hell. This kind of reaction couldn't be normal. She'd heard of an adrenaline after-burn before, but after-lust?

"I-I think I need a shower," she said. A very cold one. She'd just broken out of hell, and the first thing she wanted to do? Jump the bones of her vampire rescuer. That had to be screwed up.

Screwed. Her eyelids slammed closed. Okay, she was obviously undergoing some kind of breakdown because now she was thinking . . .

I want to screw him. Not make love. She wasn't in the mood for soft and gentle lovemaking. She wanted rough and wild. She wanted to rake her nails down his back. Wanted to feel the pounding rhythm of—

"Sabine?"

Her cheeks were burning. No, *she* was burning, from the inside out. She kept her eyes closed because she was afraid that he'd see the fire in her stare. "Something's wrong with me." Her voice was hushed as she whispered this raw confession.

Her clothes were irritating her body. She wanted them gone. Wanted only his flesh against her.

This wasn't natural. Sure, she liked sex as much as the next girl. But right then, hell, she felt like she was in heat.

Heat. Great. Fantastic. That was probably normal for a phoenix, right? Another fun side effect that she could deal with?

She heard the tread of his footsteps then felt the light brush of his fingers over her cheek. "You're sure you aren't hungry?"

Why did he keep harping on that? "Not for food," was her whisper.

Crap, she hadn't just meant to say that.

His fingers slid under her chin. "I can give you whatever you need."

The man *needed* to be careful what he offered. They'd been away from Genesis for just a few hours, and she was about to rip his clothes off.

"I think—I think you might want to get away from me." She curled her fingers down, making fists. The better not to grab him and hold tight.

"That's the last thing I want to do." Then Ryder made a very, very fatal mistake.

He put his lips on her.

Ignite.

Fire seemed to explode within her. With a gasp, she gave in to that heat. Her hands flew up and wrapped around him. Her mouth opened wide beneath his.

His tongue touched hers. Light, gentle.

Hell, *no.*

"I want more," she whispered against his mouth. She had to have more. She was desperate. Too wild. Nothing could hold back the fire.

She didn't want to hold it back.

Then his hands were on her ass—*yes!*—and he was pulling her up tight against him. There was no missing the full, thick length of his arousal. She rubbed against him, wanting more and then—

He lifted her into the air. Her legs locked around him, and she kept her mouth on his. He was carrying her someplace—the guy seemed to like doing that, and, hey, if it floated his boat . . .

She nipped his bottom lip. It was his turn to growl. She liked that rough, animalistic sound from him.

"Hold on, love, hold on."

She wanted to hold on to him, but he'd taken her into the bathroom. He eased her back onto her feet. Yanked on the water. Oh, that shower was lush. Given the size of the cabin, she hadn't expected this paradise. Big, granite, with steaming water that poured out instantly, the shower was pretty close to a dream.

And, yes, okay, she had dried blood on her clothes. On her. Not exactly sexy. Jumping into the shower with him seemed like a fine idea to her.

Sabine started to strip.

Ryder exhaled on a long breath and took a step back. He was . . . watching her.

She offered him a fast smile. One that she hoped looked sexy and not as sex-crazed as she actually felt. "You don't have to just watch." She tossed her clothes onto the floor. "I'd love it if you touched, too." In fact, she *had* to feel his fingers against her skin.

Ryder all but ripped his own clothes away, then his hands—big, strong, *yes!*—were on her. Caressing her breasts. Teasing her nipples. She and Ryder stumbled into the shower. The water was heaven. The steam whispered against her lips when she breathed his name.

He lifted her up. She was seriously loving his strength. Then his mouth closed around her breast. Her breath hissed out between her teeth. His tongue rasped over her nipple. The steam didn't seem to just be com-

ing from the water then. It seemed to be rising right off
her skin.

He sucked her breast. Kissed. Nipped lightly. She
twisted against him because he had her body aching.
She wanted more. Her fingers sank into his hair. The
water streamed down their bodies. "Ryder . . ."

She needed relief. Her sex was so eager for him. Forget the first-base routine. She wanted to head right for
home plate.

She bent her head and put her mouth on his skin.
Bite. She'd never had the urge to bite anyone before.
But in that instant, the urge was so strong. Too strong
to ignore.

Sabine bit him. Not hard enough to break the skin.
Just hard enough to show him . . . *I want to be wild.*

He shuddered beneath her. Then his head was lifting.
He pushed her back against the tiled shower wall. Her
toes curled in the stream of water.

"Spread your legs." Guttural.

Right, like she had to be told twice. Um, and, yeah,
they actually were already parted but she could spread
them a little bit more for him.

His hand drifted down her stomach. Her breath came
faster. "Don't play," she told him, tossing back her wet
hair. *"Touch me."*

His fingers slid between her legs. Found the center
of her need. Her toes stopped curling. Mostly because
she'd just jumped right up on her toes as her body went
bow-tight.

He stroked her lightly. That wasn't enough. But
then . . .

Then he pushed one finger into her.

"Tight," his growl. "Hot."

Yes, she was pretty much burning alive right then. And the fire used to scare her?

No, this fire is different. This wasn't about flames. It was about lust and need and pleasure.

He worked a second finger into her. Sabine had to bite her lip to hold back her cry. Not of pain. Not even close.

His fingers slid out. Pushed back inside.

His thumb brushed against her clit.

Every muscle in her body tightened. She'd never been one to build quickly to orgasm but . . .

He withdrew those fingers, thrust them into her once more, stroked over her clit, and she *broke.*

Broke into what felt like a hundred pieces as pleasure crashed over her. She yelled his name. Let her nails dig into his flesh. Her body pulsed and throbbed and the pleasure wasn't ending because he had his hands around her waist now. He'd lifted her again, positioned her, and the head of his cock drove into her core.

Her legs clamped tightly around his hips. His mouth was at her throat. His teeth grazing over her skin. He withdrew and thrust, and her back pushed harder against the tile.

The pleasure kept building, so much pleasure that she could barely breathe.

His teeth sank into her neck. His cock pushed into her body. He had her positioned so that every stroke took the length of his cock over her sensitive flesh, over her clit once more. Her eyes squeezed shut. She'd never felt anything like this before.

She'd died. Known pain and fear and hell.

This . . . this was consuming. Every breath was paradise. Every move, pleasure.

The sensations built, crested, and she *lost* her breath as the climax peaked.

Ryder was with her. He thrust deep once more. Shuddered. *"Sabine."* No one had ever said her name like that. Like it was life.

His head had lifted. She forced her eyes open. *Pleasure*. That was all she saw on his face. Blind pleasure.

The same thing she felt.

The steam drifted around them. Their heartbeats raced. Her sex was trembling with little after-bursts from her climax. In her whole life, she'd never, ever had sex like this.

Her body was trembling, and in the aftermath of so much pleasure, Sabine found that she felt vulnerable.

His lips brushed hers.

Her legs eased down his hips. "Ryder . . ." How did she explain that she wasn't usually like this? For a while there, it had been as if someone else took control of her. She'd only known need and lust.

The ache inside had been satisfied. Her control was back.

Her feet slid against the tile. Ryder kept a steady hold on her as he turned off the water. The shower's *drip-drip-drip* seemed too loud to her ears.

He stared down at her, frowning a bit. "You didn't . . ."

Um, yeah, she most definitely *had*. "That was more pleasure than I'd ever had before."

But he shook his head, his gaze centered on her mouth. She licked her lips, and enjoyed it when his pupils expanded, showing his desire.

His fingers rose and brushed over her lips. "You didn't take my blood."

Um, yeah. Because that wasn't exactly sexy times for her. She loved it when he bit her—*and wasn't that a huge change from their first meeting*?—because his bite sent her body into pleasure overdrive.

"You don't have fangs." He sounded shocked.

She blinked up at him. Not exactly the after-sex conversation she'd thought would come. "This surprises you because . . . ?"

"Because you had them before." His hand dropped. "What the hell is going on?"

Because you had them before. Suddenly some of that wonderful afterglow was fading.

Drip-drip-drip. The dripping water grated on her nerves. She pushed past him. Reached for a towel and wrapped it around her body. "Ryder . . ."

"I *changed* you."

She shook her head, hoping to deny his words. "No, that's not true."

He followed her out of the shower. Stalked right after her as she walked—backward—out of the bathroom. She wanted to keep her eyes on him.

"You didn't want to burn again." His words were deep and dark and he watched her with a gaze still filled with lust.

She tightened her grip on the towel. She clearly remembered the not-wanting-to-burn part. "My injuries weren't that bad. I just got better." That was the reason the flames had faded away. Not because of-of any change. *I don't want to be a vampire*. Being a phoenix was bad enough. Becoming a full-time blood drinker? *No, thank you*.

"Stir the fire," he rasped.

Sabine blinked.

"Stir the fire."

She lifted her hands. Thought of the flames. The white-hot fire.

Nothing happened.

Her hand fisted.

"You can't," Ryder said grimly. "I told you . . . *you changed.*"

Her tongue slid over the edge of her teeth. They were normal. Not fangs. Sabine shook her head.

"You asked me to *help you*," he said. His hands were clenched at his sides. His body nude, powerful. *Sexy.*

Sabine forced her gaze to meet his. She had asked him to help her. She remembered her desperate plea. She'd begged for his help, even as she knew that . . .

I'm dying again.

"I go to hell," she whispered this confession as she stared into his eyes. "The fire is so hot. It burns my flesh away. Pulls up some beast that's buried inside of me. The fire won't let me go. It surrounds me, it—"

He stalked forward and caught her arms. "You never have to feel that fire again. You'll never die again. Never age. Never get sick."

Because I'm a vampire? She'd just traded one monster for another. Her heart raced. But . . . "I don't have fangs." Her teeth were just *normal*.

"They'll grow, sharpen, when you need to feed."

She forced herself to keep holding his gaze. "I don't need to feed." The last thing she wanted to do was sink her teeth into someone's throat. She'd nipped him during sex but that had just been rough foreplay.

Right?

"Maybe you still have enough of my blood in you.

When humans change, the first things they want to do are feed and fuck."

She flinched. Um, yes, she'd sure had the fucking part down. She'd never felt a need so intense. It had taken her over. Dominated her every cell. She'd needed him, quite simply, more than she'd needed breath right then.

Was that really me? Or did those doctors do something to me? They'd injected her so many times with who the hell knew what when she'd been held captive.

"You were never human, so it only stands to reason that your body wouldn't react the same way to the change." His fingers were rubbing small circles on her arms. Did he realize that? She did. She liked it. Found the caress soothing. "It took three exchanges to convert you," he said as a frown pulled his brows low. "With a human, it just takes one."

Faint suspicion hummed in her mind. "You were trying to change me, from the beginning." *Don't be true. Don't be.* Her heart wasn't just racing. It was hurting. *I trusted him. Even with my fear, I thought he was helping me.*

His expression was blank, but his eyes were full of need. "The first time I gave you my blood, I wanted to keep you alive. That was my only goal. I *never* meant to take so much from you."

Ah, and she heard the guilt there. It would probably always be there.

"I thought that if I'd just given you more, you would have transformed. Wyatt stopped me, and I figured the change didn't occur because you didn't get enough of my blood."

But then he'd given more blood to her later. She

pulled away from him. "You *were* trying to change me." It had been deliberate. The blood drinking. The seduction. He'd pulled her in. Gotten her to trust him.

Why hadn't he told her that she'd change? Why hadn't he just *told* her what was happening?

"You didn't want to be a phoenix," he reminded her, voice flat. "I gave you what you wanted. If you hadn't been hurt, if you hadn't been lying there, dying right in front of me, I wouldn't have gone for the transformation. Dammit, *believe me*!

"I couldn't let you die again. You didn't want death, and in that moment, Sabine, I would have traded anything—even the last bit of my black soul—to make sure that you didn't burn again."

Her mouth was dry.

"I just wanted to save you," he rasped. "I haven't saved many in my life."

"Why am I special?" She hadn't meant to ask that, had she?

His gaze held her prisoner. "Because I look at you, and I see the one person that I want most in this world."

Oh, okay, that was not what—

Ryder gave a sharp, negative shake of his head. "It's *more*. I look at you, and you remind me . . . you make me long for everything I lost so long ago."

Her breath whispered out. "What did you lose?"

"Happiness. Hope. Peace." A muscle jerked along his jaw. "And when I look at you, I see all of those things."

The vampire had just stunned her.

"So, no," now his voice roughened. "I wasn't just going to stand there and let you burn, not when you were begging me to save you. Maybe it's not the method you had in mind, but the blood exchange was the only option I had available to me." His shoulders straightened. "And to be damn honest, if I had to do it all over again, I'd still try to change you. If that meant you didn't burn, I'd do it again."

She didn't know what to say to that. He was right. She'd hated the fire. Hated dying, coming back, and not knowing *anything*.

Except she'd remembered him. Even after all of the flames and death, his image had come to her. Whispered through her mind. Her vampire.

Sexy. Dangerous. So compelling.

Powerful enough to push through the fire.

A vampire.

And I'm one now, too?

"Come to bed with me," he murmured the words as his head bent and his lips feathered over her cheek. "You've been through hell."

No, *to* hell.

But he was so tempting. Still naked. All of those rippling muscles. That thick cock. *Gorgeous* male.

"I can help you when the hunger comes."

Fucking and feeding. That was what vampires did, right? The pleasure that had rocked through her before suddenly had her feeling shamed.

She'd had no control. Been just like an animal. Biting. Clawing. Would it always be that way? And when she did crave blood, would she be as desperate to satisfy her blood hunger as she'd been when she'd wanted sex with him?

What if she killed someone? Took too much?

"Sabine."

Her lashes lifted. He stared at her with such care in his eyes.

"I *will* help you."

She thought he might be the only one who could. It wasn't like she had some kind of supernatural Rolodex. He was the strongest paranormal that she knew, and, despite everything . . .

I feel safe with him.

"If you really want to help me"—she drew in a deep breath—"then take me home."

She had to see her family. Had to make sure that her brother was safe.

But Ryder shook his head, and, with regret pulling at his handsome face, he told her, "I'm sorry, love, but you can't go home again."

Her eyes narrowed. *The hell I can't.*

And Sabine knew that her time with the sexy vamp had come to an end.

CHAPTER TEN

Getting away from Ryder had been surprisingly easy. The man slept like the dead, literally. When she'd been sure that he was out, Sabine had just slipped away.

Maybe he hadn't expected her to leave. Maybe he'd thought that she was all after-sex slumberous. Maybe he'd thought she was the kind of girl who'd just turn her back on her family.

He needed to damn well think again.

She'd taken the truck. The one that he'd initially stolen. She'd ditched it at the first truck stop she came to, not wanting anyone to trail it.

She'd hitched a ride with a real sweetheart of a female truck driver. Daisy had been sixty-seven, with a grin as wide as Tennessee, and the woman had sure liked to talk.

She hadn't noticed that Sabine didn't exactly talk back much.

Sabine had thought about calling her family. Checking in to let them know that she was alive and semi-well, but when she and Daisy had stopped at an old-school diner, Sabine had glanced up at the TV installed near the counter and seen the news stories about Genesis. Fire had filled the small TV screen. The reporters had been talking about the death toll at the two facilities.

From all appearances, Genesis *looked* dead, but was it really? Maybe she was just being paranoid, but she didn't want to take any chances. Especially after the nightmare that she'd been through for the last few weeks.

She hadn't wanted to make any phone calls. Hadn't wanted to do anything that might give away her location. She just wanted—*home*.

When Daisy left her in New Orleans, Sabine inhaled the scent of the river. *Home*. Finally. Darkness was falling, but the city shone at night. So many voices. Music drifting on the breeze.

Rhett's place wasn't on Bourbon Street. No, his bar was more secret, more shadowed. She hopped on the trolley, holding tight to the bar as she slipped inside. The bell rang, and the trolley slid away from the stop. From her perch, she watched her city sweep by.

And felt eyes watching her.

Her shoulders tensed, and Sabine glanced around the trolley car's interior. A family . . . tourists . . . they always had the same eager look. Some college kids, wearing their Tulane shirts. A couple holding hands in the back. And . . .

And a guy, with a baseball cap pulled low over his head. Shoulders hunched, wearing a black T-shirt. A five o'clock shadow lined his jaw, and it *looked* like that jaw was turned away from her. As if the guy were paying her no attention.

But Sabine's body was on alert. Something was wrong.

The trolley eased to a stop. She hadn't planned to get off yet, but as soon as the trolley's doors swished open, she rushed through them.

Baseball cap jumped off the trolley, too.

Not good.

She pushed her damp palms against her jeans. Daisy, bless her sweet, big heart, had given Sabine enough cash to buy some clothes. And the lady hadn't even asked her about the rips and bloodstains in her old clothes. A *real* sweetheart.

As usual, New Orleans was hot, and Sabine was already starting to sweat. She hurried away from the trolley, wanting to find a place with as many people as possible. It was easier to vanish in a crowd.

A glance over her shoulder showed Sabine that baseball cap was following behind her. Part of her wanted to just turn and confront him. If he was a Genesis goon, he wasn't going to take her again.

But another part of her, a smarter part, realized . . . *You can't conjure fire. Ryder said you were a vamp, but your fangs still aren't there*. If she confronted him and the guy came out fighting with a stake or a gun, just what the hell was she supposed to do?

Get a weapon.

That was what she needed to do.

A crowd surrounded her as she slipped onto Decatur Street. There were always plenty of people in front of the shops. She eased through the crowd, bending and weaving, and, oh, a street performer wasn't using his cane. It was just propped against the building behind him.

Making a mental note to bring this guy back a very

serious tip, Sabine grabbed the cane. Then she rushed to the left. She made sure that her body was distanced from everyone else, that she presented a very easy-to-see target . . . *Come and get me*.

Then Sabine slipped down a side street. The flow of bodies was immediately muted. Not much to see here, so the tourists stayed away. Clutching tight to the cane, she flattened her body against a brick wall. She lifted the cane, holding it like a bat. She'd been all-state back on the girls' softball team in high school, and her hits had been pretty legendary.

If baseball cap came around that corner—

He *did*.

Sabine swung out with the cane, using all of her strength as she aimed for his chest.

He caught the cane in his right hand. He stared down at the wooden cane for a moment, then he lifted his head. "*This* is your best weapon?"

The weapon burned beneath his hands.

Gasping, Sabine tried to jump back. Unfortunately, she was already against the wall.

Worst. Plan. Ever.

She tried to sidle away then, but the man's hand flew out—the same hand that had just burned that cane—and his fingers curled around her neck. "What happened to you?"

She swallowed. He wasn't blocking her airway. Wasn't hurting her. *Yet.* "Mister, I don't know who you are, but you'd better let me go."

His eyes narrowed. "Of course, you know who I am."

There was fire in his eyes.

"I'm just like you," he said.

She couldn't speak.

His head cocked. "Or I *was* like you, but something's different. Something's blocking your fire." He dropped his hold and stepped back. *"Tell me what they did."*

She forced her shoulders to straighten. "I don't know. They killed me. Again and again—"

He waved that away. "Why don't you burn?"

Because my vampire lover bit me. Changed me.

"We kill each other," he said. There seemed to be a note of regret in his voice. "It hardly seems fair, when you won't burn."

Oh crap, he'd just threatened to kill her.

"Didn't even know that, did you?" For an instant, it almost looked as if pity flashed in his gaze. "Newborn," he muttered. "Why do you think there are so few of our kind? We're our own worst enemies."

"I-I don't want to be your enemy." She just wanted to be far away from him.

"So little can truly kill us," he said, as if he hadn't even heard her words. "The death blow has to come through the fire." His gaze narrowed. "We are the only ones who can reach through that fire."

So, um, was he saying that only a phoenix could ever really kill another phoenix? "I'm not interested in killing you." Just so they could be clear.

"But maybe I'm interested in killing you."

Hell. She'd hoped he wouldn't say that.

"I knew you'd be here." His gaze raked her. "If they haven't already, others will figure it out, too."

Others? "Genesis is dead and gone." Since that stop at the diner, she'd managed to pick up other news stories about Genesis. A reporter had been undercover at Genesis. Every time Daisy had made a pit stop, Sabine had made a point of trying to learn more of the stories circulating about Genesis.

From what she could tell, it looked like the tide was turning for the paranormals in the world. The media was giving them the sympathy, showing outrage for the suffering they'd been through at Genesis.

The government was promising a full investigation. She'd seen that particular headline on the cover of a New Orleans paper right after Daisy had driven away. Big, bold, in your face, the headline had eased some of the battle-tight tension from Sabine's body.

But that tension was back now, full-force.

The man smiled at her. "You honestly believe that crock of bull? Two labs are down, but the humans aren't going to stop. We're too powerful for them to ever just stop and leave us alone."

She held her body perfectly still. "I don't know you," Sabine said carefully. *Escape.* That was her only priority. "And I don't want to know you. So why don't you just go your way, I'll go mine, and we never, ever have to see each other again."

He shook his head and sighed. "That's not how this is going to work."

Why not? She managed to bite the words back, barely.

Footsteps shuffled in the distance. The crowd was so close. It actually seemed as if some of those folks might be coming even closer. Stepping into the alley. She thought about calling out to them, but she didn't want to risk any innocent lives. Too many had been risked already.

"You're too dangerous to be left alone," he told her, voice flat. "You're so new, I can tell."

New? She didn't exactly feel shiny and bright and *new*. More like beat down. Used. Abused. "I just want to see my family." No, she wanted her life back.

"I'm sorry," he said. Did he actually sound like he meant the words? Um, *no*. Not even a little bit. She'd definitely imagined that flash of pity earlier. "That's not going to happen." Then he reached for her again.

"Buddy, you need to step the hell away from my sister." The words were low, snarled, and coming from right behind the tall, deadly stranger.

The stranger's eyes met hers. His gaze was steady and dark. The flames were banked, for the moment. "I was hoping that he'd just keep walking."

So he'd heard the rustle of footsteps, too.

Sabine's heart ached. She couldn't see around the man—he seemed to block everything else out, but that voice . . . that deep, rich voice, roughened by the slightest New Orleans drawl. She knew that voice. Her brother. Rhett.

"Don't hurt him," she whispered to the dangerous man before her.

The stranger didn't answer.

Then there were more footsteps. Not rustling any longer. Racing toward them. And the stranger whirled to face the threat. He, wait, was he putting his body in front of her? Like he was about to protect her?

She peered over his shoulder. As soon as Sabine saw her brother's handsome but tense face, it was like a punch right to her chest. She'd missed him so much.

He had a baseball bat in his hands. The trusty bat that she knew he usually kept behind his bar. He'd been all-state, too. He'd taught her everything she knew about swinging a bat. And Rhett wasn't alone.

A crowd of men had formed behind him. Men she recognized.

Louis Marchand. Vaughn Adams. Douglas Pierce. All of the guys were regulars at Rhett's bar—and they were her brother's closest friends. The men looked pissed, and they were all armed.

Louis had a knife in his hand. *A knife?* Vaughn had a gun—well, okay, she wasn't even going to wonder how the guy had gotten that, and Douglas . . . the guy gripped a broken whiskey bottle in his fist.

"This doesn't concern you," the stranger snarled. "She's not even your real sister."

Rhett's jaw locked. Normally, he was the easygoing southern boy. A faint drawl would whisper in his words, just enough of a slow tease to make all his girlfriends smile. He had bright blond hair, a golden tan, and dimples that flashed.

No dimples were flashing.

He lifted his bat. *He'd* been the reason she'd been such a good player. The guy had been the one to teach her everything she knew about swinging a bat. "The hell she isn't." His hands had a white-knuckled grip around that bat. Oh, she knew he was about to take a swing. What would happen when he did? "And you made a fucking mistake," Rhett snarled the words right back at the man shielding Sabine, "by trying to take her away from me."

The stranger lifted his hands. Sabine grabbed his shoulder. *"Don't hurt him!"* She was so afraid fire would appear before his fingers. She didn't want her brother burned.

"He's not going to hurt me, Sabe," Rhett promised. "But I'm going to kick the shit out of him."

The man before her laughed. Then he lunged forward. Sabine screamed. Rhett swung. The bat hit hard, probably harder than the stranger expected because he stumbled back.

Rhett hadn't been the home-run king for nothing.

Rhett grabbed her hand and yanked her to his side. His buddies closed in as Vaughn lifted his gun. "Asshole, you better *freeze*," he barked. "Because I'm NOPD."

New Orleans Police Department? Since when? And when did a cop go out on the streets with men who were armed with bats and broken bottles?

The stranger's head lifted. His eyes weren't so dark now. They were starting to flame. "Freezing isn't something I've ever been able to do," he said. "But burning . . . that's a whole different matter."

"What the hell?" came the stunned question from Douglas. The redhead was shaking. Yeah, probably realizing that broken whiskey bottle wasn't going to do him much good. *"He's a para!"* Wait, what? Was that the new lingo for a paranormal?

Douglas had always been a lingo guy. He thought it made him seem cool.

He didn't exactly look cool then. Sabine pushed toward them.

Douglas was shaking harder by the second. Maybe because the stranger's eyes were burning brighter *by the second*.

"Run," Sabine whispered.

No one moved.

"Run!" she yelled. Sabine shoved Douglas. But the guy just shook his head and stood his ground.

"No one's hurting my sister," Rhett said. The leader

of the pack. Always. His bat had a long crack in it. His fingers tightened around the base. "So you come at me again if you want. I don't care what the hell you are. *No one* hurts my sister and walks away."

The man's eyes were glowing bright. "I'm not the one you have to punish. Save that for her vampire."

How did he know about Ryder?

"He's coming," the man said, a faint smile curling his mouth. "Coming in so fast. He won't give her up. What will you do then? Kill him?"

Her breath had stilled in her chest. The guy was wrong. Had to be. She'd ditched Ryder.

But Ryder knew she was from New Orleans. She glanced over her shoulder. Didn't see anything but the end of the alley and the crowd filling the main street.

"Maybe you'll come to wish that she was dead." Those words had her head snapping back toward the stranger. "Before it's all over."

"And maybe you'll wish that you'd never set foot in *our* town." This growl erupted from Vaughn. His handsome face was tight with fury.

"I'm the least of your worries." The man's burning gaze touched on Sabine. "But I will see you again."

"Not if you want to keep those eyes in your head, you won't," Rhett blasted.

The stranger just smirked. Then he said, "You should duck now."

What?

He lifted his hand and a ball of fire rushed in the air, heading right toward them.

Vaughn pulled the trigger on his gun.

Rhett's fingers locked around Sabine.

They all *ducked*.

And as the fire blazed, the stranger with the burning eyes slipped away, leaving behind a trail of smoke and drops of blood on the ground.

No one spoke. No one tried to go after the guy. They waited until the flames started to die away, then Rhett demanded, "Who the hell was that?"

Sabine could only shake her head. They were all rising, all looking around carefully. A crowd of spectators had come their way, drawn, no doubt, by the smell of smoke and the crackle of flames.

"I don't know who he was." The crowd was closing in. Sabine backed away from them, and her shoulder brushed against Rhett's chest. "Let's get out of here."

He nodded, but then, he stopped and pulled her against him. Held her in a crushing grip that threatened to break her ribs. She felt his lips brush against the side of her head. "I thought you were dead."

I was. But she couldn't tell him that. No, maybe she just didn't want to tell him. So she held him, gripping him just as tightly as she inhaled his familiar scent.

Her eyes had squeezed closed and she forced herself to open her gaze. When her lashes lifted, her stare darted over the growing crowd.

And her eyes locked on a gleaming, green gaze. *Ryder.*

He wasn't pushing forward like the others. Wasn't offering to help. Wasn't moving at all. He stood there, watching her *and* Rhett. There was so much fury in his eyes.

"Let's go," Sabine whispered again. Rhett's body felt strong and *alive* against her. She wasn't about to do anything to risk that life.

Vaughn had hidden his gun. Probably tucked it under his shirt. The others had dropped their weapons and were trying to look harmless. They managed to ease their way through the crowd—and away from Ryder—even as a fire truck's siren blared in the distance.

Rhett kept a tight hold on her as they rushed down the street. She glanced back, and, sure enough, Ryder was following her. Slow, stalking steps. She shook her head. *Stay away.* Sabine mouthed the words.

He kept coming.

Then she and her band of protectors were crossing the street. Horns blared. They ignored them. Typical. They cut through alleys, slid around old buildings, moving as fast as they could.

She looked back again.

Ryder was still there.

And she knew that ditching him wasn't going to be easy. In fact, it might just be impossible.

The bar was pretty much as he'd expected. Ryder eased inside of The Rift, following the sound of blues as the other bar patrons swept into the bar. Dim lighting sent shadows chasing over the floor. The wood creaked beneath his feet as Ryder walked. The place smelled of alcohol and perfume. Laughter floated around him, just as the drinks were flowing.

The humans were in a good mood. Celebrating.

A circle of men had gathered near the back corner of the bar, a circle that enclosed Sabine.

The humans really needed to start backing the hell off. For Sabine, he was going to try and keep things civilized.

At first.

He could just see the top of Sabine's head. Some guy with bright blond hair kept hugging her. Kissing her on the cheek.

That had better be the brother. If it wasn't, the man was going to be in a whole world of pain soon.

"Sabe, what happened?"

Ryder was close enough to hear the blond's question.

"Where have you been?" the guy demanded, emotion roughening his voice. "We were so worried. Hell, do you know how many times I checked the morgue?"

Her hand lifted, and she curled her fingers around his biceps. "I'm sorry."

The guy swore and pointed toward a door marked PRIVATE. "You're telling me what happened." Then he was marching for that door. Pulling Sabine with him.

The other men were following him.

Ryder followed, too. Until his path was blocked by a tall, muscled male with a fuck-off glare. The guy's blue eyes were a sharp and angry contrast to his dark brown skin. "Where do you think you're going?"

Ryder lifted a brow. "Trust me, you don't want to get in my way."

The guy laughed. "Looks like that's just where I am." His smile faded. "You followed us here."

Ryder shrugged. Why deny the truth? "You were easy to follow."

The man's right hand began to lift. Ryder knew the fellow was going for the gun he'd tucked into the back of his waistband.

"Do you truly want to do that here?" Ryder asked, curious, baiting. "With so many humans around?"

The man hesitated. "I'm guessing you're not *human.*"

"Good guess." Then he rushed forward and grabbed the guy's hand before he could make the mistake of going for the gun. Using his grip, Ryder twisted the man around and forced him toward the "private" door. "Now how about you and I go join the little chat in the back room?" Because he'd been away from Sabine for long enough.

She left me. Just when he'd thought they were starting to trust each other. They'd gotten out of hell together. Had some pretty fucking amazing sex. Then she'd left the minute he closed his eyes.

He'd nearly ripped down the mountain trying to find her.

As it was, he yanked back his captive and kicked in the "private" door. The door flew off its hinges.

"What the—" a man's snarling voice began. The blond. The guy had a cracked baseball bat gripped in his hand. He came up swinging.

Ryder caught the bat in his right hand. "You need a better weapon." He shattered the wood.

Then heard the faintest *click* behind him. A safety, being released. Yes, he knew the sound.

"You shouldn't have turned your back on me," his ex-captive said. "Man, you're gonna pay for that one."

"Vaughn!" Sabine's frantic cry. "Don't shoot him!"

Huh. It sounded like she cared.

"I'm not shooting him, yet." Now the guy's voice was cocky. "Douglas, patch up the door before anyone sees what the hell we're doing."

The redhead ran forward and used his body to shove the door back into semi-place.

Ryder ignored the redhead. He only focused on the one person who mattered in the room.

"Stop it," the blond snarled as he took a protective

step in front of Sabine. "Stop looking at my sister like you want to fuckin' eat her."

It was too fitting. Ryder smiled and knew that his fangs would flash.

It was the wrong move, of course, because the trigger-happy human with the gun shot him.

CHAPTER ELEVEN

Ryder didn't flinch when the bullet tore into his chest. The bullet hurt like a bitch, but after his time at Genesis, he'd rather gotten used to pain.

"You missed my heart," Ryder muttered. Then he lunged for the shooter. His hand wrapped around the guy's throat. One snap. Just one. And he'd have a dead human.

"Let him go, Ryder!"

He'd missed the way Sabine said his name. Okay, not the way she screamed it—the way she just had—but the way she whispered it. Sighed it.

He kept his hold on the human. "Others heard the shot." Even the drunks in the bar wouldn't be oblivious to a gunshot. His gaze swept to the redhead. "Make sure no one else comes in this room, or I'll tear off your friend's head."

The guy's Adam's apple bobbed, but he nodded and made his way out of the room. Then he put the door back in place behind him.

"Now . . ." Ryder sighed as he felt the blood soak his

shirt. "I'm going to need some blood." He glanced over at Sabine. She was even more beautiful than he remembered. So beautiful that he ached just looking at her.

Mine.

"Do you want to volunteer, love?" Ryder asked her softly as his gaze dipped to the elegant column of her throat. "Or shall I take a bite out of your friend?"

"You're not supposed to attack humans!" This came from the guy in the back, a thin, wiry fellow with a curly mop of black hair. "You're supposed to drink fr-from bags or get volunteers—"

"I'll volunteer, Louis," Sabine said, cutting through the man's words. Her gaze was on Ryder. "But you have to promise me that you won't hurt any of my friends."

She had too many male friends. They were annoying.

The blond was still doing guard duty near her, but Ryder now knew that, yes, that was the brother. A brother with a whole lot of fury boiling beneath his surface. Good thing the guy wasn't a phoenix. With that much rage, he would have set the whole place on fire.

"Ryder?" Sabine pushed.

He shrugged and released the human. "I'm not here for them." He knew she would understand. *I'm here for you.* He let his nails sharpen to claws, and he shoved those claws into his chest.

"Oh, the hell, *no*," her brother barked. "You don't do that kind of crazy shit in my bar!"

Uh, yeah, he just *had* done that. He tossed the bullet he'd retrieved onto the floor. He wiped the blood on his jeans and offered Sabine his hand.

There were streaks of blood on his fingers. Fitting. Until he died—an event that might never occur—he'd always have blood on his hands.

Sabine crept closer to him. Her scent reached him.

Wrapped around him. He dropped his hand before his blood could touch her. She stared up at him. "I thought you'd let me go." Her words were quiet. A little lost.

Never. "And I thought that Genesis had gotten you again. You . . . scared me, Sabine." He knew just how valuable she had been to the group. Despite the stories that the media was circulating, Ryder didn't buy that Genesis was dead. Not by a long shot.

They'd cut the head off the snake, but the beast still lived.

Sabine lifted her delicate wrist to his mouth.

The blond lunged for her. "Sabe, *no!*"

Her shoulders tensed. "It's not like I haven't done this before, Rhett."

Ryder's lips parted over her wrist. His teeth scraped over the delicate skin.

"*Don't* do it!" Rhett snapped. "You put those teeth in her, buddy, and I'll put a stake in your heart!"

A little late for that, considering he'd put his teeth into her several times before. But, right then, for *this* time, Ryder didn't let his teeth sink into her skin. He could almost taste her blood . . . that addictive flavor that was only his Sabine. But drinking from her . . . with her brother's furious stare on them . . .

No.

When he drank from Sabine, he wanted to fuck her. His bloodlust and his physical lust were too closely bound with her. And they would save that particular reunion for later.

When her brother wasn't glaring at them.

With an effort, Ryder pulled her wrist away from his mouth. "I'll feed in private." Which was code for . . . *Get these assholes out of here, Sabine.* He wanted to talk with her alone. There was much, much to say.

Things that didn't need to be spoken of in front of such an avid audience.

"You're not doing anything in private." Her brother narrowed his gaze on them. "Since when did you start hanging with vampires, Sabine?"

He heard the soft whisper of her breath, then her voice came, low and tight. "Since I became one."

Rhett's face went white with shock as he rocked back on his heels. "No!"

But she nodded, rather miserably, and wouldn't meet her brother's gaze.

Rhett turned his fury on Ryder. "You did this to her." Not a question.

And also, not wrong. So Ryder squared his shoulders and agreed. "Yes."

The human could move fairly fast. Rhett spun away. Shattered a nearby chair, and came up with a chunk of the wooden leg held tight in his fist. "I'm killing you!"

He didn't want to hurt her brother. Hurting him would only make Sabine angry.

But Ryder also wasn't in the mood to get staked.

"Would you have been happier if I just let her die?" Ryder asked. He didn't mention the part about Sabine just coming back when she died. Her brother was freaking over a bit of vampirism. Ryder wasn't sure the man was up to handling the truth of a phoenix's death. He also didn't want to be the one to tell her brother about all that Sabine had suffered.

Rhett loved his sister. That fact was plain to see. It was the reason Ryder hadn't already taken that stake away from the guy—and shoved it right into Rhett's own chest.

I don't take kindly to the threat of a stake in my heart.

If the man hadn't been family to Sabine, well, there would have been plenty of blood flowing. But for her, Ryder held back.

Sabine raised her hand, stopping her brother's advance. "I told you on the way here . . . where I've been . . . what's happened to me . . . it's a very long story."

"I've got nothing but time," Rhett threw back. "And I've been going *insane* worrying about you. Hell, Sabe, when you didn't come home, when the days passed and no one could find you anywhere, Mom had a heart attack."

Sabine's body trembled.

"She's fine," Rhett said quickly as his friends watched the exchange in silence. "But she's been crying herself to sleep every damn night since you disappeared." Faint lines bracketed his mouth. "Why didn't you just call? So you turned into a vamp. Not the choice I would have wanted, but you know I love you. No matter what you are, *I love you*."

Silence. Heavy. Painful.

Sabine rolled her shoulders. "I shouldn't have come back."

A muscle jerked in Rhett's jaw. Pain flashed in his eyes.

Ryder eyed the stake. For the moment, Rhett wasn't attacking. But the moment he did . . .

Sabine cleared her throat. "How did you—how did you even know that I *was* back? How'd you find me in that alley?"

It was the dark-haired man who answered. The one she'd called Louis. The guy who seemed to be guarding Rhett's back. "We've got eyes all over this city. Everyone has been looking for you. When we got word that you were spotted on the trolley near Canal, we hauled ass down there."

Rhett nodded. "We hauled ass, and found you up against the wall, and that crazy bastard with the fire in his eyes was about to attack you."

Crazy bastard with the fire in his eyes . . . Ryder's body tensed. "Sabine?" When he'd seen her in the alley, he'd smelled smoke, but he'd just thought—hell, he hadn't even thought. He'd reacted. He'd seen her and been damn relieved to have found her.

But now . . . was her brother saying that another phoenix had been in that alley?

Sabine glanced at Ryder from the corner of her eye.

"Was that another *friend,* Sabine?" Rhett demanded. "Another paranormal buddy that you picked up during your disappearance?"

Her gaze held Ryder's. "I'd never seen him before, but, yes . . ." Now she looked back at her brother. "I think he may have been held at the same facility I was at."

Rhett blinked. "Held?"

Behind him, Louis swore.

She nodded. Her shoulder brushed against Ryder's. His chest wasn't hurting anymore. The flesh was already starting to mend.

I want her blood. Nothing particularly new there. He always wanted her.

"I didn't leave willingly," she whispered. Her hands fisted by her sides. "I was taken, by a group called Genesis."

"Those SOBs on the news?" the one who'd been so trigger-happy before demanded.

She nodded. "Yes, Vaughn. They kept me in their facility. I only escaped a few days ago, thanks to Ryder."

Rhett's gaze drifted between them. Measured.

"I wouldn't be here without him," Sabine said.

"Hell." Rhett dropped the stake. It clattered to the floor.

"Why did they take you?" Vaughn demanded. He pressed closer. "I saw the news—they were experimenting on paranormals. Not humans. Why the hell would they—"

"It turns out that I wasn't human. Not exactly." Sabine's sigh was soft. "And they knew it."

Vaughn shook his head. "Son of a bitch."

Exactly.

Rhett kept a watchful gaze on his sister. "But Genesis is gone now, right? You're safe?"

"Yes." Her chin lifted. "I'm safe."

Her brother couldn't seem to tell when Sabine was lying.

Odd. Ryder could tell instantly. *Trying to protect the human, Sabine?* If she'd wanted to protect him, she should have stayed the hell away from New Orleans and her brother.

The scent of smoke drifted into the room. Ryder spun around, following that scent back to the broken door just as that door was tossed aside.

"Fire!" It was the human he'd sent outside. Douglas? "There's a fire in the bar!"

Rhett swore and stormed right toward the growing smoke. Ryder didn't try to stop him, but he did grab for Sabine when she tried to go after her brother.

The other humans rushed out, following the cries that had erupted from the bar patrons.

"Let me go!" Sabine twisted in Ryder's grasp. "I have to help! This bar . . . it's *everything* to Rhett."

No, it wasn't. "You're a vampire now," he reminded her, holding her tightly. "That means you burn too easily. Fire *can* kill you now."

She froze. Her eyes widened.

"And when it kills you, Sabine, you won't be coming back." There would be no more do-overs for her.

The cries grew louder. The scent of the smoke thickened.

Since she wasn't fighting him any longer, Ryder let her go.

She immediately ran for the broken door. "I have to help him!"

Damn it. He grabbed her and yanked her back—just as flames raced toward them. The bar was turning into an inferno, burning far too fast.

That's what happens when you light up a place filled with booze.

His gaze swept through the smoke and flames. Most of the humans had already gotten out. They'd broken through windows. Crashed through the front doors. Rhett was still there, trying to use an extinguisher to battle the fire that just kept rising.

"I have to help him," Sabine whispered.

No, what she had to do was get her sweet ass out of there. Ryder spun back around. He kept his hold on Sabine, knowing better than to make the same mistake twice. The room they were in was about twenty feet long, and, hell, wouldn't it figure? No windows. No exit doors.

And, just his luck, the room was filled with bottles of liquor.

The fire snaked inside the room with them.

He caught Sabine's chin. "We're getting out of here."

Because the place was about to combust. "You stay with me, got it?" *I'm not losing you again.*

"Not without Rhett! I won't go without—"

The streaking fire had nearly reached the boxes and bottles of alcohol.

Ryder pulled Sabine from the storage room. They leapt over flames, rushed over fallen tables. The exit door was in sight. Big, gaping—

"Help!"

And, yes, there was a human, yelling for help. Figured. Ryder tried to shove Sabine toward the exit.

She shoved back—and rushed right toward that screaming human. It was her brother. He was on the ground, trapped beneath what looked like a big chunk of the ceiling.

The ceiling was falling now? Talk about your bad days. Before she reached Rhett, the wood around her brother began to burn. He screamed in pain then, his face contorting as he burned.

Ryder grabbed for Sabine because he knew what she was going to do. But she moved too fast. She slipped away from him. Then she put her hands right on that burning wood and tossed it away from her brother.

Tossed it away without so much as a blister appearing on her skin.

Then she was reaching for her brother's hand. Hauling him up. Holding him easily when the guy had to weigh over two hundred pounds.

Ryder helped another human—the redhead, Douglas—get toward the door. They all stumbled out in a rush of smoke and flames.

Humans were outside. Choking. Gasping. Staring with wide eyes and whispers as The Rift burned.

His gaze swept the crowd. This fire had started too

suddenly. Erupted from nowhere. Burned and consumed.

One person in the crowd wasn't staring at the inferno with shock and horror. One person wasn't covered with ash.

A man stood with a slight grin tilting the corners of his mouth. His dark hair brushed over his shoulders and his eyes . . . they burned.

Another phoenix. One who'd followed her. One who'd just made a building burn down around her.

The bastard had a death wish.

The phoenix was turning away. Oh, the hell he was. "Ryder!"

He realized that he'd already started after the guy. Sabine had grabbed his arm, holding him now. "You can't," she whispered.

Sure, he could.

"If he's like . . ." She shook her head. "You can't kill him, but he can kill you."

Maybe.

Maybe not.

But either way, no one was going to send out an attack like that against Sabine.

"See you soon, love," Ryder whispered, and he brushed a kiss against her cheek.

She blinked and her lips parted in surprise. "Ryder?"

This time, he was the one to leave. He pushed through the crowd and didn't flash his fangs. Not until he was away from the pack of humans.

Then his fangs flashed and he started hunting.

Following him was a mistake. Sabine knew she should have just gone with her brother. Gotten into the ambulance with him. Gone to the hospital. Tried to *forget* about her vampire lover and the crazy phoenix in town.

But there was no forgetting, and she wasn't about to let Ryder head off on a suicide mission.

She made sure Rhett was all right. Minor burns, but he'd make it. The guy had suffered worse injuries on a casual Saturday night. Bar fights were bitches.

Then she raced after Ryder. As soon as she cleared the crowd, Sabine started to move fast. Too fast for a human's eyes to follow. And she wasn't even sure how the hell she did it.

Vamp speed.

Another reminder that her old life was very much over.

She rushed faster and faster, chasing after Ryder. She rounded a corner and—

The narrow stretch of road before her was empty. Dying azaleas wilted on the northwest corner, but there was no sign of Ryder.

She'd been so sure that he'd gone this way. So very certain.

"Lose someone?"

Not Ryder's voice.

The phoenix.

And his voice was coming from behind her.

Slowly, Sabine turned to face him. He stood a few feet away, arms crossed over his chest, his body propped against the exterior brick wall of an abandoned house.

"You set the fire," Sabine charged. Because she wasn't an idiot. A phoenix was in town. The Rift had just burned.

He shrugged.

"My brother could have *died*."

"Humans die every day." The words weren't even the least bit concerned. "It's kind of their thing." His eyes sharpened on her with . . . interest? Curiosity? "They aren't like us."

"I'm nothing like you." She'd never started a fire for the hell of it. Just to watch the bitch burn.

Never had. Never would.

"Did you like the darkness?" he whispered and he didn't look quite so relaxed then.

"What?" The only thing she'd like right then would be to hurt this jerk. If Rhett had died in that blaze . . .

"When you burned and you came back . . . and all you knew was the fire and fury, did you like the way you felt?"

The wind blew over her skin, but it wasn't a cooling touch. In New Orleans, the breeze was humid and hot, like a scorch on her flesh.

"I don't know what you're talking about," she told him, making sure to keep her eyes on his. She wouldn't let this guy see that she was afraid.

But if his senses were as acute as she suspected, then he could probably tell that truth, anyway.

"Pity." Now he seemed disappointed. Much less curious. "It's been so long since I talked to another phoenix. I'd hoped you'd be . . . more."

Sorry to disappoint you, jerk. "Is that why you tossed some fire my way? To see just how much *more* I could be?"

He didn't answer, but he seemed to have stiffened. His gaze darted over her shoulder.

She wasn't going to make the mistake of turning and following his gaze. The guy was probably just trying to trick her. "Who are you?" Sabine demanded.

"You can call me Dante."

"Why . . . because you start your own inferno?" She tossed right back.

A faint smile lifted his lips as he advanced toward her. "Something like that." His fingers brushed over her arm. "I do like the fire."

In the next instant, Dante was yanked back and thrown to the ground. One very pissed-off vampire stood over him. "Don't ever touch her again," Ryder barked.

Her breath came too fast. Fear could do that to a girl. Make her body tight and edgy. Make her breath pant out. She'd wondered where Ryder went, and now she was sure glad he was back.

Sabine began to inch toward him.

Dante rose from the ground. "Vampire."

Ryder flashed his fangs.

"Do you honestly think you're a match for someone like me?" Dante taunted. The flames began to flicker in his eyes. "I could kill you in an instant."

"Then why don't you just go ahead and give it your best shot?" Ryder invited, taking a step forward.

And Dante *did*. He leapt forward, his hand full of flames, and he shoved those flames right at Ryder's chest.

Sabine screamed.

The ambulance sped down the road, rushing fast as its sirens screamed.

"You're gonna be all right, man," Vaughn said as he leaned over Rhett. "The burns aren't that bad at all."

Yeah, but they still hurt like hell. Gritting his teeth, Rhett glanced up at his friend. "Where's Sabine?"

Vaughn shook his head. "I don't know. She was there with us one minute, gone the next."

Son of a bitch. "I just got her back." He tried to sit up. An EMT was swabbing some kind of gunk on his arms and hand. The EMT tried to push him back down. Rhett pushed right back up.

"I know you did." Vaughn's voice was soft. "But at least she's in the city now."

In the city, but where? And with that vampire?

Vaughn looked toward the front of the ambulance, then he peered back at Rhett. "Things shouldn't have gone down like this."

The EMT had finally backed the hell off. "Tell me about it," Rhett muttered. "My sister shouldn't be a damn *vampire*."

Vaughn shook his head. "That's not what I meant." The guy's voice was tight, heavy with tension. The way he usually sounded when he was coming off an under-cover mission.

Only Vaughn had transferred out of Vice. He was supposed to be working homicide now. And . . .

Vaughn had just pulled out his gun. "I never wanted to do this . . ."

"What the hell?" Why did Vaughn have a gun out in the *ambulance*?

"But orders are orders." He shook his head. "I'm sorry."

Rhett started to fight the tubes and wires around him. Furious, the EMT whirled to face Vaughn. "You're gonna have to help me hold—" He broke off, eyes wid-ening as he saw the gun.

Then Vaughn shot the guy.

Ryder didn't burn. Sabine had raced forward and she grabbed for Dante's hand only to realize . . .

Ryder's shirt was on fire, yeah, but his skin wasn't burning. Not even blistering.

"I think that instant's about up," Ryder muttered.

Dante's eyes had widened. His stare flew to her. "What have you done?"

What had *she* done?

But then Dante was the one screaming as Ryder sank his teeth into the phoenix's neck. The two men were about the same size, both big, powerful. Only Dante's fire couldn't seem to hurt Ryder, but Ryder's bite . . . oh yes, it was definitely hurting the phoenix.

Blood streamed down Dante's neck. It wasn't a gentle bite. No, it was brutal. Savage. She put her hand to her mouth, horrified. Was this what she'd become? "Ryder . . ." His name broke from her lips.

His head lifted and turned toward her. Blood dripped from his mouth.

Monster.

She knew exactly what she was staring at.

Ryder flinched. He shook his head, as if lost or confused. "Sabine?"

Dante shoved him away. "Fucking experiments."

Was that all they were?

Dante put a hand to his throat, trying to stop the heavy blood flow. "I'll kill you both." A chilling promise.

"No," Ryder lifted his claws, "but I'm about to kill you."

"Police! Freeze!" a female voice shouted.

Dante smirked, and he didn't freeze. "Heard them coming, didn't you, vamp?" Fire blazed above his fingers. "I heard 'em, too, and thought we could play."

Sabine spun to face the cops—three of them. Armed

and running quickly down the narrow path. "Get back!" Sabine yelled at them.

But the police had seen the blood. They'd seen the fire. They weren't turning back.

Not even when Dante sent the fire right for them.

Hell. Sabine ran for the cops, moving as fast as she could. They started yelling for her to freeze, but if she stopped, they'd die.

She didn't stop.

One of them fired at her. She moved faster, faster . . . Another fired.

The bullets missed her because she was moving so fast.

Vampire fast.

Sabine tackled one cop. Felt the heat of flames dance over their bodies.

Ryder hit the others. They went down, hard enough for her to hear the crunch of bones. The cops would all have plenty of bruises, but they'd be alive. The flames had passed over their bodies.

Sabine grabbed the gun that the cop had been *shooting* at her with and tucked it into her waistband. "You're welcome," she muttered. The guy started to fight. Sabine bit her lip. She didn't want to do this, but there wasn't much choice.

She slammed his head into the cement.

His eyes rolled back, and he stopped fighting.

"Don't worry, love, he's not dead."

She hoped not. She'd been trying to save the guy.

She just hadn't wanted to keep fighting him.

Ryder snagged her hand. "Come on. Dante's already gone."

Not surprising. Only smoke and fire were left in his

wake. But the cops would have called for backup, and Sabine didn't exactly want to be huddled over those limp human bodies when said backup came rushing to the scene.

She let Ryder pull her to her feet. But then she took the lead. This was her city, after all. She led him through the twisting maze of streets and nook-tight corners that most wouldn't know about. When they finally spilled out onto Bourbon Street, blending with the crowd was instant and far too easy.

Ryder kept a hand curled around her waist, as if he was afraid that she was about to cut and run. She had no plans to do that. Yet.

She needed to figure out just what the hell was going on.

But getting a nice, alone-time spot for a chat wasn't gonna happen right then.

Sabine turned and wrapped her arms around Ryder. He stiffened for an instant, but then immediately pulled her closer as they pushed toward the outside of a bar. His hands curled around her waist. Seemed to brand her.

Sabine breathed slowly, too aware of him then. And, um, yes, the guy was *aware* of her, too. She could feel that awareness pushing against her and getting larger by the moment. She wet her lips, *not* in preparation for a kiss, really, and leaned up on her toes to ask, "Were we followed?"

Ryder gave a small negative shake of his head.

That was something.

"I have to get to the hospital. I need to see about Rhett."

"Every time you get close to him, you just put him at risk." His mouth was inches from hers. To others, they'd look like embracing lovers.

Isn't that what we are?

"You shouldn't have come back here," he said, voice and eyes hardening. "I told you to stay away. You're not the same any longer. Your family . . ." His jaw locked. "I'm sorry, but they aren't safe with you around them."

He could have just taken a dull knife and hacked into her heart. It would have hurt a lot less.

She glanced down at his shirt. Burned. Blackened. But his chest was unmarred. "What's happening to you? To me?"

Looking up, she saw that his gaze held so many secrets. She was tired of secrets.

"You need to trust me," he said.

Sabine didn't answer.

"You trusted me to get you out of Genesis."

Yes, she had. But it hadn't exactly been as if she had tons of options then.

"Trust me now. Don't run from me again. Stay with me. Let me help you." His hands tightened on her waist. "The hunger, the bloodlust will hit you soon. If you're not careful, the first time you feed, you may lose control. I've dealt with bloodlust longer than you can imagine. When it comes to being a vampire, I'm a fucking expert."

Someone jostled her from behind. A mumbled sorry drifted to her even as Ryder snapped, "Watch it!"

She ignored the jostle. "I can't talk about this, not here, not—"

He glanced away from her. Looked up the street. To the left. The right. Then his eyes narrowed. "I know a place."

Uh, wasn't that supposed to be her line?

But now he was leading and she was following and she was tired and . . . and a dull hunger was starting to gnaw at her. *Blood? I don't want blood. I don't ever want to drink blood.*

Then Ryder was pausing in front of a small bar, one with dark windows and throbbing music. Twisting letters said the place was called BRAN, and there was what looked like the top of a castle sketched beneath that name. A bouncer stood in front of the door, and the guy didn't seem to be letting anyone in. He was a bear of a man, covered in tats and piercings, and he snarled at the folks dumb enough to head toward him.

Ryder headed right for him.

And, yes, the guy stopped snarling.

"We're here for a drink," Ryder said.

The bouncer cast a suspicious glance her way.

"We're *both* here for the drink." Ryder's tone snapped now. Obviously he was getting annoyed.

Sabine shifted from her left foot to her right. The bar wasn't on Bourbon Street. Technically it was off just one street to the side, but despite its close proximity to the infamous party street, Sabine had never been to that bar, not in all of her years in New Orleans. In fact, the place kind of looked like a hellhole. Not exactly inviting and—

The bouncer opened the door for them.

The interior was so dark. Too dark. She squinted.

"Give it a minute," Ryder advised her. "Your eyes will adjust. You just aren't used to your vamp senses yet."

Um, okay. She blinked a few times. Then everything seemed to sharpen and brighten. She saw the tables. Men. Women.

Saw the bar.

Saw the . . . blood being served?

She grabbed his arm and dug her nails into his flesh.

"How did you know?" The guy had just steered her right into a vampire bar.

He pried her nails out of his arm and led her across the room. "Because this place is mine."

The bartender stiffened when she got a glimpse of Ryder's face. She was fumbling now, hurriedly filling two glasses with red liquid, and she quickly put them in front of two empty seats at the bar. "S-sir . . ."

He nodded his thanks, but then waved her away.

Sabine's gaze darted around the bar. "Are they all . . . ?"

"They're just like us."

There was a snap in his voice.

Not like me. She swallowed back the words. She hadn't exactly gotten used to the whole I'm-a-vampire bit.

"H-how do they know to come here?" The place was a vamp bar. Got it. But did the vamps all spread some kind of secret code on the Internet? Telling each other where the blood bars were in the United States? "How did they know they could get blood here?" Because vamps were out of their closets—coffins—sure, but she'd never heard of a place like this. It sure hadn't been featured on any news shows.

"The name told them what it was."

Bran?

His fingers wrapped around the blood-filled glass, but he didn't drink. "Don't know much about Dracula, do you?"

Not exactly her area of expertise, no.

"Some folks believe that Dracula's castle was originally called Bran's Castle." His lips quirked. "And that's the name of this place, too."

So he'd named his bar after Dracula's house. Was

that supposed to be some kind of in-vamp joke? No wonder the vamps were flocking inside.

The bartender came back, nervously tucking a long lock of blond hair behind her ears. Her nails, painted a bright red, tapped on the marble bartop. "We thought . . . a lot of us thought you were dead."

Ryder just stared back at her. "Then I guess word is about to spread that I'm back."

The blonde looked scared. Of her boss?

Sabine glanced back at Ryder. His handsome face was hard. His fangs were flashing. And his eyes . . . she'd never seen them so cold. Usually, his eyes were bright. Glinting. Not icy.

His grip tightened on the glass, and a faint crack appeared, running up the side.

The blonde's attention shifted to Sabine. "You don't want the blood?"

No, actually, the sight of it was making her nauseous. Before she could speak, Ryder snagged her fingers. Brought her hand to his lips. "Sabine drinks from me."

The chick's eyes almost doubled then. "Y-you let . . ."

Ryder shoved the glass away. "And I drink from her." Then he was rising and heading for a narrow, wooden staircase in the back. When Sabine put her foot on the first stair, it gave a long, low groan.

She felt a dozen eyes on her back, but she refused to look over her shoulder. So they had the attention of every vamp in the place. So what? The way she figured it, this was a safe house, of sorts.

She didn't have to worry about Genesis here. Or about Dante.

The stairs kept creaking as they headed upstairs. Then they entered a small apartment, and Ryder locked the door behind them.

"It won't be long now," he said.

She rubbed a hand over her aching forehead. "Until what?"

"Until we see which vamps want to try to kill us."

Hell. So much for safe.

CHAPTER TWELVE

She hadn't fed.

Ryder paced the apartment, casting worried glances at Sabine. He'd yanked off his shirt, what was left of it, and tossed the fabric in the trash.

Anger hummed through him, no, rage, but he was doing his best to hold on to his control. For now. For her.

"Promise you won't leave me again." The words were an order. He probably should have tried to soften them.

Then she shook her head, and he realized he shouldn't be going easy at all.

His back teeth snapped together, and he stalked toward her. "You *need* me."

She blinked those gorgeous, dark eyes of hers. "How do you know what I need?"

Insane. That was what she wanted him to be.

He put his hands on the wall behind her, caging her between his arms. "You're a freshly turned vamp, love. You might as well be a newborn."

Her eyes narrowed at that. "Did you just call me a child?"

No, he'd called her a newborn. Even a child wasn't totally helpless. "When the bloodlust hits you, you'll—"

"But the bloodlust *hasn't* hit me," she fired back at him. "It's been days since my so-called turning, and I'm doing just fine holding on to my control."

His head tilted as he studied her. He could see the pulse racing at the base of her neck. *Drink.* He'd been injured, attacked. Lost a lot of blood. Sure, his wounds had closed. He was an ancient vamp, they'd better close, but even though his body had healed, the craving was still within him.

I need her blood.

So he'd lied to her. She wasn't the one who needed him. He needed her. Without her, the hunger would tear him apart.

He wanted to put his mouth on that racing pulse. Wanted to bite.

But she didn't?

"You fed when you left me." The only explanation. Had she killed? Not that it mattered to him.

Sabine shook her head.

And she just confused him more. "You've had no blood, no human food at all?" She had to take some kind of sustenance.

She shrugged. "I ate something at a diner."

He didn't let the shock show on his face. Vampires weren't supposed to be able to ingest human food.

"I didn't eat much," she muttered. "I just wasn't hungry."

What in the hell was happening? He'd felt her fangs before. Once. But he hadn't seen any sign of them since the moment of her transformation.

He leaned in closer. She tensed.

Ryder let his brows rise. "Are you afraid of me, Sabine?"

Her breath whispered out. "What you said before, it's true, isn't it?"

Bite her.

"You do—you want my blood."

"Love, I'm starving for it." Other blood just didn't satisfy him. Other blood made the craving for her even more intense.

Her hands rose and pressed lightly against his chest. Not pushing him away, not yet. "If I let you drink from me, then I want you to help me make sure that Rhett's all right. I have to know that my family's safe."

Trying to make another bargain with him? Fine. But he would have checked on her brother with or without the promise of her delicious blood. Those who mattered to Sabine, well, they mattered to him, too. "What is it that you want me to do?"

Her gaze held his. "I want you to make sure . . . anyone after them . . . I want you to *stop* anyone who tries to hurt them."

Easy enough. Death was always easy for him. "And you're so sure I can?"

"You're the strongest paranormal I know. Even a phoenix's fire couldn't hurt you." Her eyes searched his. "How was that even possible?"

Because of you. He knew that truth, even if she didn't. He'd taken her blood, again and again, and somehow that blood had given him immunity against a phoenix's fire. Perhaps it had even been like taking inoculations.

Maybe Wyatt had planned for him to develop that immunity. Maybe that had been the reason Wyatt first brought Sabine to his cell.

The man had created a vampire impervious to the fire. *Transformation, not birth.*

The reason didn't really matter to Ryder. Fire had been one of the few means of killing him.

Cross that one off the list.

Now his enemies would have an even harder time forcing him from this earth.

"Why doesn't the fire hurt you?" Sabine pressed.

"Because maybe I like the burn." And instead of putting his mouth on her throat, he took her lips. Her sensual lips were parted slightly, open just enough for his tongue to push inside and taste her.

Mine.

Every muscle in his body tightened at that first taste. Not sweet, but rich. Decadent. Drugging.

Her tongue slid over his and a small moan built in her throat. The sound was sexy as all hell.

Yeah, he'd tracked her across four states. Gone nearly mad on that hunt.

She *obsessed* him. Every moment, he thought of her. A dangerous situation, for them both.

Her lips opened wider. The kiss grew harder. More demanding. Her body was soft and lush against his. She made a faint moan in the back of her throat, a sound that increased his wild desire.

His tongue thrust into her mouth. His hands locked around her hips. He pulled her closer. He couldn't get close enough.

There were two things that vampires loved in this world. Blood and sex.

And if you could have both at the same time . . .

Lucky fucking day.

But she pulled her mouth from his. Turned her head away. "My . . . brother . . ."

His breath was panting. She wanted to talk about her brother *then*?

"Make sure . . . he's okay."

Son of a—

Snarling, he leapt away from her. Ryder yanked open the door and bellowed, "Grayson!"

He knew the other vampire would be there. When Sabine had left him, Ryder had contacted the other vamp. Briefed him on Genesis, Sabine, and the betrayal that had taken place in the vampire coven. New Orleans was Grayson's territory, a territory assigned by Ryder, and since Grayson was the one vamp that he actually trusted at that moment . . .

Grayson's dark head appeared as he went up the stairs.

Well, it was good to have the guy watching his back. With the hell that was headed his way, Ryder knew he could use that.

Ryder's knuckles whitened around the door frame. "Sabine's brother was taken to the hospital." Hell, he didn't even know which one. "Find him. Make sure he stays alive." Those had actually been the orders that Ryder had given to Grayson *before* he'd found Sabine in that alley.

While he'd rushed to New Orleans, Grayson had been his eyes and ears in the city. Grayson had played guard dog to the human, Rhett. Because Ryder had known that Sabine was going after him.

Grayson gave a slow nod. His dark gaze darted over Ryder's shoulder. He knew Sabine was standing there. The wooden floor had creaked beneath her feet and her lush scent teased his nose.

"So you got what you were looking for?" Grayson

asked, lifting a brow. Faint amusement had his lips quirking.

"Not yet," Ryder muttered. "But soon I will." As soon as she was under him. As soon as his teeth were *in* her neck.

He spun back around, slamming the door with his heel, and grabbing her in one fast flash. Two steps, and they were on the bed. Two seconds, and she was naked.

"Your brother's safe." Now she could focus on the heat between them. He could focus on her. He needed her blood. His fangs were burning, the hunger for her blood seeming to tear him apart.

His fingers slid over her throat. Her pulse raced beneath his touch. Throbbed. The blood so close.

"Go ahead," she whispered.

But he was caught by her eyes. She'd stared at him with fear the first time they'd met. He'd hurt her then. He never wanted to hurt her again. So as much as he wanted to bury his fangs into her and drink and drink . . . he wanted her pleasure more.

His fingers slowly slid down her body. Sabine stiffened. "Ryder?"

"Shh . . . I missed you." A confession from deep within. When was the last time that he'd missed anything or anyone?

He couldn't remember. Only her. She made him feel, yearn, as no one else did. As no one else could. Taking her blood that first time—it had been as if he'd awakened with those precious drops. Life wasn't cold and dark any longer.

The world was on fire around him, and she made him long for those flames.

He bent his head. His fingers trailed over her breast, teasing the nipple. *Take, take.*

But he kept his touch light. His fingers stroked her. He licked her flesh. Loved the way her nipple tightened as she arched beneath him. He sucked her breast, her fucking perfect breasts. Small but round, with delicious pink nipples.

His hand eased over the curve of her stomach. Down between her legs. She was so soft and warm and wet.

He licked his way to her other breast. She was shaking beneath him now, little trembles of arousal, and her nails were digging into his back. He liked her claws.

Her legs parted more, giving him better access to the flesh he craved.

He pushed his index finger inside her. Sabine's delicate inner muscles clenched down on him. Holding on so tight.

His muscles were locked. Every instinct he had was screaming for him to bite, to thrust, to claim her.

He fought those instincts. She needed pleasure. Not pain. *Only* pleasure.

His finger slid out of her. Pressed back inside. His thumb pushed against her clit. Ryder found a rhythm that he knew she'd like, one not too fast, one sure-as-hell not too slow. Again and again, his hand caressed her warm sex.

Her hips moved against him. "More, Ryder, *more!*"

If she wanted more . . .

He lifted his head. Stared down at her.

"Ryder?"

He realized he was probably looking at her like he wanted to devour her.

I do.

He pulled his hand from her sex. She shook her head. "I wasn't—"

His hands curved around her thighs. He spread her legs, holding her so that he could have the total access that he wanted.

Then he put his mouth on her. Her blood was sweet. But this, hell, nothing was *this* good.

He heard her choked scream. Felt the ripple of her release as he tasted her. He didn't stop. He licked. Kissed. Stroked with his mouth and tongue. And he could taste her pleasure.

Only pleasure.

Her breath was panting when he rose. Her eyes blind with pleasure. He positioned his cock at the entrance of her body. Slid deep into her with one powerful surge. Her sex still rippled with aftershocks of pleasure, and those little shivers of her inner muscles worked up and down the length of his cock.

Her arms wrapped around him. Sabine pulled him close. Held him tight.

Her head turned to the left, baring her neck. "Bite me," she whispered.

He wasn't strong enough to resist that invitation.

His fangs pierced her throat. Blood—*her blood!*—trickled onto his tongue.

Ryder's control shattered. His thrusts weren't easy. Not gentle. His hips pistoned against her as he thrust harder, deeper. Her hands wrapped around his shoulders even as her legs rose to lock around his hips.

She whispered, "Harder."

And he didn't know if she meant the bite or—

Ryder drove into her. Faster. Deeper. Her blood filled him, sending a surge of power through every cell of his body. Drinking her blood was like getting plugged into a power outlet. Straight energy.

Straight fucking magic.

She stiffened beneath him, and her sex clenched around his cock. *Yes*. He pulled back, wanting to see the pleasure on her face once more.

And when his head lifted, he saw that her lips were parted, her eyes squeezed shut, and—and small fangs were peeking out from behind her lips.

His cock swelled even more. "Bite me," he ordered. He wanted her to have his blood. Wanted anything that would strengthen the ties between them.

Was it fair to her? Hell, no. But he wasn't interested in fair. He was taking the one thing in this world that mattered to him.

"Bite me, Sabine," he snarled.

But she was lost to the pleasure. He could see it. And his own climax was so close. He caught the back of her head. Tilted her so that her mouth was right over his throat. She just needed to feel the pulse of his blood. Her vampire instincts would do the rest.

"You're hungry, love," he rasped. Her teeth scraped lightly over his flesh. "Let me give you what you need."

He pushed into her. So slick. So tight. He drove down again, making sure to push his cock over her clit before he sank balls-deep in her sex.

She gasped and her teeth bit into him.

Yes.

Pleasure erupted. No other word. Like a volcano, burning, blasting away everything else. Her mouth moved lightly on his neck. Lips. Tongue. Those teeth sinking into him . . .

His cock jerked as he emptied into her core. The orgasm was the strongest one he'd ever had. And it went on and on and on, sending hard pulses of sensation—too intense to just be called pleasure—through him.

He held her tight. Held her as close as he could get. When her mouth finally pulled from his neck, when Sabine eased back to look up at him with dazed eyes, he knew he'd found the one person he'd been looking for all those long centuries.

Ryder also knew that he'd destroy anyone or anything that ever tried to take her from him.

Mine.

He didn't know if Wyatt had done something with his experiments to force the intense connection that he felt with her. Maybe the mad scientist had linked them somehow.

Ryder didn't care about how he'd come to be linked to her.

He pushed into Sabine. Saw her pupils widen.

He only cared that he had her. Beneath him. With him.

He had such plans for her. This was just the start for them.

He forced himself to release her because Ryder knew he held her too tight. His hands flattened on either side of her body, sinking into the mattress, and he pushed up so that he wouldn't crush her.

Her gaze met his. She stared up at him with shock. "What did I . . . ?"

He didn't speak. Just waited for the truth to sink in.

When a tear slid down her cheek, he felt like she'd just cut out his heart.

Been there, done that before. But this time, it hurt more than when his brother had shoved that heavy sword into his heart.

"Sabine."

Her lips pressed together. Pleasure still had his body replete, but tension, fear—because of his worry for her—sent a chill through him. "It's your nature." If sex hadn't made her bloodlust come out, nothing would have. "When you fuck . . ."

She flinched beneath him.

"You feed," he finished quietly.

Her hands pushed against his chest. "You need to know that your after-sex pillow talk *sucks.*"

He blinked. "Uh . . ." He hadn't exactly had to worry about pillow talk. He didn't usually make conversation with the women he screwed.

She's not a woman I screwed. She's . . . Sabine.

"Let me go," she whispered, blinking quickly. "I can't—"

Footsteps were pounding up the staircase. He heard them, coming too fast, and rolled away from her.

She scrambled for her clothes, looking rumpled and sexy, and the last thing he wanted to do was leave her.

But a threat was coming.

He yanked on his jeans. Rushed for the door even as the wooden frame shook beneath the blow of a powerful fist.

Ryder yanked open the door. Grayson stared back at him. "Problem," the other vampire snapped. His gaze cut to Ryder's right. The floor creaked beneath Sabine's footsteps. "Her brother didn't show up at St. Mary's Hospital."

"Wh-what?" Sabine asked, pushing past Ryder. She was mussed, flushed, and smelled of sex.

Grayson's nostrils widened. He licked his lips, and his gaze drifted over her.

Locking his back teeth, Ryder stepped forward and shoved his only friend back. *"Where's her brother?"*

Grayson blinked and shook his head. The guy had always had too big of a weakness where the ladies were concerned. "The ambulance . . . it crashed. The driver was unconscious, the other EMT was shot."

"Shot?" Sabine repeated, voice rising.

"There was no sign of the human at the scene."

"It's Genesis," she whispered, her breath coming faster. "That woman . . . she told me they'd kill my brother. If I didn't do what they wanted—" She tried to rush into the hallway.

Ryder grabbed her hand and pulled her right back to his side. "You don't know it's them." Was she forgetting about that jerk Dante? And there were other enemies, enemies she didn't even know about yet.

My enemies.

Enemies who would target her because they knew . . . *I want her.* His enemies had finally found his weakness, and they would use her if they had the chance.

"Let me go, Ryder," she gritted as she tried to twist her hand out of his grasp.

When he didn't let her go, Sabine's skin began to warm beneath his touch.

Impossible.

Her eyes were still dark brown. Showing no flames. Only fear and fury.

"Where will you go?" he asked her, and Ryder damn well didn't let her go. "To your parents? Will you rush to them and place them in danger, too?"

"Aren't they already in danger?" Sabine whispered, voice tight with pain. "Because of me?"

They were. Humans were always too vulnerable. Too easily hurt. Too easily killed.

"I have to warn them," she said as her shoulders straightened.

Fine. She could warn them. Then he'd get them out of the country until his battles were done.

Ryder nodded slowly. "I'm coming with you." Because she could be walking straight into another trap.

He knew Grayson watched them far too closely. He turned toward his friend. "Find her brother." Tracks were always left behind. When it came to following a blood trail, Grayson was second only to Ryder.

Grayson nodded. His gaze swept over Sabine once more. Friend or no friend, if his stare lingered much longer, he was going to get clawed.

But, wisely, Grayson turned and headed back down the stairs.

Sabine hesitated. "Will he find Rhett?"

"Yes." But find him alive . . . *maybe not.*

"Don't tell my parents what I am," she said, swallowing.

Rage hummed beneath his skin. "Ashamed?" The public knew about vampires. They weren't just a myth any longer. Some humans loved the idea of becoming immortal. Some were all too eager to offer up their blood to a vamp.

But some thought vamps were abominations. That they needed to be sent straight to hell.

She didn't speak. Just stared up at him.

His lips twisted. "There's no point in hating what you are." What he'd made her. A sliver of what could have been guilt pierced his gut. *She didn't want to burn again. She begged for my help.*

Only he was starting to wonder . . . was she fully a vampire? Or by giving her his blood, by forcing all of those exchanges between them, had he made her into something else entirely?

Transformation, not birth.

He had to find out for certain.

"Why not?" she whispered back even as she pulled away from him and headed down the stairs. "Don't you hate what you are?"

Her words surprised him. "No, love, I don't hate what I am." Why would she believe that?

Frowning, Sabine glanced back at him.

He smiled, knowing his fangs would look sharp and deadly. "I love being the monster in the room." He'd never been one of those fools who railed against the gift of immortality. He had power. Strength that humans could only wish to possess.

Why bitch and moan about that? Why consider vampirism a curse when it could be a blessing?

As her frown deepened, a faint furrow appeared between her brows.

"Soon you'll love the power just as much as I do," he promised her. She just had to stop thinking like a human.

She wasn't prey any longer. She was the predator. At the top of the food chain.

And now it was time for anyone hunting her to realize just how powerful Sabine had become.

He was tied to a chair. Bound hand and foot with thick, rough ropes. Rhett jerked against his bonds, twisting and trying to break free. "What the hell is going on?"

Dim light spilled across the room. An old, dust-filled room that looked like it had to be in some abandoned building. The small bit of light came from a lantern, the kind you used when you went camping.

The kind Vaughn usually took when they went out into the swamp.

And Vaughn—that crazy jerk Rhett had mistakenly thought was his *friend*—was standing against the right wall, holding a gun in his hand.

Vaughn's jaw tightened as he stared back at Rhett. "Your sister . . . she's not the same anymore."

Turns out I'm not exactly human. Sabine's soft words drifted through Rhett's mind. The fire had erupted before he'd been able to question her more, but she'd been wrong. She was the same.

She was his sister. He'd been by her side when she learned how to ride a bike without training wheels. He'd been there the day she broke her arm because she'd tried to follow him up Old Man Lawson's oak tree. He'd been there when that handsy jerk Johnny had tried to get past first base with—

"Did you ever wonder about Sabine's birth parents?" Vaughn asked him. The gun's barrel was pointed at the ground, not at Rhett. At least, it wasn't pointed at him yet.

Rhett shook his head and jerked harder against the ropes. "Why should I care about them? Sabine's *my* sister. We've got great parents, we don't need—"

"Her birth parents knew they had a monster on their hands."

Rhett froze, then he snapped, "Watch that mouth, Vaughn." Gun or no gun, no one talked about his sister that way.

"So they got rid of her. They dumped her in the river."

Sabine had been found in a river, barely alive. Everyone had been stunned to find such a small child alive in that dark water. She was called Sabine because that was where she was found. *In Sabine River.*

His dad had been one of the first responders on

the scene. He'd taken care of the little girl. Loved her. Moved heaven and hell to get her brought into his home.

"I guess they hoped the water could kill her, but she was too strong." Vaughn gave a sad shake of his head. "Now she's even stronger."

"Get me out of these ropes!" Rhett yelled. His burns hurt like a bitch, and the ropes just cut right into the blisters, making the wounds throb and ache even more.

Vaughn shook his head again. "You don't understand what's happening. And I wish I could have told you. I wish I could have warned you—"

Warned me about my own sister? "You're a cop!" The guy shouldn't need the reminder. "This shit is illegal. You don't kidnap your friends!" *You don't tie them up. You damn well don't pull a gun on them.*

Vaughn lifted his hand. The gun looked way too comfortable in the guy's grip. "You don't get it. You're lucky you aren't dead already."

Rhett's heart slammed into his chest.

"She's going to come for you. When she does . . ." Vaughn sighed, a long, low sound. "I'm sorry, man."

"You're sorry?" Rhett heaved against those ropes. Screw the pain, he'd keep struggling until his body was a bloody mess. "If you're sorry, then let me the fuck go!"

"I liked her, you know?" Vaughn's voice dropped. "When we were kids, I didn't know the truth, either." He tucked the gun into the holster on his hip. "But some people are too dangerous to walk the earth. Times have changed. We can't let the supernaturals take over."

I'm not exactly human.

He strained against the ropes. He could feel his own blood dripping behind him. "You hurt my sister, and I'll kill you." It wasn't an empty threat. Rhett didn't make empty threats. He'd get out of there, sooner or later, and if Vaughn hurt Sabine, the guy would die.

But Vaughn's eyes had narrowed. "You have it wrong. If I don't stop her, then you're the one who'll be dead." Then Vaughn stalked forward and grabbed the lantern. He took it and its small light from the room. Rhett yelled after him, calling out again and again, but Vaughn didn't look back. And soon Rhett was alone in the dark, with his blood slowly soaking the thick rope.

CHAPTER THIRTEEN

Sabine nervously shifted from her left foot to her right. The house before her was just as she remembered. Tall, brick, with a long wraparound porch. Big bay windows.

Withering azaleas in the front yard. No matter how hard her mom tried, those azaleas never did live long enough.

The house was dark. Figured, since it had to be close to 3 A.M. Her heart ached at the sight of the house. She'd grown up there. Broken her arm at the house just across the street when she'd tried to climb that big, damn oak tree.

I wanted to be like Rhett. He'd climbed that tree, zipped up it in about two seconds. She'd wanted to do just what her brother could do. He'd been her hero then.

I'll find you, Rhett. I'll stop this nightmare. Somehow.

But first she had to get her parents to safety.

Sabine glanced over her shoulder. Darkness stared

back at her. Easing out a careful breath, she looked to her side and asked Ryder, "What if we were followed?"

"Their address is in the phone book. Anyone coming after you already knows where they live. They wouldn't have to follow us. They could just come up and kill them anytime."

She flinched. Leave it to Ryder not to bother sugarcoating things for her. She wasn't even sure if the guy understood the concept of sugarcoating.

Her gaze returned to the house and its dark windows. *Be alive.* The house was so quiet. She should have come here sooner.

She'd just been afraid to face her parents.

She couldn't afford fear any longer. Sabine hurried up to the front door. She didn't bother knocking. The spare key was hidden under the loose brick near the bottom of the front door. She pulled the brick out and grabbed the key. In seconds, the front door was swinging open, and the alarm was beeping. But she punched in the alarm code digits as quickly as she could and—

The lights flooded on. Sabine spun around and saw the long barrel of a shotgun staring back at her.

"Sabine?"

It was her dad. His hair stuck out in a dozen different angles. His old LSU shirt hung faded and loose around him. He blinked, as if stunned to see her. Then he lowered the gun and grabbed her in a hug that stole her breath. He and Rhett had always hugged her too hard.

"I missed you, Dad," she whispered, holding him just as tightly.

His body shook against hers. "I knew you'd come back home." So confident, but the words quivered.

Then he pulled back a few inches to stare down at

her. His gaze swept over her face, not seeming to miss any detail. She studied him in turn, noticing the new gray in his hair and the lines that appeared deeper on his face.

After a moment, her father glanced over at Ryder. She caught the faint narrowing his eyes. "Vampire, huh?"

The cool response was the last thing she'd expected. "How can you tell?"

"Because I used to be a hunter, of sorts." He pulled Sabine to his left side. His head cocked as he continued to study Ryder. "Your man there probably doesn't remember me, but I even went after him once."

Shock held her immobile. Her father? A hunter?

Ryder stood in front of the closed door. He shrugged as his gaze swept over her father. "I . . . remember your face." He paused. "You should be grateful that I let you live."

Ryder *knew* her father? That was just weird.

Her father lifted the shotgun. Aimed the barrel at Ryder. "And maybe you should be grateful that I let *you* live." A hard pause, then, "Now you tell me, was that a mistake, vampire?"

Ryder smiled, showing his sharp fangs. "All along, you knew what she was."

The ticking of the clock in the den seemed too loud. Sabine's hand tightened around her dad's arm. "Where's Mom?"

"Somewhere safe." A fast response. Again, not what she'd expected.

Sabine studied her father with new eyes. He'd hunted vampires. Hunted Ryder. But he'd never once mentioned anything about supernaturals to her while she was growing up. Heck, when the vamps had started making headlines, he'd acted as shocked as the rest of their neighbors.

He was an ex-EMT turned college professor. He spent his days digging up archaeology sites and . . .

Digging up vampires?

"Why didn't you tell her the truth?" Ryder asked, his voice flat and hard. "Why did you let her think she was just like everyone else?"

"My girl *is* just like everyone else." Now her dad sounded pissed.

"Rhett thought I was dead." The words were pushed past her numb lips. "You . . . didn't, though, did you, Dad?" This wasn't exactly the homecoming she'd anticipated. She'd thought he'd be shocked, horrified.

Her gaze darted to the mantle. Thick, wooden spears hung over the fireplace. Souvenirs—so she'd always thought—from one of her father's trips to Africa.

"Yes, love," Ryder said softly, his gaze following hers, "those have been used to stake vamps."

She felt as if she were seeing her father—seeing him *clearly*—for the first time in her life.

"Sometimes, the only good vamp is a vamp with a stake in his heart," her father muttered, "and, just so you know, I've got wooden bullets in this gun."

Her breath rushed out as she left his side. Sabine took a few stumbling steps forward, and then she turned and placed her body right in front of the shotgun.

"*Sabine.*" Ryder snarled. He grabbed her arms.

"*Don't you hurt—*" her father began.

"Those bullets can kill me, too," Sabine said, cutting across his words. Her father. She'd thought she knew him so well. But now her gaze darted around the house.

What she'd thought were travel mementoes, were they all weapons? Tribal bags from South America and faded silver spears from Guatemala.

How could she be so blind?

"Nothing can kill you, Sabe," her father said, shaking his head. "Don't you worry."

He knew. She swallowed the lump in her throat. "Were you waiting to tell me until the first time I died? When I burned for the first time, were you going to tell me then?"

He slowly lowered the gun. Ryder didn't wait for the gun barrel to face the floor. He grabbed the gun from her father's hands and threw the weapon across the room.

Her father blinked his eyes, eyes an exact match to Rhett's deep stare. "I never wanted you to burn."

"Too late." Her stark whisper. "Because Genesis made me burn, over and over again."

He paled and seemed to age ten years before her eyes. He jerked a shaking hand through his hair. "N-no. They were . . . supposed to help you."

A scream echoed in her mind. Her scream. The cry she'd made each time they'd killed her.

Her eyes couldn't look away from her father.

You did this to me.

The truth was right there on his face.

She'd never expected this betrayal. Not from him. He was her dad. Her hero. The man who had protected her all her life.

He was the man who gave me to them.

"Go outside, Sabine," Ryder said, his voice a lethal rumble of sound.

Her father shook his head. "Let me explain . . ."

"You didn't tell Mom what you'd done." *She had a heart attack.* No, her mother hadn't known. If she'd known, she wouldn't have been so shaken that she wound up in the hospital. "You didn't tell Rhett." He wouldn't have been so frantic to find her.

"I wanted to help you!"

Ryder was in front of her, blocking her view of her father. He stared down at her, his face implacable. "Go onto the porch. Wait for me there."

Her heart was breaking. "Why?" The question was stark. "So you can kill my father?"

"Yes." No lies. No denial.

"Sabine!" Her father's desperate cry. She'd never heard him sound desperate before. Happy. Loving. Even angry a time or ten when she and Rhett pushed him too far. But never desperate. Until now.

She didn't look at him. Just stared up at Ryder. She'd trusted her father, always. "But . . . he's my father." The words she left unspoken were . . . *He wouldn't do this to me. There's a mistake. My father wouldn't have let them hurt me. He protects me. Keeps me safe. Always.*

That was a father's job, right?

Not to . . . not to let his daughter get killed. Tortured. Over and over again.

"Sometimes your family members are the ones you need to fear the most." There was a whisper of something dark in Ryder's voice. A stir of memory in his eyes. But, right then, Sabine couldn't see well enough past her own pain to unlock his secrets.

He gave her a little push. "Outside."

"I can't . . ." She couldn't let her father die. Wouldn't kill him. Even if . . . Sabine rushed around Ryder and grabbed her father's arms. She shook him and was aware that his bones felt so fragile to her, brittle. "*Why?* Why did you do this to me?"

There were tears in his eyes. His hands twisted and grabbed onto hers. "Genesis . . . they were supposed to help people like you."

People like you. "They hurt me, Dad. They killed me."

His eyes seemed to sink into his face. "I saw the stories on the news. Until then I-I didn't know—"

"You're the one who told them where to find me." He'd sent the men who came for her in the night. The men who'd drugged her. Kidnapped her. Tossed her in a cell with a starving vampire and watched as she screamed.

That vampire was right behind her now. She could feel his fury. He wanted to rip out her father's throat.

Part of her wanted the same thing.

"You sent me to die," she told him.

But her father shook his head, his desperation plain to see. "I sent you to *live*. I knew what was—I knew what you were, yes, dammit, I knew. And I knew you couldn't stay that way. The fire would take you over. Drive you insane until all you wanted to do was kill and burn. But Genesis, I-I thought they could help you, baby! That was all I wanted—for someone to help you."

"No one can help me," she said, voice breaking. "They never could."

Her shoulders hunched. The home she'd loved for so long suddenly felt foreign to her. "I was . . . I was coming to tell you that you needed to leave town. The people at Genesis . . . not all of them are gone. I was told"—she stopped to lick lips gone bone-dry—"I was told that Rhett might be targeted for death."

Her father's jaw had gone slack with shock. "But Rhett's human . . ."

And you're not.

The words hung in the air. They didn't need to be spoken.

"Genesis never cared about collateral damage," Ryder said, voice rumbling.

No, they hadn't. "I was supposed to do a job for them. I didn't." She'd let Wyatt die. She hoped he was in hell. "So they sent someone to kill Rhett."

Her father staggered back a step. "I-I didn't know, I swear! One of my old army buddies, he worked for them. He said they were going to make the world *better.* I just wanted you to be normal. To be like everyone else."

"The funny thing, Dad, is that I *thought* I was normal." Until he'd served her up to those sadistic bastards. "If you hadn't told them about me, then Genesis would have never come for me. I wouldn't have burned . . . if it hadn't been for you." And she didn't even want to look at him. She *couldn't* look him in the eyes. It hurt too much. *You're not the man I thought you were.* Her gaze darted to Ryder. "Rhett's missing. I'm going to find him."

"*We* are," Ryder immediately corrected her.

If Ryder hadn't been there, she might have let the tears fall. She might have just broken. Pain twisted inside her, cutting like a knife. But Ryder *was* there. His fingers curled around hers. He was steady and solid and strong.

She stared into his eyes. Remembered the hell they'd faced. Remembered the hell they'd survived. Together.

Genesis hadn't broken her.

Genesis hadn't broken him.

They'd fought, together, and they'd keep fighting that way.

So she didn't break. She pulled in several deep, frantic breaths. Ryder's hold tightened on her.

In a world turned upside down, she found herself relying on the monster that most would fear.

He's not a monster.

Sabine realized that she didn't think of Ryder that way, not anymore.

He was her lover. He was her partner.

He was . . . more?

"I-I talked to Rhett this evening." Her father's voice was lost. "He was f-fine then."

"You talked to him before a fire tore through The Rift, and before someone hijacked the ambulance he was in and shot one of the EMTs." Her own voice sounded so calm. Odd, when she felt anything *but* calm. Turning away, she told him, "Get out of town. Go to wherever it is that you've got Mom stashed. Stay until all of this is over."

Mom. Thinking about her mother just hurt too much then.

Sabine forced herself to take slow, determined steps toward the front door. Ryder shadowed her every move.

She wanted out of the house. But a hand on her shoulder froze her.

"You were two when I found you," her father said, his hand trembling against her shoulder. "You were floating face down in the river."

Sabine River. Yes, she knew where she'd been found.

"You should have been dead. I rolled you over . . ." He turned her to face him. "And I saw fire burning in your eyes. A baby . . . with burning eyes."

She didn't want to hear any more from him.

"I loved you like you were my own. You *are* my own."

A child he'd sold to the devil. "How much did they pay you?" Sabine asked because she knew he'd gotten something from the deal.

"Nothing."

Her life had been worth nothing?

"I wanted them to fix you, baby. I saw the fire again and again over the years—it would flare in your eyes whenever you got real angry, and I was so afraid of what would happen the moment you lost your control. I'd heard stories of others like you. Supernaturals that were too dangerous to be around humans. Evil. I didn't want you to turn out like them. I wanted to help you." His voice broke.

So did her heart.

"Get out of town," she told him, the last time she'd give her father the warning. "And tell Mom . . ." She had to clear her throat. Had to choke back the lump of pain and fury that had risen. "Tell her anything but the truth." Because she didn't want to hurt her mother.

"I-I can't leave Rhett—"

"Leave on your own," Ryder told him, his tone lethal, "or I'll have my vamps drain you and drag your limp body out of this town."

She knew the words weren't an idle threat. Her father knew it, too. Glancing over her shoulder, she saw that the knowledge blazed in his eyes.

Eyes that still watched her with a sad desperation.

"Good-bye, Dad," she whispered as she walked across the porch and into the yard. Sabine expected Ryder to follow right on her heels.

But he didn't follow.

"Tell me the name of that old army buddy," was Ryder's tight demand.

"N-no."

A thud. Sounded like a fist hitting a wall. Her eyes squeezed shut as her shoulders stiffened. "Don't hurt him, Ryder. He's . . . he's still my father." The tears fell then, because she couldn't hold them back any longer. She could even taste the salt of the tears on her lips. "And I still love him." Maybe he had thought to help her. Maybe he'd thought . . .

It doesn't matter. I still love him. I love the man who played hide-and-seek with me. I love the man who read Sleeping Beauty *to me again and again and again. I love him.*

She glanced back.

Her father stood inside the house, with Ryder at his side. "I'm so sorry, baby," her father whispered.

She inclined her head. "I-I know." And one day, when this nightmare was over, she'd go back to him. When the pain wasn't so strong.

Tears fell from his eyes, too.

Ryder put his hand on her father's arm. "I want the man's name. He lied to you. He sent your daughter to hell. Give me his name, and give her the justice she deserves."

Her father's breath rasped out. "K-Keith Adams."

Uncle Keith? Vaughn's father?

Then Ryder was heading toward her.

Her gaze strayed—once more—to her father's face. "I love you, Sabine," he told her. "I always have, and I always will."

She couldn't stop her tears. "I love you." Despite it all, she did.

"Lucky bastard," Ryder snarled. "If she didn't care for you, you'd be minus a head right now." He pointed at her father. "Get out of town. Keep her mother safe."

Ryder stopped in front of her. Gently, carefully, he brushed away her tears. "Don't." His voice was gruff. "It hurts me when you cry."

Why would her tears hurt him?

He pressed a kiss to her cheek. "I told you before . . . Don't ever fucking cry for *anyone*."

She didn't know how to stop the tears.

She heard the door shut behind them. The sound was so loud. *That part of my life will never be the same*.

Ryder pulled her against his chest and held her. Strong. Steady.

Slowly, she took deeper breaths. The pain in her chest eased.

Ryder kissed her lips. Such a light, gentle kiss. "The next person who makes you cry"—his words were a rumble—"I'm killing him. Family or not."

Her fierce vampire. She was coming to know him so well. Well enough to say, "You wouldn't hurt my family." Because he wouldn't want to hurt her.

His gaze searched hers. "We have to leave here, Sabine."

Yes. She glanced at the house. She'd been happy there.

Her father was peeking out the window.

It isn't over, Dad. The love she felt wouldn't let it be.

But she loved Rhett, too, and he needed her. "I think we know our next stop now." Because Vaughn had been with her brother when Rhett vanished.

Another betrayal.

"Vaughn's place isn't far away," she whispered. It was a familiar location to her.

Why was the familiar suddenly so painful to face? *Because the familiar hides so many secrets and lies.*

She'd been foolish to think that home was a safe place.

They were being followed.

Ryder had felt the eyes on them, had heard the rustle of footsteps, ever since they'd left the home of Sabine's parents. He'd figured it was better for their prey to follow them. At least, that way, her bastard of a father would have time to drag his sorry ass out of town.

He kept his body close to her as they walked. He wasn't sure if it was his enemies stalking them, hers, or who-the-hell-knew else.

They had a tail. Soon enough, they'd get the bastard to show himself.

They were in front of a small house on the edge of the French Quarter. Time had faded the house, roughened its edges. The place was pretty secluded. Good. That way no one would hear the humans' screams.

Ryder was in the mood to make someone scream.

Sabine is hurting. That fact pissed him off.

She was standing in the shadows and gazing up at the house. Lights glowed from inside the windows. Looked like Keith Adams was waiting up for them.

A trap. Obviously.

"Who's watching us?" Sabine asked. "Is it Dante?"

Ah, so she'd noticed, too. Good. Her vamp hunting instincts were definitely starting to kick in. "If it were Dante, we'd have a circle of fire around us by now." The phoenix wasn't exactly subtle.

"Then who?"

He smiled at her. "Let's find out, love." He pulled

her close. Pressed a quick kiss to her lips. He wanted to take and taste more, but he only allowed himself that little sample of her. "Do me a favor," he said, voice rasping. "Wait one minute, then scream for me."

Her brow furrowed. "What?"

"Scream. Loud. As loudly as you can." He had no doubt that Sabine could be very loud.

Then he slipped away. Finding a perfect vantage point to watch his prey was easy. *Vampires weren't just fast.*

He leapt into the air and easily landed on the side of the roof.

They could do things that humans thought were impossible.

He crouched on his perch. Watched. Waited.

Sabine screamed. The woman had some pretty fantastic lungs.

He saw a shadow jerk away from the darkness on the left side of the property. The shadow stumbled forward, racing toward Sabine and her scream.

Do you think she's weak now? Afraid? That it's your perfect time to attack?

Think again.

Ryder leapt down and crashed right into the fool who was running for Sabine. They hit the ground, tumbling, and when their bodies stopped rolling, Ryder had his claws at the throat of Vaughn Adams. Ryder could easily see the human in the dark. Not the army buddy he'd sought, but the son. He figured one human was as good as the other.

Vaughn tried to yank up his gun. Ryder broke the man's hand. This time, Vaughn was the one to scream.

Sabine rushed toward them. "Where's Rhett?"

Ryder yanked the human to his feet. Vaughn was

groaning and trying to cradle his right hand. So weak. So human.

"Where is my brother?" Sabine demanded. She was fierce. Eyes glaring. Hands clenched into fists. Fury clear to read on her face.

Maybe the human couldn't see all of her rage. He probably could see very little in the dark.

His disadvantage.

Ryder swiped out and let his claws rip open the human's side. The scent of blood filled the air.

"Stop!" Vaughn screamed. "I don't know what the hell is happening—*stop*!"

"He's lying," Ryder said, not about to buy the man's BS. "He was tracking us, hunting us. He started following us the minute we left your father's house."

Vaughn stopped his moaning and groaning. His shoulders straightened. His chin lifted. "Damn right, I did. And I called for backup." He bared his teeth. Really? Was that supposed to be intimidating? A human's teeth? "You're surrounded, vampire. There's no getting away for you this time."

Ryder tilted his head to the right. Listened. Heard nothing. "Try again." Now, he bared *his* teeth. "Or I'll just end this game and rip open your throat."

"*Ryder.*" Sabine's snapping voice. "Get him to tell us where Rhett is, then you can have your bite." She grabbed a fistful of Vaughn's shirt. "Or maybe I'll have one." She sounded deadly.

Sexy.

He liked it when she showed her kick-ass side. That side was starting to peek out, more and more.

But Vaughn shook his head. "You won't get a chance, they're coming—"

Ryder tensed when he heard a growl. A low, animalistic sound. Not the growl of a werewolf, that was rougher, deeper. This sound . . .

He stepped away from the human and scanned the darkness. This sound was different. This sound had every muscle in his body tensing.

Then he was attacked.

Sabine screamed when a blurry form ran at Ryder. The attacker hit him, cutting Ryder's stomach open with a slash of his claws. The attacker moved fast, far too damn fast, and punched with a killing force.

Luckily, Ryder wasn't so easy to kill.

He slashed back with his own claws. Tossed the jerk into the air.

"What the hell?" Vaughn's shocked voice. A voice that shattered into a terrified, pain-filled scream.

Because someone had just taken a bite out of the guy.

A vampire was guzzling the guy's throat, a vamp with dark, matted hair and bloodstained clothes.

That human is my prey. Back the hell off.

Ryder grabbed the vamp and yanked him back. "You don't know who you're screwing with—" Ryder began, more than ready to teach the guy about the vamp hierarchy in this world.

But then he got a look at the vampire's face. At the parch-white skin. The sunken, black eyes. And . . . the fangs.

Not just sharpened canines, like vampires were supposed to have. *All* of this guy's teeth narrowed down to razor-sharp points. And the claws that had cut into Ryder before? He got a good look at them now. Those claws were like long, black knives. *Not* a vampire's normal claws.

Primal. The word whispered through his mind.

Wyatt had warned him, but getting the warning and actually seeing the primal were two way different things.

The vampire was tall, too thin, but there was a hell of a lot of strength in his body. *Too much*.

What all had Wyatt told him? Wyatt had tried to cure the primal with Ryder's blood, but that hadn't worked and—

The primal vampire's attention shifted to Sabine. He licked his lips. "Want . . . you . . ."

Oh, the hell he did.

They want . . . what you want.

The primal vampire ran for Sabine. Before he could grab her, Ryder slammed into the SOB. "She's taken." He drove his fist into the guy's gut and let his own claws swipe and tear.

The vampire just laughed. His fangs came at Ryder's throat.

I'm not on the menu.

Ryder slammed his head into the guy's nose. Bones snapped. Blood gushed.

"Vaughn?" Sabine's voice. She sounded scared. Ryder glanced over at her. She was on the ground, right next to the human. He was shuddering. Convulsing. She put her hands on his chest, obviously trying to hold him down. Her head snapped up and her frantic gaze found him. "Ryder, I think he's dying!"

The night couldn't get any fucking worse.

He focused on the vamp. Then he heard the rumble of tires. The shrill screech of brakes. Footsteps pounded toward them.

Vaughn's backup.

So it *could* get worse.

"I can't stop the blood!" Sabine cried. "It's too much. He's dying!"

No, he wouldn't die. Ryder kept his body between Sabine and the freak who wouldn't take his eyes off her.

Those teeth . . . humans should have known better than to play God. When you fucked with nature, nature fucked back.

The guy in front of him was one giant fuck-up.

"Give her . . . to me." The primal vampire's words were a growl. Not normal speech. Too rough. Too gritted. As if speaking were hard for him.

Had Ryder's blood done this? Or had the primals become this way thanks to the first experiments that Genesis had run on them? *Were they already screwed to hell and back, and my blood just made things worse for them?* Wyatt had said that three primals received Ryder and Sabine's blood. *Three*.

"Give her . . ." the primal vamp growled again.

"Not going to happen." Ryder sucked in a deep breath as he prepared for the next attack. There were three main ways to kill a vampire. First up . . . fire. *No fire here*. Second . . . a stake to the heart. *No wood*. Well, he might be able to rip off part of the fence on the west side of the house, but if he did that, he'd have to leave Sabine. The freak might grab her while Ryder rushed for the weapon. Then the guy would drink from her. *No. Not happening*.

So that just left him with option number three.

Beheading.

Could he take the vamp's head, before the guy took his?

Time to find out.

The humans were coming closer. Racing toward them.

Ryder flexed his fingers. His claws were out. This wouldn't be the first time he'd taken another vampire's head. Not the first, not the last.

But this guy wasn't like the others.

The primal vampire stalked toward them. "Taking . . . *her.*"

No, asshole, I'm taking your head.

With a growl of his own, Ryder attacked.

CHAPTER FOURTEEN

Vaughn was choking on his own blood. Sabine stared down at him, terrified. His eyes were wild. So scared and desperate.

And she remembered sitting on the couch with him and Rhett. Watching scary movies. Eating popcorn.

Swimming in the lake.

Laughing while they roasted marshmallows.

How in the hell had things come to be this way?

"You're going to be okay," she told him, pressing her fingers against his neck. His blood soaked her hand. *The blood wouldn't stop gushing out.* "Hang on, Vaughn, okay? Just *hang on.*"

They shouldn't be enemies. They should just be people. Friends.

And her friend was dying right in front of her.

"Four . . . two . . ."

She leaned toward him. "What is it? I can't understand."

"One . . . nine . . ."

He was telling her numbers? She shook her head.

"Save your strength, okay?" Sabine glanced over her shoulder. Ryder and the other vampire—*what was wrong with him? Why did he look that way?*—were running toward each other. Both had their claws up. They were yelling and they hit in a thud of bodies. Fists pounded. Claws flew.

The other vampire was going for Ryder's neck. His claws cut into Ryder's skin.

"No!" Sabine screamed.

Ryder lunged up, his claws slicing back at his attacker.

Her mouth hung open in shock, and then she had to look away.

Ryder had . . . he'd . . . just taken the vampire's head off.

Her eyes squeezed shut. That sound, that slush that she'd heard right before the vampire's head toppled back . . .

Vaughn had stilled beneath her hands. Her eyes opened and she stared back at him. His face had gone slack. "Vaughn?" She shook him.

He felt cold to her. He shouldn't be that cold, not so soon. His body should still be warm. Not so icy. Not yet. *Not ever.*

"Vaughn!" Footsteps thudded behind her. She didn't look over her shoulder. She knew those footsteps had to be Ryder's.

He'd taken the other vampire's head. With one slice of his claws. But she couldn't think about that. Not then.

Vaughn wasn't moving. The blood was thick on the ground beneath him.

Ryder's hands wrapped around her. He lifted her against him. "The humans are coming."

She felt numb. Vaughn was—

Moving?

His mouth was opening wide, and he started to groan. A low, pain-filled sound.

Relief rushed through her. Vaughn was alive!

His hands flew into the air, and—and claws were sprouting from his fingertips. Long, thick, black claws.

His mouth was open so wide because his teeth were growing, elongating into sharp points. Every. Single. Tooth.

Ryder jerked her back, keeping his tight hold on her. "Son of a bitch."

Vaughn rolled over. Slowly rose to his hands and knees as his back bowed. *"Help . . . me!"*

Sabine tried to reach for him. Ryder just wrapped his arms tighter around her. Hauled her farther back.

Then, over Vaughn's growing screams and the desperate pounding of her own heart, Sabine heard footsteps. Her head swung to the left. To the right. Men in black cargo pants and bulletproof vests were surrounding them. And leading those men, she recognized Keith Adams, Vaughn's father.

"What the hell did you do to my son?" Keith demanded. He had a small gun in his hands. A gun currently aimed at Sabine's chest.

She couldn't help but wonder if, like her father's weapon, that gun was loaded with wooden bullets, too.

"We didn't do anything." Ryder wasn't letting her go. His body vibrated with fury. "You can thank Genesis for this one. They're the ones who wanted to build bigger, stronger vampires."

Keith staggered back. His gaze went to the ground. To the fallen vampire and his disconnected head. The vamp's mouth was wide open, and you could see his mouthful of fangs.

Keith's horrified gaze flew back to Vaughn. "No, son, *no!*"

But there was no denying what was happening to Vaughn. He was screaming and crying and his body kept twisting as the brutal change swept over him.

Sabine held herself still in Ryder's arms.

"I'm going to kill them all," Ryder whispered the words in her ear, barely seeming to breathe them.

She counted seven men. All with their eyes on Vaughn, not her or Ryder. All appearing frozen with horror.

One of their own was changing right before their eyes.

"I'll kill them all," Ryder said again, "and you stay behind me. It'll be fast, I promise. Just close your eyes, and you don't even have to see what I do to them."

She had no doubt that he could kill all of those humans in just moments. She knew how fast he could move. How strong he was. He could take their heads easily or cut their throats.

"No," Sabine whispered. She didn't want more blood on her hands. She already had enough coating her fingers.

"I'm not going back into a cage." Anger now, rage, roughening Ryder's words. "Not even for you, love."

Then he pushed her behind him.

He sprang at Keith.

Only . . .

Keith was firing his weapon. Aiming not for Ryder, but pointing his gun at Vaughn.

Vaughn . . . who was on his feet. Chest heaving. Body shaking.

Vaughn . . . who was rushing toward Sabine, snarling and opening his mouth to take a bite.

The bullet slammed into his chest. Another blasted into Vaughn. A third.

Vaughn fell to the ground.

Keith looked up.

Too late, Keith. Too late.

Because Ryder was at his side. Ryder had his claws at Keith's throat.

"Tell them to drop their weapons," Ryder's voice was deadly calm.

Keith didn't speak, but he gave a fast gesture with his hand. All of the humans immediately tossed their weapons to the ground.

"Good," Ryder praised and offered a hard smile to the man. "For that, you can die quickly."

"Ryder!" Sabine hurried toward him. "Don't!"

Keith's eyes, grief-stricken, lost, met hers. "This wasn't supposed to happen."

No, she was sure that she and Ryder were the ones who were supposed to be on the ground.

"I-I wanted to help you," Keith muttered. His throat was bleeding. Ryder's claws were sinking into the skin. "When I found out what Genesis was really doing . . ." His Adam's apple bobbed as he swallowed and Ryder's claws sank deeper into him. "Since then . . . I-I've been trying to get you out . . . trying to save the others."

It was too late for saving them.

"My son . . . *my own son.*" Tears slipped down his cheeks.

Sabine realized all of Keith's guards had frozen. No one was moving. No one seemed to know *what* to do.

She took a deep breath and closed the distance between her and Keith. "Were those wooden bullets?" she asked him. Wooden bullets on vampire prey.

Keith nodded.

"He's not dead," Ryder said, sounding almost bored. "Down, but not dead. Guess you couldn't go straight for the heart with your own son, huh? And you couldn't order your men to take that heart shot, either."

Her gaze cut to Ryder. *"Stop."*

He lifted his brows.

"Take your claws away from his throat," she demanded. It was all too damn much. Rage was pumping through her own body. Hot. Blistering. Vaughn . . . turned? Keith shooting his own son? Her dad betraying her.

Too much.

Ryder's eyes widened. Then he let go of Keith. Instead of backing away, Ryder grabbed for her. Figured. When had the vamp ever backed away?

His hands wrapped around her arms. "Sabine?" He shook her once, lightly. He didn't sound so bored then. He sounded worried.

She took another deep breath and could have almost sworn that she tasted ash on her tongue.

"Sabine . . ." His voice had dropped, become an intimate caress.

She met his stare. Tried to pull more air into lungs that suddenly felt starved for oxygen.

"Breathe," he whispered to her. "Everything is going to be all right. You know I'll keep you safe."

She didn't feel like she really knew anything anymore. But she sucked in more deep breaths. Tried to calm a heartbeat that raced too fast. Her eyes stayed on his.

Finally, *finally,* the air stopped tasting like ash on her tongue.

She realized that Ryder was staring at her with a deep, intense gaze.

"Is your control back?" Ryder asked softly.

Back? When had she lost it?

But she gave a nod. His arms wrapped around her shoulders. She realized that the humans were just standing there, waiting.

For what?

Keith's head hung down, his chin almost touching his chest. Blood dripped onto his shirt. "Vaughn . . . he and I . . . we both wanted to make things right."

What was right anymore? Sabine wasn't sure she knew.

Keith's head lifted. "He was trying to protect Rhett. We knew Genesis had a hit on him. Once we realized what they were really doing, we put a plant inside the facility. *We were trying to help.*"

Ryder stared dispassionately at him. "You want to help? Get the hell out of our way and *stay* out of our way." His arm was a warm weight over her shoulders. "Because if I see you again, I will kill you." A vow.

She gazed at Keith and shook her head. "How were you going to help me?"

"There's another doctor." He licked his lips, glanced over at Vaughn's still body, and drew in a ragged breath. "She's not like Wyatt. She doesn't want to hurt anyone. She wants to *help* the supernaturals."

Right. Like she hadn't heard that one before. "Come on," Sabine said to Ryder. "Let's go."

"She's not experimenting on anyone!" Keith's voice broke. "She's just fixing the mistakes that Wyatt made."

Like she'd trust another human in a lab coat.

Her gaze darted to Keith. Before they left, she had to know one thing. "Where's my brother?"

But he shook his head. "I-I don't know. Vaughn was

sent to secure him. To get him to a safe location before . . ."

Before someone else could put a bullet in his head?

"Find out," Ryder told the man. "Find out, and you
send the location to me at Bran's Castle."

Keith nodded. His gaze swung back to Vaughn. "She
can fix him."

The words were so low that Sabine barely caught his
murmur, but when the words registered, she frowned.

"There's no going back once you become a vampire," Ryder snapped. So he'd heard the man's murmur,
too. "And you need to put him down, for good. That bite
spread the virus. Wyatt mutated his vampires. They
aren't like me. They're—"

"Primal," Keith whispered. Sick horror filled his
eyes. "I know."

"Then you know the only way to stop your son is to
kill him." Ryder's hold on Sabine pushed her forward.
"So if you really want to help him, put the man out of
his misery."

Her heart ached.

She could only imagine what Keith's heart felt like.
Maybe like it had been ripped from his chest?

Unable to help herself, Sabine looked back over her
shoulder. The humans were retrieving their guns and
closing in on Vaughn's prone body.

He didn't take Sabine back to Bran's Castle. Her
body shook against his, her rage and pain so clear on
her face that it almost hurt to look at her.

She should have let me kill them all.

But she was soft inside. Sentimental.

Still human in that respect.

He braked his motorcycle—one he'd kept stored at Bran's Castle—near the edge of the St. Louis Cemetery. "Where do you feel safe?" he asked as he turned to face her.

Her gaze was so dark and deep. But before, when she'd faced off against the humans, her gaze had changed.

For an instant, I saw flames.

Ryder knew that his growing suspicions about her were right. She wasn't vampire, at least, not completely. The power of the phoenix was still inside her, struggling desperately to get out.

Which side would win? The vamp side? The phoenix? Or would they both just tear her apart?

I won't let that happen. He would do anything necessary to protect her, even if he had to protect Sabine from herself.

"Where do you feel safe?" he pushed her. Because wherever the hell that was, he would take her there. Her trust in her family and friends had been ripped away. She needed reassurance, and he'd damn well give it to her. She needed—

"With you." A soft confession.

He blinked.

Her lips lifted in a sad smile. "It's probably crazy, I know it is, but I feel safe when I'm with you."

He could only stare at her. Did the woman realize just how much power she was starting to wield over him?

No one. No one had ever made him feel the way she did. No one else ever would.

Her legs were on either side of his. Her body hugged his.

And each breath that he took made him need her more.

He wanted to take her out of the city. Get her as far away from everyone else as he could. They could disappear. Vanish. He had plenty of money. They could start a life somewhere else.

Anywhere else.

Jaw locking, Ryder turned away from her and revved the motor. Her arms curled around his stomach, and he felt her put her head over his shoulder blade. The woman *fit* his body. So well.

Too well.

His gaze cut into the dark. Were more enemies watching? Seeing the weakness that he couldn't deny?

The motorcycle flew away from the corner. Ripped through the waning night.

He took them from the city. Away from the lights of the town and away from the danger that waited in New Orleans.

"A cabin." Her voice came quietly, barely rising over the growl of the motorcycle. "At the edge of the swamp. We'd go there all the time when I was a kid."

Her safe place?

I'm her safe place.

"Take the next exit," she told him as her hold tightened. "Then turn right."

The motorcycle sped off the exit ramp. Rushed around the narrow turn.

"Go straight. Drive until the road ends."

He'd do anything to make the sadness leave her voice.

He followed her instructions, taking the turns, and glancing back to make sure that no headlights appeared in the distance. The road looked empty.

Appearances could be so very deceptive.

Then they were barreling down a small, dirt road. A gate waited up ahead with a No Trespassing sign hanging from its gates.

Ryder drove right through the sagging gates. The cabin waited near the edge of the water. Small, but it looked clean.

He parked the bike in the back. Then Ryder let Sabine lead the way inside. She took a key from beneath a brick—did they always hide their keys in such a spot? And she opened the door, ushering him inside.

He expected the cabin to smell musty, closed-in, but the area was filled with a sweet, light scent.

The place was as clean on the inside as it was on the outside. A tidy table. A comfortable couch. The walls were lined with pictures of a much younger Sabine and her brother.

Damn but she'd been a cute kid. A heartbreaker, even when she'd had long pigtails.

"I was happy here. Always . . ." She rolled her shoulders. "But I guess it was stupid to come here. My dad or Rhett could have told Genesis about this place."

He pulled her into his arms. Pressed his mouth to hers. "Let them come." Didn't she understand yet? No one was going to take her again. He wasn't leaving her side, no matter what the hell happened next.

Her hands rose to his shoulders. Held tight. He liked the bite of her nails on his skin. Liked *her* bite more.

He kissed her again and his tongue pushed into her mouth. The kiss wasn't wild or rough, not like before. Because this time, he wanted to comfort her.

To make her feel safe.

He kept the kiss light. A hard task, when his instincts demanded that he take. When Ryder felt his body tightening, he pulled his mouth from hers. Ryder pressed his forehead against Sabine's. "You're not alone."

She'd never be.

He caught her hand. Pulled her toward the couch. She looked up at him, so sexy that she made him ache. His cock was fully erect, eager for her.

But this time, she needed more.

"My family betrayed me, too." A confession that few had ever heard from him, but he wanted to share his past with her.

She sat down on the edge of the couch and stared up at him. Waited. Her lips were red from his mouth.

"I've walked the earth for a very, very long time, Sabine." Longer than she probably realized. He'd stopped aging long ago. "As far as I know, I was the first vampire."

Her eyes widened. "You—"

"I took a sickness when I was human. A disease that ravaged through me, seeming to consume me from the inside out." He could still hear the sound of his own desperate screams. His mother's wild pleas for help.

Help had finally come.

But it hadn't been what he'd expected.

"The disease spread to others in my family." A plague, that was what they would call it in the Middle Ages. A virus. A sickness, now.

"I recovered." Flat. He held her gaze. "Most did not. Only my brother and I were spared. Everyone else . . . they perished." The deaths hadn't been easy. So much suffering. Agony. The bodies had been twisted. Spotted. Blackened. The rotting stench had filled the air. Death had come to his land.

"My brother was weakened from the disease. He could barely walk. His skin was mottled, scarred, but

I—I was fine within a few nights." His body had been strong.

Too strong.

"My blood has always been different." Or else the virus would have ravaged him, too. "Something was . . . off with me." He'd known it from the time he was just a child. There had been a darkness in him. An instinctive urge to *hunt*. To be the predator.

To destroy prey.

Evil? Maybe. Maybe that's what he was. But he'd always tried to fight his deadly instincts, as best he could.

"Within just a few days, I noticed the new . . . hunger."

Her gaze locked on his. "For blood."

He nodded. "My teeth burned in my mouth. They stretched. Sharpened. My senses became more acute. When I touched my servant's neck, I could hear the whoosh of his blood." His hands fisted. "The first time I drank, I killed."

She swallowed.

Tell her all. Show her the beast. "I enjoyed the kill."

The silence in the room was deafening, but though Sabine tensed, she didn't try to run from him. She just kept sitting there, staring up at him with those dark eyes of hers.

So he told her more. "I killed others. My hunger was insatiable. I wanted the blood. I gorged myself on it. In those first days, I was half-mad. A beast that had survived hell and wanted only blood."

Human food had no longer been able to sustain him. "Many tried to kill me."

But their weapons hadn't worked against him. Not any longer. They could slice his flesh or break his bones, but he quickly healed from those injuries.

"I was stronger, faster, so my attackers were the ones who died." And the blood kept flowing.

"Why are you telling me this?" Sabine demanded.

"Because I want you to *see* what I am." *And to stay with me anyway.* The whisper came from deep within. He ignored it. She had no choice. She had to stay with him. Too many were after her. To survive, Sabine needed his protection.

"I know what you are." Her words were stark. Sad.

He flinched. *I killed you, so yes, you do know.* His hands fisted. "I told you . . . one of my brothers survived, but he was weak from the sickness." Weak and still diseased. The scent of death had clung to him. "I . . . wanted to help him." Because even though the bloodlust had created a monster in him, the man inside had still fought to rise to the surface. "My body was different. I knew that. So I thought that my blood must be different, too."

There had been no doctors then. Just those who dealt in false magic and barbaric "healing" techniques. Even before he'd gone to his brother's side, Malcolm had been bled. Again and again.

By the time Ryder had gone to him, Malcolm had already been near death.

"I wasn't sure how to transform him. With the others, I hadn't cared." Humans, but he'd tossed them aside like they were nothing. *See me for what I am.* "But I wanted to save him." No, he'd needed to save Malcolm.

"I gave him my blood. Forced him to drink, but nothing happened." He'd been so furious. He'd paced in his brother's room for hours and hours. But Malcolm had stayed pale and weak. "I gave him more. Kept forcing him to drink. He . . . fought me."

And that was when it had happened.

"When I fought back, my hunger rose." The scent of blood had been all around him. He hadn't been strong enough to hold on to his control. "I bit his arm. His blood poured into me. He started to shake and convulse. I-I gave him more of my blood, still thinking it would help him."

And, in a way, it had.

"That's how you learned how to create other vampires," Sabine said softly. "When you saved your brother."

"Malcolm didn't exactly think of it as a saving." But Ryder nodded. "But it was after that moment, when I took his blood and gave him back my own . . . it was then that he changed." Already so close to death, Ryder had thought that he'd lost his brother.

But Malcolm's pallor had changed. The stiffness had faded away from his body. His eyes had opened. He'd . . .

Had the same consuming hunger that Ryder felt.

And the same loss of control.

How many had they killed in those first months? How much blood had they taken? There had been screams. Death.

Then they'd realized that there was more they could do. Not just drinking and killing.

Control.

"We learned that if we fed on humans and let them live, we could slip into their minds. We could control them completely, with just a thought." A heady power. One he'd abused. One he'd abuse again.

She pulled her lower lip between her teeth. Bit it lightly. Then asked, "Can you control me?"

He stared back at her.

"*Have* you?"

He wouldn't lie to her. Others, sure, without a qualm. But not to her. "I tried."

Her eyes narrowed.

"But you weren't human. Your mind didn't work like theirs. Every time I tried to reach you, I just saw a wall of fire." He hadn't been lying when he told her that before.

She rubbed her hands over the couch cushions. "And now? Since I'm like you? Do you still see the fire?"

"You're not like me," he muttered. He was still working that part out. "And I haven't tried to control you since we left Genesis." Not even when she'd left him. It had felt wrong.

"Try now."

He shook his head.

Her brows rose. "Why not?"

"I don't want to control you." Control . . . that had been Malcolm's thing. The more blood he'd taken, the more control he'd wanted. Ryder knew that he and Malcolm had both changed. All of a sudden, it had seemed that they'd had the power of gods, while they were surrounded by mere men.

Sex. Blood. Death.

But Ryder had finally found his control. Finally pulled back.

Malcolm hadn't. "My brother was older than me." By a year. "He'd always been the leader, the one who would rule after my father, but . . . with the change, he was weaker—"

"Weaker than you?" she finished, head tilting back.

He couldn't read the emotions in her eyes, and he wanted to know what she was thinking.

"My blood made him, but though he was strong, I was stronger."

"Because you were the first." Her whisper. And she seemed to finally understand.

I was the first vampire.

Long before the legend of Vlad the Impaler, Ryder had been roaming the earth. Ryder didn't know of another who'd been cursed by the bloodlust . . . until he awoke with the hunger.

Hell, it had been at least a few centuries later before he'd met Vlad on a blood-filled night.

"My brother didn't want someone else to be stronger than him. Malcolm wanted to rule. He wanted the humans at his feet." Malcolm had wanted to change the world. To show the humans just what they should fear.

And the stories had started to spread then. Stories about men who hunted during the night. Who drank blood. Who killed. Who terrified.

"I saw what happened." He turned his back to her. Paced across the room. His gaze fell on a picture of Sabine. She looked about sixteen. Smiling from ear to ear as she stood on a sun-soaked deck. "The humans turned on each other. They killed, *each other,* because they thought the monsters were among them." *And they were. Only the fools were killing the wrong ones.* "They tortured innocents. Slaughtered. And my brother was there, laughing at it all. Even holding court over some of the proceedings."

Malcolm had enjoyed it all. Enjoyed having those he *knew* to be just humans brought before him. Malcolm had ordered their blood drained. Ordered them sliced open. Ordered so many atrocities.

His shoulders stiffened as the memories flooded through him. "Malcolm could have taught Wyatt a great deal about torture."

He remembered the screams. Bones—broken. Bodies—slowly cut in half. The Middle Ages had been the worst time. So many ways to torture, ways that made the victims take so long to die.

The screams stay with me.

"I knew I had to stop him." Malcolm's madness had infected the humans, not just because he was controlling their minds, but because the hysteria spread so widely and quickly. "I wanted to stop the death." It had sickened him, and the knowledge that pained him the most . . .

I started it. His blood had transformed Malcolm. If he'd just let his brother die, then so many other lives would have been spared.

"I went to him. Got him away from the followers he kept so close." Malcolm had always been eager to make more vampires, though they hadn't actually been called vampires, not back then. No one had called them vampires until centuries later.

Back then, they'd just been blood drinkers. Monsters. Later, his kind had become *vykolakas* or *strigoi*. And, finally, vampire.

"You killed him," she said, her voice without emotion.

He glanced back at her. "Actually, he tried to kill me first." A perfect setup. "I was still trying to save him. Trying to stop his madness, when he drove a sword into my heart."

The blade had been silver. *Silver didn't kill me, brother.* But the blow had weakened him. "During his tortures, my brother had been experimenting."

Just like Wyatt. His jaw locked. Ryder hated experiments. And the monsters who enjoyed them. "He killed humans, but he also made vampires . . . made them, then killed them, just so he could learn our weaknesses."

You don't understand. You've changed. Malcolm's charge to him. *We can have everything. We can drink this world dry.*

Ryder hadn't been thirsty any longer. He'd controlled his cravings. Been able to think past the bloodlust.

"He used the sword to maximize my blood loss, to weaken me." If Ryder had been a normal "transformed" vampire, the attack would have worked. But Malcolm's "experiments" had been off. Because Ryder wasn't like the others. "While I was on the ground, bleeding out, he went for my head." His brother hadn't wanted to take any chances. He'd attacked quickly, going for a brutal kill. Ryder rubbed his neck, remembering that long-ago day. Time couldn't erase some memories. Not the darkest ones.

Sabine rose and came toward him with slow steps. Her hand lifted and touched the skin of his throat. Her fingers felt like they were wrapped in silk. "But you stopped him."

He offered her a small smile. "No, love, Malcolm drove that sword's blade into my throat, and I choked on my own blood."

Her lips parted in shock.

"But the first blow of the sword didn't completely sever my head. My brother should have used a sharper blade." *His* mistake. "So I fought back. Not with my body, because it was all but useless. I used my mind." He'd made a shocking discovery then. "I could control the others. Every vampire he'd made. Every vampire I'd made." His control hadn't been limited to humans.

"In those desperate moments, I reached out, and I could feel them all."

Every single one.

He'd felt a rush of power so intense then that his body had shuddered.

"I sent out one order to the vampires. Just one . . . kill Malcolm."

Her fingers trembled against his throat.

"And my brother stared into my eyes. He took the sword, and he plunged it into his own chest even as he screamed at me."

"Ryder . . ."

"The others came. He wasn't dead. They attacked him. Hitting. Punching. Clawing. Tearing into him. He kept screaming, but he wasn't fighting them. He could scream, but he couldn't fight."

She didn't stop touching him. Why? He was telling her everything. She knew his darkness. But she was leaning closer to him. "How did you get away?" Sabine asked.

"I made them give me blood." He'd taken and taken. "They dragged my brother's body away. Buried him." What had been left of him.

"Then what did you do?"

"I tried to stop the monsters I'd made. Tried to pull them back, but by that point, there were too many of us." He expelled a rough breath. "I hunted the worst of the vampires. Killed them. Staked those who slaughtered innocents and enjoyed the bloodbath." *Confess.* "Though I was little better than they were. But I tried to be. I swear, I *tried to be.*"

Her fingertips rested over his pounding pulse. "How long did you hunt?"

"I'm still hunting." A dark truth. "I'm the one who created the vampires, so it's my job to take out the monsters who live to torture and destroy." His job—his penance.

"I know the rage you carry," he said, and Ryder was careful not to touch her. "You feel betrayed. You trusted your family." This she had to understand. "But family can and will turn on you. Especially if . . ."

"If you're a monster?"

"If *they* are the monsters. And humans can be just as evil and twisted as any beast stalking in the night."

"Yes," she agreed with her steady gaze, "they can be." Then her fingers slid over his neck, lightly caressing his skin once more. "How close did you come to death that day?"

"Too close." Close enough to know that he didn't want to see whatever hell waited for him on the other side.

She leaned up on her toes, and her lips brushed over his throat. Over the phantom wound that had long since faded. "I'm sorry."

She was apologizing to him? What the hell for?

"I couldn't imagine killing my brother."

No, she loved Rhett. Once, he'd loved Malcolm. Looked up to his brother. Fought death to save his brother's life.

"But what would you do . . ." Ryder had to ask her this. He'd told her his story, and he had to ask, "If your Rhett tried to kill you?"

Her lips pressed over his racing pulse. Then she pulled back, just enough to look up into his gaze. Her lashes were long and dark, shadowing her eyes. "I don't know."

"Could you kill him? If it came down to a choice . . . you or him . . . *could* you do it?"

"I hope I don't ever have to find out."

It wasn't an answer. He needed more from her. "Your father sent you to those men at Genesis. What if your brother comes after you? You want to save him, the same way I wanted to save Malcolm." Maybe this was really the reason he'd told her about his twisted past. "When the time comes and you're forced to choose, will you choose death for him? Or will you sacrifice yourself for him?"

She just stared back at him, and Ryder realized that she didn't know what she'd do.

He understood then just what he'd have to do. If Sabine couldn't fight back against those who would betray her, then he'd damn well take them out.

She could hate him. She could fight him. But she *would* live.

All of the others would die.

Vampire law. His law. *You don't hurt what's mine*.

No one would hurt her and keep living. No. One.

Rhett yanked his hand free of the rope, sending blood spattering behind him. His wrist was ripped open, thanks to all the sawing he'd had to do on the rope. But he was free now.

He'd shouted until his throat ached. That rat bastard Vaughn hadn't come back. No one had come.

He used his bloody hand to yank at the other bonds. His ankles were raw, more damage from the ropes, but with some tugs and twists and a hell of a lot of hoarse "fucks," he managed to get free of those bonds.

Then he was on his feet. His first step almost sent him tumbling right down on his face. The ropes had been too tight. There wasn't enough circulation in his feet. They were numb. They were—

On fire as feeling surged back into them.

His teeth ground together as he forced himself to move. He had to get out of there. Had to find a phone and call for help.

Got to find Sabine. Because if Vaughn had gone after her . . .

The floor creaked. Not the floor he was standing on. The creak had come from the other room, just beyond his door. The building had been dead silent for so long that the quiet sound shocked him.

Rhett's heart slammed into his chest. *Vaughn was back*. Rhett scrambled back. Light streamed into his room now, faint light that came through the cracks in the boards that lined the windows. He grabbed the chair he'd been sitting in and lifted it over his head. It wouldn't be much of a weapon, but he'd do whatever the hell he had to do—

In order to survive.

But the man who opened the door wasn't Vaughn. The guy was some big, rough-looking bastard with black hair and glinting eyes. The guy smirked as he took in Rhett's weapon and bloody form.

I know him. Rhett's eyes narrowed. This was the SOB who'd burned down The Rift! Rhett had seen him.

"Good thing I was the one to find you and not some vamp." The man lifted one black brow. "Or else feeding time would be going on right about now."

"Who the hell are you?" Rhett didn't attack, not yet. Mostly because his arms weren't exactly feeling steady. *Need another second. Just gathering my strength, then I'll attack*.

"What do you think your sister will do in order to get you back?" the man asked, lifting a hand to scratch his chin. "Do you think she'd trade her life for yours? Maybe trade the life of her vampire lover?"

"Who the fuck are you?"

The guy's smirk just got bigger.

And Rhett had gathered his strength. He attacked, launching forward with the chair.

The guy grabbed the chair before Rhett could slam it into his head. The man's fingers wrapped around the wood. "I'm someone you *don't* want as an enemy."

His eyes weren't dark any longer. There was a circle of orange—red?—around his pupils. As if . . . as if his eyes were burning.

The wood began to smoke beneath the man's hand. Tendrils of smoke drifted into the air. Then the wood caught on fire. Big, bright flames erupted along the surface of the broken chair.

Rhett jerked his hand away and leapt back.

"I told you, be glad I'm not a vampire." The chair burned to ash in a blaze that matched the fire in the man's eyes.

No, not a vampire, but . . . "What are you?" Rhett's voice was hoarse, thanks to all the damn screaming and yelling he'd done.

But the guy wasn't answering him. He was too busy touching the wall to his right. Just his touch sent flames licking up the old wood and rushing toward the ceiling.

"Stop!" Rhett yelled—or tried to yell. But, oh hell, screw stopping the guy. He just needed to get away from him. So Rhett rushed forward. He plowed his fist into the guy's face—shit, that blow scorched his knuckles— and tried to lunge through the doorway.

But the hulking guy just laughed and grabbed hold

of his arm. "It's not that easy." He looked over at the flames. They were burning bright and hot. "We'll send a little message to your sister, then we'll let her find us."

"If you're killing me, do it," Rhett snarled. The guy's hold was burning into his skin. "I'm not going to let you use me against Sabine." The way Vaughn had wanted to use him.

"Of course, you will." He said it as if there had never been any doubt. "You're just human." The guy shrugged. "What else are you gonna do?"

Kill your ass. He was just close enough to do the job. Cocky supernatural. Thinking humans weren't a threat. "I didn't know if Vaughn would be coming for me, or if it would be someone else."

Blisters were on his skin. Blisters and blood and he was tired of being a punching bag.

Rhett said, "But even if a vampire had come through that door, I wasn't gonna go down without a fight."

That stupid smirk was getting on his nerves.

"Why fight?" the man asked. "The result will be the same. You'll lose."

"No." But Rhett stopped fighting. For the moment. *Let him think I'm weak.* "You will." Then he brought up his left hand—with the broken chair leg that he'd kept hidden—and he stabbed that chunk of wood right into the pyro's chest.

The guy's eyes widened with surprise.

"Guess you didn't see that coming," Rhett said as he twisted the chunk of wood.

The SOB's hand fell away. His body sagged to the floor.

"Stop underestimating humans," Rhett bit out. He turned away. Rushed through the door.

The crackle of flames grew louder behind him. Rhett didn't bother trying to pull the man's body from the fire. Even a vamp couldn't rise with a stake in his heart.

The fire kept spreading.

Rhett rushed away from the flames.

CHAPTER FIFTEEN

Dawn had come. The light spilled through the thin curtains at the cabin. Sabine knew Ryder wanted something from her, she could see it in his eyes.

She just didn't know what he needed.

Would she kill her brother? No. She wouldn't. Not Rhett. Never him. But it wasn't going to come down to that. "I trust Rhett."

"The way you trusted your father?"

He was pushing her. If he kept that up, she'd push back.

"Betrayal hurts, it's a wound that doesn't heal, not with any kind of time."

She wouldn't step away from him. Right then, Sabine wanted to be close to her vampire. "How many times have you been betrayed?"

"Too many to count."

Brutal.

"But I made sure to always pay back those who betrayed me."

Yes, she was rather sure his payback was a biting bitch. She kept her hands on his shoulders as she eased back down until her feet were flat on the floor. *Don't kiss him again. Not yet.* When she kissed him, she just thought of sex. She needed to ask him more questions. This was her chance to actually unravel the mystery that was Ryder.

She wasn't giving up this chance. Even if she did want to strip him naked.

He looked good naked.

Sabine cleared her throat. "How did you wind up in Genesis?" He knew how she'd been tossed into that cage. What about him?

"Another betrayal." He inclined his head toward her. "Some vampires sent me right into a trap. One I stupidly didn't see."

"Have you gotten your payback?"

His gaze seemed to see past her. "A human owned the motel they sent me to. They said . . . said there was one of our kind there who needed my help. I went, but the human just sprung the trap. You see, he *sold* paranormals to Genesis. He sold me. Probably dozens more, too."

"What did you do to him?"

"I sent him to hell."

She should have been afraid of him. Any sane woman would have been scared.

She wasn't afraid. Maybe she wasn't sane, either. "Do you know who the others are that betrayed you?"

"Two vampires are already dead, but there were more."

The puzzle pieces slipped into place for her. "When we went into that bar, Bran—"

"I wanted word to spread that I was free. Those who worked against me . . . now they'll know that I'm back. Soon I'll be hunting them."

"Or they'll be hunting you." Would they just sit back and wait for death to come? Not likely. They'd fight. Try to attack first.

He simply stared back at her. "Let them come. There isn't another vampire on this earth who is stronger than me."

She had a flash of the vampire who'd attacked Vaughn. Her heartbeat kicked up. "What about that freak who came after us before? The one who bit Vaughn?"

"I can handle the primals."

Primals?

"They're . . . after you." His words were halting.

Surprise barely flickered in her. Because, sure, whatever, *of course* they would be. Was there anyone who wasn't after her? "Why?" Sabine asked. But she really wanted to know . . . *why can't they all just leave me alone*?

"Wyatt made them. At least two others that I know about. I can't control them, but I can kick their asses."

Her heart kept beating too fast. "Made them how?"

"He used my blood. He injected it into test subjects that he'd been experimenting on for years. The blood amped up their power. Made them into something else."

Something right out of a nightmare.

"But why do they want me?" Maybe she would be better off not knowing this part, but sticking her head into the sand wasn't exactly an option that she wanted to take.

"Because I do." Gravel-rough. "With my blood,

somehow, they got my cravings. I think Wyatt linked you and me. Made me want you. Made me—"

"Crave?" His word. But wasn't that just the way she felt? Like she craved his touch? His body? The wild pleasure he could give her?

She'd worried that the emotions she felt were too intense around Ryder. Were the feelings she had the result of some experiment? Was she not even controlling herself any longer?

"I've never wanted anyone this way before," he said. His pupils spread, pushing darkness across his eyes. "So badly that I'd do just about anything in order to have you."

"J-just about?"

"You know all of me."

She could taste him.

Could feel him.

Her breasts ached. Her sex . . .

"If you want to run from me, that might be wise."

She tried to control her breathing. Tried not to look like she was panting.

Ryder shook his head. "But the truth is that even if you ran, I'd follow you."

Because he craved her? Because Wyatt might have drugged him? Her?

"I don't even care why I'm this way." His hands finally came up. Curled around her hips. Brought her against the—wow, yeah, that was some serious arousal there. "I just want you. I *need* you, and to hell with the reason why."

Okay. Her mouth opened for his. His tongue pushed past her lips even as her fingers sank into his hair. Their bodies brushed, the need spiked higher, and Sabine realized that, right then, she didn't care why she wanted him so much.

She simply needed him.

His hands went to the snap of her jeans. She heard a *pop,* then the *hiss* as her zipper was lowered. His hand pushed inside her jeans. Eased past her underwear. His fingers brushed over her sex.

She stiffened, then tried to widen her stance. Sabine wanted to feel more of him.

"Already wet," Ryder whispered against her mouth, "and you feel so damn good when you squeeze around me." His tongue tasted her. "So. Damn. Good." His fingers thrust inside of her.

She pushed against his hand, wanting a harder touch. Arousal had her blood pumping faster in her veins. Her nipples were tight points, and she wanted his mouth on them. Wanted the wild rush of pleasure that he gave to her.

He gives the pleasure.

Her hands slid to his shoulders.

The last time they'd been naked, he'd given her so much pleasure that she'd gone a little crazy.

His fingers pushed into her. She gasped into his mouth.

In another few minutes, he'd have worked her to orgasm. Just with the skillful roll and thrust of his fingers. The man knew how to touch.

She knew how to kiss. She'd always been good with her mouth.

Her tongue slid lightly over his. Teasing now, when she wanted to sink into him. *Hold back. Give to him.* Sabine knew it was time for a fair exchange between them.

Time to blow his mind.

No, maybe it was just time to blow him.

She caught his lower lip between her teeth. Bit lightly. Sucked the small wound.

His hand pushed harder between her legs. Two fingers were in her now. Stretching, thrusting.

She lowered her hand and wrapped her fingers around his wrist, stilling him.

Then she bit his lip again. Because she could. A harder nip.

They both needed the rush of pleasure. Life was hell. The devil was chasing them. Maybe they couldn't trust anyone else, but they had each other.

"I want you." She breathed the words and knew the desire she felt had to be reflected in her gaze.

His gaze promised so much pleasure. He tried to pull his hand free.

Sabine shook her head.

He frowned.

Then she pushed his hand away from her. Slowly and *ah*—she couldn't quite hold back that little moan of pleasure when his fingers brushed over her clit.

His lips parted.

She swallowed and kept lifting his hand. Then she pressed her hand against the wall, right beside his. "Lift the other one," she told him.

Raising a brow, he lifted his other hand and pressed it back against the wall.

"Stay just like that," she told him.

"Why?" Not moving. Obeying, for now.

"Because when you touch me, I lose control, and I need that control." Her hands went to his jeans. Unsnapped. Lowered the zipper. "For now," Sabine added.

His teeth had sharpened. He wanted to bite her.

She wanted his bite.

But she wanted to taste him, more.

She lowered his jeans. Ryder kicked them—and his boots—away. He kept his hands up on the wall.

Good.

His cock pushed toward her, rising from the dark thatch of hair at the top of his powerful thighs. His cock was long, wide, the head already glistening with moisture. Her hand curled around the thick length, and she stroked him, from root to tip. Slowly. *Slowly.*

Then . . .

Harder.

Faster.

"Sabine." His voice was deeper. She liked that. Her head was leaning forward as she caressed him and—

His teeth nipped her throat.

A pulse of pleasure shot straight from the small bite right to her core. She trembled. Her sex clenched. "Not . . . yet." Her head tilted back. She stared into his face, was stunned by the stark need she saw there. No one had ever looked at her that way before.

Because of some drug? Because of an experiment? No, she wouldn't let that be the reason. Ryder would want her, Ryder *did* want her because of the way they made each other feel.

Keeping her eyes on him, Sabine slowly lowered to her knees. She kept her hand wrapped around his cock, and, with their gazes locked, she put her mouth against the head of his arousal.

A shudder worked through his body. *"Sabine."*

Her lips opened over him. Her tongue snaked out, tasting the moisture on his tip. Her fingers curled around the base of his cock, the perfect position to let her maintain control, then she began to lick him. Again and again. Tasting his flesh, then parting her lips and taking him inside her mouth.

His cheeks hollowed. His whole expression altered. Lust. Animal need.

His hands jerked away from the wall. Locked around her shoulders.

She kept tasting him. Her head moved up and down. Sabine sucked his flesh, took him in deeper, and let her tongue swirl over him.

He grew even bigger in her mouth. His hips were thrusting, driving his cock harder against her, but she tightened her grip around him. Didn't take him all the way inside of her mouth. Instead Sabine just tasted and teased and tormented.

"Need. More." His growl was one of the sexiest things she'd ever heard.

As a reward, she gave him a little more.

His hands tightened on her. "Fucking . . . good."

It was about to get better.

She sucked him, harder. Took a little more of that heavy shaft—

And he pushed her away. Sabine blinked. "What—"

He yanked her jeans off her. Shredded her underwear. Spun her around and lifted her against the wall. Before she could even say his name, Ryder was plunging into her.

Then she could only sigh his name. Could only lock her legs around his hips and shove her body back against his as hard as she could.

This wasn't some tame need. Wasn't something made in a lab. This was lust. Raw. As wild as it could be. Desperate.

Her nails bit into his shoulders. She could feel her

canines stretching, sharpening, as the telltale ache filled her mouth. Being like this . . . with him . . . it made her want to bite. She wanted his blood because she wanted him. Wanted him in her. Wanted him to be a part of her.

She sank her teeth into his neck. He pumped harder. Her back shoved against the wall. His blood was on her tongue, and the taste was strangely sweet, but rich. Like decadent chocolate.

Pleasure hit her, not a crest or a spike but a shattering explosion that wrecked her. Her mouth lifted from his throat, and she tried to suck in some desperately needed air, but all she could do was pant and shudder because the pleasure had left her too weak.

Pleasure unlike anything she'd ever known. The kind of pleasure, well, that people just might kill for.

And Ryder was with her. She felt the hard jerks of his hips. His hands tightened even more around her as he emptied into her core. When his head lifted, she saw the blindness in his gaze. Pleasure.

Then his mouth was on hers. Stroking. Licking. Kissing.

Her heartbeat struggled to calm down. She kept touching him, because she didn't want to ever stop.

Her legs were still tight around his hips. She should probably try to stand. Probably, but she wasn't.

"You only bite me," he began, his words growling out, "when we fuck."

She felt a blush stain her cheeks. "Guess that's when you bring out the animal in me."

His gaze searched hers. "You always seem to bring out my darkness."

He was thickening within her once more. She tightened her inner muscles around him. "Is that all I bring out?"

"No."

She'd hoped to get a smile from him, but his face seemed even tenser than before.

"You make me very, very dangerous." He withdrew his cock, then pushed back into her. Her already too-sensitive flesh loved that push. "Because you make me need you too much."

Was it possible to need someone too much?

"I warned you," he said, pushing into her again, and the rush of pleasure started to pulse through her once more, "but it's already too late."

She licked her lips. Wanted to lick him. "Too late for what?"

"To get away."

Did she look like she was running?

Another withdraw, then a hard thrust of his flesh into hers. "You're mine now," Ryder said, "and I won't let you go."

The words were fierce and possessive. Before she could speak, he was kissing her again. The rhythm of his thrusts grew faster. The passion flared again, and Sabine forgot about warnings.

She only thought of pleasure.

The bar emptied out at dawn, the way it always did. If it was a normal bar, maybe the patrons would linger. There was always some kind of party in New Orleans.

But Bran's Castle wasn't normal, and even though their flesh didn't burn in the sunlight—total Hollywood BS—vampires didn't exactly love hopping around in the daylight.

They hunted better at night.

Grayson Hughes stalked around the empty interior.

He'd expected Ryder to return by dawn, but Ryder always loved doing the unexpected.

Tricky SOB.

"What happens now?" The soft, feminine voice came from behind him.

Ah, so he wasn't quite alone.

He glanced over his shoulder and saw that Julia, the sexy little bartender, was edging away from the stockroom. Stockroom, blood freezer, whatever you wanted to call it.

He raised a brow at her. He'd wondered when this conversation would happen.

"I mean . . . I thought this place was yours." She smoothed her hands over the front of her jeans. Julia was new to the vamp life. She'd only been changed a little over a year ago. "But the dark Ryder comes in and just takes over."

The Dark Ryder. Dark Rider. Yes, that had been the name he'd gotten centuries ago. When he rode into towns and fought vampires, then left, covered in blood.

Ryder was the vampire judge, jury, and executioner. If you crossed a line, he came for you.

And, of course, he was the one who drew the lines to begin with. The vamp with all the power.

Because he'd been created first.

"What happens?" Grayson repeated as he turned to fully face her. He knew exactly how to play this game. Over all the long years, he'd gotten so good at playing roles. "What happens is that we keep our mouths shut and our minds as sealed as possible."

Julia's eyes widened. "What if he finds out about what we've done?"

What did she think would happen? Ryder would try

to kill them, obviously. So he just stared back at her. She swallowed and glanced away.

After a moment, Grayson said, "If you're smart, you won't talk about that again, not here."

But Julia shook her head. "It doesn't matter what's said or not said. He's going to push with his power. He's going to scan us all. Then he'll know."

Ryder would know that they'd been in on the plan to kill his ass? That they'd helped to set him up?

"He won't know if we take him out first." And wasn't that supposed to be the goal, anyway? To stop the vamp king before he stopped them? "Call the others," Grayson ordered her. "Set up a meet. Ryder's distracted by his lady, so we have time to move, now."

Her lashes flickered. "His lady?" she repeated. "I'd wondered if he—"

"Ryder is obsessed with her." Obviously. The vamp could barely keep his fangs off her. "That buys us time."

A faint smile curved Julia's full lips. "Yes, it does. I'll get all the others, and we'll do it—we'll kill him." Her face didn't look so soft or so sweet as she said, "Let's see how he likes it when all of his power is ripped away. When he becomes just like the rest of us."

CHAPTER SIXTEEN

They'd made it to the couch. Lost the rest of their clothes. Her body was so sated that she never wanted to move, and Sabine could admit, she rather enjoyed the way Ryder's arms felt around her.

"What's going to happen?" Sabine asked him because she couldn't help herself. "Is there any way out for us?"

Frowning, he raised his head to look down at her. His fingers skimmed up her arm. "We're going to kill our enemies." Said with perfect certainty. "Make them beg for death. Then we're going to walk away."

Her lips had curled into a smile at first, then she realized he was dead serious. "Uh, I haven't exactly ever made anyone beg for death." Her smile dipped down. "Genesis . . . that lady there tried to turn me into a weapon, but I couldn't even carry out one job. The werewolf . . ." Her fingers rose to her stomach. The wounds were gone, but the memory would always be there to terrify her. "He just ripped me open."

Ryder shifted their positions, moving so that she lay

beneath him on the couch. Then he slid down, pushing between her legs. His mouth lowered over her stomach, and he pressed a light kiss to the skin there. "You scared the hell out of me then."

She stared at his bent head. To be so fierce, he had his tender moments. She'd never felt more cherished in her whole life than she did in that moment.

She could feel his arousal, but he wasn't pushing her. He was just . . . kissing a wound that wasn't there. And his kisses were making it all better, well, almost all better.

"I would have just burned," she said, and her fingers brushed through his hair. "Even if your blood hadn't turned me, I would have come back."

His head lifted. "You were terrified. You didn't want to die." His jaw locked. "So I didn't let you."

His words sent a whisper of cold blowing around her heart. "You can't always stop death."

"I can try."

She swallowed. Trying and succeeding were two very different things. "What happened to the were-wolf?" She hadn't cared to ask before. Sabine had just been glad to get away from the beast.

"Why? Do you want me to kill him for you?" Said so simply.

Sabine couldn't speak.

"He wasn't always like that," Ryder said. His fingers brushed lightly over her stomach. "Wyatt experimented on him, too. Pushed his beast into taking over. I'm not even sure that any part of the man is left within him now."

"Is he loose?" she asked, as her heartbeat kicked up and she finally found words.

Ryder nodded. "Him . . . and dozens of other monsters that Wyatt played God with in his labs."

Other monsters . . . like the primal vampires.

"Do you want me to kill him?" Ryder asked again. "Because I can hunt him. I can—"

Sabine put her fingers to his lips. Part of her wanted to kill the wolf herself. A very, very big part. But another part of her had recognized the animal in him. An animal that had been in such horrible pain. She'd looked into his eyes. Seen rage and hate and fear. He hadn't been trying to kill her. She'd been in his way. But . . .

"We deal with the immediate threats," Sabine said, because they had to create a plan. "Then we'll start dealing with Wyatt's mess." Someone would have to clean up after him.

Why not them?

Clearing her throat, she said, "W-we can't hide here forever." *Our enemies will find us sooner or later.*

He blinked at her. "I'm not hiding. I hide from no one."

Now she did smile. "Of course you don't. We came here because—"

"Because you needed to remember your life. Who you are on the inside hasn't changed."

Her smile faded.

"You're still the girl who fished with her father. Still the girl who jumped from the pier. The girl in all those pictures that line the walls." His gaze searched hers. "And you're also the woman that I fucked so well here all morning."

Okay, now that sent a ripple of surprise through her.

"You're not some monster. You're still *you*. And, Sabine, that's—" He broke off as his head jerked up. Then his gaze flew to the door.

She strained, trying to use her new, enhanced senses.

Yes, she could hear a car's engine, but the sound was faint, still far away.

Ryder was on his feet in an instant. He yanked up his jeans. Sabine scrambled for her clothes. The last thing she felt like doing was facing an enemy naked.

She hopped as she put on her jeans and snatched the shirt over her head. Ryder wasn't waiting for the enemy to come in. He'd already run out the front door.

Typical. Her vamp always attacked first, then asked his questions later. Provided, of course, that his enemies were still breathing and *could* answer any questions.

The engine had come closer. A few moments later, a car door slammed. She caught a raised voice, a male who asked, "What are you—"

Her blood froze. She knew that voice.

Sabine raced outside. The two men had stilled, facing off against each other.

Ryder and . . . Rhett?

She didn't realize she'd whispered her brother's name, but then she was running as fast as she could and throwing her arms around him. He staggered back when her body collided with his, but then his arms wrapped around her. She smelled blood and ash, and she was afraid for him and so happy and she was laughing as she held him.

Not dead. Not dead. Not dead. The litany repeated over and over in her head.

"It's okay," Rhett told her. "Sabe, you're squeezing the life out of me. I swear, I'm all right."

But she didn't want to let him go.

She also didn't want to hurt him.

So she eased back, just a little bit. "How are you here?"

His face was pale and tired. "I tried to figure out a safe place you'd go."

Where's your safe place?

She glanced back at Ryder.

He gave her a little nod.

Her breath heaved out. Ryder had known. She swallowed. He'd known that her brother might break free of whatever prison held him. And he'd wanted to take her to a place where Rhett would be able to find her.

He'd found her.

She squeezed him again.

"Don't break my ribs!" Rhett gasped out.

Whoops. "Sorry," she mumbled. She'd have to be more careful with that vamp strength.

"We should move this inside," Ryder said, his voice mild. "There's always the chance that he was followed."

She eased away from him, but Sabine kept a strong hold on Rhett's arm. She didn't touch his bloody wrists or the blisters on his flesh. Sabine was as careful as she could be.

"There's no chance I was followed." Rhett came easily with her. "I staked the bastard who came for me."

Her gaze met Ryder's. "A vampire attacked you?"

"No, that asshole from The Rift—the SOB who burned down my bar. He can touch things and they *burn*."

Dante.

Ryder let them enter the cabin first. His gaze swept behind them.

"You killed him?" Sabine asked, just to be sure. "You saw him die?"

"I drove a chunk of wood into his heart." Rhett's shoulders sagged as soon as he was in the cabin. As if he thought . . . *I'm safe here*. But he wasn't. "The fire was burning all around us. He was dead when he fell, I know he was, and the fire was just going to burn right over him."

Not exactly.

Sabine's gaze met Ryder's. "Was he followed?"

"I wasn't!" Rhett immediately huffed. "He was dead, I tell you, he was—"

"He'll come back." Sabine tried to keep her voice steady. "That man, his name is Dante, and he isn't dead."

Rhett shook his head. "Bull. Even vamps can't come back if you stake their hearts. I took out that guy and—"

"He wasn't a vampire. You killed him, yes." She cleared her throat. "But after he burns, he'll come back. He's a phoenix, and death doesn't stop him."

It just pisses him off.

Her brother shook his head. "That's insane! A phoenix? Like the myth? The big bird that burns and—"

"Not exactly like the myth," Ryder interrupted as his gaze studied Rhett. "But close enough."

"He's *dead*." Rhett was definite. A faint flush stained his cheeks. "We have other things to worry about instead of focusing on a corpse. Like Dad—he's gone. The house is empty. What if Vaughn grabbed him, too?"

Tell him. "I know Dante isn't dead because"—she inhaled slowly and made her gaze hold his—"because I was like him."

Rhett had finally stopped talking. His head tilted as he studied her.

"Dad isn't in town," Sabine continued. "He's gone because I told him to leave. I didn't want anyone coming after him."

"And he just what—picked up and left? Left you? Left me? That's not the way this family does things!"

"He sent Mom out of town to keep her safe. He's gone to be with her." She straightened her shoulders. *Tell. Him.* "He's the one . . . he's the reason I vanished, Rhett. Dad knew what I was. All along, he knew."

"Yeah, he knew you were his kid so—"

He wasn't listening. After everything that had happened, did he just not want to hear this? Denial could be a powerful thing.

"Dad knew that I was a phoenix." She kept her voice calm because she had to, but Sabine wanted to scream. "He thought . . . he *said* he thought that by sending me to the Genesis facility, he'd be helping me."

Rhett's eyes had widened. "No, you—you were missing. We were all worried. Mom . . . she went in the hospital—"

Ryder crossed his arms over his chest. Watched. Waited.

"He didn't tell you what he'd done. Didn't tell Mom. Didn't tell me." She pressed her lips together and remembered the terror of waking up and being tossed at a vampire. Her gaze slid to Ryder's.

The memory was between them.

A muscle flexed in his jaw.

"Dad said he wanted to help me, but, Rhett, Genesis didn't help."

"I saw the news," he muttered. He ran a shaking hand over his face. "They were torturing—" He broke off and sucked in a ragged breath. "Did they hurt you, Sabe?" Now he was the one to grab her. To hold too tight. "Did they?"

"Yes."

He blanched.

She wouldn't tell him what had been done. There were some things that a brother didn't need to hear.

Some things that a sister couldn't say.

But Rhett was a smart guy. Always had been. "You know . . . you know the phoenix guy is coming back because they killed you and you came back."

She nodded.

"Dad . . . he did that to you?" Whispered. Humming with fury.

"He thought . . . he said he wanted to help me. To make me normal."

He yanked her against his chest. Almost broke *her* ribs with his fierce grip. "Fuck normal. You're perfect just the way you are, even if you burn."

Or bite?

Over Rhett's shoulder, her stare met Ryder's. "I want you to leave town, too, Rhett," she whispered.

He pulled back, fast. "Hell, no."

"Hell, yes," she shot right back, voice gaining strength and volume. She eased away, putting some space between them. "You can't handle this fight."

His chin notched up. "It sure looked like I handled that Dante fellow pretty damn well."

Had he? Or had it been a trick? Was Dante tracking them even now? And why? Why wouldn't he just let her go?

But Ryder strode to her side then, and he faced off against her brother. "You can't handle vampires. Can't handle the flames when they come. You'll die. She'll mourn. Is that what you want?"

"I *want* my sister back! I want our life back!"

But Sabine had realized something. Something Ryder had told her before, but she just hadn't been ready to hear. "That life is over." Even once the bastards after them were gone, returning to her old life . . . *not an option*. "I can't be the same any longer."

She looked down at his hands. Already, she'd brought him pain. "You need to get away from me."

"No, I need to stand by you."

Didn't he see? "Vaughn was your friend. He—"

"Was?"

Hell.

Rhett's whole body had tensed. "Did something happen to the jerk?"

"A vampire happened," Ryder told him, and Sabine was glad he took that burden from her. "One with a very powerful strain of infection."

"So vamps have an infection now?"

"These do," Ryder said, voice flat. "Wyatt created them. Screwed with things he should have left alone. One of those vampires attacked Vaughn."

Rhett rocked back on his heels. "That's why he didn't come back for me."

Because he was dead.

And if Rhett didn't get far away, he'd be dead, too. "Please," Sabine whispered. "Get out of town."

Rhett shook his head. "I'm not leaving."

They had to make him go. Had to *make*—

Ryder caught her hand. Her head turned toward him. She knew exactly what she had to do. What she had to ask. "Ryder, make him leave."

"He can try," Rhett snapped and he pushed his way between them. "But it's not happening. I'm here, I'm staying in this fight, and, shit, that had *better* not be your panties on the floor."

And in the midst of everything, oh crap, she'd forgotten her underwear.

Rhett was beaten, exhausted, and . . . furious.

He whirled on Ryder. "Did you just have sex with my sister?" His voice had dropped to a deadly whisper.

"All this other shit, *and* you think you're good enough to touch her?" His hands were fisted. "I don't care if you're a vamp, I don't care if you're the freaking king of vampires—"

Um, yes, well, he kind of was.

"—you don't mess with—"

"He didn't have sex with me," Sabine said as she hurried to step between them. Rhett needed to seriously focus. Killers were after them. Life-and-death situations were happening every minute.

And she wasn't sixteen. If she wanted to screw her vamp, then she would.

"Sabine," Rhett began.

"I seduced him. And I liked it."

Ryder gave a choked laugh. "Trust me, I liked it, too."

But Rhett's face was still flushed. Protective big brother. Trying to fight every battle for her. Not caring if she was human or phoenix or anything else.

Loving her, either way.

"I'm sorry," she told Rhett, "but it has to be this way."

"What?"

"Bite him, Ryder," she said. She didn't know how to control someone through the blood. Couldn't even begin to figure that out right then. But Ryder knew just what to do.

Rhett's face went slack with shock. "What?"

"I have to keep you safe." There was no other choice for her.

Ryder grabbed her brother. Easily held him while Rhett thrashed. "Are you sure?" Ryder demanded.

"Sabine!" her brother snarled.

"Yes," she said, staring into her brother's eyes, "I am."

And she turned away while Ryder took her brother's blood.

Keith Adams pounded his fist against the front door of Bran's Castle. He hated coming to this place, but his options were slim and fucking none.

The door opened.

A man stood before him. Tall. Bored-looking.

"Where's Ryder?" Keith demanded. He didn't have much time.

"Not here."

Great. "He told me to come. I have information for him."

"Do you now?" Still no real interest on the guy's face.

Keith frowned at him. "Who the hell are you?"

"I'm Ryder's friend. Name's Grayson." Grayson opened the door, indicating that Keith should come inside.

Why? Because he looked stupid?

"I've got five men with guns pointing dead-on at this place right now," Keith snapped. "You make a move at me, vamp, and you'll find wooden bullets in your heart."

Now the guy didn't look *quite* so bored.

"I need to talk to Ryder." He needed the guy *now*. "I can help him, if he'll help me."

"And how can a human help a vampire?" the one called Grayson wanted to know. "Unless, of course, you're going to bleed for him."

"I know where Sabine's brother is, okay? Tell him . . . *I know*. I can take him to the warehouse. I can get the dogs off Sabine and Rhett, but Ryder's gonna have to do something for me."

"Sabine," the guy whispered her name. "Doesn't she just come up a lot in conversation?"

"Ryder has to meet me. He *and* Sabine. Tell them to come to Forty-Nine Chartres. We can work out a deal."

"Doubtful." Grayson sounded dismissive. "Ryder doesn't exactly deal with humans. Unless he's eating them."

"Tell him," Keith snarled. He should be handling this better. He just couldn't. Not with his son . . . Keith cleared his throat. "Tell him. Tell him to come at midnight. We can make this nightmare go away."

"What if he doesn't want to make it go away?"

"He will." Then he played his trump card. Actually, the only card he had left, especially since he was bullshitting about Rhett. He had no idea where that guy was. Hopefully, the hell away from New Orleans. "And tell Ryder that Malcolm sends his regards."

The vamp frowned at him. "What?"

"Malcolm." He'd already been out in the open long enough. He didn't trust the vamps not to attack. The primals were out there on the streets of New Orleans, two according to his intel, but if those two had already bit and infected other humans . . .

We have to stop this.

Ryder was his only hope.

Keith turned away. "The guns are gonna stay on you until I'm clear." Not his first ball game with the undead.

But the coming battle might just prove to be his last.

"I'm going back to the bar," Ryder said. He glanced at Sabine's brother. The guy was pale, but not fighting.

Why would he fight now?

Sabine lightly touched Rhett's shoulder. "I'm sorry."

She kept apologizing to the guy.

Ryder shook his head. "Rhett, I want you to take your car and get out of New Orleans." The link was effortless. Humans were so easy to control.

Rhett rose to his feet. His gaze drifted to Sabine.

"Go to Memphis," Ryder instructed. He could just *think* the instructions and Rhett would obey, but he said them out loud so Sabine would know all of the plans. "Find a club called The Blue Jay. Tell the bartender that I sent you." Rhett would fit right in there, and Jay would make sure the guy was safe, until Ryder sent for him again.

Rhett nodded. "I can . . . feel you." He rubbed his temples. Almost clawed at them.

Stop.

Rhett's hands dropped. "In my head. You're . . . in my head." His eyes were wide with horror, but he made no move to attack Ryder.

You want to fight me. You can't. So you just need to walk out that door. Get in your car. Drive to Memphis.

Slowly, very, very slowly, Rhett started to walk. But then his gaze drifted to Sabine. Guilt was written all over her face.

Tell her you love her.

Ryder didn't even know why he sent the command, but Rhett's voice rasped, "I love you."

Sabine's eyes squeezed shut, as if she couldn't bear to look at her brother. "I love you, too, and I swear, I'll make this up to you. *I swear.*"

Rhett lifted his hands. Pushed hard against his temples once more. "In . . . my . . . head."

Stop.

"Hurts," Rhett whispered, sounding lost.

Sabine opened her eyes, frowning at him. "What hurts?"

Perhaps this human wasn't as weak as he'd originally thought. *Walk away, now.* Ryder focused harder and actually got the guy to move. One foot. Another.

A few more steps, then Rhett opened the door.

Don't look back.

Rhett's body trembled. The human had one strong will. Stronger than any Ryder had encountered before. "Keep her . . . safe," Rhett rasped. "Or I'll . . . stake you."

You can try. Ryder gave another hard mental push, and Rhett left the cabin.

Sabine stared after him. She didn't speak until she heard the car crank up. Then drive away.

"Thank you."

She shouldn't really thank him. Once Rhett got far enough away, the guy might just be able to fight that compulsion.

And come back.

So they didn't have time to waste. "We need to get to the bar."

She nodded.

He crossed to her. Caught her shoulders in his hands. "I'm going to have to kill today."

Her breath whispered out. "Keith—"

Perhaps, but first he had a few other priorities. "I can't let my enemies go any longer." The longer he waited, the more dangerous they became. When you were betrayed, you had to strike back. A fast and brutal strike. "If I don't go after them, they'll come for me. And for you." Because needing her so much was a weakness that others would try to use against him. "Wyatt and his scientists used you against me in Genesis. No one else can do that. Ever."

"Wh-what do you mean?"

"Vampires sold me out before, so vampires are dying today." The trap should be set. He'd given the orders. Put the plan into motion.

Now it was time to kill.

"If you don't want to watch what's coming, then you need to stay here."

"They're—you think they're going to try and kill you?"

He laughed at that question. "You're not the only one with enemies on your trail. They'll try. They'll fail. I'll succeed." Because the minute he got close enough to the traitorous vamps, the battle would be over.

He'd compel them. Control them. End them.

Maybe he didn't want Sabine to see this fight. Watching him control her brother had been bad enough. Watching him get a group of vamps to stake themselves . . . well, that wouldn't exactly be a warm and fuzzy memory for her.

"Stay here," he said, voice deepening. Not so much a question any longer, but an order.

She shook her head at him. "You need me. I'm coming."

"I don't—"

"I'm coming with you, Ryder." Shrugging, she said, "Besides, if I stay here, all alone, who knows what could happen? Maybe Rhett was followed, maybe—"

Hell. "Just don't try to stop me."

She shrugged again. The shrug was no answer. They both realized that.

"Sabine." Her name came out on a sigh. "Don't try to stop me. They've got this death coming."

Her brows lowered. "How can you know that you'll be targeting the right ones?"

"Because I have a spy in their camp." One who had been assigned the job of rooting out the vamps who'd sent him to hell. "And that vamp is ready to serve the others up to me."

He just had to go in.

And deliver his justice.

CHAPTER SEVENTEEN

Bran's Castle didn't look nearly as . . . exciting during the day. There were no glasses filled with blood. No vamps lurking in the corner.

There wasn't much of anything happening there. The place could have been any human bar.

"Ryder."

Okay, so maybe there was one vampire lurking around. Sabine turned and saw Grayson heading out of the back room. The scent of blood followed him.

"We've got a big problem," Grayson snapped. He shot her a quick glance.

She tried to look cool and in control.

"Where are they?" Ryder demanded. He *sounded* cool and in control. She wanted to be like that.

"Julia's getting—shit, *forget* about them a minute, okay?" Grayson ran a shaking hand through his hair. The mussed look suggested he'd been yanking a hand through his hair for a while now. "A human came by, looking for you. He said that he had what you wanted."

"Keith," Sabine whispered. But how could he have what they wanted? Rhett was gone. Safe.

"The guy asked that you meet him, at midnight tonight, in some place on Chartres."

"Screw him," Ryder said as he headed toward the bar. "I don't need—"

"Malcolm."

Ryder froze. Then he turned, his movements tight, and stared back at Grayson. "Why the hell did you just say his name?"

"Because your human friend told me that Malcolm sends his regards." The vampire was sweating. His hands shoved through his hair again. *Fear.* "But that's total bullshit, right? I heard the stories. Your brother is dead."

"Dead and buried," Ryder agreed. His jaw had locked.

"So why did the guy say that?"

"Because he's trying to rattle us." Ryder rolled his shoulders as if pushing away tension. "Keith knows that he doesn't have what we really wanted, and he's trying to draw me out for a fight."

"Who the hell *is* he?" Grayson wanted to know.

"He's just a human who thinks he can manipulate me. But that's not going to happen." Ryder shrugged. "Now where's Julia?"

Grayson opened his mouth to speak.

Sabine beat him to the punch. "You're just going to ignore this? What if—what if Malcolm *is* somehow alive?" *Malcolm.* The guy scared her. Scared her more than Genesis, and that was saying a whole lot.

"He isn't alive."

"How would Keith even know—"

"Because we all use spies to get our dirty work done." Ryder cast a quick look at Grayson. "Keith said he had a person at Genesis. That person could have talked to some vamps there. Could have heard about my brother. His existence wasn't exactly a secret."

"More like a legend," Grayson mumbled.

Ryder frowned at him. "Malcolm isn't a threat that we need to worry about. The vampires after me—"

"The ones who are planning to cut off your head," Grayson supplied, rather helpfully, Sabine thought.

"They're the threat that we eliminate first." Ryder crossed his arms and studied Grayson. "So what did you find out?"

"There are six . . . here in New Orleans. They're all young, fairly new changes, and they—"

The bar's front door flew open and slammed into the wall. "And they're not as stupid as you think," Julia snarled as she rushed inside. "I knew all along you were still sided with this bastard!"

Sabine eased back, taking a few fast steps closer to Ryder.

She wasn't fast enough.

Because Julia wasn't the only vampire to come rushing in that door. Three others followed her and two burst in from the bar's back door.

Ryder just stared at them all. The vamps were armed, some with guns, some with stakes. They looked pissed and scared and determined.

Ryder laughed at them and said, "You're exactly as stupid as I thought. I just needed Grayson to get you all together, to pull you out into the open."

He glanced at the vampire with the stake. Ryder's eyes narrowed.

Sabine knew exactly what he was doing. *Telling him to kill himself.*

The vampire raised the stake. Started screaming, "Stop it! Stop it!" His hand curled toward his own chest.

Ryder glanced away from him. Stared at a redhead with scruffy hair. The man lifted the gun he held to his head.

She didn't want to see this. Ryder had been right when he'd tried to get her to stay away.

"What are you doing?" Julia screamed. Her scream wasn't directed at Ryder. It was directed at the vampires—her men—who were turning to flee.

But those men suddenly froze in place.

Ryder.

"All vampires have blood that links to me," he said simply. And his control, his power, it was terrifying.

Terror was exactly the emotion reflected on Julia's face. "That's why we have to kill you," she whispered, licking her lips. "If we're ever going to be free, you have to die. He was right."

He?

But Sabine didn't get to question her. More glass exploded because more *vampires* were attacking, only these vampires were different.

Too many teeth.

Too many claws.

Primals. And not just the other two that had escaped from Genesis. At least seven primals had just leapt through the broken glass of the windows and rushed into the bar.

"We brought some backup," Julia said. She smiled, flashing her fangs. "I bet you didn't see that coming."

No, they hadn't.

The primals ran forward, attacking, but they weren't going for Ryder.

All of those black claws, those sharp teeth—

They're coming for me.

They closed in as Sabine screamed.

Keith paced around the small apartment. Midnight would be coming all too soon. They had to be ready. He glanced to the left, at the woman who stood so still and silent near the window. "You're sure you can do this?"

She turned toward him. Small, with golden skin and wide, almond-shaped eyes, she didn't look particularly strong.

But sometimes, strength wasn't physical.

For her, it was all mental.

"If you bring me the phoenix, I should be able to save your son."

Yes, he noticed her very careful *should be.* Because Cassandra Armstrong wasn't going to make a promise she couldn't keep. She was already nervous, already so scared he'd caught her hand shaking when she'd injected Vaughn with a sedative.

But Cassandra wasn't going to break and run. She'd dealt with plenty of supernaturals before.

And she was his only hope. "She's coming." Little Sabine Acadia. Who would have known that she'd be the key to saving so many people?

"Is she coming . . . willingly?" Cassandra asked carefully.

Not exactly. But he nodded anyway. When it came to his son, willingness didn't matter. Nothing mattered but saving Vaughn. Stopping him from being a monster.

But he didn't tell Cassandra that part. She wouldn't

understand. She hated what Wyatt had done. She was on some quest to help the supernaturals, to make up for all the wrongs that Genesis had done to them.

Good fucking luck to her.

He just wanted his son back.

And he'd do anything, use *anyone,* if it meant that Vaughn could be more than just a killing machine.

When those bastards closed in on Sabine, something broke inside of Ryder. He didn't care about control or caution. He had only one thought.

Kill them.

So the vampire with a stake at his own heart and the vampire with the gun at his head—they both turned instantly . . . and attacked the primals.

Julia screamed, even as she, too, lifted the weapon she'd tucked in her jeans and fired on the primals.

All those vampires who'd thought to take him out, Ryder turned them on the primals.

Take them out. Get their attention. Stop them. Kill them.

"Fucking bloodbath," Grayson muttered. He tried to run forward and attack the primals, too.

Ryder grabbed his arm. Grayson was his oldest friend. That meant something. Even in the roar of his fury. "Stay back or you'll die, too."

"Staying the hell back," Grayson agreed as he jumped behind the bar's counter.

A primal sank his teeth into Julia's throat. She screamed and fired her gun right into his heart.

One primal was already on the ground, a stake in his heart. Another primal had just ripped a gun away from his attackers.

But there were still others. Still too many vampires . . .

Get them away from Sabine.

Because he couldn't hear her screams anymore. She had to be okay. Too many bodies were in his way. He couldn't even see her.

Ryder tried to reach her mind. *Sabine.*

A wall of flames flickered in his mind's eye.

Still flames. With her, he was starting to realize that would always be the case.

Then a vampire—a primal—flew back through the air. A stake was embedded in his heart.

"I'm not"—Sabine shoved her hair back over her shoulder and wiped away the blood that dripped down her chin—"helpless anymore. Not human . . . So back away!"

But they weren't backing away.

The primals were slicing right through the other vampires, the other fools who'd been stupid enough to think they could control these predators.

But Ryder could attack. He could kill. Now that he knew Sabine was alive, he could actually think again.

He shoved his claws into the chest of one primal. Had his heart before the man could scream.

There were so many screams around him.

Ryder sliced the throat of another.

Sabine had a chair in her arms. When a primal vamp came at her, she shoved it at him. The chair leg sank into his chest.

The vamp fell to the floor.

The primals were dying. Those still living should have tried to run, but they just kept trying to get to Sabine.

Ryder grabbed the next bastard who was attempting to bite *his* woman.

"Need . . . her . . ."—the primal's eyes looked blind— "her . . . blood . . ."

"You're not getting it." Ryder sliced his throat. Took his head. Dropped his body. Moved on to the next target. "None of you are getting to her."

But the primals were so close to the one thing they wanted most—Sabine's blood. And they were fighting with a wild ferocity as they realized that death was stalking them.

Because he sure as hell was.

Then one primal made the mistake of driving his fist into Sabine's jaw. He yanked the makeshift weapon from her hands and shoved his fangs into her throat.

The world became a sea of red rage for Ryder.

He tore through everyone in his path. His claws sliced. His teeth bit. Flesh tore. Screams surrounded him.

Get to her.

Sabine's arms came up. *"Get away!"*

The faintest tendril of smoke appeared between her and the primal.

Ryder reached out and grabbed the bastard—even as the primal started to howl in pain.

The primal's chest was burning.

From the inside?

Ryder swung him around. The guy sliced out with his claws, digging deep.

And Ryder just laughed. Then he picked up the still-smoking bastard and tossed him across the room. The man slammed into the bar.

Grayson lunged up and staked him.

Ryder stood there, chest heaving, fury boiling his blood. His head turned, and he met Sabine's wide-eyed stare. She had her hands at her throat. Her lips were trembling.

As she stared at him, there was no missing the fear in her gaze.

His racing heartbeat began to slow. Ryder shook his head and glanced around. Bodies littered the floor. Blood. So much blood.

All of the primals were dead. Their eyes stared sightlessly ahead. Some of them . . . His chin lifted. He didn't remember even making the brutal attacks, but he knew the kills were his.

I lost it. When they went for her . . .

And the vampires that had thought to attack him? All but one of them had already died. The only one left was Julia. She lay sprawled on the floor, a giant chunk of wood in her chest. Her gasping breaths seemed to echo in the room.

Ryder didn't want to touch Sabine. Not yet. Not with so much blood on his hands. And there was still one more piece of business to finish.

He turned away from her. Walked toward Julia's desperate form. His shoes slid in the blood that surrounded her.

Then he was bending over her. Her gaze met his. A faint smile lifted her lips. "You think . . . won?"

Yes, he fucking did. His hands closed around the stake.

"Did you . . . give her a . . . choice?"

Ryder's eyes narrowed. He heard the faint rustle of steps behind him. Felt Sabine standing at his back.

Julia's gaze wasn't on him. It was on Sabine. "Did you . . . ask to be . . . like this?"

Grayson had come from his position behind the bar. He stood on Julia's right side. Not touching her. Just staring at her with a mix of pity and fury in his eyes.

"Did . . . you?" Julia pressed as her chest heaved.

"I asked to live," Sabine said, her voice soft.

"But you didn't know . . ." Julia's lips curved in a faint smile. "The price he'd . . . make you pay."

Ryder stiffened.

"I . . . didn't . . . know . . . I didn't . . . ask . . ."

"Is that why you sent me to Genesis? Because you and the others hadn't asked to be vampires?" Ryder asked, voice rough. "I didn't turn you, I didn't—"

"You . . . started it. You turned . . . him. Made us all."

Him. Malcolm.

"Some things . . . shouldn't be made."

His fingers were curled around the chunk of wood in her chest. One twist of his hand, and she would be dead. "And here I thought it was all about you wanting to be free of me. Because I controlled you all."

"They wanted . . . said you couldn't control them."

They? Would that be the dead vamps on the floor?

"I wanted . . . free . . . in different way."

"She didn't want to be a vampire," Sabine said, sadness tingeing her words. "She just wanted to be normal."

"Normal's overrated," Grayson muttered.

"There's no going back," Ryder said. Surely Julia realized that. "You can't be human once you've changed."

"I know . . ."

Ryder stared at the wood in her chest. She'd been in on the plan to take him out. Not the leader, he sensed that, so maybe one of the broken vamps behind him had planned everything. But Julia . . . she'd known.

And she wasn't fighting death.

It would be so easy to take her out.

But Sabine was touching the back of his shoulder. Gentle fingertips. Sabine . . . who also hadn't known exactly what she was getting into when she became a vampire.

Ryder hadn't been given a choice.

He'd just woken to bloodlust. A new life.

Julia . . . he remembered her story. She'd been attacked by a vampire. Raped. Bled nearly dry. But then that vamp had transformed her.

That vamp . . .

"I killed him," Ryder said as his fingers slid away from the wood. "I killed the vampire who made you." And she'd still come after him?

Julia laughed. The wood shifted deeper. Blood trickled from her lips. "Judge . . . jury . . . executioner. You're the vampire . . . l-law."

He tried to be. They needed law. They needed—

"Why didn't you . . . stop him . . . sooner? Why didn't . . . you . . . save me?"

And that was it. That was fucking it. She blamed him for not killing Moses, the vamp who'd attacked her and four other coeds in Mississippi.

Shame hit him then. Yes, he could see what she meant. Every vampire . . . *they all come back to me*. If he'd never bit Malcolm, never learned to spread this fucking curse, then monsters like Moses wouldn't have preyed on the humans.

Julia *would* still be human.

Ryder rocked back, stood, and stepped away from her.

Hundreds, *thousands* of others would still be alive.

If I'd just died.

"I'm . . . gonna be free . . ." Julia whispered. Her gaze came back to Ryder. "You . . . won't be . . . Retribution . . . coming."

Then her fingers lifted.

Too late, Ryder realized what she was doing.

He reached for her.

But Julia had already shoved the wood deep into her heart.

She died with a smile on her face.

Ryder's fingers were around hers. He yanked the wood free from her chest. Tossed it aside.

Then his fist slammed into the floor near her body. Again and again and again, he beat the floor.

All because of me. Everything. All the death and pain. *"My fucking fault,"* he snarled, and Ryder leapt back to his feet.

He grabbed the nearest table. Smashed it. Hurled chairs. Threw glasses.

So many deaths. On him.

Every fucking one. It all went back to him.

"Someone needs some chill time." Grayson's tense voice.

He'd made Grayson into a monster. Found him on a battlefield. Moments away from death. A hero's death.

He'd turned the guy into a killer instead.

Ryder whirled and grabbed Grayson by the throat. "You didn't want this life."

Grayson's eyes widened. "You . . . don't see me . . . complaining, do you?" He gasped out the words.

"Ryder, *stop!*" Sabine.

Sounding more furious than he'd ever heard her before.

He dropped Grayson.

"Definite chill time," the guy muttered as he began to edge toward the back door.

Ryder turned away from him. Faced Sabine. She had her hand at her throat. Over the damn *bite* the bastard had given her.

Ryder took a step toward her. Almost slipped and fell in the blood. So much blood.

And she saw me do this? No wonder she's afraid. She'll always be afraid of me.

And he'd always need her. Would never be able to let her go.

He laughed. Wasn't that just a bitch? He really was the monster. Sabine had been right about him from the beginning. He'd always thought Malcolm was the one with no control. The one who'd brought hell, but all along . . .

It was me.

"She was wrong," Sabine whispered. Her hand dropped. The wounds were still on her throat. Seeing them just made his fury deepen.

His hands clenched into fists. He wanted to rip this whole fucking place down. "Get out." He backed away from her.

She blinked. "Ryder?"

"I don't want . . . to . . . hurt you." Because he was too wild. Too uncontrolled.

Too much of a killer.

The evidence was all around him.

But Sabine didn't walk away. She walked toward him. Grabbed his arms and shook him. *"Look at me."*

He didn't want to see the fear in her eyes.

"She was wrong, Ryder. Do you hear me? *Wrong.* Yes, she was pissed and hurt, and she got a terrible,

terrible hand dealt to her in this life . . . but what happened to her, the change, it wasn't your fault."

"I started it all. I made—"

"That is such a load of crap," Sabine's annoyed voice snapped. "No matter what you might like to think, you aren't God."

He blinked. His gaze met hers.

"You can't control everyone or everything."

He could actually control a pretty good number—

"If the guy who attacked Julia hadn't been a vamp, did you ever think that maybe he'd just be a straight-up killer? That he was screwed to begin with? Humans have plenty of freak tendencies, that's why there are so many serial killers out there. If that guy hadn't been a vamp, he could still have killed her. Could still have tortured and raped because the sad fact is . . . evil is real. It comes in all kinds of forms."

The form of a vampire. The form of a human.

Her hand lifted. Her fingers touched his cheek. "You aren't responsible for every evil that walks the earth. We all have choices."

The room reeked of death because of the choices he'd made. She'd seen all that he could do. And she still touched him. Looked at him like there was someone good inside of him.

He turned his head and pressed a quick kiss to her fingertips. He'd thought she was his weakness.

Maybe . . . maybe she was his strength.

The fury began to fade. His lashes lowered as he sucked in a deep breath. He needed to get her out of there. Had to wash the blood from her skin. Get her clean and safe. "Sabine—" His lashes lifted. He stared right at her.

There was so much fear in her eyes that he lost his

breath. She touched him, comforted him, *calmed* him, but Sabine was so afraid of him that she was shaking.

"He . . . bit me," she whispered. Her hand pulled from his. She touched the wound at her throat again. "Ryder, I'm sorry."

He shook his head, not understanding.

"Julia . . . she didn't want to live the way she was . . . I-I understand. I *don't* want to be like them. I don't want—"

He stiffened as understanding dawned. The fuck *no*.

"I don't want to be like them. Please, help me now." She straightened her shoulders. "Kill me."

CHAPTER EIGHTEEN

"Never," Ryder barked, his response instant. Now he was the one to grab her and hold on tight.

"If I change, if I'm like them—" She shuddered. "It just takes one bite to get infected by them, doesn't it? Just one. He bit me, so that means that I'm going to become primal."

"You're not changing. You're already a vampire." Mostly. "You *can't* change." He sure as hell hoped not.

But fear was whispering through him. Sabine wasn't like him, not like the others. With her, what if—

No. It had taken three exchanges just for her to become a vampire in the first place, and he was still seeing signs that her phoenix side wasn't gone.

"If I do change, then promise me that you won't let me—"

He pressed his lips to hers. Kissed her hard and deep. Drank the gasp from her mouth. Gave her his breath. *I'd give her my life.* "I promise that I'll always protect you." That was all she'd get from him.

And he'd protect her any way that he could. Every way.

Glass crunched. The scent of gasoline hit him.

Keeping a steady hold on Sabine, Ryder turned his head and saw that Grayson was back. And carrying gasoline containers in both hands.

"Since we don't keep a lot of alcohol here, I planned ahead," Grayson said, lifting the containers. "Don't want to leave any messes behind." He started pouring the gasoline on the bodies. On the walls. Everywhere.

Sabine shuddered. "More fire."

When you needed to wipe away the scene of a mass attack, yeah, fire could do the trick.

"Go," Grayson said, jerking up his chin. "I got this."

Ryder hesitated. Grayson had always been there for him. Steadfast. True. But he had to ask, "Do you wish I'd left you on that field?"

Grayson hesitated. "Some days."

Because Grayson never pulled his punches, Ryder felt that hit right to his gut.

"But most days, I'm glad to be alive. Glad to see the sky, glad to screw pretty women, glad to do all the damn things that *I* want." Grayson bared his fangs. "Julia made her choice. We all make our choices. And I choose to keep living."

Ryder's breath eased out as some of the tension left his shoulders.

"Now get your lady out of here." There was concern in Grayson's gaze as his eyes dropped to Sabine's throat. "Take care of her."

He thought . . . Grayson thought that she was going to change.

The hell she was.

Ryder laced his fingers with hers. Led her away from the blood- and gasoline-soaked scene.

Before he left the bar, he glanced back, just once, to see the clock.

Two hours before midnight.

Two hours . . .

"Sabine just ignited Bran's Castle," Keith said as he shoved his cell phone back into his pocket. "The place is burning, with flames reaching up to the sky." Now why the hell had she burned her lover's place?

Cassandra frowned. "You're sure she was behind the attack?"

"You know another phoenix in the city?" Keith demanded. It wasn't like their kind was heavy on the ground. "The flames are burning, it's a vamp bar, hell, just connect the dots."

"Do you think she killed Ryder?"

If she had, their plans were about to be screwed. "The local cops aren't even at the scene yet. There's no way to tell if anyone was inside when the blaze started." The tip he'd just received from one of his watchers had been fast and frightened.

The guy had been hauling ass away from the fire, not trying to get close and see if any victims were burning.

Keith looked at his watch. "She'll come." She had to come. Sabine was his key.

"And if she doesn't?" Cassandra asked. There was sympathy in her green eyes. "Then you'll need to prepare yourself for what must be done."

Killing his own son?

No, he wasn't prepared to take that step. Not yet.

Sabine's father had been ready to do anything to "cure" his little girl. Keith was ready and willing to do the same thing.

Anything.

She wanted him.

Sabine was afraid and furious and ripping apart on the inside.

Don't want to change. Don't want to change.

Her neck had finally stopped throbbing, but she felt like a ticking time bomb was inside her, just waiting to explode and destroy her. She didn't want to change. Didn't want to become one of the primals.

They didn't seem to have any emotions. Only basic needs.

The need to kill.

Ryder was running with her. They were rushing down an alley. Dark. Away from the scent of fire.

Away, away, away . . .

"Stop!" Sabine cried.

Ryder whirled to face her just as the dark clouds over them erupted. Rain fell down on them, beating hard, pounding in a fury.

Maybe the rain would stop the fire at the bar. Maybe the rain would wash away all the pain swirling inside of her.

The rain fell and the blood washed from her hands. *Now for the pain, please.*

Her hair clung to her neck. She lifted her fingers and wrapped them around his shoulders. "I want you."

Ryder blinked. Desire flared instantly in his eyes, but he shook his head. "Sabine, you need to be safe, you need—"

To feel alive. The way he'd always made her feel, even as he brought her death.

She stepped toward him. The rain kept hailing down on them. Thunder rumbled in the distance. Angry. Threatening.

Kind of the way she felt.

All she'd known before Genesis . . . that life was gone.

All she had left . . . *the way I feel for him*.

Sabine kissed him. She tasted the rain on his lips. The richer flavor that was his alone.

He went still beneath her touch.

"I don't have a lot of control right now," Ryder whispered.

She let a smile lift her lips, even though she knew the smile wouldn't be reflected in her eyes. "Good. Because I don't want control." She didn't want a safe lover.

She wanted him.

The most dangerous man she'd ever met.

The only man who made her feel *safe*.

Maybe she was screwed up. Maybe she was broken inside because of everything that had happened to her at Genesis.

She didn't care.

Sabine kissed him again. This time, he broke.

His arms locked around her. His tongue thrust into her mouth. Her hands pushed between them. Desire was desperate, a greedy bitch swamping her. Sabine wanted to touch him. Needed to feel his cock push deep, so deep inside of her.

But Ryder grabbed her hands. Two steps, and he had her against the brick wall. He locked her wrists above her head, pinning them there with his right hand.

His mouth kept kissing hers.

She could hear voices. Laughter. The crowd was close. She didn't care.

Someone could walk into the alleyway. Someone could see her and Ryder.

I don't care.

His left hand had opened her jeans. Pushed between her legs. She hadn't put on underwear. No, Ryder had grabbed it and tossed it somewhere before they'd left the cabin.

So his fingers touched her sex.

"Wet."

And she knew he wasn't talking about the rain that kept falling.

The rain was making the humans scatter. That was where the voices and laughter were coming from. The humans were running in the rain.

She and Ryder . . . they weren't running.

Two of his fingers pushed into her.

She rose onto her toes. Tried to yank her hands down so she could touch him, but Ryder wasn't letting her go.

His fingers thrust into her, again and again, as his thumb worked over her clit. She twisted her hips in an attempt to demand more of his touch.

He gave her more.

His mouth stayed on hers, his kisses deep and drugging as the rain fell, and his fingers kept stroking her. Light and easy then deep, demanding. Pushing and taking until her sex was clamping eagerly around him and then—

She came.

A release that shook her body and had her hips thrusting hard against his hand. A release that sent pleasure spilling through her and driving deep the realization that—

I'm alive. I can feel. I can want. I can need.

I can love.

He still had her hands pinned. His fingers stroked her, softly now, as the aftershocks of pleasure hit her.

His jaw was locked. His eyes blazing. His control was still there, hanging by a thread.

He'd held on to that control, for her. But she didn't want that control. She wanted all of him.

His fingers slid out of her. Gave her one last caress. He started to lift her jeans back into place.

"No."

Now she did pull her hands from his hold. Because he let her. "Ryder, *I want you.*"

"I'm . . . trying to be stronger."

She put her hands on his chest. "You don't always have to be strong with me." Her whisper. "With me, you can break."

He wanted to. She could see the struggle on his face.

So she made it easier on him.

She spun around. Slapped her hands against the wall and kicked away her jeans. Sabine lifted her hips, arching so that her ass—

Ryder growled. Then his body was surrounding her. Cradling her. Covering her. If anyone saw them now . . .

I don't care.

He adjusted his clothes. Parted her sex and pushed deep into her.

The pleasure hadn't stopped. When he thrust into her, when he drove deep, the sensations nearly ripped her apart.

Too much.

So good.

So . . . Ryder.

Her next release contracted around him, tightening around his cock. He thrust. Withdrew. Thrust.

The rhythm was frantic. Desperate.

Then he was stiffening behind her. Holding her even tighter. Coming.

In the rain.

In the alley.

With her.

His body shuddered. His arms curled around her and hugged her. And he pressed a kiss to her neck. Not a bite. A kiss. Right over the wound that was finally healing.

In silence, he withdrew from her. Ryder straightened her clothes, his. His hands steadied her when her knees wanted to tremble.

Then he turned her around and stared into her eyes. They were soaked through.

And she was so sated she just wanted to sink into his arms.

"When you come for me, your eyes burn."

Sabine blinked. That wasn't what she'd expected to hear.

"When you touched the primal who attacked you, smoke rose from your fingers. His chest . . . it burned."

She didn't remember that. She'd just been afraid. Desperate.

"When I kiss you, I can almost taste the fire."

Was that good? Bad?

"You're so much more than I ever expected."

So was he.

He put his forehead against hers. Held her tighter. "If I could go back, I'd change it all."

"There isn't any going back." She didn't even want to look back. Why see the scars? "I just want to go forward." She drew in a breath. "I'm ready to leave this town. Let's forget about Keith. He doesn't have my brother. He doesn't have anything that I need."

"He'll hunt us." Ryder shook his head. Raindrops slid off him. "I don't want you always looking over your shoulder. I can finish this mess. If he's the last tie connecting you to Genesis, then we sever the tie and make you free."

Her laughter was weak. "There's always another tie and another . . ." She just wanted to start new. To do that looking-forward bit, with him. "I want . . ."

You.

They'd never talked emotions. Just lust and need and power.

But it was more than just lust. What she felt for him was so much more.

A sudden ache stabbed at her, as if a knife had just been plunged into her stomach, and twisted. She sucked in a sharp breath and her nails sank into Ryder's arms.

Her nails . . . her nails were turning black.

He bit me. The primal . . .

"Sabine?"

She pushed at Ryder. "It's . . . happening." The virus—whatever the hell it was—it was *in* her. She could feel it. Twisting. Cutting. She ran her tongue over her teeth. They felt normal, but her nails . . .

She held up her hands. "It's happening," she said again.

His face blanched. "No, no, it's fucking *not.*"

Her gaze met his. She was so glad she'd taken the pleasure with him. So glad that they'd stopped in the rain.

The rain . . .

It was just a sprinkle now.

"You promised you'd help me," Sabine reminded him. She fumbled, adjusting her clothes.

He had to help her.

But his face had locked into tortured lines. "I'm *not* killing you."

The knife was stabbing her again. "It . . . hurts, Ryder."

He shook her. "We can stop it." He laced his fingers with hers. "Come on. Genesis made them. We can fix them. Hell, Wyatt said that you were the key—"

She wanted to tell Ryder that she felt more than lust for him.

But she couldn't seem to speak. The stabbing was gone, but she felt as if she were burning up from the inside. *Burning.*

A moan slipped from her.

Ryder lifted her into his arms. "Hold on, love." He started running then, moving so fast. "Please, hold on."

Her vampire.

The fire built within her. Burning more. Hotter. Her hands curled around his neck. If she changed, he wouldn't kill her. Sabine knew that.

Because she also knew, though he'd never said the words . . .

He loves me.

Which was only fair, since Sabine was sure that she loved her dark vampire.

Loved him and was very, very afraid that she might soon turn on him.

The others had no control. They killed.

Her black nails dug into his skin. Her teeth began to ache.

I don't want to hurt him.

But when she turned fully primal, her control might not last.

It wasn't midnight. Not even eleven o'clock yet. Ryder didn't give a fuck. He kicked down the door at 49 Chartres, and when the humans turned toward him, he bellowed, *"Adams! Keith Adams!"*

Keith came running, his eyes wide. As soon as he got a good look at Ryder, and the woman lying so still in his arms, Keith stumbled to a halt. "Sabine?"

Ryder's hold on her tightened. "One of the primals bit her. I thought . . . I thought the bite wouldn't change her."

"But it is." A woman's voice.

Keith backed up.

Ryder saw the woman walking toward him. Her hair hung in a long braid. Her eyes—green, focused—were on Sabine. "The virus is pushing through her body now."

Clinical. "You're the doctor Keith mentioned."

She nodded. "My name's Cassie, and I'm here to help you."

He stalked toward her. "Don't help me. Help *her.*"

Cassie's stare drifted over Sabine. Worry flashed on her face. "Bring her to the next room. There's a table in there that we can use."

Ryder followed her, hurrying inside the small room. Keith shoved some papers off the table, and carefully, Ryder put Sabine on the table. He took her hand. Wanted to roar when he saw the dark nails.

The woman—Cassie—reached into a black bag.

Ryder swiped out with his left hand and caught her fingers. *"She's been sliced open enough."*

He saw the pulse jump in her throat. "Please, I-I'm not like Wyatt and the others at Genesis."

But he didn't believe her. There were secrets in her eyes. Lies.

"I just . . . I need to check her blood. Get it under a microscope." She had a needle in her hand. "I need to see what's happening on a deeper level."

Sabine moaned. "Burning . . ."

Cassie frowned down at her. "How long ago was she bitten?"

"Thirty minutes." He rubbed his fingers over her knuckles. Her nails. Shit, they were . . .

Not as dark.

His breath stilled in his lungs.

Cassie leaned over Sabine and looked into her mouth. "Her teeth aren't changing."

No.

He lifted her hand. He could see the pink in her nails now.

He could actually *breathe* again. Whatever was happening in Sabine's body, she was fighting off the attack.

Hell, yes, she was *fighting*.

Cassie tried to push the needle into Sabine's arm. Ryder grabbed the syringe. Tossed it. "She's fine."

He'd been frantic moments before. Ready to trade and barter and demand, but her claws were turning back into regular nails. The stark paleness of her skin had faded back to a normal hue. Her lashes opened.

She was back.

"Ryder?"

His Sabine. So strong, when she didn't even realize it.

"Get away from us," he snapped to the woman and Keith. He didn't need them. He should have stayed away, for a little longer. But the panic had made him crazy.

Didn't matter.

She was *back*.

Sabine sat up. Ryder pulled her into his arms. Held her close.

"Amazing," Cassie whispered. "Her body fought off the infection at such a rapid rate."

"How!" The desperate cry came from Keith Adams.

Ryder lifted his head. Stared at the red-faced man.

"How'd she do it?" Keith asked, his voice lower. *"How?"*

"Her genetics are no doubt very different from a human's," Cassie said as she tilted her head and swept an assessing gaze over Sabine. "We already knew the primals were after her blood, but maybe . . . maybe it wasn't for the reason Wyatt thought. Not because they were linked to Ryder, but because . . ." Her eyes narrowed. "Maybe they realized she was the key they needed. Their cure."

Ryder pulled Sabine from the table. Pushed her behind him. "You're both going to want to get the hell out of my way now."

Cassie shook her head. "Maybe it was something in her scent, some kind of trigger that their enhanced senses picked up on. They had an instinctive response, not even knowing why . . . but perhaps it was because they were ill. She was their cure—"

Ryder didn't give a fuck as to the whys of the situation. "I warned you," Ryder growled. Then he shoved Keith out of his way.

Cassie yelped and hurriedly jumped back. Good. Time to get the hell out of there.

"We have your brother!" Keith yelled at him.

Ryder hesitated. His gaze swung back to meet the human's. Keith was rising off the floor. No guards were in the room. Just Keith and the doctor.

Easy prey.

Ryder smiled. "My brother is dead. I sent him to hell a long time ago." *The first time I bit him. When I destroyed the man he'd been.*

"You think so?" Keith challenged. He was back on his feet now. Looking too desperate. Desperate men were often the most dangerous. "Then why don't you just check behind that door?" He waved to the right. To a wooden door that had been painted white. "Because Genesis found him. They *found* him, buried in Russia. The guy was nearly decapitated and had a stake shoved in his chest. Only he wasn't bones in that grave. Wasn't a rotted corpse. When they took that stake out, when those Genesis fools there gave him blood, he came back."

Impossible.

"Ryder?" Sabine's shocked voice.

"They wouldn't have even known where to look for him," Ryder said. He wouldn't fall for this BS.

"They had dozens of vampires imprisoned in their facilities. Vampires that they tortured for weeks. *Years.* With enough pain, don't you think those vampires would have shared the information they had? Told anything? Everything?" Keith's voice rushed out. "One of them . . . some guy named Lawrence . . . he knew."

Lawrence. The name was familiar. Ryder had a flash of a vampire. Thin, small. With shaking hands. Hands that had helped to kill Malcolm so long ago.

"You didn't finish the job on your brother," Keith told him. "Or hell, maybe he's too powerful to ever die, just like you. Too powerful . . ." Keith lifted his chin and straightened his shoulders. "At Genesis, they injected him, gave him their fucking tainted blood, and he became just like the others. *Primal.*"

Ryder shook his head. Impossible. He wasn't gonna believe this story. "If my brother were alive, he—"

"*You* were the first!" Now it was Cassie who spoke. "But when you gave your blood to others, you started diluting its power. Every exchange, every vampire created after that was weaker."

And that was why Wyatt had tried to give Ryder's blood to the primals in his lab? Because the doctor had thought the pure blood could heal them?

It's not blood that . . . was the cure. It's Sabine. Her tears. A phoenix's tears . . . found out . . . really heal . . . Some of Wyatt's last words seemed to echo in Ryder's mind.

His gaze darted to the door. If his brother was in there . . .

"Go look," Keith yelled. "Look!"

He could hear sounds behind the door. Desperate breathing. Scratching. As if someone were clawing against wood.

"How would you have him?" Sabine demanded. She was at Ryder's side now. Not looking so weak. Looking strong and beautiful. "If this story is even true, how would he be here, with you?"

"I was smuggling subjects out of Genesis," Cassie confessed quietly. "Trying to help. I was going to get you out, too, but Genesis burned before I could help you."

She sounded so sincere. But no one had been there to help him. Or to save Sabine. "Lies," he rasped.

"Well, there's one way to know for sure," Sabine said and she stalked toward the white door.

But before she could rip open the door, Ryder jumped in front of her. If his brother was in that room, no way would he let her go in first. He grabbed her hand, curling his fingers around hers, around the doorknob. His gaze met Sabine's, and he knew she'd see his fury. "My brother was a butcher." His head tilted toward Cassie. "Do you even have any idea what he did *before* I put him in the ground?" *My brother . . . alive?*

"He isn't the same man now," she whispered, looking tearful. "I started . . . I figured out the cure, using teardrops that were recovered from Subject Twenty-Nine—I mean, from Sabine. I used those drops to begin treatment to eliminate the primal virus from his system. Your brother has changed. He's—"

"Open the door," Sabine whispered, her soft words cutting right across the doctor's words.

But Ryder pushed her back. He made sure his body was shielding hers, and only then did he open the door. With a squeak, the knob turned beneath his hand and the wooden door opened.

The inner room was big, much bigger than the other room. Inside, there were lab tables. Test tubes. Cages.

Been there. Fucking done that.

In one of those cages, he saw the hunched form of a man. The man's body was in the shadows. Ryder began walking toward him. There . . . that was where the scratching sound was coming from. He could see the man's long, dark claws scratching at the floor near his feet.

"I know what he was like before, but he's different." Cassie followed close behind Ryder. "Since I started his treatment, there's been no aggression. I think the original vampirism virus created a serotonin deficiency in him that—"

Malcolm wasn't in the cage. As he watched, the man in the cage surged toward the bars and gave Ryder a clear view of his face.

"Vaughn?" Sabine whispered. "He's . . . dead."

"There's a lot of that going around," another voice said.

A voice that came from the right. The man standing there had made no sound at all, hadn't even *breathed*, so Ryder hadn't picked up on his presence as he stood cloaked in the shadows.

But that voice had haunted Ryder for so long. He turned his head even as his hand reached out and curled around Sabine's arm.

And his eyes met a gaze the exact shade as his own. A gaze that had last looked upon him with fury and hatred.

"Hello, my brother," Malcolm said quietly. "It's been a long time."

Screams and blood and agony. Women and children slaughtered. Cries that wouldn't end. So many broken bodies. "Not long enough," Ryder responded as battle-ready tension pumped through him. He'd defeated Malcolm once, and he'd do it again.

"You see?" Cassie was there again. Rushing in front of Malcolm. Gesturing excitedly with her hands. "He's cured! His fangs have returned to normal. His claws— normal. He has his control back. There haven't been any attacks from him, any—"

"Did you hear that?" Malcolm asked with a smile. One that showed his sharp canines. "I'm normal."

Easy words. Flat. But . . .

"Sabine, go back into the other room," Ryder ordered.

Cassie blinked. Some of the excitement left her face. "But we need Sabine's assistance. It's her tears, they're the key. A phoenix's tears can heal anything, anyone."

So he'd heard.

Cassie glanced toward Sabine. "The tears have to be shed willingly. They can't just be harvested from the tear ducts. That's why it's so hard to get them."

Wasn't that just a damn inconvenience for her?

Cassie shifted nervously. "If we can just get a few more then we can help so many others."

"I-I haven't cried since Ryder changed me," Sabine said, shaking her head.

"Changed you?" Now Keith had come into the room.

"Ryder's blood . . ." Sabine swallowed. Ryder saw her gaze dart to Vaughn. The primal was yanking at the bars of his cage. Snapping his teeth. "I'm a vampire now, not a phoenix. I *can't* help Vaughn."

Cassie's eyes widened, and then she glanced over at Vaughn. "B-but we need . . ."

"You *will* help my son," Keith demanded as his hands fisted. "He's not dying!"

The snarling, fighting beast in that cage screamed. An inhuman cry.

Then Keith charged for Sabine. Ryder yanked her back and stepped forward. So instead of attacking Sabine, Keith shoved the stake in his hands into Ryder's chest. Or rather, the fucking fool tried to drive it into Ryder's heart.

Ryder stopped him. He caught the wood. All but disintegrated it in his fist. "*Never* come at her!" he roared.

Then he heard the laughter.

Ryder stared into the human's eyes. They looked a little . . . lost. Unfocused.

And that mocking laughter had haunted so many of his dreams.

"You always were too impetuous . . ." Malcolm's voice. Ryder turned slowly and found Malcolm holding Sabine in his arms. His brother bent to smell her hair. "You just could never see the real threat that was right in front of your face. The threat that's been there, all along."

His brother.

Ryder grabbed the human's head. Turned it to the side. Saw the faint bite marks on Keith's neck.

Son of a bitch. Malcolm had just forced Keith to attack, in order to distract Ryder.

"They're just puppets, aren't they?" Malcolm murmured. "Puppets and food."

Ryder pushed Keith away. He faced off against his brother. Cassie was still there, her frightened gaze flying back and forth between Malcolm and Sabine.

"Wh-what are you doing?" Cassie asked Malcolm. "Let her go!" The woman was scared, but she didn't appear to be under Malcolm's control.

Appearances could be so deceiving.

"Of course." Malcolm smiled. His fangs glinted. "I'm not desperate for her blood like the others, so I *should* just let her go. It's the right thing to do." His fingers were wrapped around Sabine's neck. "But fuck the right thing."

He snapped her neck.

"I never gave a shit about right," Malcolm said. "Not after my change, and, sorry to ruin this for you, brother, but not before, either."

He had a stake in his hand.

The broken neck . . . that wouldn't have killed Sabine. Ryder rushed forward. She'd recover from the break. *She'd recover.*

But not if his bastard of a brother staked her.

He grabbed Sabine's hand. Yanked her body away from Malcolm. When he turned to shield her with his body, Ryder felt strong fingers close over his neck.

"You love her."

Carefully, because her broken neck hadn't healed yet, Ryder lowered Sabine to the floor. Cassie gave a wild cry and rushed toward her.

When Ryder stood, Malcolm moved in a flash and put the stake right over his heart.

"I didn't think you could love. I thought you were like me." Now Malcolm sounded disappointed. But he'd made a mistake. He hadn't attacked when he'd had the chance.

"I used to think that I was just like you," Ryder told him. "But then I realized I wasn't broken."

The tip of the stake pushed into his skin, drawing blood.

"They *buried* me. I wasn't dead. I could feel everything. Do you know what the worms and insects did to me?"

Ryder's jaw locked. "You'd lost your head. You were *staked*." He should have been dead.

"It takes more than a stake to kill you and me. Let me show you." Then Malcolm shoved forward with that stake.

Only . . .

Ryder's hand flew up. He stopped the wood before it could do more than—*fuck me*—press against his heart. The pain pulsed through him, burning and white-hot.

Malcolm's eyes widened in surprise. He tried to push down with the wood. "You're . . . stronger."

"I was always stronger."

He heard a gasp behind him. Sabine. Coming back to him. Healing. Bones cracked.

Ryder yanked the stake from his chest. Malcolm jumped back and gazed at him with furious, desperate eyes.

"None of this was my choice!" Malcolm bellowed. "You should have let me die with the rest of our family. It wasn't your call to make! *You should have let me die then!*"

Ryder nodded. "Yes, I should have." Malcolm's words were so familiar to him. His head cocked even as the blood continued to pour from his chest. "Julia," he murmured, understanding so much more now.

Malcolm smiled.

"You're the one," Ryder said with a slow nod. "You wanted them to take me out."

"I wanted you to wind up in hell, with me," Malcolm snarled back. "Those Genesis bastards found me. They took my blood and kept me prisoner in their cells for *years.*"

Ryder stared at him. When he looked hard enough, he could almost see the brother that Malcolm had once been, back when they were both still human.

I never gave a shit about right. Not after my change, and, sorry to ruin this for you, brother, but not before, either.

But maybe he'd never even known him then.

"I told them about you," Malcolm confessed. "Told them that if they wanted real power"—his lips twisted— "then they wanted you."

And Genesis had begun hunting him.

Vaughn was yelling behind them and still thrashing against his bars.

"Ryder?" Sabine whispered.

He eased out a slow breath. "Richard Wyatt kept us both at the same—"

"You're *not* listening!" Malcolm yelled at him. His brother's face flushed. "I said . . . *years*. Richard was just a whelp when they brought me in to Genesis. It wasn't him. It was the old guy who found me. His father. That's the asshole who dug me up. I thought he was going to help me. Stop the pain. He just made it worse."

Ryder saw that his brother's hands were shaking.

Malcolm lifted his hands and pressed them against his temples. "Everything makes it worse."

A soft hand curled around Ryder's wrist. Ryder didn't look at Sabine. He couldn't. Malcolm had already tried to use her against him once. "Go to the other room, Sabine."

Malcolm's hands dropped. "So she doesn't see you clean up this mess? So she doesn't see you kill the primal? Kill the human?" He pointed toward a frozen Keith. "And drain the doc?" He tossed a glare toward Cassie.

Cassie was crying. Tears trickled down her cheeks, but she didn't make a sound.

"And after you dispatch all of them, you'll have to kill me. But a stake didn't work before. A beheading didn't. What else can you try?" Malcolm seemed mildly curious.

Fire. "I think I have a few options," Ryder said as he rolled his shoulders. There would be no room for emotion here. No sympathy could stir in his heart.

Do you know what the worms and insects did?

"Go, Sabine," he urged and pushed her away. Pushed her away, when he wanted to pull her close. To make certain that she was whole and healed.

Her steps were hesitant.

But just as she reached the door, Malcolm spoke again. "Do you think Keith is the only human I . . . sampled?"

Hell.

"Sabine."

She stopped at the door.

"What did you do?" Cassie whispered, her voice hoarse. *"Why?"*

Malcolm shrugged. "It's good to hedge your bets. And I have always enjoyed being in control of my own little army." His arms lifted and spread around him. "I've been building my army for quite a while. After all, I was in Genesis for over twenty-five years."

Fuck.

"But . . . you were a primal," Cassie said, swiping at the tears on her face. She came closer to them, with slow, hesitant steps. "You weren't in control. You only knew the hunger."

Malcolm turned his stare on her. "A mindless beast."

She flinched.

"Isn't that what I was *supposed* to be?" Malcolm growled at her.

"It's what the others were . . ."

"The others were made from *my* blood. Humans, who thought that they could become bigger, better warriors with some vampire blood and DNA thrown into the mix. I *made* them. *Me.* They just couldn't handle my power."

"B-but . . . I found you . . . in that cage . . . you looked just like the others."

Ryder knew she had to be talking about the black claws. The mouthful of razor-sharp teeth.

"You mean . . . I looked like this?" Malcolm's head bowed. His body convulsed. Shuddered.

"The tears . . . *They healed you!*" Cassie cried out.

Malcolm's head lifted. His eyes were pitch-black. His teeth—*hello, mouthful of fucking fangs*. When Malcolm raised his hands, Ryder wasn't surprised to see the flash of black claws.

"I can change anytime I want." Malcolm jumped forward, moving lightning-fast. His claws wrapped around Cassie's neck and he hauled her against him. "I *told* you, I made them. My blood. Genesis wanted to play with genetics and mutations, but before they even started experimenting on humans, they first played with me."

And his brother had become even more of a monster.

"Old Man Wyatt tried to punch up the vampire evolution." Malcolm's hold tightened on Cassie. "The scientists understood what I could be. How strong. How deadly. But I could change back, any fucking time I wanted."

From the corner of his eye, Ryder saw Sabine crouch and pick up a chunk of wood.

Vaughn was still screaming. Snarling.

"After they experimented on the humans, they realized—too late—that they couldn't change back." He bent his head and licked Cassie's neck. She held herself statue-still within his arms, eyes stricken and terrified. "They couldn't do anything because they weren't strong enough. They weren't like me."

Or me. Ryder realized as he stared at Malcolm. No wonder Richard Wyatt had been so desperate for his blood. Malcolm's blood had sent the test subjects straight to hell. Richard must have thought that an infusion of blood from the first vampire—untainted blood—could help them.

He'd been wrong, so Richard's only option had been . . .

Ryder's gaze jumped to Sabine. She'd hidden the stake behind her back.

The tears of a phoenix.

"I made my army," Malcolm said, as he looked up to smirk at Ryder. "One victim at a time. I controlled the humans. Even from inside my prison at Genesis, I sent the humans out to find vampires who would aid me."

Vamps who would be willing to turn on me. Ryder stared back at his brother and didn't allow any emotion to show on his face.

"When my army was strong enough, when I knew Genesis had *you*," Malcolm continued, "I escaped."

By acting like a victim. By using Cassie.

He hadn't realized his brother was such a damn good actor.

"I've been wanting to taste you for a while," Malcolm muttered as his mouth lowered near Cassie's throat once more. "There were always too many cameras on us. Too many watching you so closely."

Ryder saw Cassie's eyes. The fear faded and gave way to . . . satisfaction? But when Cassie spoke, her voice trembled. "Don't," she said. "Please."

Maybe his brother wasn't the only good actor in the room.

Malcolm sank his fangs into her throat.

Sabine screamed and ran forward, with her stake clutched tightly in her hands. "Leave her alone! No more! *No more!*"

But Ryder grabbed Sabine around the waist and hauled her back. He held her against his chest.

She didn't need to save Cassie. Malcolm was already shoving the doctor away and trying to spit out her blood.

His claws retracted. His mouthful of fangs vanished.

"Surprise, surprise," Cassie said, her voice sad. "I'm not what you thought, either, bastard."

Malcolm stared at her with horror blazing in his eyes. Blood dripped from his chin.

And then he fell to the floor, his body frozen, apparently stone-cold dead.

CHAPTER NINETEEN

Ryder's hands were like steel bands around Sabine's stomach. Her neck ached and fury clawed at her gut.

And Malcolm was dead?

"You're like Richard Wyatt." Ryder's voice came out, low and deadly, from behind her.

Cassie gave them a sad smile, even as her gaze dipped back to Malcolm's still figure. "No, Richard's blood contained a diluted poison. Mine is much more potent, as you can see."

Poison? In the woman's blood? What the hell was going on there?

Sabine tried to pull free. Ryder just held her tighter.

"I made sure that Malcolm never got my blood while we were in Genesis." Now Cassie's voice sounded sad. "Because I thought I could help him. I knew if he tasted so much as a sip . . ."

"He'd be dead," Ryder finished.

She nodded slowly and said, "I wanted to save him. Genesis had already hurt so many, killed them." Her chin lifted. "I'm truly trying to make amends."

Yeah, well, good luck with that. Sabine stilled in Ryder's arms. "Some things can never be fixed."

Cassie's stare turned to Sabine. The woman's eyes were green. A familiar green. *The same shade as Richard Wyatt's eyes.* "No," Cassie sighed out the word. "They can't."

Ryder slowly eased his hold on Sabine.

"I was created as a weapon," Cassie told them, turning her back on Malcolm. "A way to stop the vamps. With the right serums, human blood can become toxic to vampires. Just one sip, and it's a real killer drink."

Sabine put her hand on Ryder's chest and shoved him back. She didn't want the guy anywhere near Cassie's blood.

Wait, come to think of it . . . *I don't want to be near her blood, either.* So Sabine backed up a few steps, too.

She just wanted to get the hell away from Cassie. Only, if the woman was a walking vampire death kit, could they just let Cassie leave that place?

"My . . . boy . . ." The broken sob had Sabine glancing over at Keith. He was on his feet and looking about ten years older. Malcolm's hold on the guy was gone, and now Keith was blinking and staring at Vaughn's snarling figure in horror. "We can't . . . fix him?"

"Not without phoenix blood," Cassie said quietly. "I'm sorry."

There was another phoenix in town. Sabine compressed her lips, knowing that if she mentioned Dante, he'd be hunted. But if she didn't tell Cassie and Keith about Dante, then Vaughn's life would be over.

What loyalty did she owe to Dante? He'd tried to kill her before. Multiple times.

So she could easily offer him up here. Right?

The scent of smoke teased her nose.

"Why the hell not?" Ryder muttered as his body tensed. "Everyone else is here. Figures he'd join the party, too."

Then the door burst in. Sabine realized that she wouldn't have to reveal Dante's presence in the city. The phoenix had just stalked inside. Fire burned in his eyes. He stared at them all with fury. And flames burned above his hand.

He lifted his hand and aimed the flames right at Cassie. *"You."*

The flames tore from his fingers and flew toward her.

Cassie screamed and lifted her hands.

Sabine moved before she realized what she was doing. She jumped in front of Cassie and the flames hit her in the chest.

"No!" Ryder yelled.

Sabine fell to the floor and rolled. Her clothes were smoking, but—but the fire hadn't injured her.

Cassie was there, trying to slap at the flames on Sabine's body. She gasped and glanced up at Sabine. "No burns." A shocked whisper.

So the fire hadn't burned her. Big deal. "You're welcome," Sabine mumbled as she jerked her head to the right to find Dante and Ryder fighting it out. Flames and claws and fury.

"He wasn't aiming at either of you," the low voice whispered from behind Sabine and Cassie. "I think that fire was meant for me."

Even as fear pulsed through her veins, Sabine spun around.

And she felt a sharp, hard thrust in her chest.

Sabine looked into Malcolm's eyes. Eyes that were very much aware, and then her gaze fell to the chunk of wood that had been shoved into her chest.

Blood pumped out of her.

"No!" Cassie yelled.

Malcolm swiped out with his claws and sliced right across Cassie's throat. Her yell choked off. Blood sprayed. In the next instant, Cassie was tossed across the room.

"Told you all," Malcolm growled, "it takes *more* to kill me."

Sabine's fingers were fumbling with the stake. Attempting to wrench it out of her. But . . . her fingers felt numb. Uncoordinated. She couldn't seem to grab hold of the wood. And she was falling, slumping, hitting the hard floor.

She tried to keep her eyes open. They wanted to sag. She wanted to sleep.

No, not sleep.

Die.

"Sabine?"

Ryder was there. Crouching over her. Ignoring the threat right behind him. Didn't he see Malcolm? He couldn't turn his back on that bastard. Malcolm was evil. Twisted.

Unstoppable?

"You're going to be all right," Ryder said.

She hadn't realized he was such a liar.

He pulled out the stake. The fast removal hurt, and she moaned.

And more blood gushed from her.

Ryder put his bleeding wrist over her mouth. Tried to give her his blood.

But she couldn't take it. She was too cold. Her body . . . She couldn't even drink.

It was just like before. Her body had shut down, and

she was trapped, screaming on the inside but making no sound for anyone else to hear.

Just like before . . . the first time she'd met Ryder. She'd lost her blood and been so cold, *just like this*.

Malcolm drove his claws into Ryder's back. Ryder didn't let her go. He had to let her go. He had to fight his brother.

Ryder's blood rained down on her.

No.

He wasn't fighting back. Malcolm was slicing Ryder's back, ripping into his flesh, but Ryder was just holding her tight. Whispering, over and over, "Don't leave me, Sabine, don't ever leave me."

But she was already leaving. She knew what death felt like. Knew its cold touch so very, very well. Almost as well as she knew her lover's touch.

Her breath had stilled in her lungs. Her heart had stopped beating. Maybe it had stopped the instant the stake plunged into her . . . or the instant it was pulled out.

She couldn't move her body. Couldn't speak and say the one thing that she needed to say. *I love you.*

But perhaps she didn't need to say the words. Perhaps Ryder already knew. Because in that last glimpse she had of him, Sabine saw his eyes. His gaze was filled with fear, yes, but also filled with love.

He loved her.

She hoped, *hoped*, that he knew . . . *I love you, too.*

Then the cold deepened. Such terrible cold.

She was leaving him.

Leaving . . .

Why did the cold burn?

* * *

Sabine was gone.

Ryder held her tight, ignoring the pain as Malcolm sliced the flesh from his back.

"Fight me!" Malcolm roared.

Ryder held on to Sabine. Her blood soaked him. She'd been gone, even before he'd pulled the stake from her chest. Her eyes had already been empty. The fierce passion that was Sabine . . . *gone*.

Another slash over his back, then Malcolm's claws drove straight into Ryder's spine. *"Fight me."*

Ryder didn't feel the pain from the attack. He was already in enough agony. *Lost her. The only thing, the only person that I needed . . . Lost. Her.*

His heart was gone. He'd tried to hold on to his humanity. Fought for it.

But . . .

Gone.

There wasn't anything left within him. Just a roar of rage that was building. Hollow. Cold.

Sabine had never been cold. She'd been fire. She'd been life.

Carefully, gently, he released Sabine. He pressed a kiss to her lips.

Malcolm was laughing.

"Did you love her so desperately, brother? Is that why you made her into a vampire? Did you think she'd be with you forever?"

She will be. He'd never love anyone but her. In his heart, Sabine would *always* be there.

His gaze lifted. The human, Keith, was near the cage. His eyes were anguished as he looked back at Sabine's body. In shock, he stood frozen.

And the other phoenix was on the ground. Ryder

had broken his neck. The flames were flickering around him, and Ryder knew Dante would rise soon.

But until then . . .

I have plenty of time.

His hands trembled as he closed Sabine's eyes. He didn't want her to see what he'd do.

She's not there to see . . . The whisper slid through him, but he ignored it. He could feel his mind splintering.

Without her . . .

Why?

His spine should have been severed by his brother's claws, but Ryder rose to his feet. He'd found that he healed faster and faster these days.

Because of Sabine? Because of her blood? Her tears?

She'd done nothing but make him stronger.

He'd be nothing without her.

"I love her." Love, not *loved.* Because his feelings weren't just going to magically stop.

Malcolm's lips parted in surprise. "You—"

Ryder drove his fist into his brother's jaw. Sent him sprawling back to the floor. "Have you ever loved?" Ryder demanded.

Malcolm scrambled back.

"I hadn't . . . not until her." He grabbed Malcolm. Yanked him to his feet. This time, Ryder drove his fist into his brother's stomach. "She made me stronger."

Malcolm was spitting up blood.

"Do you think I've never wanted to close my eyes? To end this nightmare?" Ryder snarled at him.

The roar within him built.

Splinter . . .

"I've tried . . . my body heals . . . heals so fast, even

faster now . . ." He slammed his head into Malcolm's, breaking his brother's nose. "You think you're the only one who has ever felt insects crawling on you? Eating you? I went to ground in the fourteen hundreds, so tired of the slaughters committed by men and vampires alike. You were gone. And I hated what I'd become." He'd ordered his own entombment. He'd finally clawed his way out of that imprisonment after a year. "But we can't change what we are."

Malcolm watched him with wide eyes.

We can't change.

Ryder glanced over at Sabine. "I wanted to change for her."

Sabine . . . his Sabine . . . she was . . .

Burning?

The scent of ash and fire hadn't come from Dante. Dante was still lying on the floor, not moving. But Sabine was burning.

We can't change.

Her eyes had still flickered with flames when she made love with him. When she'd touched the vamp's chest back at Bran's Castle, he'd seen smoke drift in the air.

He'd tried to convert Sabine, but the phoenix part of her hadn't died, not completely. Maybe it could truly never die.

And the phoenix was rising again.

"What the hell . . . ?" Malcolm's shocked voice cried out.

"Not hell," Ryder muttered. Sabine was his angel, and she was coming back to him. *Yes.*

The fire spread over her body. Burning slowly at first, then blazing hotter, higher, until he couldn't see her at all. Just the flames. Red and gold and beautiful.

"She's burning." Malcolm grabbed Ryder and spun him around. He put a gun to Ryder's chest. Ryder didn't even bother wondering where the guy had gotten his weapon. "You'll never have her again!" Malcolm swore.

He'd have her in minutes. Ryder smiled at him. "Wooden bullets?" Because, of course, what else would you use against a vampire?

"They'll knock you out," Malcolm said, snapping his teeth. "Then I'll take your head. I won't leave it hanging with some tendons and flesh, the way you did with me."

The smell of smoke filled the room. The crackle of the flames grew louder. Sweet, wonderful fire. "Was that my mistake?" Ryder asked him, holding his body still. He didn't want Malcolm focusing on Sabine now. He'd heard that the moment of change was the weakest moment for a phoenix. They were vulnerable at that time. According to old whispers he'd heard centuries ago, the only time they could be truly killed was when they burned.

Sabine was vulnerable then. And—

And Dante had wanted to kill Sabine. The phoenixes . . . they kill their own kind.

The cold suspicion iced through him. Dante had come to New Orleans in order to find Sabine. He'd been tracking her. Trying to find the perfect moment to kill her? A moment like . . . now?

But he'd snapped Dante's neck. Hadn't he?

"Yes," Malcolm hissed. "That was your fucking mistake, that was—"

Ryder yanked the gun from him. Fired the wooden bullet straight into Malcolm's heart. "Good-bye, brother." He wouldn't feel the grief or the rage. Not then.

And he *would* finish the job, but first . . .

Ryder spun around. Dante was on his feet—*tricky*

SOB—and advancing toward the flames that enclosed Sabine. Ryder ran for him and tackled the guy. "Stay away from her!"

Dante shoved him back.

That was when he noticed Cassie was in the corner. She watched them with pain-filled eyes as blood pulsed from her neck. "S-stop," she whispered.

Dante and Ryder rose to their feet.

"Is this what you wanted?" Ryder demanded. "To attack my woman? To kill her when she was weak?"

Dante craned his neck, popping it as he turned his head to the left and the right. "Had to see . . . wasn't even sure if she could burn anymore . . ."

She could burn just fine.

"You're staying away from her," Ryder said because he wasn't about to let anyone get close to her when she was weak.

"She's not even going to know you." Dante smiled at him. A hard, evil grin. "When the fire dies away, I'd say you've got about a five percent shot of her even remembering who you are. Do you know that? The fire can take away our memories. Leave us with nothing but ashes. She'll see you, see your monster and just want to run from you. That is, if she doesn't go for your throat first."

"That's a chance I'll take." Maybe she wouldn't remember him, then, fine, he'd just make her fall for him again. This time, things would be different. She wouldn't have to know the pain of their first meeting. She wouldn't remember the bite or the blood or—

No.

He didn't want any memories taken from Sabine. She deserved to have every instance in her mind, good and bad and everything in between.

Dante's eyes narrowed as he studied Ryder. "I don't understand you."

Ryder shrugged. "What's to understand?" *Sabine, hurry, come back to me.*

"I've seen you, over the centuries . . ."

Dante's words shocked Ryder into silence. As far as he knew, only vampires lived for that long a period of time. Every other being he'd encountered had seemed to have an expiration date.

"You've killed," Dante said, voice expressionless. "You've fought. You've left a trail of death in your path."

Ryder lifted his chin. "Looking to throw some stones? What have you been doing for your *centuries?* Protecting the innocent?" Doubtful, given the way this guy enjoyed tossing around his flames.

Dante waved that away. "I know what you are, on the inside. Because I'm the same. The darkness. The need to kill, to fight, to destroy. It's in us both."

"I *don't* want to destroy Sabine."

His brother's blood was on the ground. How long would he have before Malcolm rose? How long before Sabine came back to him? *Hurry, love. Don't keep me waiting.*

He had to stand guard over her burning form. He couldn't leave, not even to finish his battle with Malcolm. Or rather, not even to *finish him.*

"Why not?" Dante asked. "What makes her different?"

Cassie started to choke. No, she'd been choking all along, slowly dying as she tried to beg them for help. Ryder saw that now as his gaze flew to her. She couldn't speak. Her eyes screamed for her. Keith had finally shaken from his stupor and run to her, but there was nothing he could do to help.

"Will you save the human?" Dante asked as he cocked his head. "Will you rush to aid her, trying to even that bloody scorecard that you carry around with you? Saving human lives, to make up for all the ones you slaughtered?"

Cassie was dying in front of him.

"Or will you keep standing guard," Dante murmured. "Over the phoenix who burns so brightly? A phoenix who may soon come for your heart."

"She already has my heart." Sabine could do with it whatever the hell she wanted.

Cassie had tears streaming down her cheeks. Her eyes were desperate, but she shook her head when she gazed at Ryder. Her lips moved, just the faintest bit . . . *Stay with her.*

Sorrow had his own lips tightening. Cassie wasn't like the others from Genesis. Perhaps she really had wanted to help.

For that kindness, she was receiving a slow and brutal death.

Then Ryder saw her eyes dart to Dante's form. Her stare changed. Flickered with an emotion that he was becoming too familiar with these days.

Ryder's breath left him in a rush. "She saved you."

Dante frowned. "Sabine has done—"

"Not Sabine." He didn't want the man even speaking her name. *Stay away from her.* To keep Dante's attention away from Sabine, Ryder said, "The human, Cassie, she's the reason you escaped Genesis."

Dante shook his head. His gaze darted to Cassie. His frown deepened.

"You don't remember," Ryder said as his heart raced. "Because they killed you, again and again." The same lack of memory that Dante was using to taunt him, well, that same darkness, that *nothingness,* had erased Dante's past.

A past that was dying less than three feet from him. And the guy didn't even realize what he was losing. *Not what, who.*

A woman with love in her dying gaze.

"How do you think you got out?" Ryder pushed.

Dante's stare was on Cassie. Her shirt was soaked red from the blood that had poured from her neck.

"Do you remember her? At all?" Ryder knew the emotion he'd seen in Cassie's eyes. That kind of consuming need and longing was exactly what he felt for Sabine.

Dante turned away from Ryder. He gazed only at the woman before him. A woman who was wheezing as she tried to catch her last breath. "Cas . . . sandra? My . . . Cassandra?"

There was a *whoosh* of sound. Ryder whirled around. Sabine was on her feet. Surrounded by flames. Standing, with her hands up.

Malcolm was clawing at his chest, rising again, shouting, but Ryder couldn't make out his brother's words over the crackle of flames.

Flames that were snaking out. Racing over the walls. The ceiling.

She doesn't have control.

Keith yelled as he ran back to the cage and fought to free his son. But if he let the beast out, what would happen then?

Vaughn would attack. Would kill others, infect more humans.

Dante crouched over Cassie. His hands were bathed in her blood. "Help her!" he roared.

But who could help her?

If the phoenix cried, perhaps his tears would heal Cassie.

Or my blood, maybe I can transform her. But no, Ryder couldn't transform her, not with the poison that had been placed within her body.

And Sabine's flames were growing. She'd kill all the humans there, if he didn't stop her.

Ryder straightened his shoulders. Took a step toward the flames. They wouldn't burn him. They hadn't before.

But even if the flames did burn, wasn't she worth the pain? Wasn't she worth *everything*?

The flames licked around his feet. Rose over his legs. Burned his clothing.

Didn't touch his skin.

"Sabine."

Her head whipped toward him. He saw the fire in her eyes. Fire, but no recognition.

"Pull it back, Sabine, before you hurt the humans."

She smiled.

The flames grew higher.

She was so fucking beautiful—and the deadliest thing he'd ever seen in his very long life.

"You don't want to hurt them," he said, closing in on her. Her flames were orange and gold. Big. Bright. "You don't want—"

She lifted her hands and held them, palms out, toward him. "Stay back."

No. "Do you know me?"

Sabine shook her head.

"I know you," he whispered as he kept advancing. "This isn't what you want. You don't want to kill."

But her smile said otherwise. "I like the fire. I want to burn. Destroy."

She turned her head. Keith was struggling to open the cage. Fumbling with keys. Sabine frowned and sent fire racing toward the cage. Vaughn screamed when the fire licked over his arm.

"I only know the flames," she whispered. Her voice was husky. Deeper than before. Flowing with power. Darkness. In her eyes, he saw rage and pain and fear.

And he remembered another time. The first time she'd burned before him. "I thought you'd died then, too," he said.

Malcolm rose to his feet. A gaping hole filled his chest. He'd dug the bullet out of his heart. Now Malcolm was coming for him again.

"One of us is dying, brother!" Malcolm swore as he charged at Ryder. "One of us is—"

Sabine put her hand on Malcolm's chest. He howled in pain and . . . he burned.

Quickly, too quickly. He fell to the ground, tried to roll to put out the fire, but the flames wouldn't die.

Instead, *he* died. In mere moments.

Then there was only . . . ash left.

There'd be no returning from that.

Sabine lifted her hand and asked Ryder, "Are you ready to die, too?"

He shook his head. "You can't kill me." Malcolm was truly dead now. *Rest in peace, brother.* Finally. Maybe there would finally be some peace for him on the other side.

Or maybe there would only be more fire.

"I can kill anyone." She had flames at her fingertips. "I can burn you, from the inside out."

"Pull it back," he told her, keeping his voice calm with every ounce of his strength.

For an instant, her expression flickered.

Did she remember? Another time, another place, but he'd spoken those exact words to her before.

The fire died above her hand. She touched her temple. Rubbed it. "*Destroy. Burn*. It's what the fire whispers to me."

He had to get Sabine to ignore that insidious whisper. He had to make her remember. So he told her the same thing he'd told her the first time she'd risen for him. Ryder lifted his hand to her and said, "I thought you were dead."

Her lips moved. She looked scared, lost. "*I was*." Then she shook her head. "Who are you?"

"Ryder." And he closed the last of the space between them.

She raised her hands again, as if to ward him off, but the fire didn't burn from her palms. Not now. "Stay away from me!" Sabine shouted.

"Never," he whispered.

Sabine slammed her palms against her head. "Hurts . . . *burn* . . ." Her eyes locked on his. "What is happening to me?"

She'd asked him that before. When she'd burned in his cell and returned to him. Now he just told her, "You're coming back to me."

Flames were on the ceiling. All around them.

He didn't risk a glance at the humans. But from the corner of his eye, he saw Dante running from the room. With . . . Cassie cradled in his arms?

But Vaughn and Keith would still be trapped. Sabine's fire was raging out of control. If he didn't stop it, how many would die? How many humans were in the building? Would the fire spread to the rest of the block?

To the whole city?

Her power was limitless, he saw that now. Everyone else needed to fear her.

But he . . . he just loved her. Ryder reached for her hands. *"Sabine."*

She blinked at him. "I've heard your voice . . . calling to me . . . through the fire."

Yes.

He swallowed. Kept his hands light and gentle on her feverish skin. "Stop the fire," he told her softly.

"I-I don't know how!" Tears leaked down her cheeks.

His heart ached. They'd been through all of this before. But this time, he knew what to do.

She knew fury and fear and pain.

He would remind her of something else. *Love.*

"Help me," she whispered to him. "Please."

"I will," he promised. Then Ryder put his lips to hers. He kissed her, pushing all of the love and need he felt into that kiss.

But she jerked her head away from him. Her eyes were even more afraid. "Why don't you burn?"

"Because you'd never hurt me." She was shaking. Hurting so much. He had to stop her pain. "And I won't let you hurt."

"Why?"

"Because I love you, Sabine." He kissed her again. Soft, gentle, even as the fire crackled and raged. She stood tense and scared at first, but then her lips parted just a little. Her breath eased out. He took that breath, as he'd take anything that she'd offer to him.

His lips were careful on hers. He held back his frantic need. Held tight to his control. He just wanted her to return, his Sabine, with her memory. Her fire. Her wit. Her beautiful spirit.

Her hands pushed lightly at his chest. He lifted his head.

She stared at him, and the flames seemed to have dimmed in her eyes. "Y-you . . . you have fangs."

His heart squeezed at the familiar words. That was what she'd said to him before, too, when they'd been trapped in his cell, and that time, he'd told her, "And you're burning the room around us." His voice was husky.

From the corner of his eye, Ryder saw a dark form dart through the doorway. Another man. He ran toward the cage. It looked like the man was trying to help Keith. Trying to save Vaughn.

Ryder focused on Sabine once more. If he didn't stop Sabine, there would be no saving anyone. "Pull it back, love," he told her, deliberately using the words he'd said in his cell in order to jar her memory. *"Pull it back."* Then he kissed her again. "Focus on me." Just like they'd done before. "Breathe," he told her. "Slow. Deep." His hand moved to rest over her heart. "Too fast," Ryder told her. *"Breathe.* You're safe with me."

Her breath whispered out. Her hands weren't pushing against him now. They were digging into his chest.

"I . . . remember you."

He wanted to yank her against him and hold tight. "Good because *I love you.*" He'd tell her forever. Every day for the rest of their lives.

The flames were gone from her eyes. Around them, the fire was dying. "Vampire," she whispered.

He nodded.

"You . . . bit me."

He had, several times.

"You . . . love me."

He would, always.

Another tear leaked from her eye. "I remember you . . ."

The good? The bad?

She smiled then, and it wasn't the deadly, dangerous smile from moments before. It wasn't the phoenix smiling. It was the woman, and her smile was beautiful. *She* was beautiful. "My vampire," Sabine said.

Hell, yes, he was hers. *Always*.

Then her body trembled. He caught her in his arms, lifting her up when she would have fallen. Holding her so tightly against his chest. His heart.

Then he saw the others. Keith and—*Rhett? Hell, that crazy bastard who'd run into the flames had been Sabine's brother?* If Ryder hadn't been so busy trying to stop the inferno, he would have recognized the man instantly. But he'd been a bit . . . distracted.

Rhett and Keith had just opened the door of the cage. Vaughn was rushing out at them.

They were going to get bitten. Become primal. He yelled out a warning.

Even as a shot fired out. The blast hit Vaughn in the chest, and he fell to the floor, unconscious.

"It's safe now," Cassie's voice called. "You can carry him out." She stood in the broken remains of the doorway, a gun in her hands. "I gave him a tranq."

The wounds on her neck were all but gone.

She'd been at death's door, but now she was back. Moving. Barking out orders. That sure as hell wasn't a normal recovery. Not even normal for a vampire, much less a human.

The tears of a phoenix. Had she really made that SOB Dante shed a tear? It sure looked as if she had.

"Rhett?" Sabine's stunned voice. "I almost killed my brother!"

Ryder kissed her. "You didn't," he said fiercely against her mouth. "You *didn't*."

Her lips trembled. "I did . . . kill . . . your brother."

Ashes to ashes.

"You gave him peace." The peace he'd sure never found on earth.

The last of his family was gone now.

"I'm sorry," Sabine said as she hugged him.

He realized then that, no, his family wasn't gone. His family was right in front of him. In his arms. Sabine was his family. The life he'd wanted for so long.

Keith was sobbing as he hauled out his limp son. The human . . . a human Sabine had known for most of her life.

Ryder glanced back at her lovely face. He could still see the tears on her cheeks.

"Cassie," Ryder snapped out the other woman's name.

She rushed to him. One look, and she understood just what he wanted from her. She ran away for a moment, then came back with a small vial clutched in her hand. She reached for Sabine.

Sabine flinched away. "What—"

"Your tears may be able to heal him." Ryder wouldn't promise her that Vaughn would survive. Not yet. He didn't know what Cassie could do with the primal infection, what she could do for any of those who'd been hurt by Genesis. Malcolm had faked his recovery, so they had no proof that the tears would have any effect on the primal.

But perhaps Cassie could do *something* for them.

Sabine stared into Ryder's eyes, and another tear slid down her cheek. "I could have lost you. Rhett. Everything."

Cassie took that tear and hurriedly stepped back.

"You remember," Ryder whispered.

Her lips rose into a faint smile. "You're pretty unforgettable."

The ceiling was groaning. Cracking. The building couldn't withstand the punishment from the fire. Ryder carried Sabine out of the room. He took the lab coat that Cassie gave to them and covered Sabine's golden skin. The fire had burned away her clothes.

It had burned away everything.

"Start again with me," he said. *I can do this right.* "You have the memories, but this time, I swear, I can make things better."

Her smile widened as she shook her head.

"Please," he whispered, when he'd never begged anyone or anything.

"I don't want to start over."

They left the ash and blood and smoldering fire behind. Rhett and Keith and Cassie came after them, pulling out Vaughn's body.

There was no sign of Dante.

Ryder took Sabine outside, where she could breathe the fresh air. Hear the sights and smell the scents of the city she loved so much.

He didn't know if she was back to being a full phoenix or if part of her remained a vampire. And, really, he didn't care *what* she was. He loved her. That was all that mattered.

"What do you want?" he asked her.

Her lips stretched into a smile. "I want to be with you."

She probably deserved better. No, she *damn well* deserved better, but he'd kill any man or supernatural who ever tried to take her from him.

So Sabine was pretty much stuck with him.

If she wanted to leave me, could I let her go?

It was a dark thought, and one he didn't want to examine too deeply. He needed her so much. Too much? Maybe he wasn't what she—

Sabine's soft laughter stopped him. "You just faced me and my fire, so why worry now? Don't you realize, vampire, you're all that I want? The only man who can get through the flames and *get to me*?" She pulled his head down toward her. "I want to go where you go. I want to be with you."

And the only place he wanted to go? Wherever the hell she was.

If she wanted to stay in New Orleans, he'd make the city safe for her. If she wanted to fucking fly to Paris, he'd buy her a jet. He'd do anything for her. Risk anything.

Give anything.

His forehead pressed against hers. "Don't ever die on me again." Because he'd wanted to cut out his own heart when her eyes had gone blank.

"If I do," she whispered, "I'll come back. I swear, I'll never leave you."

He believed her. After all, his Sabine had never lied. She'd also never said . . .

"I love you, Ryder."

He kissed her.

Then heard the disgruntled, "Hell," that came from Rhett. "Looks like I'll have a vamp brother-in-law."

Yes, he would.

Ryder ignored the human. Rhett had managed to shake off his compulsion, just as Ryder suspected he might do. He'd come back to the city, ready to face any enemies.

Ryder could respect him. But even though he had that respect, he wasn't about to stop kissing Sabine. Because she was all that mattered.

Fire. Blood. Fury.

Life. Death.

Lust.

Love.

She'd given him the world, and he'd spend the rest of his days laying the whole damn world at her feet.

EPILOGUE

Cassie paced down the narrow corridor. The fluorescent lights barely flickered over her head. She'd
made the serum from the phoenix's tears, and the primal cure had actually *worked*.

The tears from the phoenix were amazing. She'd
been able to inject Vaughn Adams, and, while he hadn't
become human again, he'd managed to leash the beast
that had been created within him. He could function
once more. Could control his ravenous hunger.

He didn't have a mouthful of fangs. Actually, he only
had two fangs now. Just like any other vampire. His
knife-like claws had vanished. His eyes showed sanity,
not the delirium of the beast.

And there was enough serum left that she could possibly treat five other primals. *If* any others were still out
there.

The tears had been just what she needed. But a phoenix couldn't exactly cry on demand. It seemed that only
a life-or-death situation could bring forth the tears of a
phoenix. The phoenix had to care, had to *love*.

And had to break before the tears would fall.

Ryder wasn't about to let his phoenix break again, so Cassie knew there would be no more tears from Sabine. But Sabine had done more than any other before her. She'd shed tears to save Ryder, and the female phoenix must have also cried to save Cassie's life.

Because Cassie knew that she'd been about to die. She'd felt the cold touch of death sweeping over her. But she'd recovered. Cheated death. All because of a phoenix's tears.

Thank you, Sabine.

The floor creaked behind her.

Cassie froze.

She should be alone on this level of her lab. She'd been working with a wolf shifter—one who'd been the unfortunate prisoner of Richard Wyatt—but she was making headway with him. He was housed downstairs, but that creak . . .

It came from steps behind me.

Slowly, she turned around. In the shadows at the end of the hall, she could just make out the tall, dark form of a man.

And she could see his eyes. Glowing, burning with flames.

Her heart slammed into her chest.

Those eyes had haunted her memories. Her nightmares.

"Hello, Cassandra," his deep, rumbling voice seemed to pour over her, "I've missed you."

Then Dante stepped forward, and Cassandra was pretty sure that her world stopped.

He couldn't have cried for her. Dante didn't care about anyone. Not anything.

He *couldn't* have.

He was coming for her. Stalking slowly out of the shadows. Cassie didn't know if she should scream or reach for him.

"Cassie?"

Another voice. Coming from the opposite end of the hall. Cassie whirled around and saw Ryder striding toward her. He'd just come up the stairs. A frown pulled down the handsome lines of his face.

Ryder . . . right . . . he'd said that he would stop by to check on the serum's progress and on the status of the werewolf. Somehow, Ryder knew the wolf. Seemed to actually want to help him, too.

He's making amends, just like me.

Ryder glanced over Cassie's shoulder, then he looked back at her. "Is everything all right?"

What? Of course, things weren't all right. A phoenix was stalking her, he was—

She looked behind her. The hallway was empty. There weren't even any shadows there. Just a too-bright fluorescent light.

Cassie shivered.

What was happening to her?

He touched her arm, and she flinched. "S-sorry . . ." *A phoenix is haunting me. Wherever I go, I feel like he's with me.* She forced her shoulders to straighten. Cassie cleared her throat. "I need to tell Sabine how much I appreciate all that she's done."

"Sabine wanted to help Vaughn."

Because Sabine was a good person. Sabine wanted to help everyone.

And she was doing it all out of the goodness of her heart. Not just because she was trying to erase the black sins from her soul. *Not like me.*

"She saved me," Cassie continued, clearing her

throat. *I imagined Dante. He wasn't there. I've just been working too hard.* That was the story of her life. "I was a stranger to her, I—"

Ryder's tightening expression told her all that she needed to know.

Not Sabine.

"It took Sabine a while to get her control back." Ryder shook his head. "You . . . you wouldn't have lasted that long."

Her lips were numb. Her cheeks. Her hands. "What happened to me?"

"Dante took you from the room." A muscle flexed along the hard line of his jaw. "Then the next thing I knew, you were rushing back inside and shooting at Vaughn."

Because she'd woken to the smell of fire. Her throat had still been bleeding. Her fingers rose and traced over the healed skin. She'd heard the screams and she'd rushed into the burning back room.

Sabine had been alive then, the only phoenix she'd seen there. And Dante, he *hated* her, so why would he have brought her back? Why would he have wasted a single second on her, much less actually shed a tear?

A shiver skated over her. *Impossible.* The wounds just must not have been as severe as she'd thought. Ryder was mistaken about what he'd seen. Obviously, the guy had been distracted as he focused on saving Sabine. There had been so much fire and smoke. He hadn't seen clearly.

I dragged myself out of the room. Yes, that's what happened. Then I got . . . I got stronger when I breathed some fresh air. I was able to go back inside and help the others.

"Why do you look so scared?" Ryder asked her as he

tilted his head to study her. "Has someone been threatening you?"

She remembered eyes that burned. "N-no." Cassie forced a smile. "Everything is fine. The patients are getting better." The nightmare that was Genesis—it was over.

Dead.

She wouldn't tell Ryder about Dante. Besides, there was nothing to tell. Just the nightmares that were now haunting her days.

And the dreams that haunted her nights. Dreams of Dante touching her. Calling for her.

She grabbed her stethoscope. "Let's go check on the wolf."

Her steps tapped over the tile. Cassie didn't look back, but she could have sworn that she smelled . . .

Smoke.

And where there was smoke . . .

A phoenix often waited.